THE SIMPL

In the early 1920s, in the grim days preceding the humiliation of the Armistice, a Prussian naval officer finds himself in despair at the lack of repentance he sees around him. Leaving his young son Joachim and his socialite wife, Commander Thomas von Orla takes a job as a fisherman amongst the lakes and forests of East Prussia. Here, living simply in a wooden hut on an island, a period of catharsis begins, and the horrors of the war are gradually purged through hard work.

His friendship with a naturalist, Count Pernein, encourages him in his search for knowledge and an understanding of fate. The widening gap between the youth of the day and the generation who had lost the war is portrayed by Wiechert in the person of Joachim, whose dogmatic approach to life clashes with the philosophical outlook of his father. It is a young girl, however, who brings von Orla closest to achieving the 'happy heart' he longs for, though at a cost he could not foresee.

ERNST WIECHERT

The East Prussian poet and novelist Ernst Wiechert was born in 1887. Throughout the First World War he fought in the front line. From 1933 onwards he devoted himself to writing, and his outspoken criticism of the dogmas of the Third Reich led to his imprisonment at Buchenwald in 1938. He spent the last years of his life in Switzerland, and shortly before his death, confided that *The Simple Life* was the novel he was most glad to have written, although he had had more than forty books published.

ERNST WIECHERT

The Simple Life

With an Introduction by
MARIANNE JETTER
Translated from the German by
MARIE HEYNEMANN

QUARTET ENCOUNTERS

Quartet Books

Published in Great Britain by Quartet Books
Limited 1994
A member of the Namara Group
27 Goodge Street
London W1P 1FD

Originally published in German under the title *Das einfache Leben*

ISBN 0 7043 0185 7

A catalogue record for this title is available from the British Library

Printed and bound in Finland

INTRODUCTION

The life and works of Ernst Wiechert have aroused the admiration of many readers, who recognize and are grateful for the pertinence of his message to our times. In emphasizing the worth of every human being, he has the courage to stand up against the dangerous tendency of modern man to submerge his own individuality in a group-consciousness. In the sense of belonging to a group of some kind the individual believes that he can find the security he lacks when alone. By integrating himself with the personality of the group he hopes to rid himself of his awareness of the deficiences of his own personality. But the security he achieves is a pseudo-security. To find real security he must, as Wiechert points out, find himself again, know himself, accept himself. He must acquire the ability to be alone so that he may quietly contemplate the world, his relationship to it and his role in it. He must have the courage of his convictions, the mental independence which can develop only in mind. The man who is able to enjoy his own company can achieve that self-realization which is the first step towards self-perfection by withdrawing from the world either physically or spiritually. By working through his conflicts he becomes more and more objective towards himself until he reaches the point at which love and consideration for others become the dominant forces within him. When the individual has matured to a stage where his concern for others is stronger than his concern for himself he is ready to serve mankind either physically or spiritually as the need may dictate.

In his works Wiechert frequently allows those characters in search of self-perfection to retreat, either literally to an island or, frequently, to a spiritual isolation into which no outsider can intrude.

In this retreat his characters succeed in overcoming their hostile feelings towards the world, and in so deepening the resources of their personalities that they are able to meet hate with love, mistrust with confidence, war with peace, egotism with altruism. They are able to live lives which are meaningful both to others and to themselves. They have indeed become so secure in themselves that they influence others in a positive way and even combat destructive and hostile feelings in others.

Wiechert did not immediately arrive at this conception of life. He himself had to undergo a maturing process, which, as it proceeded, paralleled the development of the theme of isolation (the 'island motif') so that his work in all its phases is a faithful mirror of the poet himself.

How Wiechert struggled with life's problems becomes apparent in his two autobiographical books: *Wälder und Menschen* written in 1935 and *Jahre und Zeitan* written in 1947. From *Wälder und Menschen* it is obvious that, as a young man, the poet felt different from other people and found it exceedingly difficult to make effective contacts with other human beings, who on their part looked upon him as an outsider. It is only natural that his feeling of isolation, both physical and emotional, caused a state of anxiety which he solved at first by a conscious withdrawal from the world, by flight. This is the time when the poet depicts the 'island' as an escape from the world, as a place where man continues to brood over his painful isolation without being able to rise above himself. He enlightens the reader as to the reasons for his feelings of isolation which go back to his earliest childhood. But in discussing those reasons it becomes clear that the poet, even at an early age, saw isolation as having not only a depressive, but also a strengthening effect upon the mind. Wiechert interprets isolation as a necessary though painful technique of survival, and also as a latent opportunity for enjoying life more fully and for even heightening one's capacity for experiences of all kinds. During his childhood and early youth, isolation appears to have provided a greater number of painful than of pleasant associations. Some aspects of his isolation, such as his home, appeared to be both painful and pleasant at the same time. Recollections of the less pleasant aspects of this isolation are numerous:

Wiechert's home stood remote, in the beautiful woods of East Prussia, surrounded only by forests and moors, 'in complete isolation'. The beauty and grandeur of the countryside impressed itself early on Wiechert both positively and negatively. He and his family lived among a Polish-speaking population, a circumstance which, to some extent, isolated him from other children, but brought the members of the family closer together. There seems to have been a certain tendency towards melancholy on his mother's side. The mother herself suffered deeply from the dark loneliness of the country and her outlook is reflected in Wiechert. As a child he seems to have been rather quiet and very sensitive, 'always in a corner, taciturn, preoccupied and even when visitors came I am said to have sat on a small stool in the most remote corner, my head resting on my hands, absorbed in watching and listening'.

Even in his games he preferred those in which he could dream by himself. This tendency was further increased by Aunt Veronika, the most beloved of his relatives in Wiechert's youth, but a woman who was somehow mysterious in her way of telling fairy tales. She believed Wiechert destined to become a poet. In many of her stories made up around the lives of the children she seemed to set Wiechert apart from his brothers which gave him at an early age the feeling of being different. She encouraged his love for the unreal, the imaginary, thus perhaps offering a more constructive way of living to the lonely child.

A great part of Wiechert's childhood was lived in a dreamworld, and at an early age there appears to have developed a division into an outer and an inner life, into the real one and the more satisfying one he built for himself.

Several incidents in the poet's youth contributed to his painful feeling of loneliness – quite apart from his countryside and his inherited disposition. One such incident was the death of his youngest brother, apparently the most gifted of the sons. Another was the decision of Wiechert's parents to send him to the city for his schooling, recognizing in him at an early age a talent that ought to be cultivated. Life in the city allowed his previous years to appear in a new bright light. Wiechert became terribly homesick. 'For the first time a hopeless loneliness engulfed me, not one of pain but rather of joy.'

Wiechert remarks that because his home appeared to him to be the only star in the dark night of his schooldays, he developed a capacity for giving himself entirely to his dreams of home, 'the ability to yield completely to a world, not always an imaginary world, to be sure, yet a world removed'. Instead of going to sleep, Wiechert began his real life at night, when '... I left the real world in which I was forced to live and went whither I wanted to live alone'. He withdrew from his unfriendly environment into his own world which he seemed to enjoy.

On the one hand, city life strengthened Wiechert's awareness of the difference between nature and civilization, deepening his feeling of isolation and separation from nature, but on the other, a visit to his home four times a year overjoyed and overwhelmed him.

During these weeks at home he worked as a shepherd, a huntsman and a fisherman – all occupations which required self-reliance and the ability to be alone with nature and in nature. Wiechert praises the solitude of these occupations, gaining strength and pleasure from them. But the occasions when he suffered from a sense of isolation became more frequent just the same. When his brother, with whom he lived in the city, finally left school – he did not get on well – Wiechert felt once more orphaned. 'I was an individual, a human being all by myself.'

Also in interpreting his first love experience – a love that was returned by the girl for some time – Wiechert says: 'in the last kisses lie already the pain of separation, of loneliness, the complete sense of being lost'. For Wiechert the end even of love was solitude.

In looking back on his last school year Wiechert refers also to the difference between generations. 'How dreadfully lonely I am, at this age, on the bridge between two generations . . . how foolishly proud one is of one's loneliness and how deeply does it burn the soul so that the ear becomes alert to every sound from the forest . . .'

But Wiechert also kept apart from his schoolmates and acted like a lonesome revolutionary hero among them. He deposed everything from its pedestal, God, Christ, Church, Emperor, state, parents, teachers, women. The world consisted only of himself and idiots. The young man, however, had now begun to feel confident of his own capacity. He asserted himself and may have derived from that self-assertion more satisfaction than he had formerly done from flight and withdrawal. Now, although isolated, he was capable of taking a more positive attitude towards his environment. Later, he interprets this stage as a transition to a more rational approach to life. Wiechert remarks that although he eventually returned to the ordinary ways of people 'still as one in a deep dream', he had decided to become a poet and to start to live.

This retreat into isolation was due to his poverty. He could afford to eat only very modestly and none of his student friends ate in such cheap restaurants. Besides, he felt that his critical mind would not permit him to follow one teacher or to accept implicitly one system of ideas. Consequently his friends looked upon him as 'an odd one'.

The world of science, the *ratio*, seemed to him in deep contrast to his woods and the fires in which he used to roast potatoes and mushrooms – to nature as a whole. He felt strangely out of place in the city among university students and professors. Yet in observing some professors he also noticed their 'being different' and came to the conclusion that they wanted to appear original, that the source of their 'being different' was pure vanity. Certainly Wiechert never considered vanity a source of his own sense of difference and we must agree with him. Wiechert at no time seems vain.

On Sundays he used to get away from the city and went alone into the country, sometimes taking a book with him. Perhaps – as Wiechert concludes – this solitude was necessary to the development of his character and simply served as a maturing ground. Even if he did not get away from the city, in his imagination he could always find his way back to the rustling trees, moors and lakes of his East Prussian home. They never lost their influence over him.

Wiechert also ascribes a great deal of importance in shaping his personality to his devotion to the Eastern world. He felt that it was a world that was not yet undermined by modern civilization and that 'he who came from it had to remain permanently a stranger' – meaning a stranger in Western civilization. At this stage he accepts himself clearly as an outsider.

His feeling of strangeness wherever he went must have created a sense of not belonging, almost a permanent state of anxiety and desire for security. A stranger feels insecure wherever he goes. All his life Wiechert tried to find security and at the end of his days he finally found it when he lived alone in a simple house in Switzerland and when he wanted simply 'to write unto his very death'. Because of his feeling of not belonging he had to recognize physical and spiritual isolation as a basis for the development of his own personality. It was in seclusion that he produced the idea of the function of an 'island' in an artist's life and there he was able to find peace.

Wiechert discusses the artist as such. When we consider Wiechert himself as an artist, the analysis of the 'fundamental elements of creative life' throws further light on his love for and appreciation of isolation. He feels that an artist has to have these 'fundamental factors', a certain amount of quietness, absolute silence, without concern for the day and its duties. He cannot forgo 'his quite lonely and secluded inward life'. This consideration applies only to artists, but Wiechert goes a step further and allows every human being to have his 'lonely and secluded world', attributing a great deal of importance to it. Only a person who has achieved that world can be creative, be it in a literary sense or by 'giving' to others of himself in a personal one. Seen in this way seclusion assumes an important functional meaning – a far cry from the time when the island served the poet only as an escape.

His longing for companionship, or duality, is important – fulfilment brings security. At this moment Wiechert becomes a real poet. His description of his friendship with a Russian girl throws some light on his feelings. The relationship was a deeply platonic one which lifted Wiechert above everyday occurrences. 'It was as if we were on a desert island, the ocean roaring monotonously around it.' This feeling of being on a lonely island in the ocean was experienced when Wiechert sat in a popular café in the city. But he calls it the 'emerging from a great solitude'. Somewhat later he emphasized the redemption, or at least the hope of it, that he saw in the 'companionship'. 'The emerging from the terrible encirclement of the individual to find in it (companionship) that entity which a creative human being desires more passionately than others.' Wiechert did not find what he expected in his first marriage, which was nothing but an uninterrupted series of painful experiences. He attributes a great deal of importance to this unhappy relationship and its influence on his work. He felt that he remained egocentric at all times, and that this preoccupation had its repercussions in his writings. Only after he met his second wife could he establish constructive relationships with other people. 'The gift of being able to go hand in hand with another person was seldom bestowed upon him', but after this meeting, referred to in 'Der Mann von 40 Jahren', he succeeded in becoming the great poet he aspired to be. He had found that security he needed in his marriage. Wiechert describes his first impression of his second wife: 'She was very beautiful, but more than her beauty mattered her absent expression, her absorbed gestures, her complete isolation in the midst of people and sounds, colours and lights.' Only after he knew her could he make the 'decisive step from the subject to the object'.

The poet's struggle to understand the essence of religion, the essence of God, was part of his longing for 'companionship' or as he calls it the 'entity'. His parents were very religious, his father depending upon the Bible as the only authority. Wiechert rejected every kind of dogma. He recognized an 'all-embracing magnificent and unchanging necessity', but whether he called this necessity God or Buddha seemed irrelevant. Consequently Wiechert was a tolerant and deeply religious person but in a somewhat unusual way. This lack of sympathy with his parents' beliefs must have increased his feelings of isolation, his 'being different'. It took courage to rise above the ordinary concept of religion. The orthodox do not feel isolated but rather secure in their chosen church community.

'Life' had a tremendous impact on Wiechert and he acknowledged that fact, perhaps overestimated it in a wider sense. He certainly recognized the danger for the poet in creating a world of fantasy. The door must be open day and night to everything which can fill the heart: books, ideas, people and their fates, but isolation is still needed in order to be creative. 'That great loneliness which we require from time to time. That complete immersion into another world, that turning away from the people and things of your own life, that great silence in which only Pan's flute is heard.' Such isolation requires renunciation of all kinds, but it is essential. 'Blood must be dried and tears must be wiped away before beginning to write a book' so that the book may gain power and become a blessing to the reader. Isolation is not a goal in itself but a means to an end – to create books to help people in their distress and to serve them in the best possible way. Together with the creation of his books goes Wiechert's service to others, either in the form of his books, or of talks, letters, newspaper articles. This service to others, to *Humanitas*, which began when Wiechert was eighteen years of age and was employed as a tutor in the house of Baron Grotthuss, developed into a *conscious* way of living when he wrote *Der Knecht Gottes Andreas Nyland* and remained one of his guiding stars throughout his entire life. 'The human being, that is what matters,' says Jons in the *Jerominkinder*, and indeed Wiechert remained more than faithful to this motto during his years of teaching until his death.

Wiechert's own life was filled with hardships and disappointments of all kinds. His four years of war service, his years of learning as a young teacher, his unhappy marriage, his later imprisonment under the Nazi Government, the curtailment of his writing, and finally his illness, are only some of them. But Wiechert's philosophy of life survives everything and he emerges as an even greater man. He says the only way is to remain master inwardly. 'One must remain master of one's inward emotions and not become their slave.' Wiechert achieved it because he had an unmistakable sense of right and wrong, true and false, never falling prey to mass suggestions of any kind, a deep sense of humility towards the Universe, acquired in his physical or sometimes only emotional seclusion. When Wiechert became ill with tuberculosis he was able to get six months leave of absence and in 1933, after the Nazis had come to power, he was retired on a pension on account of his illness. The poet had perforce led a quiet life, but he had not wasted that life. He felt that he had moved the hearts of young people towards truth, fortitude and love. His illness seemed to have done more for him than he discusses in his autobiography. He says only that his teaching years had come to an end and that the time had come 'to go into retirement and there cultivate my field'.

Wiechert enjoyed his 'separateness' and appreciated the fact that he was left alone but he knew also that he was being observed by the government which had come into power in 1933. What a great decision it must have been for him to step out from his isolation and make his stand in the new world. He had a premonition of what he was doing when he accepted the invitation to speak to the university students in Munich.* More and more Wiechert and his wife felt the growing wall of solitude around them. Wichert was travelling a great deal, thinking that he could

* '*Der Dichter und die Jugend*' in *An die deutsche Jugend*, 6 July 1933

give comfort and advice to people who had lost their direction. In 1936, however, the family moved into a house of its own.

Wiechert wrote *Das einfache Leben* after his return from Buchenwald Concentration Camp. He wrote it with all the love left in him. The island of the blessed ones was created here amidst a terrible world. It was a symbol of Wiechert's way of absorbing the experience of Buchenwald into his life. The tenderness and love that emanate from this book were created in solitude. No previous book had the island motif as the predominant one and never again did Wiechert achieve a similar atmosphere. Writing the book gave him refuge from the world and offered to himself and his readers a solution to life's turmoil.

Only in solitude could his roots grow once more into life and help him overcome his suspicions, fears and concern for the world. Wiechert was never the same again. Solitude had become more and more important in his life. In referring to his native world of East Prussia he says: 'That was my world, it was an aloof world and in it I always remained aloof.' When hardships became too depressing he 'could always withdraw into silence like a fish that submerges in deep water'. But he withdrew not to flee from the world but to gain new strength from his isolation and to be better equipped to 'give' his best to the world.

The poet actually returned to the solitude of his childhood, so to speak, in his last years when he lived alone in Switzerland. 'But it has been this way with me from childhood: I was alone and the solitude of childhood and youth limited but also protected me.'

He recognizes that his longing for solitude, for living on an 'island', was uppermost in him and that he could never rid himself of it. His solitude in old age differs from his solitude in his youth. Although he lives alone in his old age at the same time he knows he will never be entirely alone because he has so many admirers, far and near, who surround him with a wealth of love and gratitude and to whom he can stretch out his hands, welcoming them to his home.

Thus Wiechert's yearning for solitude represents not only the central conflict of his life but also of his books. And since this theme of the isolated individual finding his true mission in the world is found in practically all of Wiechert's prose works as the underlying thought, it is important to note the stages of its development in the poet's own life.

During the first stage, the 'island' is an escape from the world which cannot be mastered by the individual. During the second, the 'island' is thought of as a place where man might mature. In the third stage, this possibility becomes a certainty. So far, emphasis has been on the individual's attempts to solve his inner conflicts. The fourth, fifth and sixth stages enter upon the relationship of the individual to the world. Having reached maturity, the human being has an unconscious healing effect on his environment which develops into a conscious effort to help others, and finally culminates in the desire to serve mankind – the only desirable goal of man.

Marianne Jetter

CHAPTER ONE

ON AN EVENING early in spring, not long after the Great War, a man stood at one of the west windows of his home. He raised his eyes from an old much-thumbed volume which he held in his hand, and became lost in thought. The cloudless evening sky glowed with distant flames which, reflected through the wide window, filled the whole room with a soft crimson light. The coloured bindings on the bookshelves glowed and the strange weapons and masks in an adjoining cabinet shone with an almost wicked radiance. In the only picture the wall could boast a cruiser was firing its guns dense with smoke and appeared to be rushing straight into the flaming abyss of a twilight of the gods.

The light also fell on a huge globe standing on a pedestal in front of the rows of books and seemed to weave magic spells on its surface. The mountains appeared outlined in brown relief; the plains were tinted like meadows interwoven with a network of rivers and the blue oceans shone with a purple glow in the rays of the setting sun.

The man turned his eyes away from the window towards the shining image of the earth. The small groups of islands were swimming in the Indian Ocean like so many pearls, and Adam's Peak threw a pointed shadow over the sea. The coasts looked as if finely outlined in red, whilst beyond the Himalayas over the yellow country of Tibet the dusk seemed to await the coming of a strange star. The man remained lost in thought before the globe; its outline became vague in the diminishing light as the shadows gradually faded to grey and greenish tints. The coast outline became blurred, the valleys darkened, until at last there was nothing to be seen but a large orb, like a distant star floating in space.

In the growing stillness of the evening the faraway roar of the metropolis became audible over the sururban gardens, like the sound of distant breakers rising and falling almost imperceptibly in the growing darkness. The trunks of pine trees towered dark and motionless into the pale green sky; white lamps sprang into light over a far-off street in rapid succession. He who had lived long on the high seas imagined himself standing on the bridge listening to the low hum of the ship's engines, while the lights on the land moved silently in the distance and gliding away became extinguished by the earth's curve, while the bows furrowed a menacing sea never sailed before.

In the fading light the man raised the book once more to his eyes as if he wanted to make sure that certain passages were still there and had not become effaced by the twilight of the world. Still grasping the book, he turned again to the window, leaning his left temple against the curtain's edge. The last rays of light caressed his features; shadows gathered beneath his brow and in the deep wrinkles lining his nose; so his face seemed not unlike the world which appeared suspended in mid-air in front of the rows of books.

Suddenly the door opened and the light from the passage broke with an almost cruel insistence into the silent room. The man turned slowly towards a woman who was standing on the threshold, but before his eyes reached her he became conscious of some of the things now illuminated in the room: the picture of the cruiser as if held in the beam of a searchlight but still firing its dark red volleys, a clearly defined strip of light on the purple carpet, and the curve of the globe as a thin white line like a sickle. Only then did his gaze fall on the woman in her evening-gown in the doorway with her naked arm stretched out to the light-switch.

'Don't!' he said sharply. She arrested her movement without dropping her arm, and even if she had not been standing in the light he would have known that she smiled in slight mockery yet not without indulgence.

'Is the captain dreaming again?' she asked.

'He has been reading,' he replied, going to the desk and putting the open book down carefully, 'a psalm which he had not read since confirmation and there he found the verse, "Swift as a breath our lives pass away." He has been meditating on it.'

'Heroes and thinkers,' she said in her deep voice, 'these are left to us; the Great War has taken all the others.'

'There have been generations who would have been proud of such a heritage.'

'Yes, former generations, but we, after all those terrible years, do not wish to fight, nor to think, but only to live, just *live.*'

'Exactly like animals,' he replied.

'Just so, that is what is so healthy and beautiful about them; they neither read psalms nor dream into the twilight.'

'Sometimes,' he said, staring at the shining edge of the globe, 'I understand why primitive men feel the urge to beat their wives.'

She laughed happily and carelessly, and without warning switched on the light, so that it shone down from the ceiling with a crude glare.

'I must have a look at the man who feels that urge at the present moment.'

'I was not speaking of myself,' he replied, frowning at her

from the far end of the room. She had become slimmer during these years of austerity, her features sharper and her eyes more brilliant. Only her mouth, like that of a child, had remained the same in spite of the vivid make-up she used, small with its corners slightly drawn down, so that he never knew whether they would start quivering with anger or with tears.

His thoughts went back to the time of their first love and he realised of how much the war had deprived them.

'Go now,' he said kindly, 'it's no use. It doesn't lead to anything.'

Her hand, sparkling with rings, stroked the red bindings of the books near the door.

'I only wanted to remind you that it is time to change. They will be here in half an hour and you know that the admiral is coming too. He may be of use to you; he has great influence.'

He crossed to the switch and turned out the light. Then he took hold of her arms and turned her round gently and pushed her into the passage. Her cool skin was nearly as strange to him as that of a dead person.

'Put your Nelson on my globe,' he said, 'then kneel down and worship him and his influence. I am disgusted with all these ghosts. Can't you understand that? He who has lost the game must admit it as I do and not pretend that the game was played unfairly.'

'Oh, Thomas!' she said, smiling back over her shoulder, 'What an incredible fool you are.'

He closed the door, but the room seemed different. The flickering light of a street lamp shone into it and the shadow of the globe lay like a black circle on the wall of books. 'That's it,' he murmured. 'A dark world which they illuminate with their vanities. He who has lost the battle should be silent, and we have all lost more than a battle.'

He listened to the tinkling of glasses and cutlery in a distant room. Then he went cautiously into the passage, took his coat and hat and opened the door of the nursery. The nurse was sitting on the bed trying to pull a small wooden boat from underneath the blanket. But the boy's little hands held it fast at the other end.

Both turned as he entered. He stopped and looked at the child's furious face in silence. Yes, it was his face, reproduced once more out of an enormous number of possible faces, slightly modified, with a firmer forehead and harder lips, and yet reproduced. His own face and not hers – the only thing saved from the war for the future.

'What is it, Joachim?' he asked seriously.

The nurse opened her lips as if to answer, but the child put his little brown hand over her mouth. 'Nurse Beate says,' he shouted in his high-pitched voice, 'that I can't go to sleep with a warship, and I have said that a captain's son can go to sleep with twenty men-of-war. Tell her it's right, Daddy.'

Thomas went to the bed and took hold of the clumsy toy. Obediently the little hands let go, and he lifted it to his eyes as he had lifted the book a little while ago. 'A captain's son can sleep in a warship, Joachim, or even under a warship, but I think only little girls would sleep with a warship and think it a doll. A boy puts his ship on the cupboard where the morning sun will shine on it, and when he wakes up there it stands and calls him to his duty. Don't you think so?'

He saw how the boy wrinkled his brows in an effort to understand each word, and he turned with the little ship in his hand towards the toy cupboard to hide his emotion. He had seen children so rarely during the war.

'You are the cleverest man on earth, Daddy!' said Joachim, taking a deep breath as his doubts disappeared.

'Not quite, Joachim, but at least not the most stupid. And now you will go to sleep, won't you?'

'All right, Daddy. Portholes screwed down and off to sleep, is that it?'

'Yes, that's right.'

'And where are you going now, Daddy? Aren't you staying to meet the admiral?'

'No, I have seen many admirals in my life. I must now go and look for something.'

'What are you looking for?'

'That I will tell you later. One must never talk about what one is looking for until one has found it. Have you said your prayers?'

'Yes, sir,' replied the nurse, straightening the blanket. His thoughts began to wander again. 'Later on, nurse,' he said, 'you can use for his prayer the psalm with the verse, "Swift as a breath our lives pass away"–that is a good prayer. I only discovered it today.'

Tears came into her eyes as she looked at him. But he was already at the door. 'Do you know, Nurse Beate, that there is an epitaph with your name? Listen: "Here lies a woman named Beate, but she preferred to be Beate." Yes, it is by Lessing himself. I found it the other day. "She preferred to be Beate." Now good-night and sleep well.'

With an absent-minded smile he closed the door.

Outside he stood for a little while under the pine trees in the front garden and looked up to the early stars. In his imagination he was on the ocean and involuntarily he searched the horizon for the guiding constellation. It was a misfortune that his wife had already moved to the town at the outbreak of war, but from the beginning she had hated the seaport in which they lived. She had never loved the ocean nor the great winds nor his life regulated by a strict duty. She had been fond of his uniform and of her dream that one day he would be an admiral, and a young admiral at that.

He was already walking along the street towards the underground. No, it did not seem quite fair – there had been love but without any trial or suffering – that's what it was. They had both grabbed at life as at the ripe fruit of a good tree. God had planted it in their garden and they plucked from it and ate. Woe to him who dared say that they did not deserve it! And yet they did not deserve it, none of them. The result had proved it and also the manner in which they had snatched at it – without dignity. For he who is without dignity is without value.

I must go away, he thought, as if this were a town stricken by plague. She will not go with me, but I must go. I do not want to be one of those 'undefeated heroes'. They do not realise how defeated they are but, by God, I know how defeated I am! Only the child, the child –

Suddenly he found himself in a cool tunnel staring at the ticket in his hand. An enormous price was printed across it. Where did she get all the money? For the home, the servants, the nurse? 'Gambling on the Stock Exchange is unworthy of an officer.' Is that what they say? But she was certain to gamble day and night. Not only admirals were her guests; the old gods were being dethroned. An incredible fool – no doubt that is what he was.

And why did he wait for one of these trains? For one of these roaring monsters with dazzling lights, carrying stale air and ravaged faces which stared into empty space? Why did he wait for them nearly every night in order to drive aimlessly and senselessly through this town which he hated? Hour after hour, this way and that? By underground, bus or tram? Through slums, past palaces (but these were more miserable than the slums), looking from one face to the next as if searching for something irretrievably lost? Could he not bear any longer to be alone, hopelessly alone amongst these accursed and lost? Some bought drugs – one could buy them at dark street corners or in obscure gateways. So he travelled on and on, got out, got in again, more benumbed than any of them, and yet with an ice-cold fear in his heart than it might escape him, that he might not find what he was looking for: a face, a revelation, peace, he knew not what. 'Well, that will come to an end too,' he said aloud. He sometimes talked to himself now.

He had not looked at the illuminated indicator and he did not know where the train was taking him. He did not want to know. He sat in his corner, well-dressed and erect, and his eyes travelled from face to face. He had known some of them for a long time. The man with the wooden leg who would be selling shoelaces outside the big church later on; the actress going to her theatre, and from her lifeless expression one could guess that she was going to act her part tonight for the hundredth or two-hundredth time; the factory girl with the red scarf; and the old aristocrat whose whole body seemed to quiver incessantly; only the eyeglass, which seemed to shine in front of a dead eye, did not tremble.

Doors were opened and slammed like traps closing on prisoners. Then the motor roared and the subterranean lights flashed by like a torn ribbon. Sometimes the train rose to the surface, light shafts appeared and windows in decaying walls, and scraps of illuminated signs shot over the roofs. Then the walls of the tunnel closed in again; damp air came through the half-open windows and white faces appeared outside like fish behind glass walls, moved up and down by an invisible current.

Now and again Thomas saw a sailor in an unkempt uniform which he had had altered to look like a civilian suit, and he looked at him with half-closed eyes. He saw the rebellious triumph in the other's face, but behind it there was nothing but an awful loneliness and a longing to consort with similar faces, to form a protecting mass and to hide in anonymity.

Further on they got out, to work or to fritter away an idle hour – the man with the wooden leg, the actress and the aristocrat. The train rushed northward and new faces appeared, some frankly vicious, others laid waste by bitter experience. It seemed as if the train were gathering up the harvest of the last few years – hastily bound together in rotting sheaves: mothers who stared with glassy eyes as if seeing tombstones and sunken crosses; foreigners who wrote illegible signs on pieces of dirty paper, and cripples, many cripples, the bloody witnesses of the great sacrifice, who looked at the sound ones with resignation or hatred; for they had been told that they were heroes and now they imagined they could read in the eyes of their fellow men that they had been fools and were an encumbrance to be carried along the road to a new goal.

Thomas closed his eyes. He was healthy, upright, well-dressed. He was like the only living man in a mortuary, one who could get up and walk away while the others seemed to be writhing on their slabs full of hatred and longing to hold him back. Either all should have to die or none. Nobody ought to be rich and he who was in good health was a thief.

'The gentleman has an appointment, I presume?' asked a man opposite. The skin over his hollow cheeks was taut as if drawn over a wire frame and Thomas thought that when the time came for the finger of death to touch it, it would give a hollow sound. But the tone in which the question was asked was full of malice, irony and the hatred felt by the defeated.

'Yes, with an angel,' said Thomas quickly.

The other man's eye fell and glanced along the windows on which warnings were printed in silly verses. Then he turned again slowly: 'There are no angels any more.' His voice sounded tired and hopeless.

The brakes were applied and Thomas got out. 'Yes, there are,' he said. 'There are still angels, but they wear armour.'

'He was buried and dug out,' mumured a voice as he got out. He turned into a side street, which seemed like an endless passage leading to a faraway desert. A greenish moon hung over the roofs, unreal like all the light in this town. The sound of footsteps echoed from the walls, and one could distinguish those people who still wore wooden soles. The lights behind the windows were dim, and when one of the large doors leading to the backyards opened, the air seemed to come from a cemetery, laden with the smell of withering wreaths. Gramophones screeched in the distance, as if muffled under wet blankets; high above the invisible roofs a broken neon sign turned its circle rapidly, flashing red and green alternately. It looked like a mutilated symbol of eternity.

Thomas walked along the street with his hands in his pockets and his hat pushed back on his head. Then along another and yet another. He passed squares, gardens and crumbling walls, a railway line, a bus which disappeared into a cave like a fiery dragon. He wished to walk on and on like that, but he did not enjoy it. He was like a ship driving before the wind. Five years had been wasted. The war had been the great test and he had failed. There must be many like him but that was no consolation. However, he wanted to start all over again and that made him different from many others. He did not know yet where to begin, but he hoped to find out. Perhaps here, and if not here in another place. He knew that others studied or worked in a bank or a factory. But he did not want to do that, because it was not a new beginning. They had thrown him overboard when he seized the flag. The waves had closed over him; he was only saved by a miracle. The angel had looked at him and had passed on, but he would meet him again. Perhaps at the next street corner where a white signboard was to be seen above the pavement. Perhaps near the globe which stood in front of his books, perhaps only at the moment of death. But he would find him one day.

The dim stars showed him that he was walking towards the east and the appearance of the town confirmed this. War had been more disastrous here than in other quarters. The houses looked eaten away, as if leprous. The windows were blind, the people demoralised, and those who crept from the doorways into the street had livid faces and walked with cautious steps as if crossing deserted battlefields. Girls accosted him and followed him for a while; it was as if he could see through their eyes into an abysmal depth. He heard very few coarse or wicked words, and even these sounded as if they came from behind closed doors. He was not afraid of being robbed, for he had no possessions. He was as lonely as these outcasts who lived in cellars and backyards, and what they considered as his property was to him as stale as the air they breathed.

He did not want to investigate their lives or convert them. He only wanted to experience a world which was unknown to him. He knew all that people talked about in his own house behind the dark curtains, their thoughts and desires. But this life was new to him, and he wanted to learn all about it and to understand this strange world, the whole world which turned silently round and round in front of his rows of books. War, death, destruction that could not be the sum total of life. Somewhere the reins of this driverless carriage were trailing on the ground. He felt the urge to keep on moving until they swept near him, so that he could grasp them in his hands. He must try to find some meaning in all this, not necessarily the full solution, but at least some sense, even an inkling of a plan. Then he would be willing to start afresh in God's name.

His road led over a bridge which spanned the railway lines and he saw express trains rushing into the silent blackness which covered the fields and the woods. In the west the signals were close together: red and green lights as at the entrance to a harbour. A soft breeze fanned his hands as he grasped the cold iron railings, and he felt as if he were sailing towards a foreign shore with damped-down fires, steering between treacherous sectors of light, where death, silent and watchful, lay in ambush beneath the twinkling stars.

A little later he found himself on top of a bus. The illuminated advertisements became more frequent and raced by at greater speed; the streets became more crowded; hotel-porters stood like kings in entrance halls of marble. Above the heads of the crowd, coloured arms holding newspapers were lifted and hoarse voices cried the news of the day: the rate of exchange, the murders, the strikes, the revolutions.

Thomas got out and walked on aimlessly. He soon disappeared in the crowd, swallowed up like a drop of water in a broad stream. Cripples squatted near the railings of the gardens and their songs fell on the ears of the crowd with the montonous regularity of a machine. Coins jingled, and the hands of the givers were drawn back quickly, as if fearing to be caught stealthily paying ransom to the stone-faced god of war who still stared down from the damaged roofs. Now and again the broad caps of the Salvation Army could be seen emerging from well-lit doorways. The faces underneath them looked calm and detached from the world, as if they had already forgotten the sneers and the pity which had greeted them inside.

An idea crossed Thomas's mind and made him smile. 'What would they say at home, if I suddenly appeared in the uniform of a Salvation Army officer?' Thomas the lieutenant of God! God had gone away but the prophets had arrived. They came out of the cellars; they lifted their naked, withered arms in the pulpits, in the parliament they spoke of the realm of love; they read wisdom and man's fate in the stars. But the angel had disappeared, and he was the only one who could cast lots and knew.

A policeman in white gloves stopped the traffic at the crossroads. Somebody hailed Thomas. He approached the halted car reluctantly. A comrade from his last ship moved aside in the car to make room for him. But Thomas shook his head; a visit to a bar did not appeal to him. He preferred to remain in the open air. What was he doing? Oh nothing, he was waiting. The other man smiled. 'You ought to come on to the Stock Exchange with me, Thomas,' he said. 'I assure you they make money there, and the whole thing is like a night-battle. You never know how you will come out but if you are successful it's well worth while. Shall I give you a tip, Thomas? It will be worth more to you than a year's pension.'

Thomas refused that also. The road cleared and the car moved on slowly. 'All the best, Thomas, until the next war . . .'

For a while he looked after the car. Then he went down the next street to the underground. All of a sudden he longed to see the river, and its dark water, in which the masts were reflected and above which the stars shone brightly. No, success could not be the last word. Gamblers were successful, too, but nothing was recorded of their lives in the books from which children learned how to live. That man had been a good officer and a good comrade, but when you discarded your uniform you ought to be more than that. Life demands more than is required on board a warship. He was again overcome by doubts and for a moment he thought that it must be good to write addresses, distribute parcels, anything that made the blood circulate in your fingers. There are no holidays for young hands.

He stopped in front of a flower shop and stared at the vases of hothouse lilac. 'If I had only fired,' he meditated, 'they would have killed me and all would be well . . . a second, nay half a second and the decision was missed . . . that is why the angel does not come . . .'

In the underground an old man sat opposite to him and stared at a sheet of paper, which was covered with circles and signs. His hair fell down to his shoulders and he wore queer 'reform' shoes, which had been patched up in many places. 'How rich and patient are these times,' thought Thomas. 'There must be a place for me somewhere and an object in life. One must wait for the needle of the compass to settle in one direction . . .'

The man sighed and looked at Thomas. He had good brown eyes, slightly watery, and with the astonished look of a man who had suffered much. Thus might a cow which is milked out of turn stare, thought Thomas. But no sooner had this thought entered his mind, than he reproached himself for having thus judged a fellow creature. The man raised his forefinger and whispered: 'Capricorn, is it not? Between the 23rd of December and the 23rd of January, is that right?'

Thomas forgot his good intentions, when he was accosted with such unwanted familiarity. 'No,' he replied bluntly and changed his seat.

The astrologer got out at the next bus stop. When he reached the door, he bent over Thomas, obviously quite unoffended and whispered behind his hand: 'The knees are critical under Capricorn – even dangerous – always take good care of your knees, dear sir.' With a friendly smile he raised his forefinger once more, warningly, and disappeared.

The street sloped slightly towards the river, and when Thomas went down the steps to the quay, he though of his knees and smiled. Then he walked slowly along the waterside. The river flowed lazily in the darkness and mirrored the trembling stars whose reflection always remained in the same place. Boats were moored along the embankment; the deck-planks shone and the ships' lanterns threw a dull glimmer on tackle and wood. Now and again a watchdog barked, first one then another, until the call was taken up right along the stream. Then it became quiet again, and only the soft lapping of the water was to be heard and the gentle breeze in the branches of the birch trees.

'It ought to be water,' he said, 'but calmer than the sea. I would not like to hear breakers again . . .'

He sat on one of the pillars of the embankment for a long time smoking and folding his hands idly over his knees. The air was warm and smelt of reeds and alders. In the distance the trains glided through the night like bands of light, in almost complete silence. The sky was bright as embroidered silk and once he thought he heard wild geese in the distance. He forgot everything now, the events of the last few hours as well as those of the hard years. He sat there like a peasant on a boundary stone and listened to the stirring of life on earth. However much the upheaval had destroyed, all men were still able to keep their feet on the cool earth and to see the stars revolve. Joachim should learn that too as soon as possible, before they spoilt him with their questionable knowledge.

When he began to feel cold, he got up. The lanterns were

still burning and a thin haze hung over the water. The nearby town seemed to be only a guest on this river bank.

Nobody spoke to him on his way home. He went a long way round in the hope that the guests would have gone when he returned. However, he found all the windows still bright and went away again. Midnight struck from a nearby church, and he listened to the sound fading away. Suddenly something came into his mind, and he walked quickly through a few streets to the church. The steeple rose like a dark needle in the bright night, but in the vicarage at the back of the garden two windows showed lights. Thomas climbed over the fence and went towards the glow. The windows were on the ground floor, and when the gravel crunched under his feet, a man stepped into the light. He wore a dark suit and Thomas thought that he had never seen such a big, heavy man before. Of course, he had not been to church.

'It is late, sir,' he said, 'but I would like to have a word with you.' The clergyman bent down in silence and tried to recognise the face on which the light fell. Then he withdrew without a word, and Thomas heard his steps approaching the front door, which he unlocked. 'Do not make a noise,' he said, 'they are all asleep.'

The room was large and full of books. A life-size figure of Christ carved in grey wood hung between the windows. Thomas took a seat, perturbed by the size of the figure. But the vicar did not seem to notice anything. He looked at him calmly. 'Quite a few people come to me at this hour,' he said. 'You need not excuse yourself. I realise that it must be serious.'

Thomas looked at him. His father might have walked behind the plough, but he, too, would have been a thoughtful man. This tendency seemed to have come to the surface in the son. His forehead and the lines around his mouth bore the traces of mental suffering, but above his smooth grey hair one might imagine the same halo as over the wooden figure on the wall. His face betrayed no feeling, but his grey eyes were old and understanding. They looked at Thomas with a friendly gaze, and he felt young and foolish under their scrutiny.

He sighed before he began. 'I am not a churchgoer, sir,' he said apologetically. The parson raised his hand.

'Let us speak of what is important,' he interrupted.

'Nor have I read the Bible for a long time,' Thomas went on, 'not since my confirmation. My service was hard and somehow Bible reading did not seem to go with it. Today I found the Psalms among my books, quite an old edition in large print. I inherited it during the war. I turned the leaves and found the Ninetieth Psalm. I remembered it, most of it at least, but there was one verse which I did not know. As a child one passes over such things, besides this verse was not written for children. "Swift as a breath our lives pass away." First I went on reading, as if it did not mean anything special, but then I turned back to it and read it once more. I could not go on reading – it was as if a mast had crashed down on me. The weight is so great that one cannot get up.'

The parson nodded. He supported his head on his right hand and looked at Thomas without moving. 'Yes,' he said, 'of course you will say that you happened to read this psalm by pure chance. I myself when these things happen to me – and they do happen quite often – look upon them from a different angle. From my point of view that verse was waiting until its time had come. Do you understand? A man lives his life, and a verse lives in its own sphere, and it may be that their paths cross at some time. It means – of course in my opinion only – that the verse has been waiting for its man and the man for his verse. When a certain phase of one's life has been accomplished, be it a collapse or a success, or even only a period of gloom and uncertainty, then all of a sudden the verse appears. The right page opens of its own accord and reveals itself in our path. It conquers us. Do you not think so?'

'Yes,' said Thomas in a low voice, 'it has conquered us, that is how it is.'

'And now you want me to tell you what you are to do about it, don't you? The verse oppresses you; it is like a dull, persistent pain, always present. You read something, or you go for a walk for many hours in the daytime or preferably at night. Or you think of the Skagerrak or of your end. But it is always with you, it is no longer outside, in a book which remains at home when you go out. It is already deep within you, in your blood; you are no longer its master.'

'Yes,' said Thomas, 'that's it.'

'Now you must look at it like this,' the vicar went on, 'or rather it would be well to try to look upon it like this: the verse has done its duty; it is as if it had risen from death and was resurrected for your sake. Now it is a question whether you will do your duty. I will not call it resurrection after all, for that is a very great word. Are you going to bury the verse again, strangle it, so to speak, and cover it with earth . . . yes, I said strangle it – then it will twitch for a little while, like the child in Tolstoi's book – at night, when you wake out of a dream, or at a party, or perhaps when you look at your boy. But after a while it will become quiet, as quiet as it was before. It knocked and you did not open. You set the dogs on it, and now it is dead. It is lost to you – irrevocably – for ever.

'That is one way. The other is just as clear, namely that you do your duty. Which means that you stop wasting your years as a breath. If you do that, the verse will lie still. Its warning, its reproach and its accusation will have been heeded by you. It is no longer meant for you; you have silenced it. As far as you have been concerned, its mission has been fulfilled. In a fairy tale the dragon is changed into a princess; in real life one simply ceases to be what one was hitherto and becomes a different man, not necessarily a saint or a prophet, but just different. Do you not agree?'

'Yes,' said Thomas, 'but one cannot change oneself just like that, I mean become religious or have faith, as one calls it.'

'Become religious? Have faith?' The parson bent forward and looked at him in surprise. 'What made you think of that? One must work, work! Do you understand? Nothing but work – that's what the verse means.'

'But you as a clergyman. . . .'

The big man got up and stood in front of the crucifix. He was almost as tall as the image of Christ, and they seemed to look into each other's eyes, which were on the same level.

'HE', said the parson in a low voice, turning half round, 'will forgive me for mentioning his name so rarely; that I only speak for the one thing needed so badly today – of work. Also in church, especially in church. For four years we have abused His name, now we should not pronounce it for another four years. We have killed and now we should start working with the sweat of our brow, nothing but work. Then we shall see whether we shall become worthy to pronounce his beloved name once more.'

'How do you mean work, sir? What kind of work? I myself. . . .'

The parson lifted his hand. He was standing with his back to the window, as if he had just come out of the darkness of the night – a peasant whose fields kept him awake. 'Cabinet ministers and road sweepers live in this community,' he said. 'Neither of them comes to church but both work; the work of both is equally dignified. The one I can see when I leave my house, the other I cannot see. I only guess or read about him in the newspaper. I personally believe that the road sweeper is happier with his work than the minister. He has his district, his broom and his barrow. Nobody trepasses on his preserves. The cabinet minister is not so lucky. Horse droppings are easier to remove than intrigue or political enmity. Besides the road sweeper can always hope to become a minister one day, whereas for the other there is no star in the sky to which he can reach out. But all these things are quite unimportant. You must not ask: what work? Look at my table! Do you see these letters? Dozens, hundreds of letters written with blood, yes, I say so explicitly: written with blood. Do you not know how God has chastised us? Chastised us frightfully and without pity? Oh . . .' He lifted his hands and wrung them over his grey hair, and for a minute his face was more despairing than that of the grey image on the wall.

But then his hands dropped, and he smiled as if apologising. 'It overwhelms me sometimes,' he said, 'and will pass presently. . . . I have been watching you for a long time, Herr von Orla, for nearly five years. Nothing remains hidden in this community. When you go out with your boy, or when you walk alone – long and lonely walks. But I always felt confident when I thought of you. He is sure to meet his angel, I thought. He who walks about so much is sure to meet him some time. I did not call on you – those are new-fashioned things. When the churches are empty, the vicars go to homes to give away admission cards. No, no. The farmers also wait until we come to them. But you did not want "the Word of the Lord" as it is called. You only wanted confirmation that something is not quite right in your life. And you thought that a vicar who is still awake at midnight might perhaps know. . . .'

'I have been home already,' said Thomas, 'and only when I saw that all the windows were still lighted and the cars parked in the street did I turn away again.'

'Yes, they live like Belshazzar and his servants . . . it was always so in times like these . . . one must must not scold, one must always be present, always there.' He leant his head against the back of his chair closing his eyes. Every feature was relaxed in deadly fatigue.

Thomas got up. 'Thank you so much, sir,' he said.

'You should not thank me, Herr von Orla, until you are sure that in the morning you will not regret this. And even then it is unnecessary. We do not deserve it, you know. Very few people deserve it, and I am not one of them.'

He accompanied him to the garden gate, locked it behind him and looked up to the stars once more. 'I visited a murderer today,' he said almost as an afterthought as he was already half turned towards the house. 'Yes, you must not be astonished; it was my duty . . . Tomorrow he will be executed. I sat with him for an hour and prayed – alone – for he did not want to pray. He did not want to speak either, not a word. But I thought perhaps he felt that it was good to have somebody with him, so that he was not alone with those terrible walls. But when the warder came to fetch me – and I looked back once more on his bent figure, he sat up and said: "It's a blessing that there are no parsons where I am going." He said it in quite a friendly tone, but how much must my profession have sinned, Herr von Orla, to justify such an utterance! Do you understand? But mine is not the only profession to sin, believe me. We never know how guilty we are, and how far we are responsible for everything that happens. For everything, do you hear? Yes, for everything. . . .'

Then he went back to the brightly-lit windows, and Thomas saw how rounded his heavy shoulders were.

Later on Joachim ought to go and see him, he thought, as he walked down the street slowly. When I am working again – and it will certainly not be here – Joachim ought to sit now and again in that large room and see what that man is doing. How alive his features are among all the dead ones around us.'

Nurse Beate was standing in the door of the flat as he came upstairs. 'Madam has been taken ill,' she whispered, obviously very alarmed. 'I do not know what it is.'

He went in without taking off his coat. At a glance he took in the tables with glasses and ashtrays, the folds in the carpet, the crumpled cushions on the sofas and armchairs. Coming out of the clean night air, he felt sick in the stale cigarette smoke. 'Please, open all the windows, nurse,' he said in a low voice. Then he went to the fireplace, where the fire was still burning.

His wife was cowering in one of the low armchairs. She had drawn up her feet, and her head was lying against the back of the chair. Her face looked white and exhausted with small drops of sweat on her wrinkled forehead. As he stretched out his hand to stroke her hair, she opened her eyes and smiled. Her gaze was dull; she was half unconscious, her features were distorted by the smile like those of a mask. 'Tho – mas,' she whispered with difficulty. She was drunk.

His hand stopped in its movement and he stared into her face. He felt his skin grow cold, and a bitter taste came into his mouth. 'We are responsible for everything' – went through his thoughts, 'yes, for everything. . . .'

They carried her into her bedroom and Thomas sent the

nurse for a glass of milk. He remained standing at the foot of the bed until she came back. 'A slight poisoning,' he said. 'After this she will be better. Call me if she should get worse.' He held her gaze until she appeared to understand.

'I am sure I can manage alone now, captain,' she said.

In his room he sat down on a narrow divan and rested his head on his hands. He knew that it was hopeless. The aftermath of war was as merciless as the years of bloodshed. Ten years ago he would have thought it his duty to go down with his ship. He did not believe that any more. His father had never believed it.

'A man, Thomas, who suffers himself to be drawn into the whirlpool by his wife, has ceased to be a man.' They were standing at the coffin of a ploughman who had drowned himself, because his wife had deceived him. Thomas was still a cadet, but his father had shown him the dead man. He saw him standing there, his hands resting on his stick looking past the dead man at the green field. White clouds sailed through the sky and threw dark shadows over the young crop, and in the distance there was the sound of a scythe being sharpened. 'You will remember, Thomas,' said his father. 'There will be a time when your life will not belong either to you or your wife, to neither of you. . . .'

Now he did remember. It was not good that his father had died so early.

He fetched a pillow and a blanket from the spare room. Before he put out the light, he went once more to the globe. He put his finger on the summit of Mount Everest and moved it slightly. The big ball began rotating on its axis with a whirring noise, and mountains, plains and oceans passed before his eyes. They rose and sank, a patch of colour, a network of lines, light and shadow. He bent forward in slight surprise; he seemed to be looking down on his earthly home from another star – far away, in icy space, and destiny seemed as strange as a fairy tale of days long gone by.

Then the rotation grew gradually slower until at last it stopped. His own part of the world lay spread before his gaze, but its image did not show the conflagration and devastation of the last few years. The continents and oceans lay quiet, the streams found their way as thin, blue lines over the curved plains, and the town in which he lived lay like a small, dark circle between water and woods. Towards the east the large, empty plains spread out becoming more and more empty the farther his eyes followed them to the mutilated boundaries of the German empire, and there in the blue and green of many lakes and forests his eyes rested once more, until the curvature of the globe caused it all to disappear into infinity.

CHAPTER TWO

AFTER TRAVELLING through the night and half the next day, Thomas alighted at a small wayside station and collected his bicycle from the luggage van. Outside the station he consulted his map once more, strapped on his knapsack and cycled down a road bordered by birches towards a forest which looked blue in the distance and seemed like the end of the world. Though the country was not unlike that near his home, he seemed to have travelled during the night over strange, wide streams and he thought that this country was not like any he had ever seen.

As he glided along almost without sound, assisted or hindered by a soft breeze according to the windings of the road, he turned over in his mind the possible reasons why he appeared to feel so at ease in this countryside, although at first sight the landscape seemed harsh, open and forbidding. He noticed that the air was stronger, that vegetation and agriculture were less flourishing here than in his birthplace. The houses and villages which nestled in the hollows were more poverty-stricken and less attractive. Roads and paths appeared more deserted, implements simpler and more workworn; the whole standard of life seemed humbler, as if the rule of nature was tyrannical here and more reluctant to yield to the demands of man than in other districts. He had the impression that here man must rely on his own strength and on the power within him, without that support from others which is accepted as a matter of course elsewhere, especially in towns.

Here the sky seemed infinite. Clusters of clouds sailed in stately dignity across the canopy of heaven, their heavy shadows trailing on the brown earth. Isolated trees stood on hillocks in the fields, their branches often bent to one side by the prevailing wind. As the trees were silhouetted against the sky they gave even the poverty-stricken fields a look of pride, for they seemed untouched since creation, save by wind, rain or a kindly sun.

He thought that the cries of the birds were pitched higher here; nowhere had he seen so many birds hovering or circling over the fields on the lookout for prey. Gradually they seemed to him to merge with the forests which he was approaching, the home of all that moved in the skies searching for food.

Whilst he had not yet reached that tranquillity of mind which he hoped to attain, he already felt that his thoughts were freer, and that he was ready to cope with anything that fate might have in store for him. He noticed with joy that his whole being faced the future with confidence, ready to accept whatever he might have to meet. The thoughts which had worried him in the last few days and during the night journey seemed to have been dissipated like mist by the rising sun.

The outline of the forest became clearer and more defined, and it seemed to him that hidden in its twilight lay not only the real meaning of the landscape but the goal of all his searching.

Even at a distance he realised that its oppressive silence could never be broken and that combined with the fields and the village it formed a monumental landscape comparable only to the vastness of the ocean or the majesty of high mountains.

Already he was able to perceive how straight the grey trunks towered, so close together that they seemed to make a solid wall. Above them the rounded treetops had the appearance of the granite shapes of a mountain chain.

As he drew nearer, the details, which up to then had been merged in the landscape, became clearer; he noticed pine plantations looking as if an oblong had been carved out of the forest and sunk into the earth, and next, a grove of beeches and a hill whose side was overgrown with light birch trees and dark juniper. Further on, they grey wall of the lichen-covered treetrunks appeared unbroken, except where it opened to swallow up the road.

Here Thomas got off his bicycle, as if it were quite the natural thing to do, so as to take a last look at the open landscape through which he had just come. He sat down on a treestump, around which the hepaticas grew like clusters of light-blue stars, and filled his pipe slowly. As the smoke drifted with the soft breeze, he looked back. The landscape appeared to him calmer, and in view of the rise in the road, more extensive than when he had cycled through it. Things which he had passed at intervals now seemed to be lying close together.

The vastness of the space, the soft contours of the landscape, the scarcity of houses, the calm of the atmosphere, the apparent infinity of the horizon, all combined to produce in him again that feeling of tranquillity and happiness which he had already experienced. He tried to visualise how a change of season would alter the appearance of the country, how such a change would affect himself, whether it would allow him to retain the feeling of happiness, or whether it would produce uncertainty once more, whether the first impression would remain fresh and become permanent, if instead of being a passer-by he were to settle down in this land and become a working part of it instead of remaining a spectator.

Even from this point of view the picture spread out before him seemed to inspire the same strength and comfort. When he turned round, his gaze encountered the multiplicity of treetrunks. There the sunbeams played over the moss and the bilberry leaves, causing the treetrunks to take on a red glow and to appear to recede deeper and deeper into the bluish twilight. The tapping of the woodpecker broke the silence, and yet seemed to render it more intense. Then a feeling of contentment came over him, and he thought that in spite of the vicissitudes of a hard life it might be possible for him to recapture the peaceful happiness of his childhood. Indeed, the tranquillity inherent in the landscape produced in him the feeling that the blissful peace of his early years had returned, and that he only had to reach out to grasp and recapture it completely. He knew, of course, that it is not given to man to put the clock back in this manner, and that each age must acquire its own peace of mind. Nevertheless he allowed himself to revel in this dreamy retrospect, fully realising that in a short time the hard facts of everyday life would demand his attention and call for a practical decision.

He cycled on, and when he reached a wooded height, he stopped once more. For on either side of the road he saw one of those large lakes on which his eyes had rested when he turned the globe in his library. The landscape as it appeared in reality was different, but he had an even more vivid impression that he was standing not only at the borders of the German empire, but on the threshold of a new experience. The inlets of the lakes were still covered with ice. Their shores were framed with the trees whose bluish tint merged gradually into the reddish-brown hue of the reeds, where echoed the plaintive note of the grebe. This land appeared untouched by the conflagration of war and its tragedies. As if its purity had been preserved by a layer of ice, which had only now disappeared, permitting it to emerge in immaculate serenity. To him it seemed unlike all other parts of the empire, not like a page which had been written on, crossed out and then written on again, but one which was ready for a new beginning, like a field ready for the first furrow made by the hand of man, over which the birds would gather and rejoice.

He thought of his child who was growing up at home, well looked after, and yet surrounded by an atmosphere of decadence and pleasure. He knew he would have to leave him there for a few years more, but one day he hoped to bring him to this place or to one like it to show him what one should live for – on this earth – where man was still striving.

At dusk he put up at an inn by the roadside, which was marked on his map. Scarcely ever in his life had he seen poverty and decay so close at hand; they seemed to be a good and useful beginning for this journey of his, which he hoped would not remain only a journey. His room was small but clean with a view on the plantations bathed in the setting sun; this gave him a feeling of contentment, so that the only request he made was to sit by the kitchen fire while his meal was being prepared.

A woman busied herself silently at the kitchen stove. A boy and a girl sat on a wooden bench and stared at him with wide eyes. They were about the same age as Joachim. The father remained standing behind the table with his back to the window, and after hesitating, went on mending a net with a wooden needle. He was dressed in a suit of coarse, grey material and wore high boots like the men Thomas had met on his way. Even in the warm room he wore his scarf.

To Thomas's eyes the faces of the innkeeper and his family appeared heavy and tired, as if the vast landscape had helped to mould them.

When asked what work he did, he told them that he had been helmsman on a large steamer and had spent nearly all his life at sea. But having lost his job, and disliking life in the big towns, where the wind only drove dust and bits of paper along instead of the salty surf of the sea, he had made up his mind to look round in this district to see whether he could rent a fishery, where with hard work he might earn his daily bread, food at least, for paper money was losing its value faster and faster.

'You might well be able to find something,' said the man slowly, though he did not think that there was anything in this district. He offered to put Thomas on to some people who might help him. He told him there was a lot of unrest in the neighbourhood, because of the fear of the Poles, and because the young people were throwing up their jobs under the impression that it was no longer necessary to work, or that those should now work who had never done so. He himself was left alone with his wife, both his farmhand and maid had left for the country town where, no doubt, they were reaping a golden harvest.

He noticed that in spite of all his heavy work at sea the gentleman had very delicate hands, and he was doubtful whether with the best will it would be easy for him to take up such a hard trade.

However, Thomas reassured him about this; he wrote down the names which the man mentioned in his book and asked for permission to have his meal with the family in the kitchen. His idea was to save them trouble, and he also felt that he might just as well get used to the world in which he proposed to live.

The woman said grace before dinner, and during the meal he heard that they belonged to a religious sect like many others in the district, and that they were worried when they saw what was happening in the world. Some of them even thought that the vision of St John was about to be fulfilled.

Thomas did not agree with this and expressed the opinion that the German nation was sure to rise again from the confusion of the times. He also told them of his visit to the vicar who, as a matter of fact, had pointed out the way to him, and in whose house he had learnt how dangerous it is to condemn classes and professions carelessly on the basis of our knowledge of individuals only.

Then the conversation shifted to his seafaring experiences and the naval battles of the war and back again to the lives and customs of the people in the area. He and the innkeeper smoked their pipes, whilst the woman knitted, and the children listened breathlessly, as if Sindbad the Sailor had suddenly appeared in their pinewoods and brought romance into their lives.

After Thomas had said 'Good-night' and mounted the narrow staircase to his bedroom, candle in hand, the whole evening seemed to him a fine opening to a new world, full of good augury, and separated as if by decades from everything he had been accustomed to in the past.

The longer he stayed in this part of the country the more it grew on him. Day after day he cycled from one village to the next, sometimes staying for a while when something attracted him. At the equinox the weather changed; gales and heavy rains became frequent, and one evening snowflakes whirled round the grey trunks. Then the sun got the upper hand again and dried roads and paths. The ice in the inlets melted, and warbling larks rose into the blue sky, high above the young crops. Always Thomas was surrounded by large forests – sometimes leafy trees, sometimes conifers. He saw them in the pale light of the early morning, in the blazing glare of noon and on the gradual approach of darkness. The air was pure and bracing; it made breathing easy and seemed to evoke the carefree years during which he had stood high above the sails and the ocean at the masthead.

The advice which the man at the inn had given to Thomas turned out to be good. Some offers he found very attractive, and yet he hesitated to accept them, because he did not feel in his heart that they were what he needed. To him the approval of his heart seemed more important than the cool calculation of his mind.

Late in the afternoon of the tenth day Thomas came to a milestone on the road, where a narrow path branched off leading to a forester's house. The wood was rich in fine old oaks and nurseries of birch trees and seemed to him more beautiful than any he had passed through. He took this path feeling quite convinced that he would find a place to sleep, if not in the house itself, then in some barn or even in a haystack. The air had become milder, and a south wind blew quietly through the wood, bringing the scent of wild flowers which blossomed on the sunny slopes.

The forester came to the gate of the yard as Thomas drew near. He was a tall man walking with a stoop; the hair above his temples showed white from under his hat. The gaze of his very bright eyes pierced Thomas as if they were not seeing him, as if they were looking at somebody else, who had followed in his footsteps, behind and unknown to him. He seemed so lonely in front of the silent house, that Thomas hesitated to speak to him and ask for a favour – with the result that he stood there dumb, with his hands on the handlebar of his bicycle and his foot resting on the left pedal, as if ready to turn back, if the forester so wished.

However, unexpectedly, the forester came towards him, touched his hat and asked him in a low voice whether he was a seafaring man. Thomas somewhat bewildered said 'Yes', then the forester took his arm gently and asked him to come part of the way with him. When they got back into the wood, he begged Thomas not to be surprised that he had recognised him as a sailor and explained that each hard profession had its own characteristics. In this case they were a certain brightness of the eyes and some sharp lines from nostrils to mouth. Besides he knew something about sailors, his own son had been one, and he was pleased to meet someone who had probably 'been there'.

'Certainly I have "been there",' said Thomas.

'I thought so,' said the forester, 'and you need not turn back, you are very welcome to stay. First you must come with me, however, while I shoot snipe, as I should like to be alone with you to start with. For my wife is strange, indeed very strange – as quite a few people were left after the war – it is as if Death did not want them after all the young blood he had drunk.'

At first Thomas was silent, strangely affected by the manner of this man who spoke as if he had been ill for a long time, hurriedly and in a low voice, as if he did not yet know whether the spectres of fever were still standing around him, or whether he could speak with confidence about his visions and dreams to those who were healthy and wide awake.

Then Thomas told him who he was – a helmsman on a large steamer – and what he had come here for. He also told him that he had intended to cycle along the road to the next town, and something, he knew not what, had impelled him to take the path to the forester's house. It may have been that the wood was so beautiful and had filled him with such confidence or perhaps only because the south wind had tired him.

The old man nodded as if wishing to convey the impression that he knew the real reason and said that he felt sure they would get on well together. He did not doubt that his guest had reached his goal here; they would talk about it later, now they had to attend to the shooting.

They walked along a path, overgrown with grass, which led past plantations to a small swamp, where the evening sky was reflected in the pools. They stopped among the junipers; the forester opened his shooting-stick and sat down, and Thomas chose one of the tree stumps which had been warmed by the sun.

The untouched virginity of the forest would have filled Thomas with awe, had it not been for the song of hundreds of thrushes and for the strange cries of the birds of passage which were carried over the wood by a gentle breeze. His thoughts went back to the forester's words 'we shall get on well together' and from time to time he stole a shy glance at the man sitting in front of him. His rifle was resting on his knees, but instead of being on the look-out for birds, his eyes were lifted to the evening clouds which were sailing towards the northern horizon, long and narrow, bordered with crimson, like a silent squadron leaving the field of action.

Gradually the thrushes stopped singing, one after the other; only now and again a sound like that of a flute came from the far side of the swamp and faded into the general silence. Thomas's mind went back to the days when as a young man he had gone hunting, and he thought that it was now time to concentrate on the shoot and to be on the alert for the cry of the snipe which in spite of all its softness thrills the heart of the hunter.

As he was about to get up, the forester began to speak and it became immediately apparent that his thoughts had been far away all the time.

With some diffidence he asked whether Thomas had taken part in the battle of the Skagerrak. And when Thomas said 'Yes', the forester asked if he had been on one of the cruisers? perhaps on the *Seydlitz*?

'Not exactly on the *Seydlitz*, but on a sister-ship,' replied Thomas, and he began to guess what questions would follow. At that moment a snipe was heard to cry over the plantations; then it seemed to be above the swamp, until the grey shape of the bird was silhouetted against the evening sky. It was turning its head from side to side – as if searching for something. Now the bird's soft cry seemed to be immediately above them, and in a twinkling it had passed and disappeared.

Thomas had jumped up and had stretched out his hand towards the man sitting in front of him, but when he saw the expression on the forester's face, he dropped it, abashed. The man's eyes seemed to be watching something that was happening far away and a vision of which he seemed to perceive in the evening sky.

'Did you see the fire?' he asked in a low voice.

'Yes.'

'From the turret in front?'

'Yes, everybody saw it.'

'A column of fire?'

'Higher than the masts, but nobody there suffered, nobody. It must have struck them like a flash of lightning with such swiftness that they felt nothing.'

'That's what they say and that's what they write, but there was nobody there who had only his hair or his eyebrows singed and might live to tell the true story.'

Now Thomas put his hand gently on the bent shoulder

before him: 'We should not let our imagination dwell on these things,' he said, 'otherwise we cannot find the courage to go on living.'

'Yes, yes . . . that's what I tell she who has become strange . . . only . . . he was so afraid of fire, you know. Something terrible happened when he was a child . . . we had heated the oven to bake bread. The red embers had already been taken out and the loaves, too. The oven stood isolated in the garden, far away from the house. He came running along with the dogs chasing a cat, just playing, and the cat jumped into the oven. He laughed and slammed the door and did not know that it was red hot. That very moment it happened I shot a henhawk at the garden fence – that made him forget all about the cat and the oven and the dogs. He always lived for the present. Two days later he happened to think of it. He found the cat . . . And now the same thing has happened to him. The water is cool and deep, and I imagine it would be good to sleep at the bottom of the ocean, where strange plants move with the currents – but to be burnt and blackened – God's image destroyed and desecrated –'

He did not put his hand to his eyes, he still stared straight ahead to where the evening star shed its soft rays over the forest.

'No,' said Thomas with decision, 'then you have been told wrongly. We brought the cruiser, riddled with shells, into the harbour; and some of my comrades were there when they opened the turrets. Nobody was disfigured, they were – they crumbled into dust and ashes as one tried to move them. I tell you the truth and you must believe me.'

'Dust and ashes,' whispered the old man, 'that's better, much better – that is as God ordained it in the Bible, dust and ashes, that is good, and I need resent his fate no longer.'

He remained seated until an owl came out and circled

silently above them. Then they walked back along the dark path.

'His name was Gruber,' he said. 'Valentin Gruber – but I suppose you did not know him? No, the ships were so large. Neither of us understood why he wanted to go to sea – there are no sailors in our family. The lake had thrown a spell over him, there near the house, not the wood, only the lake. You will feel its spell also. He was called Valentin because I am Catholic, and he was baptised and brought up in my faith. My wife always maintained that we worshipped a false God, and that that was the cause of it all. Don't tell her anything and do not be surprised at anything you may see. Everything must be forgiven she who suffers, must it not?'

'Yes,' said Thomas in a low voice.

The table was already laid and the woman was looking out of the window. She only turned round when Gruber said that he had brought a guest. 'Welcome,' she said, holding out her hand. It was cold and almost wooden, and her voice sounded as if coming from a machine. Then she dropped her hand and went past Thomas to fetch a third plate. She did not see him. Her face was not careworn but gave the impression of a death-mask. She seemed blind and deaf to the outer world.

When they went to the table the woman folded her hands to say grace. Gruber made a movement as if to stop her but collected himself and lowered his eyes. The woman looked at the bread basket on the table. Her lips moved mechanically as she prayed:

'As guest, dear God, do come to us
And see what you have done to us.
The dead you have destroyed with water and fire–
The good and those of evil desire.
Are they all to enter your fold

Whilst suffering we endure untold?
As guest, dear God, do come to us,
Enjoy what you have done to us.'

Then she sat down. Her black silk frock was torn, and rustled at each movement. When she took a bite, it looked as if strange hands were feeding a rigid idol. She did not know that a stranger was sitting at the table. She had already forgotten. Maybe she saw a child running with an oar through the wood down to the edge of the lake, or perhaps she saw the columns of fire shooting out of the gun turrets, or she saw the figure of a god eating the dead with bloodstained hands. She had stepped out of all that was human. Thomas seemed to feel a cold blast as if from a tomb. He shivered and remained silent.

After supper she cleared the table and did not come back.

'That's how it is,' said Gruber, when they had lit their pipes. 'Seven years, my dear sir, seven years. Others would start drinking or cursing but I can't do that sort of thing. He was my son too, wasn't he? And so I am responsible too, am I not? Sometimes when I walk in the wood alone, I talk to myself aloud and for quite a time, just to see whether I can do so still, and I smile, too, for we don't want to forget that. I speak to him as I used to when we walked together through the wood. He was always merry and we laughed. He is not dead for me, you know. Here, at home he's always lying in state. I don't want that. The war has taken him from us, but he is always with me, and as you have told me that about dust and ashes, I will try to be happy again. It is good that you have come.'

'If he could see her,' thought Thomas, and in his mind's eye he saw the vicar again standing before the wooden Christ, 'but even he would not be able to help her. Seven years, and I have dared to complain.' He almost felt as if he loved this old man who wished to be happy again. The hair on his head was still black, it had only become grey round the temples, and now he also understood why the son had gone to sea: it must have been the eyes. He must have had the same eyes for which things were always too near and which wanted to find out what was beyond the horizon. He thought that one could learn that at sea, the only element which was infinite. But he had only learnt that death is at home in all elements.

'And can nothing be done for her?' he asked.

The other shook his head. 'The activities of doctors and clergymen are confined to certain ideas, which have ceased to have any meaning for her: God and duty and willingness to co-operate and so on.' He looked round cautiously. 'I am a simple human being,' he continued in a low voice, 'but I know. There are mothers and children who are not separated by the cutting of the umbilical cord. That was so with our child. They were always one, never two. She knew of the accident as soon as it happened. She came to me in the yard as pale as a ghost and pointed with outstretched arm towards the wood. "Now they have torn him from me," she said, "My life's blood is flowing away." And so it happened that she became as if lifeless. One must accept things as they are, sir, and therefore it is a blessing that you will be staying here, so that I may sit with you from time to time. What is your name, sir?'

As he bent forward and looked into Thomas's eyes with a smile, his face seemed to be illuminated by an inner light.

'Orla,' said Thomas, 'Thomas Orla; it's a Brandenburg name. But what makes you think that I am going to stay here?'

'You have been sent to me, dear Herr Orla, sent like an

angel of the Lord, that is what I believe. You see, in these seven years, there were times when I doubted the existence of God, but never that of the saints. They have been with me since childhood always, that is the basis of our faith; we are nearer to the saints than to God. He is so far away, so terribly far away. But they are near, almost by our side, for they, too, have suffered, just as we have or even more so. God, you see, does not suffer. Well, the saints have sent you. They saw that I am at my wits' end, therefore they sent that message about dust and ashes through you. That is a new start for my life, for I believe it. And as a reward for what you have done you will find here what you are seeking. In human life everything is preordained, and every good deed finds its own reward. The lake here is to be let, or rather I should say is not to be let, but the post of fisher is vacant, fisher and hunter in one person. It's an easy post–even though the general is somewhat strange. Everybody here is a little strange. There is a small house over there on the island, no farther than a bullet can carry. Its roof is thatched with reeds, it has a big hearth and a shed for the nets. The wood on the island is beautiful, young pine trees and birches interspersed by old oaks with withered crowns, where the herons perch at night. You will be quite alone there, you know, all alone, surrounded by wood and water. Nobody can come to see you without using a boat.'

'And the general?' asked Thomas. His pipe had gone out and he was listening as to a fairy tale. A spell seemed to emanate from the old man and to fall over him.

'Yes, all this belongs to him, dear sir. The castle, the estate and the lake. A poor man who lost both sons in the war. They often used to sit on my knees. Only a granddaughter lives with him, and she is like an angel in that sad house – and you will get the post. I will speak for you myself. He who has it now is a Bolshevik. One who wants to be called "Sir", and years ago his mother stole potatoes from my field. He calls the general a bloodsucker, and every child knows that the old gentleman only drinks red wine. However there are cannons in the hall of the castle, and two servants wearing uniform like soldiers stand near them. The Bolshevik says that he wants to lead a revolt, but everybody knows that the cannons are not loaded.'

'Can we go and see it?' asked Thomas, and got up. 'I mean the island and all that. The moon is shining, and perhaps by tomorrow it may all prove to have been a dream.'

The old man smiled. 'He was just the same,' he said, 'everything had to be done at once, without any delay, lest it might have disappeared by the following day. Nothing disappears, dear sir. If one is old, one knows that nothing disappears. But let us go; by moonlight the place will throw its spell over you even more deeply than by day.'

The air had become warmer and a few raindrops fell from a stray cloud on to the dry leaves under the oak trees. 'Is anybody there?' asked Thomas in a whisper. 'No, no that noise is made by the rain and it is part of the magic. In this neighbourhood at night it always sounds as if somebody were walking. But there is nobody; the wood is quiet and empty. It may be that the dead have risen from the earth and the water, but of these things we cannot claim to know anything.'

The moon was still low in the sky, so that they only saw its reflected light. The heavens were bathed in a soft glow which seemed to come from a portal far away. Every now and then a spark flared up in the wood when a moonbeam fell on moist bark through a gap in the branches. Owls hooted and an unknown bird twittered over the water as if asking its way.

The path led downwards, and soon they were able to see

the lake which lay in darkness like a dull disc in an irregular frame. In the distance it seemed to become more grey and dull, until it merged into the blackness of the night. A moonbeam reached down to their feet and between the slowly drifting clouds they could see the stars. On earth everything was still, even the moonbeam was immobile, and at the edge of the lake the bulrushes stood like spears with glowing tips. Then again it seemed as if somebody were walking softly through the wood and over the water, secretly and breathlessly, now on the right, now on the left.

'There it is,' whispered the forester.

Thomas saw the island, fairly close to the shore. It lay like a black spot on the disc which was the lake, except that the line of the treetops was picked out in white by the moon which made the withered branches of the oaks appear like masts. On them dark birds sat motionless.

'Here is the boat,' said the forester. But Thomas did not want to get in. He knew intuitively that this was where he must live and probably also die. He saw it with his eyes and he knew it with his heart. But he did not want to go and see it in the magic of the moonlight, for too much was at stake. He was forty-five years old, and he wanted to see all this in daylight. It would still be there in the morning, and it would be a good thing if it were to rain and if a sharp wind were to blow, so that everything would look grey and real. 'No, tomorrow morning,' he said.

They stayed there for a short time and gazed over the water. One of the big birds on the island rose and flapped its wings. A hoarse cry came across the water, then complete calm reigned once more.

'Those are the herons,' said the forester. 'The general doesn't like them, but they are noble birds, and their company is all you will have on the island.'

'That will be all right,' said Thomas. Then they walked back the way they had come. The house was in darkness, and Thomas went upstairs with a candle in his hand. 'His room was next to yours,' said Gruber. 'She doesn't allow anybody to go into it. But it is quiet there and you needn't be afraid.'

Thomas stood at the open window lost in thought. Most assuredly he was not afraid. The place he had seen was meant for him. He felt that all this had been waiting for him, otherwise he would have cycled on to the town. One need only accept one's fate without resisting. He left the window open and in the darkness he looked up at the low ceiling. The big bird, how it had opened its heavy wings and had then sunk back into sleep. The moon shone on its closed eyes, the stars glowed, all was good and peaceful there. He felt the urge to go there and to work, never before had he been alone; ships, men, houses. He had no more ambition and very little faith – swift as a breath – but there he would talk to himself, as lonely as the big birds. Then he fell asleep.

CHAPTER THREE

WHEN THOMAS woke up the rain was pattering on the roof, and somebody was walking about in the next room. He realised this from the creaking of a floorboard at regular intervals. It sounded as if two trees were rubbing against each other in the wood. There was a faint light behind the windows but it was still night. You could only distinguish the outlines of things in the room.

Thomas sat up and listened. The steps were slow and quite regular, and when his breathing became quieter, he thought he heard the rustling of a silk frock. So it was the woman who was in her son's room. He did not know whether she slept there. The rain was streaming down; there was no wind and the wood stood motionless under the falling drops. There was only one deep sound round the house, soothing like the sound of breakers in the distance. Then a deep, soft voice became audible, as if humming a tune. The woman was singing as if she had just lulled a child to sleep. But her singing was in sharp contrast to the pattering of the rain, for it was full of feeling. It had nothing plaintive in it, but sounded like a child who had remembered a marching song and was unconsciously singing it softly to himself while walking along the road at sunset.

Thomas thought he knew the song, yes, he knew it as well as he knew his name, but in the uncertain light of the breaking dawn and in the apparent unreality of everything about him, he could not remember the words. Dream and morning merged into each other, and as he listened he felt that all this belonged to his new life – the singing of the woman as well as the rain. Grief did not hide itself here as it did in the towns, but sang in the night, careless of being heard even by a stranger whom it woke from his sleep.

The singing ceased or melted into the swish of the rain, and the creaking of the floorboard seemed to come from a great distance, like two pine trees rubbing against each other in the wood and shivering in the early morning air. Then it seemed as if on the other side of the wall somebody were softly laughing, somebody who was all alone, all alone, from whose memory this soft sound escaped. Then Thomas dropped off to sleep again.

When he went downstairs later there was nobody in the room, but the forester had left a note beside his plate. Thomas was to take the boat to the island and wait for him there, or later on at the house. The handwriting was firm and upright, and Thomas thought again of the song he had heard in the night, and how strange the woman's handwriting would look next to her husband's. 'Seven years, my dear sir –'

He left the house quietly. The rain had almost stopped but dark clouds were still drifting over the wood. The drops ceaselessly fell off the trees on to the dead leaves, and each gust of wind made a heavy spray. It was still warm, and an acrid smell arose from the damp soil. A light haze covered the lake and the island lay gloomy in the grey water. The house was visible now; it was no bigger than a large hut – really just a heavy thatch over a low white wall, but smoke was rising from the chimney. There was a small wooded hill crowned with oaks behind the house. The withered treetops became indistinct in the haze.

Thomas stood at the water's edge and listened for a sound from the woods or from over the water, but all he could hear was the call of a reed-warbler and the dripping of the raindrops in the wood. He stood for a long time looking at the island. He felt quite reassured. His heart throbbed quietly and the thought came into his mind that his first job would be to get a small, light boat for Joachim when he came in his summer holidays. Now that he had settled everything in his mind, it seemed to him the natural and obvious thing to do.

As the seats in the boat were wet, he rowed to the island standing up. The boat had a flat bottom, and each movement of his long oar caused the bow to rise out of the water with a hissing sound. At first he was able to see through the clear water to the sandy bottom of the lake which showed the ridges of former wavelets. Then the water became darker, nearly black, and green plants growing up from the bottom waved to and fro. Now and again a heavy fish jumped into the light and a silver sheen flashed through the grey air. Then thin circles spread over the lake, came as far as his boat, and vanished again. It seemed to him as if he had been rowing here for ever, as if he need never stop, as if the ships and the ocean had been only a dream, some ghastly nightmare of a restless sleep, and now everything was coming back into proportion in sober and orderly reality.

The flat keel grounded noiselessly on the sandy shore and Thomas got out. He went straight up the slope to the house without looking round and knocked at the door. As nobody answered he went inside.

In the dim light he could only see the fire in the stove and a dark figure of a man who seemed to be staring into it. The man's arms were on his knees and his hands supported his chin. As there was no reply to Thomas's greeting, he went past the man and sat down on a wooden stool in front of the stove. The man looked sullen, but not evil, and sat motionless. His head was crowned with a tuft of grey hair. The flames were reflected on the dome of his forehead and in his eyes which had an almost melancholy expression. His beard, grey and unkempt, hung down over his chest. The room seemed to be filled with a smell of smoke and fish.

Here it was even calmer than on the water; the only sound came from the fire crackling behind the half-open door of the stove. An opaque light fell through the narrow windows on to the dark timbers of the walls. Nets were hanging on wooden pegs and oars stood upright in the corners.

'What do you want?' said the man looking up reluctantly.

Thomas said that he wanted to become his successor.

'Successor is good,' said the man, looking at Thomas out of the corner of his eye. 'Successor to the throne would be even better, for thrones are shaky nowadays and this one especially.'

'Well, I never wished to sit on a throne,' said Thomas.

'What do you want to do?'

'To work. I can't find a job at sea any more, and I can't stand the noise in the big towns.'

The man took his pipe out of his mouth and looked at Thomas for some time. 'You're a funny fellow,' he said thoughtfully. 'I wonder whether you are somebody other than you seem.'

'No, I'm not,' said Thomas with a smile.

'Anything is possible nowadays. From the right and from the left. You needn't be afraid of noise here. No soap-box orator has ever come to the island to talk of the suffering proletariat. You want to work? That you can do here if it pleases you to work for the bloodsuckers. It doesn't suit me.'

'When we were at sea, we never asked whom we were

working for,' said Thomas. 'Just to be at sea was a joy, and if I work here I hope to feel the same way.'

'I see,' said the man. 'Have you already been across there?' and he pointed with his thumb over his shoulder.

'No.'

'The general is not half bad in his way, but stupid. I can't tell you how awfully stupid. He's still living in the times of the crusades. "My lake, my wood, my castle." Can't understand that it belongs to me as well as to him. *Property is theft*, he has never heard of that. I must admit that we often spoke frankly to each other – about everything – except the flag.'

'Which flag?'

The fisherman slowly unbuttoned his coat, on which fish-scales shone, and carefully took out of his breast-pocket a piece of red cloth. It was folded many times and split in places in the folds. He spread it out over his knees and smoothed it with a heavy hand.

'This one,' he said. 'Every time I hoisted it over the roof, they came and pulled it down, he and his minions. At last I gave notice. For there must be a flag.' He cupped his chin with his hands once more and stared at the red cloth.

'But here on the island?' asked Thomas. 'Is it really necessary?'

'Everywhere the flag must fly,' replied the man sullenly. 'Over the island and over the coffin. . . .'

'And what are you going to do now?'

'Don't know. Probably I shall go to the town and lash out on all sides with an oar. I don't want to work any more. I have been working sixty years for a pittance and, after all that, one is not even allowed to hoist the flag when one wants to.' He spat into the fire and took a swig out of a white bottle.

He offered it to Thomas, who refused. 'You will learn all

that, my friend, here you will learn all that,' he muttered gloomily.

Thomas took a small parcel from his wallet. It was wrapped in tissue paper and was as thin as a letter. He unfolded the paper and took out a piece of cloth which was no larger than a hand and torn at the edges. It was black all over except for one corner in which a white spot seemed to be stitched on. 'Look here,' he said, 'that is my flag. They hit me over the head and threw me overboard, but I did not let go, and with my hand I tore a piece off it. It was still in my closed hand when somebody pulled me out, and I have kept it. It doesn't look worse than yours, does it? Only smaller and more insignificant. But I am not allowed to hoist it any more; that we have in common.' He smiled and allowed the light of the fire to play on the cloth.

'Disguised after all,' said the fisherman bending forward and looking at the torn piece of flag in Thomas's hand. 'Bad colours,' he said sadly, 'many had to pay the last penalty for them. They were all colour blind, rushed in with a cheer and went to the bottom head first. The world is stupid, so very stupid.'

'In town you too will go to the bottom head first,' said Thomas.

The fisherman waved the idea aside with his hand. 'What does it matter?' he said. 'Anyhow I shall take some of them along with me, and this will be laid on my coffin.'

He folded up the cloth and put it back. 'When one is sixty, one is no longer afraid, my friend; put yours in a safe place, too. I like you even though you are not what you seem. He who lets himself be hit over the head rather than leave go of his flag is a good chap. Others just sneak away, their tail between their legs, like dogs.'

He was willing to show Thomas everything but there was

not much to show. At the door he turned round and looked back. 'Change of flags,' he said, 'what a joke–you and I.' Then he went in front of Thomas along the narrow path which led through the plantation to the oak trees. A ladder was leaning against one of the treetrunks. They climbed up and found a small platform with a rustic seat among the huge branches. From here could be seen the whole island, the lake, the woods and a distant village between meadows and fields.

'The captain's bridge,' said the old man and leant against the railing. 'From here you can see them coming, whether reds, or blacks, or blacks, whites and reds. It is a proper place for a machine gun, but I hadn't one. Now listen to me! The nets should be put in those two bays; when the wind is in the east you should use that one, when in the west this one. If a storm is brewing, you can fish anywhere. When the wind is in the north, it's useless to try, it's better to stay at home and dry your nets. The nets for crayfish should be put there, two or three metres down. If there is anything you don't know, don't ask the general, but row through that small stream into the next lake. A man lives there who must be well over eighty, perhaps even a hundred. His name is Peter–the people call him St Peter. But I haven't seen him walking on the waves. He understands all about the fish, he talks to them, knows when they migrate and when they don't, looks into the future and takes snuff. By the way, what's your name?'

'Thomas.'

'Well now, there we are, all the saints together, my name is Christoph, and I can carry you over the water. By the way the boss doesn't want you to catch much. His idea is that the people in the town can starve. You will have a good life here if you have done something and have got to hide yourself. Nobody will spy on you here, not even the fishery-inspector. He is afraid of the old man. But it isn't always as it is today, my friend. There are dark days when the blizzard howls in the chimney. You think of all the mistakes you made in life, and there is nobody who will smoke a pipe with you. The ice cracks and grinds in the lake, and the foxes bark, and sometimes a wolf howls in the plantations. Then you will start drinking, my friend, because you know there is nothing else between you and madness. He who has not lain in a golden cradle can spread his nets for sixty or eighty years and yet he will not catch the fish with the golden crown. Whether you hoist the red flag or the black, white and red flag doesn't matter, you will grow silent here, as silent as a stone at the bottom of the lake.'

He made a gesture with his hand and started climbing down the ladder. 'The nets are all in order,' he said when they had come to the door of the house, 'they're all three as I found them. In the winter you must look out for mice and see that they don't do damage. I'm leaving tonight, and I shall fasten the boat to that tall pine tree over there.'

He stood in the doorway and to Thomas he seemed to symbolise the spirit of the island – grey, weather-worn and bent – and thought he himself might look like that standing there in twenty years' time. The door which hid the future seemed to turn on noiseless hinges, and for the space of a heartbeat he saw himself as in a vision standing in the doorway just like that other man, turning round and going in and sitting in front of the fire. The light of the flames playing over the globe, countries and oceans, mountains and streams. His head supported in his hand, he looked past it, without any desire, with many experiences behind him, but with very little prospect for the future, a lonely man, mute as the stones at the bottom of the lake.

'I shall catch it, Christoph,' he said, 'the fish with the golden crown. I shall catch it.'

The other only made a grimace, waved his hand and went inside.

An invisible clock struck eleven as Thomas arrived at the foot of the steps leading to the castle. It was nothing but a large manor house with two wings and a brown roof. It stood in an imposing and stately position overlooking a bay of the lake. The ivy which had climbed to the windows of the second storey made it appear old and very secluded. The coat-of-arms above the heavy door was so weathered that you could not recognise more than a mailed fist holding something, but it might just as well have been the stalk of a lily or the handle of a battleaxe. The park behind the house was bordered by woods and in the distance a thin haze rose over dark fields, the extent of which seemed to be bounded only by the horizon. A gap appeared between the moving clouds, and a ray of sun fell on the wet earth, on the glistening roofs and on the flagstaff over the centre of the house.

Thomas went up the steps and rang an old-fashioned bell. The heavy door was opened by a giant in uniform whose white belt and gold braid looked as if it had been designed at the time of Frederick the Great. The man was not wearing a busby; his hair was close cropped, and he looked as if he had just been taken from behind the plough where he must have felt much more at ease than in his present occupation.

'The general wishes to see you,' he said in a mournful tone, and helped Thomas out of his coat. It sounded as if the general were lying on his deathbed.

Thomas found himself in a lofty hall which ran the length of the whole building. He saw a fine, broad staircase of brown polished wood, palms, antlers, stuffed birds, arms, ancestral portraits and an enormous fireplace where an entire tree stump was smouldering. In the background two old cannons stood on either side of a double door, their dark muzzles pointing towards the entrance menacingly. But there was no artillery man with a slow match near him, as Christoph had said, ready to open fire on anyone whose attitude and ideology he did not like. Thomas almost expected to see a regimental band with all its instruments but they were not visible. He followed the tall grenadier, or whatever he was, with confidence, though a little confused at all this gloomy solemnity. They went through an anteroom full of books to an oak door at which the giant knocked distinctly but with due respect.

A somewhat hoarse voice called: 'Come in.' The tall servant opened the door, stepped or rather jumped over the threshold with astonishing agility, clicked his heels, and announced in a high-pitched voice: 'The successor of Mr Christoph, sir.'

A short, thickset man in undress uniform raised his head from the papers on his desk, said: 'Idiot' and beckoned Thomas to approach. He pointed to a chair at the side of the desk, waited until the giant had left the room, and then looked at Thomas.

The general's face seemed familiar to Thomas. He almost imagined that he had seen it in the many-volumed *History of the Conquest of India* which had stood in his father's bookcase, right at the bottom. Six dark brown, heavy tomes, in which he had particularly loved the pallid watercolours – a medium quite insufficient in depth for the glow of those landscapes – filled with strange men, animals and plants. There amid jewel-bedecked Maharajahs and demonic temples, were also portraits of the conquerors. Soldiers, captains and merchant princes, with bronzed skins and white bushy hair, stern, sometimes cruel lips and bright, blue eyes of childish candour. When these men returned home to their green misty island, they sat before the great open fireplaces of their mansions and drank the heavy wine which had made the journey to and from India time and again in old oak casks, so mellowing into that soft warmth which gave their faces a florid, bronzed contentment. He had pictured these men to himself, surrounded by a pack of hounds and countless grandchildren, for whom there had been in his childish thought but one mysterious and almost tropical name: Nabob. He did not know where this word came from, nor what it meant, but something threatening and at the same time stimulating wafted from these syllables: power and loneliness and an exotic and strange fascination. Once, he had made his schoolmaster stare at him in helpless astonishment when, on being asked what he wanted to be when he grew up, he had answered loudly and without any hesitation: a Nabob!

Sitting here he had almost to conceal a smile when he reflected how he had failed to redeem that childish promise to attain the outward show or the inner self-confidence, or that bearing which conveys the impression of omnipotence. Today he was as far removed from a pack of hounds as from a bevy of flaxen-haired grandchildren. This man facing Thomas across the table with features which seemed familiar to him from the pages of those books, might also well be far behind those imagined Nabobs – in actual fact as well as in memories, power and wealth – except perhaps that he might possess in the cellars of this house a considerable, but ever-diminishing store of that wine which, consumed before roaring fires in long winter evenings, might produce a complexion seeming to have been tanned and bronzed by an Indian sun.

These thoughts made Thomas feel that he would get over the barriers of age and rank quite easily and that he could put up with the peculiarities for which he was prepared and some of which he had already experienced.

'The name is Orla?' the general asked in a hoarse voice. The words came out abruptly like bullets from a rifle.

'Yes, sir.'

'Served in the forces?'

'Yes, sir.'

'Any medals?'

'Yes, sir.'

There was a short pause during which the general surveyed his visitor piercingly – not from mistrust but from an old habit which had been useful when inspecting the ranks. Thomas was convinced that he would stare at an orphan-child or a new-born calf in exactly the same manner. So he was not put out and did not flinch under the gaze of those blue eyes.

'Gruber tells me,' said the general, 'that you have been in the battle of the Skagerrak and that sort of thing. I distrust all sailors. They were the first to be beaten. Hope you will be an exception to the rule. I can only do with reliable people; do you hear, re-li-able?'

'Yes, sir.'

'All right. Your predecessor was an ass. Fair distribution of property. World peace, red flag and similar nonsense. Not a rascal, but an ass. He will die at the barricades. These are glorious times for rascals and asses. The island is part of our defences, and if an enemy comes that way, you must die rather than let him through.'

'Yes, sir.'

After this assurance the expression on the general's face relaxed. There was a second pause in which Thomas tried to remember which of the Prussian kings had spoken like this. Now he began to feel that the post would be his, the image of the island rose up before his mind and a feeling came over him that he would find there a haven of rest after all his nerve-racking experiences. It was a feeling of blissful safety and happy lassitude. He had no desires except to see the glow of the fire in the stove reflected on the dark boards and to hear the wind blowing around the thatched roof.

However, Thomas now had to give careful answers to the somewhat hesitant questions of the general about his education, his travels and his family. Then he was instructed as to the protection of game, and at last he signed the short contract, which his employer copied from an old, faded parchment, forming with his pen large, old-fashioned letters.

Thomas read the details of his rights and duties, the amount of his salary and the additional remuneration he was to receive in kind, read that he was entitled to flour, potatoes and fruit for the winter (this seemed to him unusual) also to a grey fisherman's overall, together with a pair of waders once a year. It also contained an old-fashioned clause stipulating loyalty to his employer at all times, whilst on the other hand the employer agreed that he would satisfy his needs of body and soul. The contract as Thomas read through its contents slowly, might have come down from the times of that laconic monarch, Frederick the Great. At the same time there seemed to him something touching in the old-fashioned phrases, which he had never experienced before in his dealings with landlords or tenants. As he was about to sign, he looked once more into the eyes of the general and felt that never had an agreement been signed with more goodwill on both sides, and that he would be happy to do the work entrusted to him.

The general held out his broad hand, and as Thomas jumped up to grasp it, he felt that 'if necessary he would die' for this queer old man whom the memory of passed times seemed to protect like armour.

'That's right,' said the general. 'I saw at once that we should get on well together.'

They went to the rifle rack and the general showed Thomas a small rifle and a double-barrelled gun which he intended to send to the forester's house for him. 'I took it away from that ass,' he said. 'He was standing on the oak tree waiting for capitalists. Be lenient to the poor, but strict with rascals. They think that the word Property has no meaning any more. Keep good order and discipline. I was trained like that myself. Remain a soldier even in a fisherman's overall.'

'Yes, sir,' said Thomas.

They agreed that Thomas should start work in a fortnight, but not begin fishing before May. 'I shall come to see you on the island,' concluded the general, shaking hands with him once more. 'It is not surrounded by the sea, but at least it is good water. "I serve" is not the worst motto.'

Then the general signalled to Thomas to go. The giant in the Frederick the Great uniform was leaning listlessly against the muzzle of the gun. He helped Thomas in a friendly way to put on his coat.

'Isn't it uncomfortable?' said Thomas, pointing to his uniform.

'No, sir, but the children in the village follow me calling out "Punch", and throw mud at me.' He smiled sadly and accompanied the guest to the door.

'At that time,' said Thomas, pointing to the white bandolier, 'they used quite different missiles . . .'

'Yes, sir, and one day I shall give them a good hiding.'

He opened the door, and as Thomas went out, a young girl dressed in black came up the steps. She must have been about thirteen years old, held herself very straight and was shaking the hair out of her eyes. She was accompanied by a young man, also dressed in black. He was very thin, wore glasses and was just finishing a sentence, from which Thomas gathered that they had been talking about the position of women in Germany in olden times.

They stopped, looking at Thomas, the young man absent-mindedly, as if still in the midst of his argument, the girl interestedly and without embarrassment.

Thomas bowed and was about to stand aside to let them pass, when he changed his mind and turned towards them introducing himself as the new fisherman. The young man seemed surprised, returned his bow and murmured a name he could not catch, the child inclined her head in an old-fashioned manner and without taking her eyes from his face asked: 'What is your name?'

Thomas repeated it.

'Is that a name out of a fairy tale?'

'No, it is my real name.'

The child's left hand played with a string of wooden beads. 'My name is Marianne von Platen,' she said. 'All the girls in our family are called so. This is my tutor, Herr Bergengruen, but Orla – I have never heard a name like that in my life – are you going to fish with Christoph?'

'No, Christoph is leaving; I shall live on the island alone.'

'Christoph is a poor man,' said the child. 'He always meant to be nasty to me, and yet he was always kind.'

'Surely that is better than the other way round,' said Thomas.

'That's true, but would it not have been best to mean to be friendly and to be so?'

'You are undoubtedly quite right there.'

'Herr Bergengruen,' Marianne went on, 'always says that men are generally different from what they seem. But I don't believe that. Herr Bergengruen always looks like a startled elf, but that's what you are, aren't you, Herr Bergengruen?' A soft smiled played round her lips, and she put her right hand with a caressing movement on his arm.

'That is just one of our jokes,' he said apologetically, 'but we should be glad if we might come to the island now and again. Christoph had his peculiarities. . . .'

'And so have you, my dear friend,' thought Thomas. He replied that he would be pleased to see them.

'And you are really going to fish there?' asked the child.

'Yes, I am, and I told Christoph that I shall catch the fish with the golden crown.'

'Is there such a thing?'

'The fairy tales say there is.'

'And what next?'

'Then I will make you a present of it.'

She took a deep breath and Thomas saw how the necklace round her little throat moved. Then he bowed to her, as if she were a grown up and went down the steps.

Only when he got to the wood and had filled his pipe did he realise that now everything was settled. Indeed more than that–he had pledged himself to die in defence of his employer, if necessary, and to give away a golden crown, should he find it.

He sat down on a tree stump in the sun and started calculating how far his money would go. He had always been methodical in such matters and he knew exactly what a man needed for bread, meat, tobacco and clothing. He also knew what he did not need here, and where the borderline came between intentional simplicity and unavoidable poverty. He found that he could leave his pension to his family without keeping anything back for himself, and that he would have a little left over each month to buy a few books or to spend on the garden, so that beauty and joy might come to the grey house, should he feel the need of them. He might even be able to entertain guests properly; the serious, little lady who had probably come out of one of the gilt frames in the hall and her biblical companion who spoke as solemnly as if he had wandered through the wilderness with the patriarchs.

The house with the pine trees in the front garden, the thundering trains of the underground, the boats with the lanterns on the river seemed already as far away as if years had passed between. He thought how easy it was to detach oneself from all that–from all, except from the child, and that thought gave him a shock. His past life seemed to him like a brittle tapestry that fell to shreds in one's hands. This was not due to the fact that he had said goodbye to that life during the first nights of the Great War. The threads which had bound him and his comrades at those times had not been cut, for they all had wished to return, that had been their constant hope. But the trouble was that they had returned with different eyes, at least he had, and the old world seemed strangely changed: men, ideas, even those we loved best on earth. The happiness of old days no longer existed, it was like a withered plant which, whilst not lacking water nor sun, still remained withered. That's what it was: a withered plant! They did not throw it away and replace it by a fresh plant, a different and unknown one. For the others did not see that it was faded, to them it appeared glowing and sparkling as before. They did not see the worm drinking its sap, but he saw it. Something must have been wrong when they came back, but he could not explain what it was. He felt that he had lost his balance, and there was nothing to which he could cling to save himself.

But now he had made up his mind to leave all that, and the others would call him a fool. His father would have understood, but he was dead. Now he had to understand it all alone. Possibly the secret lay in the ability to go to bed with gladness in one's heart and with an eager expectation of the morrow, without the help of adventure, without having to play a hero's role, without a laurel wreath on one's brow. For him it would be enough to spread out the nets, to haul in the fish, to keep house and island tidy, to read a few pages in the evening, to sit by the water's edge, to look up at the stars and to carry out the agreement which he had signed.

He tried to think back to the last time he had been truly happy. He examined each year and put the memory of it aside; in this way he went back to his childhood. He remembered his father coming to say 'good night', the open window through which he heard the subdued noises of the farm, the smell of cigar smoke coming from the next room, where his father sat over the account books or reading a volume by Fontaine. Pictures which became more and more confused, the wheatfield in the blazing sun, the lake stocked with old pike, riding on the roads with a slight feeling of fear, the clock on the tower ringing out its chimes over the fields which lay in a thin haze and the long echo after the last stroke, wave after wave, getting more and more indistinct; by that time he had fallen asleep with gladness in his heart, and with gladness in his heart had awakened in the morning.

But that never happened again, not when he was a cadet nor when he was a lieutenant. His duties always felt like armour which restricted his breathing, and sometimes even hurt him, the sails, the masthead, the guns, navigation, figures, formulas, curves, calculations, faces which were either solemn or mocking, and then the war. He had responsibility for human lives and for ships, and he did not always feel equal to it. There was no gladness in his heart, not even among his friends, an odd fellow, quiet, shy, reticent. The war, a bitter trade without any glory, killing and destroying, and then the end and the emptiness of days and nights, like a board bobbing on the ocean–up and down and up and down–swift as a breath our lives pass away.

But what he saw here was good. High grey treetrunks like masts, the treetops misty from the rain, the woodpecker tapping the trees behind the hill, as industrious as a lonely man, the lake glittering through the trees and birds singing over its brightness, clouds high in the blue sky across which cranes flew in arrow formation, a good and quiet life governed by old laws of nature which all creatures obey by night as well as by day. War and suffering were here also, but they were caused by the law of self-preservation, not by an arbitrary power.

The signature of the agreement made him part and parcel of this world; the work of his hands would fill his hours. A simple task which required nothing but industry and good-will and submission to the order of nature. Even those who still carried the old arms could fulfil it, those who strove after simplicity because they felt like strangers in the present confused times, those who wanted a roof over their heads and a hearth secured by their own work and gladness of heart.

Although he was of a different faith, it occurred to him that he had always admired monks who in olden times made the soil fertile and painted large letters on yellow parchment by candlelight. They would take up the sword in the defence of the Lord and of their fields and would sheathe it again when thc danger had passed. The world to them was far away like a stream swirling behind willow trees and they were content that it should be so. They only wanted their plough, the picture of the Virgin and candlelight on the white walls of their cells. They were satisfied to live unseen like the stones at the bottom of the lake, but the work of their hands lived through the centuries. No wasted life was theirs, no excitement, no idle gossip. They were faithful servants who now slept under slabs of stone, but the heavenly Father had collected and remembered their names.

'When Marianne is older', thought Thomas, rising, 'she will know that the golden crown is invisible, and perhaps even Joachim will also know it. She will know that it is the last thing in life that we understand; its real meaning is drawn out of the net of many experiences. It means that one ought to be good and wise and without desires, and strive to make peace – an eternal peace. Perhaps I shall find it, so that I can show it to them, only to her and to him, two human beings are enough, and I myself am the third – three – what a big number for the hand of man.' It would be hard to leave the child behind, much harder than all other sacrifice, but there were roads which had to be taken unaccompanied – without one's wife and also without one's child. First he himself had to stand firm, like an acrobat in the circus, before he could lift his wife and his child on to his shoulders. A few times each year Joachim would come to see him. He would try to teach him what he had learnt in the meantime. He would share faithfully. He only wanted to keep back a very little for himself. His life was already on the decline, but the child would have to go on into a new life.

The forester who was standing at the fence beckoned to him. 'This is a good year, dear sir. The corn is growing well, and there will be life on the island again. A ghost lived there and now a human being is moving in. A good year.'

They had a silent meal and then Thomas spent the whole afternoon on the water. He rowed along the banks and visited bay after bay. He looked down into the water and saw a sandy bottom broken by occasional stalks of waterlilies and decayed tree trunks whose branches stretched towards the surface. On the shore he saw a narrow path through the long grass and the tracks of an otter in the soft soil. He rowed round the edge of the wood and farther on to the stream, behind which a second lake began. All round there were woods and meadows, and in front of a bluish strip of pine trees, fields and a village – a piece of country with a character of its own, caressed by a soft wind.

He saw Christoph leaving the island and getting out of the boat at the tall pine tree. He carried all his belongings in a sack on his back and disappeared, grey and bent, into the wood near the lake – most certainly his flag was wound round his body – a soldier after a lost battle.

There was nobody on the island now. The sun set behind the tops of the oak trees; dark thunder clouds rose over the wood; no smoke came from the chimney; a big bird circled over the grey roof and disappeared into the dark clouds.

Thomas fetched the empty boat and rowed back to the forester's house. They intended to look over the house together and to make a note of what should be altered in Thomas's absence. He was to leave the next morning and to return within a fortnight.

There was nobody in the yard but once more he heard the sound of low, dreamy singing coming from the garden. The woman was strewing seeds in the broken soil of the newly made beds. She was wearing her black frock and had a scarf round her shoulders. Her hands were empty, but there was meaning in her gestures. Her song sounded monotonous in the calm air, simple and almost gay, like a lullaby. Thomas fancied he saw him kneeling there, him whom the fire in the dark turret had burnt to dust and ashes, a small figure trying to catch the seeds, and ignorant of the future harvest.

The air was close as on the previous evening; clouds covered the sun, and a dull light shone from their glowing edges over the earth. In this light the woman dressed in black went slowly to and fro, up and down between the rows of the beds, strewing imaginary life over the soil.

Thomas shivered again and went into the house quietly. 'Yes, a storm is brewing,' said the forester. 'Then she gets restless and will not say indoors. She cannot see the fire over the wood, for she covers her eyes with her hands, but she does not go to bed as long as the storm lasts. Perhaps she sees him in the fire, dear sir.'

They rowed over the lake in silence and entered the house. It was as empty as before, and there was no sign that a human being had lived there. They looked at everything and Thomas wrote the measurements down in his book. He knew what he needed. They made the necessary calculations for new floorboards and a small kitchen stove to be installed in the adjoining room; the window was to be made higher and four times as wide. Everything else was to remain unchanged and the forester promised to see that this was done within a fortnight. 'A palace, dear sir,' he said with a smile, 'and in the winter I shall see your light through the trees. God bless your coming, dear sir.'

Thomas walked round the island over sand and brown grass, past the reeds and back again. He was as lonely as on the ocean. His heart throbbed as it had throbbed before the battle. He found a place on the west side of the hill, below the oaks, where heather and young pine trees grew right down to the water's edge. There he could sit on a tree stump and look out over the wide waters. It was like being on the bridge of a ship with the masts towering behind.

It had grown dark over the woods, and the glow from beneath the clouds flashed over the water, in a sharp and crimson reflection. The wind blew over the reeds, then dropped, and Thomas heard the low rumble of distant thunder from behind the wall of clouds. Now and then a pale light appeared over the island and the wood, then there were menacing flashes of lightning which seemed to come from long gun barrels over a grey armoured wall, a sharp flash shot through the sky and long afterwards a clap of thunder was heard, which shook the earth on which Thomas sat.

With wide-open eyes he looked into the light. He thought he saw soldiers clad in grey attacking, and the foam-covered ocean. He imagined hearing again the sound of bell signals and human cries. He sat as in a dream; his past life seemed to rise up before his eyes and ears, the test of many years, the crisis of young trembling hearts: the battle.

Then he heard the wings of great birds and their hoarse cries. In the light of the next flash he saw them stretching their slender necks upwards, while the dry treetops rocked under them.

Then he went down to the lake to his boat. A few raindrops fell, warm and heavy, and he stood there a little longer before leaving, his face raised and his eyes wide open.

CHAPTER FOUR

THE CLOCK over the courtyard of the castle measures out the time for the district round the lake. The farmyard lies high above water level, and the steeple on the roof of the stables towers high above the yard. When the air is calm, or when only a soft breeze blows over the woods, the bright sound of the clock, as it strikes the hour, penetrates far and wide, and people sit up in bed or stop work for a moment counting the strokes and time their sleep and their daily work by them. The church is far away, the railway is far away and so are the sawmills. But the castle clock is in their midst; the previous generation also knew it well. Its age cannot be traced in the legends of the district. It only becomes silent when somebody in the castle is dying, so that the striking of the clock may not disturb the sufferer's last hours.

The first to be awakened by the clock are the valet and the agricultural student in the castle, Thomas and the fishing eagle. The two former rub their eyes and are not always cheerful. The two others wake up easily and are keen on their daily work. Thomas has his breakfast at the table in front of his house and smokes his first pipe there. The sun is red over the black pine trees, and the haze over the creeks looks like glowing steam. At their edge he can see the sticks from which the bow-nets are suspended at the bottom end of the lake.

The eagle comes from the east, high above the wood,

silent, flying fast in a straight line. He flies over the island and only turns over the western part of the wood. When the sun shines on his breast it appears as white as snow. Over the other creek he circles for the first time; the water is motionless there, and the old fish are just below the surface. Then he folds his wings and pounces on his prey. Out of the foam he rises slowly, shaking his wings. Higher and higher he rises until the prey in his talons is silhouetted against the bright morning sky. His scream is heard high above the island before he disappears in the sun.

Again the stroke of the clock is heard over the lake. The cuckoo calls and the hup hup hup of the hoopoe sounds like a child's toy in the wood. The carts leave the farmyard, and the girls go tramping over the dewy paths of the wood, their naked feet in heavy shoes, for they cannot kneel on the damp earth in their stockings. One or the other of them grumbles, but then they sing a song that sounds over the shining plantations, for life is stronger than bad moods. The forester takes some frayed bark off the trunk of a pine tree, where a roebuck has cast its antlers, and Thomas rows to the shore with the first of the wet nets.

The sun rises above the forest, and in a room on the east side of the castle Herr Bergengruen tries to demonstrate the rotation of the earth with the help of a small globe. Marianne von Platen looks at it seriously and asks him whether he thinks that Herr Orla has caught the fish with the golden crown in the black water. The general sits on horseback, and the soldier of the time of Frederick the Great goes back to the muzzle of the gun.

The clock strikes, a flight of white pigeons rises into the blue air, and in fields wood-brown hands pull the corks out of tin cans of cold coffee. The bodies of the horses steam and the morning sweat of man and beast dries in the warm wind.

Thomas spreads out the wet nets; he wears only a shirt and shorts; his skin is brown and fish-scales sparkle in his dark hair. The woman with the lifeless face walks to and fro in the attic and sings the merry marching tune without words. When the sun shines on the split silk of her old frock, it glistens with a greenish sheen on her lean shoulders.

The clock strikes and smoke comes out of the chimneys, also from the chimney on the grey roof of the house on the island. Thomas cooks his fish soup, and the blue tench do not break to pieces any more as at his first experiment. The carts drive home, the girls in the plantations rest in the shade, and Gruber tells his pale wife how much he enjoyed his meal today. She turns her head as if listening – but her gaze goes through him, far away, to the dark ocean on which they throw wreaths now to the memory of the dead, and where the loud scream of the gulls sounds over the ships. The general raises his wine glass to the light and asks his granddaughter what she would like for her birthday. Bergengruen mumbles that a great fuss is being made of a new edition of the fairy tales of the Brothers Grimm, and the child nods in agreement. The melancholy giant stands straight as a ramrod at the sideboard, and some obstinate flies rest on his white straps.

The clock has finished the circle of the hours and starts anew with the high-pitched sound. The hand of the clock advances, and work follows, slows down as the workers tire and finishes at last. The eagle has been over the lake three times, and Thomas returns from spreading out his nets. His small rifle lies at his side on the bench, its barrel is still shining. He has collected his letters at the forester's house, a newspaper full of discord and rumours and a postcard from Joachim on which he writes that he is very good at arithmetic now, and that the form master has asked him whether he will not remove the black, white and red flag from his bicycle. He adds in brackets in his big, stiff hand-writing: 'He's got a hope!' Then he writes that there are only another fifty-two days until the summer holidays. On the front of the card he has written obediently: Herr Thomas Orla.

Thomas hears the clock sound over the lake, six bright strokes, so he still has another four hours to himself. At ten the lamp is put out. Door and window are wide open in his house, and he remains for a while on the doorstep looking into the room to see whether Christoph stands in front of his books shaking his head. For his books have arrived now, five broad high shelves all along the dark boarded wall. The globe is there too, and the brass ring of the equator sparkles in the sun which shines into the room through the wide, open windows. Two heavy armchairs stand in front of the fireplace; a narrow folding bed is at the other wall as well as the cabinet with the arms and masks, and in the corner near the window stands the heavy grey table and a wooden bench. There is nothing on the walls but the picture, in a gilt frame, of the cruiser firing its guns.

And all this belongs to him, to him alone, and is filled with his own life, with memories of the days and nights he has spent in reading, thinking, pondering, existing. They belong to him like the clothes he wears, like the air he breathes. He saved all this from shipwreck so it is doubly precious. He carried them to the island with his own hands, as if he had saved them from the breakers of the ocean. Christoph had been afraid of the blizzards and the wailing in the chimney, the fog and the hoarse cries of the beasts in winter. He had only his pipe, his fire and his brandy and the burning vision of a future which would remain a future for ever.

But Thomas had more. He had work which he liked; his hands had become hard with rowing. He had the clock which accompanied his daily work, and he had the bench from which he could see the sun setting. He knew that it only went down for those who were tired. He had his globe which rotated softly through infinite space when his hand touched it. He had everything that had gained immortality on that globe. All the immortal ones stood on the shelves in front of the wall darkened by smoke from the fire; they looked at him; they were near and familiar, for he was like the guest of them all; they knew the look of his eyes; they knew how carefully he turned the pages, how he bent his forehead when he looked at them. Their past belonged to him and all future lay embedded in their past, a pure future full of coincidence, purged from hatred and pride, the great calm for which they had striven to the end of their lives, and after which he, too, was striving, a humble scholar learning from them.

The clock strikes, and all those who hear it know what curfew means. Thomas sits on a tree stump under the oak trees and understands why man has praised God. He remembered that as a child he had known how beautiful the world was, so beautiful that it made your heart ache. He sees the last crimson light on the lake, the sleeping forest, the young birch trees silhouetted against the white sky and smells of their scent which cannot be compared with any other. Then the owls begin to hoot; the mist rises; the stars come out. The calm of the night spreads like circles in the water from a fallen stone, further and further, and he himself sits in its midst, motionless, and his blood flows and sings as in the fountain of a dream.

The clock strikes – the light of the lamp falls on the pages of the book in his hand which the flame of the fire illuminates. When he looks up he sees through the open window a distant trembling light in the forester's house, and it is the only light in sight. The old man would probably be sitting at the window, too, smoking silently. 'Seven years – dear sir.' In the attic the woman would be singing. The floorboard creaks, and the man at the window does not hear it any more. Or he thinks of his trees in the wood and how gently the wind touches them, and he thinks that he has a neighbour with whom he can sit sometimes at this time of the day, when the roof stifles him, and the low singing fills him with horror.

The 'Nabob' lifts his glass of red wine towards the flame in the huge fireplace and sees its purple shine, like dark blood. He has buried two sons. The big house lies dark and dead. The hall above him is like a church. A gilt frame sparkles, and the stuffed animals stand like saints on their pedestals. The flame quivers and seems to go out, but flares up again. So many visitors – laughter and low singing. A face with a golden helmet, first pink, then grey, then white – the helmet falls to pieces, the forehead dissolves, the vision disappears. Pull yourself together, general! All right, all right. The coat-of-arms is broken, but the dead remain, the dead and the king. He lifts his glass; it shines red.

The clock strikes, and the lights are put out. Sleeps falls like dew on the eyelids. A heron flaps its wings and folds them again. It sees the stars reflected in the water like silver fish – motionless. A toad sits on the doorstep.

The clock strikes, and Joachim von Orla starts up from his slumber. He had dreamt that he was in a battle, and a bell had called him to the bridge. But all is dark; there is no admiral who gives him the great command after which he – Joachim von Orla – will direct the battle. In the faint light that falls through the window the ship carved from limewood glimmers. Father said that you ought to look at it, for it calls you to your duty. Father is far away on a large lake, where he is the master of eagles, herons and fish, and in only fifty days I will see all that. And perhaps in another thousand days I will become a cadet and be trained as an admiral or a commander of the navy. Father resigned too soon, but I will make up for that – and tomorrow there will be lemon pudding as Nurse Beate has promised – nurse is kind and feels like the white sheep which Mother gave me for Christmasmothers never understand what a boy wants. He stops breathing for a minute to listen whether Nurse Beate is asleep in the next room, the door of which is half open. When he hears her moving softly under her blankets, he turns on his side and closes his eyes – she preferred to be Beate to being called Beate – what funny things Daddy sometimes says.

The clock in the church steeple behind the pine trees strikes, the alarm clock whirrs, and Joachim jumps out of bed, his eyes still blank and heavy with sleep. But only women may turn over on the other side again to cheat the clock and the day. The cold shower pours on his back, the blackbirds pipe in front of the narrow window. Nurse Beate still staggers with fatigue, and he splashes cold water into her face.

Then he eats an egg with his Latin grammar beside his plate. His bright eyes are quite awake by now and race over the pages: 'I shall do the best excercise today, Nurse Beate,' he says. His alertness and confidence make her a little confused. His father would not have believed that he was going to do the best exercise.

'You are so sure of yourself, Joachim,' she says with a sigh. He looks at her out of the corner of his eye and smiles.

'You have to be if you want to get on,' he says very wisely. 'At school they would like to see all those of good birth as stupid and lazy, but as far as I am concerned, that is a vain hope, my friends.'

Nurse smiles and in her imagination she sees the sad

absent-minded eyes of the captain. 'Quite right, Joachim,' she thinks, 'try to be as efficient as possible, then your father will be happy.'

Then he cycles along the quiet streets, his arms crossed over his chest. The streamer on the handlebar flutters in the wind.

The clock strikes. The lessons pass by. He does write the best exercise, and during break he settles a quarrel with the banker's son once for all. His nose is bleeding and a long scratch runs across his left cheek, but his opponent is counted out after a good punch on the chin, and he bumps his head against the wall of the passage when he staggers back into the classroom. A beastly chap! Driving up to the school in a great, big car, and stuffing cake–no good to the country, people like that!

Joachim is popular, though his classmates are a little afraid of him. His grey eyes flare up too quickly. But he never puts up with anything coarse, neither in behaviour nor in character. 'Orla said it is impossible' put an end to everything. Most teachers think him a little uncanny, he is like an arrow on the taut string of a bow, ready to rush forward. But his headmaster, a major in the militia, likes him better than his own child.

'Have you heard from your father, Joachim?'

'Yes, sir; he fishes from morning to night and is as hungry as a wolf.' The grey eyes beam and his hands, covered with scratches, press against the seam of his knickerbockers.

'That's right,' said the headmaster, stroking Joachim's fair hair, 'he shows the people what work means. Your father is a wonderful man.'

At the end of the gym lesson Joachim distinguishes himself again. He climbs up the rope like a cat, and the gym master who is always a little sullen looks at him askance. 'Don't go through the ceiling,' he says.

But Joachim has glided down already. 'The shrouds are higher,' he answers carelessly.

The finches are singing as he cycles home for lunch. At the corner of the street he rings his bell shrilly and nearly runs down the neighbour's dog. He comes up the steps beaming.

His mother happens to be in which is unusual. He does not like the make-up on her face, and only holds his right cheek up for her kiss. At lunch she wants to know everything that happened at school and how he likes the other boys. She knows nearly all of them; the surburb is like a village.

He is ready to tell her everything, without vanity, but always conscious of his own value. There are some 'first-rate' chaps in the form, but they do not always come up to his standard completely. He also tells her that he considers wealth and daydreams of no importance, possibly even to be looked down on.

Dark rings show round Frau von Orla's eyes. She listens to the boy half seriously, half amused. She does not interrupt until he mentions his contempt for money. 'You shouldn't despise the realities of life and power so young. Your father has strong views about them.'

'Marvellous man, your father,' the headmaster had said.

'Of course,' a smile crept over her face, 'but usually headmasters do not have to judge the values of life, that is generally left to bank managers. Would you like to live like a fisherman at the age of forty-five?'

He thinks for a while and the frown reappears on his forehead. 'No,' he decided at last, 'I shouldn't. That life is not enough, though it might be very nice for one summer. A cruiser is better than a boat, and a squadron better than a cruiser. Father has retired a little too soon, but he must know best.'

'Yes,' murmurs Frau von Orla, 'perhaps he never started a career.' At that moment the pudding was brought in, so Joachim did not hear her.

Only Nurse Beate feels slightly embarrassed, and she nearly hands out fish forks and knives for the dessert instead of spoons. Her big eyes which fill with tears so easily see once more as in a vision the captain's face as he turned round for the last time on the staircase saying: 'And the boy, nurse, look after the boy by day and by night.'

God knows she does what she can, but so much is said which ought not to be said, like that remark just now, and for many things it is already too late. She knows that children are often as clever as their elders; parents do not take this into consideration, but she does. She has brought up other people's children for a good long time now and she is counting the fifty days to the holidays just as Joachim is. When the pudding is put on the table, then at least he behaves like a real child.

As Frau von Orla takes Joachim's plate for a second helping, the lace of her loose sleeve gets caught in a fold of the tablecloth, and the flimsy material is pulled back over the elbow.

'Are those scars, mother?' asks Joachim, stroking her arm with his finger.

She takes it away hastily and pulls her sleeve down. 'No,' she said, 'those are gnat-bites, the maid must put wire gauze over the bedroom windows again.' She has turned pale and looks at Nurse Beate, who however is bending over an empty crystal plate and is tracing the lines of the cut glass with her finger.

The church bell tolls, three strokes one after another in sad succession. Nurse Beate drops her mending and thinks, 'Who has died in the neighbourhood?' So many die in these times, not only of disease, but of misery, despair, starvation. Time has swallowed up all they possessed so rapidly – and now that currency notes are printed in millions – comes the aftermath. The old aristocracy is hit as badly as the new rich, but the former pass away more quietly. The country is like a diseased wood where the trees are marked, and the bells toll every day. She sighs and steals a quiet look at the child.

Joachim sits over his books, his brow is wrinkled and he is deeply absorbed. When he is working, games and dreams do not exist for him, and he allows nothing to interrupt him. His forehead looks like that of an old man, and when he lifts his eyes to the window, he does not see Nurse Beate there, but a word or a missing figure seems to appear on the shining panes, and in a mysterious way becomes clear. The pupil, Joachim von Orla, gives the nurse no trouble; sometimes she is afraid of so much industry and precocious tidiness. There is also a small globe on his bookshelf, and he stands in front of it often with a book. When he touches the globe, he does so with a quick movement, and the rotation of the earth stops where he wants it to stop. She does not hear the low humming any longer with which the many-coloured globe in the captain's room rotated round its axis without being arrested by his hand. Never will she forget the gaze of his eyes following the rotation, old eyes which seemed to rest once more on the radiance of a soap bubble.

When he has finished his homework Joachim spends his time either in the wood or on the water until dusk. He and three of his friends have a small sailing boat, and he nearly always acts as captain. They do not play, for them there is no pirate's island in the river. They work and learn, and many a thoughtful gaze follows them from the pleasure yachts. In the evening he builds models of boats, learns flag-signals, registers tons and lists of ships' armaments. Then he talks in English to Nurse Beate for half an hour, and he tries to speak as correctly as possible. He does not play, he reads very little, and as soon as he pulls the blanket over his shoulders, his eyes begin to close.

The clock strikes, and the vicar stands in front of the wooden Christ and looks at Him for a long time. He would like to know whether the dead look different from the living. He does not know. He sighs a little and looks out of the open window into the night, he thinks of Herr Orla's island, where he would like to go to sleep, just once, to sleep so deeply that neither dreams nor worries could trouble him any longer, to sleep like the dead – just once. However, what does he know of the sleep of the dead?

He takes a sheet of notepaper and writes a few lines to the helmsman, Thomas Orla. He tells him that his son has called on him, brought kind regards and has told him everything. He was glad to know that he was working. He did not think that Joachim would come to the vicarage often. He was looking forward to life on the ocean, and had no time for dark aisles, which after all was quite natural. He happened to remember a verse from the Proverbs of Solomon and he would finish his letter with it: 'He that is slow to anger is better than the mighty; and he that ruleth his spirit than he that taketh a city. The lot is cast into the lap; but the whole disposing thereof is of the Lord.' Perhaps Herr Orla would like to think about it over his nets.

At that hour a car stands in front of the house – in tune with the times Frau von Orla now owns a shining, roaring vehicle. She is about to leave the house and is putting on her gloves when a man dressed in blue comes through the garden gate, a sailor apparently, but without any badge and without the name of a ship on his cap. His neck is brown, his bell-bottom trousers cover the toes of his boots, and the black ribbons of his cap hang down over his back. His face is broad and his expression benevolent, but there is something untamed and adventurous about his whole figure. He walks through the garden as he would walk a deck, with a careless yet eager gait, and he looks as if he were ready to sit on a boom over the green ocean with his hand grasping a rope, whilst above his fair head the gulls would circle.

When Frau von Orla comes towards him, he clicks his heels and pulls off his cap. She only recognises him after she has come right up to him, and with a smile she shakes hands with him. 'Hallo, Bildermann, I have not seen you for a long time. Have you been on a spree again?'

He smiles back at her without embarrassment. 'There are no more sprees, Frau von Orla,' he says, 'now we have got to get things straight.' He drives his right hand, in which he holds his cap, into the open palm of his left with a bang.

'Yes,' she says, 'these are sad times, Bildermann – and the captain is not here. God knows whether he will ever come back. Have you heard?'

No, the sailor had not heard anything, and all of a sudden his face looks serious and attentive. 'Indeed,' he says, after she has told him the main facts, 'the captain is a wonderful man, to be sure. First rate! Goes away and catches fish. Who else would do that?'

'Probably very few,' she says and smiles in a peculiar way. 'He will certainly be alone in his new trade.'

The sailor looks far beyond her into the evening sky. He does not smile any longer, he has 'sea-eyes' again.

'Well, Bildermann,' says Frau von Orla at last, fumbling in her little handbag, 'here is his address, if you want to write to him, but I think the captain would like to be alone there for the time being; lately he has been a little bit unsociable, you know.'

'No wonder,' says the sailor, looking round the garden absent-mindedly. 'No, thank you very much, I am not starving yet. If I ever sink as low as that, I shall hold out my hand.'

He accompanies Frau von Orla to her car, shuts the door behind her and asks for permission to go and see the young gentleman for a little while.

'By all means do so, and ask Nurse Beate to give you a decent supper at least.'

An hour later she asks the admiral whether he has ever had his life saved. No, not he, but he has often seen it done, he answers. There have been opportunities enough to see that–with others.

'They are a little tiresome, these life-savers,' she says thoughtfully, 'like quiet creditors who do not say a word, but are always present–and one cannot send them away.'

About this time the sailor is on his way again from the western suburb to the allotment gardens in the north. His hands are in his pockets, he holds his pipe between his teeth and seems to be lost in thought. First he tries to calculate whether the wear and tear on his shoes will cost more or less than the fares for the underground. Then he counts on his fingers the months to the beginning of the autumn storms, how many kilometres, how many days' marches would be necessary to take him to the captain and how much employment pay he would get. At last he takes his pipe out of his mouth, spits on the ground in front of a gentleman in a fur coat–says 'Damn you' and jumps on the steps of a moving bus, where he stays until the conductor appears. Then he jumps down, waves his hand and waits for another vehicle. He thinks that he alone knows when the captain needs him.

He alone and nobody else. He never arrived too early and never too late.

The clocks strike all over the country, the stars rise and set. The homeless ones wander on the roads, and the fish migrate in the dark water. Before dawn the cuckoo begins to call. Towns lie like bright islands on the dark earth and the white lines of the railways run like a spider's web over plains and mountains. The woods are still asleep just as the lakes, the swamp and the green crops. Fog rises and the birds of passage can be heard in the fog. The sap rises in the trees, and dew falls from the stars. It is written in the Bible: 'The lot is cast into the lap; but the whole disposing thereof is of the Lord.'

CHAPTER FIVE

NOT MANY visitors called at the island. Before Joachim came at the end of June, the general had been once and his granddaughter several times with Herr Bergengruen. The general came in the evening in a light, narrow boat. He sat at the helm, a simple coat over his shoulder and a soldier's cap on his white hair. The giant rowed. He was not wearing his uniform. The water foamed under the bows. From a distance it looked like Blücher crossing the Rhine.

Thomas had no flag to hoist but he stood on the board which served as a landing stage, held the bow of the boat fast and helped the general ashore.

'I would like to see how everything is going,' said the general looking round threateningly. Then he relaxed: 'You look well, everything looks well–good management–' He went to the poles where the nets dried during the day and looked down the long line. They were hanging in rank and file. 'I knew it,' said the general, and leaning on his stick, he looked over the island as over a parade ground. 'I knew it–you are an old soldier–and reliable–look at it, Johann!'

Johann stepped behind his master, did not know exactly what he was to look at and stood like a pillar in the sand. 'Let it be an example to you,' said the general. Thomas smiled and led him up to the house.

He saw the broad, new window immediately and stopped to examine it. 'Gruber told me,' he said, 'but you mustn't pay for it alone. Wait until summer; we will share the expense.'

Then he stood still on the threshold in surprise. Several times he tapped the floorboards with his stick cautiously, as if he wished to make sure that they were real. At last he turned round slowly and looked at Thomas.

'Did you give a false name, Orla?'

'No, sir.'

He scanned every line in Thomas's face, then he looked round helplessly. 'You wouldn't deceive an old man, Orla, would you?' he said in a low voice and almost pleadingly.

'No, sir,' said Thomas seriously. 'There are still some things . . . which I would like to tell you a little later. For the time being I beg you to let the matter rest there, sir.'

'Are you in hiding?' asked the guest.

'No, sir.'

'Well, let the matter rest there, but don't deceive an old man.'

The general nodded and entered, looked at the picture of the cruiser and folded both hands over his stick. Then he stood for a long time in front of the globe, which reached as high as his chest. Once he put his finger on the blue lakes which showed like tiny dots on the surface and turned the globe carefully. Almost noislessly the countries disappeared behind the horizon, and new countries and oceans rose from behind the earth's curve. 'Very peculiar,' he said – 'the whole world. . . .'

Then he stood in front of the books and cast a furtive glance at the titles, went into the next room, stopped again in front of the cabinet with the arms and masks and finally went up to Thomas and said thoughtfully: 'Herr Christoph's successor, let us drink a bottle of wine.'

Johann brought the bottle and two glasses, gaped at the

changed room with open mouth, was given a cigar and disappeared along the shore.

They sat on the bench in front of the house. The wine sparkled in the setting sun, and tiny drops of resin glittered like gold on the grey table. The reed-warblers were noisy and the swallows carried bits of straw under the grey roof.

The general with his coat over his shoulders sat very erect, his hands on his stick, and looked across the water. 'I have lost much, Orla,' he said quietly. 'Emperor and empire, wife and two sons. But the sunset and my estate are left to me, and I must not complain. I will start again from the beginning; a new generation will grow up.'

'It is already growing up,' said Thomas.

The other nodded. 'I will not grow bitter as so many do. They only curse and complain. Nobody is without sin. Nobody. But we will not make compromises. We will remain honest and set an example. Why did you come here?'

Thomas turned the glass slowly with his fingers. 'First there was a psalm, sir, which I read. No, that was not the first reason, that was the last. There I found the verse which we often skip when reading: "Swift as a breath our lives pass away." It was as if a hammer-blow had struck me. The same evening I went to see our vicar. He maintained that God, Christ and the church were nothing. "Work", he said, "is all that counts, hard work by the sweat of one's brow." That was his Gospel, and so he sent me away. For the next few years, perhaps even for the rest of my life, I will do nothing but work. The angel has looked at me, and what he requires of me is simplicity. I never was very efficient, but here I shall be efficient. I shall gain happiness, sir.'

The general pondered for a long time. 'It's a good plan, Orla,' he said at last. 'To be content is the beginning of wisdom. Once we rushed to the attack to gain the laurel wreath, but the best wreath you can have is the sweat of your brow. I have no heir, my sons are dead, the coat-of-arms is broken – only a grandchild, but she comes of good stock, look after her, Orla, will you?'

'Yes, sir.'

'I shall send her here often. Bergengruen is too pious, a lamb in spectacles. But here she will have the globe, books and fresh air. She shall learn to swim, to shoot and to fish – swift as a breath – it is a good saying. I am very grateful to you, Orla, do you hear?'

'Yes, sir.'

They looked at the setting sun. The evening breeze moved the reeds, and a cool current of air came from the lake. The general got up and wrapped his coat around him. 'I have sent many to their death, Orla,' he said. 'But it was my bounden duty. Nor did I spare myself. Everybody knew that out there. We had a singer on the Staff, a first-rate bellower, and he sang a song with the chorus: "To die is the most beautiful death." Those who have passed away are all right, they did what they were ordered, and finished!'

He put two fingers to his mouth and whistled. Johann's answer came from behind the oak trees.

Marianne and her tutor called the same week. They took the boat at the forester's house and Bergengruen's course was far from straight. Thomas found out that the general had not told them anything about him; he only had asked them to bring coffee and bread with them and had given them leave to stay for as long as Herr Orla would have them.

While Bergengruen walked round the island like another Robinson Crusoe, cautiously as if it were a breeding ground for snakes, Thomas remained on the doorstep after he had let the child go into the room. She stood motionless, and the sun threw her shadow over the hearth. 'Be a good angel to me, Marianne,' said Thomas seriously.

She turned her head and looked at him. Her hair was full of sunshine, and her delicate face appeared as under a golden helmet.

'Has your mother been dead a long time?' asked Thomas softly. She nodded without taking her eyes off him.

'Eight years,' she answered. 'Her horse fell with her. Does all this belong to you?'

'Yes, all this is mine,' replied Thomas, 'and you can think of this as your own house and everything in it.'

As her grandfather had done, she went to the coloured globe and put her hand on it. When the globe started rotating, she stepped back in fright. 'It moves so easily,' she whispered. Then she looked at the rows of books and again at Thomas. 'Do you read every day?'

'Yes, every night.'

'Why are you a fisherman if you have so many books?'

'Books are my evening prayer,' replied Thomas. 'As you can only say your prayers when you have been good, I can only read when I have been working all day long. We have to earn the pleasure of reading.'

'So you do not say your prayers in the evening?' The question was asked shyly as if from behind a veil.

'Perhaps I do not pray as you pray,' he replied with a certain embarrassment. He thought that the child looked at him strangely. He felt as if he were looking at a closed book.

Then he showed her the adjoining room with the kitchen stove and the few pieces of china he used. 'Yes, I have to cook everything myself; the mermaids have not yet offered their help. And I wash up, too, but after all water is my element.'

Again she looked round in silence as if she were in a museum. When she came back into the first room, she stopped in front of his camp-bed, straightened the bedspread and looked at the picture of the cruiser. She asked whether he had ever been on board that ship.'

'Yes, I stood there once.'

In a low voice she told him that she has asked Herr Bergengruen what the fifth commandment meant but he did not know.

'Nobody knows that,' Thomas replied.

When they were about to leave the house, he let her go ahead, and she bowed as she had done on the steps of the castle some time ago. He became convinced that she had already lived another life in this world.

'Why did you say that I was to be your good angel?' she asked while they were unpacking the basket outside the house.

'I need one sometimes,' he said. 'It will be good to think of you. The shadows disappear where you enter. You are hardly a year younger than Joachim.'

'Who is Joachim?'

'My son; and in four weeks he will be here for his holidays.'

'Is he like you?'

'I don't know – he is happier and a little more noisy.'

'Have you got a wife, too?'

'Yes.'

'And won't she come to see you?'

'No, not yet.'

The string of beads moved again on her young bosom. They unpacked the basket together and called Bergengruen.

The tutor proved to be a collector, although not a very selective one. The pockets of his coat were full of shells; those of his trousers were filled with stones, and in both his hands he carried some beautifully shaped fungi which he had found growing on tree stumps. 'It's like Paradise, Herr Orla,' he said full of enthusiasm. 'Not even the birds on their nests are afraid.' His glasses had slipped from stooping, pine needles and cobwebs were tangled in his hair, and he looked as if he had come back from an expedition to the source of the Amazon.

'Wait until the savages kill you,' said Marianne, wiping his face and suit with a handkerchief.

'Oh no, there are no savages here, since Christoph left.'

'Was Christoph a savage?' asked Thomas, smiling.

'A scoffer, Herr Orla, and an unbeliever. If he had not been in the general's service, he would have impaled me on a sharp stake. Scoffing is the worst evil on earth.'

'Perhaps there are things still worse,' said Thomas, 'but now you must have your coffee with the master of the house who is so poor that you have to bring your own.'

'But our host is wonderfully kind,' said Marianne. 'Afterwards you can go into the house, Herr Bergengruen; it is even worse than it was in Christoph's time.'

After they had drunk their coffee, Thomas asked her whether she would like to go swimming with him.

'Yes, Grandad specially asked me to swim.' She fetched her bathing suit from the boat. Thomas took the small rifle and told Herr Bergengruen that he might look round as much as he liked. They went behind the hill, where there were no creepers.

They changed behind the oak trees and then went down to the water's edge. The grass was warm under the soles of their feet. Thomas put the rifle against a low pine tree near the water. Then they took each other's hands and stepped on the soft sand. The water was motionless and after a few steps it became greenish and the bottom disappeared in blackness.

'You need not be afraid,' said Thomas. 'I will stay beside you.'

She was a little uncertain but she nodded and smiled, and with outstretched arms she let herself fall forward into the water. She had no bathing cap, and her hair floated behind her like a strange golden flower.

They swam for a little while. Below them lay the reflections of the white clouds broken by the movement of their arms. The surface of the water was warm, but cool currents came from the depths, and sometimes they felt little fish playing round their feet.

Thomas was always close to her. When they turned to swim back, the island seemed to be higher out of the water than before. The shore looked strange, severe and untrodden, and a blue bird shot like a flash of lightning over the reeds and disappeared with a soft cry behind the trees.

'A kingfisher,' said Thomas. 'I've never seen one here before.' He noticed that her breath came faster, and asked whether she wanted help.

She looked straight ahead and shook her head. Near the end she swam very slowly and before they stood on the bottom again, she asked whether she might call him Thomas.

'Of course, you may. I shall always remember this lovely day.'

'Let's not say we saw a kingfisher,' she said after a while, letting the water run through her fingers. 'Let's call it, "The Bird", shall we?'

Thomas agreed, and looked at her thoughtfully. When they reached shallow water, he supported her body on his hand and showed her what she still had to learn to become more certain of herself and to feel as much at home in the water as on the land.

After that they lay in the sun, she wrung out her hair, and

he told her of other islands, where he had been, where palms grew, where coral reefs sparkled and brown men lived like children. She cupped her chin in both hands and kept her eyes on him, while he lay on his back and lifted his eyes towards the clouds which sailed above them white and high.

He spoke slowly and dreamily, as if he were talking to himself, but sometimes he turned his head and looked into her eyes, as if he wished to make sure that she was still there. 'Yes, the earth is beautiful,' he concluded, 'everywhere where men are happy in their hearts.'

She did not want to practise shooting today; next time she would; today she had experienced three times as much as she ever had with 'the wise man from the east'.

'Who is the wise man from the east?'

'That is Herr Gruber, the forester with the sad wife.' She called him so, because she thought he looked like one of the wise men from the east. 'Was his son on that ship, too?'

'Not on that one, but on another close by.'

'The woman thinks that he will come back one day.'

'He need not come back, for he is always with her.'

'Are dead people always here?'

'Not always, but sometimes, when we have loved them deeply.'

'My mother is never here, but my father sometimes appears to me in a dream – he wears a tall shield in front of his chest and a black helmet – he nods to me and then he is gone; it is as if he were falling to pieces.'

The blue bird flashed past them once more. Then they got up and dressed. The shadows of the young oak leaves moved softly over the child's skin.

'Thank you very much, Thomas,' she said, as they went down the path to the house.

He turned round and stroked her hair with his hand. She had grown this spring and reached nearly to his chest.

They found Herr Bergengruen lying at full length in front of the bookshelves. His fists were pressed against his temples and a large book with coloured pictures of tropical butterflies was open before him. He had pushed his glasses up on his forehead and his eyes were sparkling as if reflecting the colours of these marvellous insects. 'All this is enchanted,' he said, looking up to them. 'It is as if an angel had touched the island.'

'Oh yes, but now we must go back to our boat, perhaps the angel will help us row,' said Marianne.

He got up with a sigh and put the book back in its place, let his glasses drop on his nose and looked at Thomas. 'Who are you?' he asked.

'Thomas Orla, helmsman pensioned off.'

'That I do not believe,' said Bergengruen, 'and I shall never believe it . . . probably you are Sindbad the Sailor.'

The child looked from one to the other and smiled. Little golden grains seemed to lie in the grey iris of her eyes in the light of the setting sun.

From that day on they came twice a week and sometimes oftener. The boat for Joachim had arrived, a small, narrow skiff, and one could put up a small mast with a white sail on the front seat. Bergengruen was soon dismissed, he always pulled the wrong rope and always sat in the wrong place. He admitted it without trying to find an excuse and he lay on the floor, the books with the coloured pictures open in front of him.

The child became sunburnt and her eyes sparkled. She rowed, sailed and swam, shot at fir cones and sat poring over charts. She let the nets glide with the wind from the side of the boat and washed the china in the kitchen. 'When Joachim comes,' she said in the last week of June, 'you will do this all without me.'

'But Joachim will do it with you,' Thomas replied. 'He can do most things better than I can.'

She smiled indulgently, bent over the side of the boat and let her hand glide through the water.

'You will like him,' said Thomas, 'most people like him better than they like me.'

She looked up, then her gaze travelled again over the water. A fine fold formed between her eyebrows. 'Perhaps –' she answered, lost in thought.

Joachim came and she did not hide her pleasure in him. He was so full of health and joy that he infected them all. It was as if he brought new life, certainly not that of the towns, but that of youth, a youth disturbed neither by thoughts nor by emotions. Even Marianne, who was younger, said after a few days: 'He is so young, Thomas.'

'Yes, dear,' he replied, smiling. 'We have been playing at old folk for a little while, haven't we?'

He had met him at the station with Gruber's one-horse carriage, and it was as if they had separated only yesterday. He felt as if they had never been apart. All Joachim's thoughts were of the island, the lake and the daily work. Thomas was surprised that he only asked about the things which were awaiting him, and hardly at all about the people. He seemed to believe that his father was king here.

Thomas encouraged him to talk and asked very little, only once in a low voice inquired after his mother. 'Oh, she is very well; she only coughs a little, at least Nurse Beate says so. I only see her at lunch; in the morning she is still asleep and in the evening she is out.'

'And Nurse Beate?'

'Oh yes, she sends you her best regards. Of course she cried when I left.'

'You should be very glad to have her,' said Thomas seriously. 'There is not much faithfulness to be found nowadays.'

'Certainly, Daddy, we get on very well together; she speaks marvellous English.' However he was a little surprised at his father's admonition.

He shook hands with the forester like old friends. His wife stood at the garden fence and looked at him with startled eyes. Her hands kept gliding over the tops of the fence-posts. Joachim had to shake hands with her, but he tried to get away quickly. Her clammy fingers held his so fast that it seemed as if she would never let go.

'The water,' she whispered, 'the water–'

'Oh, that's it,' said Joachim, when Thomas had told him her story. In the forest he turned round a few times.

Then they stood at the water's edge and Joachim forgot everything. He uttered a shrill cry of delight, and entered his new world with joy. Thomas was filled with pleasure, yet he realised with some misgiving that at the same time he was feeling a certain apprehension. He had always been considerate with the child and had taken Joachim's likes and dislikes, his opinions and judgments into account. But there had been hours, many hours, when Thomas had experienced only a feeling of joy at Joachim's directness and outspokenness. Yet he always found himself appraising and watching the child in an unobtrusive way, as if he were following the needle of a compass, whilst his hand rested on the wheel, ready at any moment to alter his course. Thomas justified this to himself by remembering that they had been separated for a considerable time and would have to learn to fall into step again with one another. He could not disguise from himself the fact that for Joachim happiness meant adventure. The daily work – by no means easy with the many nets – in all its novelty appeared to Joachim like a game, as did the daily routine: the preparation of the meals, the washing up of the simple crockery, the cleaning of the two rooms – all this seemed to Joachim like the whims of a hermit or the hardship of two castaways to be accepted cheerfully. At first the hidden meaning of the new work and the new life was not apparent to him, and Thomas did not attempt to enlighten him. He had never educated by precepts; he understood that a child looks at everything with a child's eyes and not with the eyes of an adult who is trying to save his life from the general shipwreck. He was glad that when Marianne came as usual, Joachim accepted her without question, having first carefully tested her physical qualifications to go on his expeditions, in fact as carefully as if she were a domestic animal.

They loaded the small sailing boat with provisions, the girl took her seat in the bow, and after a final scrutiny Joachim went on board with his little rifle slung over his shoulder. He seized the tiller and ordered Marianne to hoist the sail with a movement of his hand. The white sail tautened slowly in the wind and then flopped as they went through the shadow of the island to become taut once more. The boat rocked and a thin white wave appeared at the bow; the two sailors waved their hands a last time and then glided away into a world of their own.

Thomas went about his work lost in thought, rowed to the fishing places, pulled in the nets. Now and again he raised his eyes to look over the water so that he could see the white sail in the far distance – sparkling in the sun or becoming almost invisible in the dark shade.

Suddenly he felt grey and old, but he suppressed that

feeling firmly and concentrated on his work. Later in the day he could not refrain from looking out of the window now and again, to see whether the white spot had not reappeared in front of the blue forests.

When they came home it was evident that they had each profited in a different way from their adventure. Joachim always brought back facts: some new experience in sailing, some observation of wind and weather, some knowledge he had gained; for him it had not been an excursion but an expedition.

Marianne would listen to all this in silence, looking at Joachim with thoughtful eyes. Sometimes she would turn her gaze from him to Thomas, who also listened in silence, as if she wished to find out whether he was really the father of this bright conqueror of the world. Now and again she threw in a word, in order to bring back to plain facts some exaggerated report, but generally she seemed to agree and seemed to be more interested in Joachim's story-telling than in the actual experience they had had together.

However after the first weeks full of adventure, she began to refuse to join in Joachim's expeditions and preferred to remain on the island. Joachim only showed mild surprise and went away just as happy as before. Marianne appeared to be a little lost, she tried to find some work to do, but soon came back to the house, sat on the bench near Thomas making a wreath of flowers like a child, or turning over the pages of a book without giving them much attention, or she walked about the house singing softly to herself and moved the globe carefully, or let her hand glide over the rows of books. Sometimes she stood in front of the picture on the wall, her hands behind her back looking up at the wild and violent happenings in the picture with a kind of gloomy devotion.

Thomas took good care not to disturb her. When he asked

whether she would like to go bathing with him or look for 'the bird', he saw her face light up with pleasure, so that he treated her as tenderly and carefully as if a princess out of a gilt frame were walking at his side and not a sunburnt child who had grown up in the world of men.

Once when they were resting in the grass after a swim, and only the monotonous chirping of the grasshoppers was to be heard, she said, looking away from Thomas over the wood: 'It is so good when all is quiet.'

Thomas looked at her out of the corner of his eye, at her pure features which showed all too early some delicate shadows, at the soft throbbing of the blue vein under her ear, at her hair which lay wet on her shoulders. He felt deeply troubled when he wondered how she would be able to direct her life and keep her individuality in this dark world so full of passions. He put his hand cautiously on the hair at her neck and turning her head gently towards him said in the voice he always used in speaking to her: 'Dear child, the utmost we can achieve in life is to be without desire' – and after a while he added, 'even in love.'

She sat quite motionless and Thomas thought he saw how the idea entered her mind and then her heart, as if falling into a well through the golden sunlight at the top down to the twilight of the depths.

Then she nodded in agreement, and when they got up she touched his hand gently with her fingers. It was like the brush of a young bird's wings.

When she said goodbye Thomas promised to bring Joachim to the castle the following day.

Now it so happened that Thomas wished to ask the steward to tell the fish merchant to come to the castle as usual and to have the fish collected which were filling the tanks. So he told Joachim to wait for him in the park near the house. He had to go as far as the big barn, where the steward was supervising some women who were cleaning the racks for the new harvest.

In the meantime Joachim examined the big house, its steep roof, the old oak trees behind it, the buzzards which circled over the park. He stood there upright and firm like a little admiral on his bridge who sees a new country looming up near his bows.

Suddenly a menacing voice from behind asked him who he was and what he was doing here, and the point of a stick was poked against his back. When he turned on his heels, somewhat frightened, he saw an old man standing in front of him in a well-worn hunting suit, with a rifle over his shoulder and a weather-beaten hat pushed back from his forehead. Joachim recognised the general at once, for his father had often spoken of him, the grandfather of Marianne, his companion on the lake. So he clicked his heels in military style, put his hands on the seams of his knickerbockers and without thinking shouted in his high-pitched voice that he was Joachim von Orla, the son of the commander of a corvette, Thomas von Orla, now retired, and that he was waiting here for his father who had gone to discuss some business with the steward.

The old man stared at Joachim as if he were a foreigner speaking an unknown tongue. He saw his grandchild coming down the steps towards him and said: 'Listen, Marianne,' and then ordered the boy to repeat his answer.

Joachim was a little nonplussed at the stir he seemed to be causing, and perhaps he had also an intuition that his father might not be pleased that he had said all this. After a moment's hesitation he shouted out the answer again – a little resentfully – in his high-pitched voice.

'Did you hear, Marianne?' asked the general. 'Keep it to

yourself! Do not be as talkative as this young man!' However he stroked the boy's fair hair and asked: 'What do you want to be? A naval commander!' He nodded thoughtfully and then crossed the yard to meet Thomas, who came from the barn.

'I've been hearing things, Herr von Orla,' he said. 'He has a quick tongue, that young man of yours, but bears himself well. What are we going to do about it?'

For the first time in his life Thomas was angry with his son, but he controlled himself and asked the general not to let it make any difference and to keep his secret. The child he saw had given him away before he was ready to speak himself.

'I was a fool, Orla,' said the general. 'I ought to have kept my eyes open. Be a friend to my child. And keep a little friendship also for an old man, will you?'

Thomas bowed. He had to go home now, as the fish merchant was already on his way. 'Rest assured, sir, that there is nothing behind this, no "disguise" as Christoph suspected.'

The children stood on the steps of the castle. Thomas only waved to them and went through the park down to the lake. But when he unfastened the boat, Marianne caught up with him. She had been running and her breath came fast. 'Joachim ought not to have said that, and he knows now,' she said, without greeting Thomas. 'Perhaps he thought we would appreciate you more, if we knew who you were.'

'He thought,' replied Thomas seriously, 'that you would appreciate him more, when you knew it. He was a little ashamed of me all the time.'

She nodded like a grown up. 'Will things be different now, Thomas?' she asked in a whisper. He smiled and took her hand in his.

'We two old people will always be the same, Marianne, won't we? Even when you find the golden crown.'

She squeezed his hand hard with her small fingers and slowly went back to the house.

Joachim returned in the evening as originally arranged. Thomas was sitting on the bench in front of the house when he furled his sail and made it fast. Thomas was tired, for emptying the tanks had been hard work. However, he was pleased to see how quick and neat Joachim was in all his movements. He was deeply conscious that each child's life springs from two sources – and what did he know of the other?

Joachim sat down at his side immediately and said: 'I've done wrong, Daddy, do forgive me.'

Thomas watched the smoke of his pipe and nodded. 'Joachim, there are two things I would like to say,' he said calmly. 'He who wants to command must learn how to obey. And the other thing is that it's not the name that makes the man but the man that makes the name. You thought all that was a game, but it isn't. It's something exceedingly serious; do you understand?'

Joachim nodded and again Thomas saw how he wrinkled his forehead in an attempt to understand everything.

'And Marianne?' asked Thomas after a while.

'Oh – she was so condescending,' replied Joachim a little annoyed.

Thomas laughed. 'Well, that's the unexpected, old man.' Nothing more was said.

The holidays passed peacefully. There were some wonderful highlights; the general invited them both to a duck shoot; then there was a garden party at the castle, a crayfish picnic over an open fire under the oak trees and some night fishing with large dragnets. There was a supper in the house on the island in honour of Joachim to which the general and his grandchild were invited. After it was over, they sat round the open fire, the guests in the armchairs, and Marianne turned pale with happiness when Thomas waited on her as if she were a grown up.

However, work and holiday came to an end. Joachim packed his trunk and spoke of the autumn holidays, as if they were already imminent. He paid a farewell visit to the castle, and at last he stood bravely on the small platform with Thomas, as if he had lived all his life on departure platforms; for the future Naval Commander a word like 'emotion' did not seem to exist.

Thomas stood by the compartment window asking Joachim to remember him most heartily to all at home, and only when the engine whistled did he knock his pipe out on the side of the carriage and say: 'By the way, Joachim, last night I read something in the Bible which I have been thinking about a good, long time: *He that is slow to anger is better than the mighty*. It is a curious saying and well worth thinking over, and now goodbye, Joachim, and do your job well.'

Thomas kept the horse at a slow trot on the way home and saw very little of the woods. When he went down from the forester's house to this boat to unfasten the chain, he saw a bunch of flowers on the seat, such flowers as can be picked in the wood: campanula, sweet William, wild roses and quaking grass. There was no note nor letter with the flowers.

CHAPTER SIX

THE CUCKOO called no more. The days grew shorter, and when Thomas climbed up the ladder in the oak tree he could see the poverty-stricken village in the distance and yellow stubble in the fields. Now and again he saw a triangular bird with a long waving tail, the first kite, rise high above the blue forest. Early in the morning the grass on the island was covered with cobwebs, and the dew lay so thick on it that it looked like hoar frost. Storms still broke over the woods; every night the nets were full of fish, and bats tumbled against the grey roof. Shooting stars darted across the sky – singly or in clusters. They drew sparkling lines on the blue sky and disappeared as rapidly as if they had been extinguished noiselessly in icy seas lying above the clouds.

Thomas noticed the decline of the year by his lamp which he had to light earlier every evening. He took a greater liking to his fire as time went on, and the books rested longer and longer in his hands. It seemed as if for him also it were harvest time and though there was not much worth bringing home, he was able to look forward to winter with a happy heart. He did not believe that the general wished to have Christoph or any of his predecessors back. He did not believe that there was anybody in all the world who longed for himself, so that he had no compunction in staying on the island and not seeking a better post and greater honour. He did not think it worse to catch fish and to keep order on the lake than to manufacture rope or keep a bank account.

He fetched his winter wood from the forester's house – birch and beech – sawed and chopped it and piled it up in the shed for nets. His body had become obedient to his activity; he was at home in everything that his life demanded. If during his work his thoughts sometimes ran away to Joachim or to the child in the castle or further back to raids and battles, they always returned without effort or regret to the smell of wood under his hands, to the view across water and forest, to the globe mysteriously illuminated by the fire. Here he held the world locked in a small space, and it was more obedient to his eyes and hands than it had ever been before.

When he read about foolish, painful, or even shameful events in the outside world, he saw above all his bitterness the vicar's face and remembered what he had said about work. He came to the conclusion that man while growing more mature can only do right in the small circle of his own life and perhaps set an example to two or three of his fellow creatures.

In these days of Indian summer, when the rowan berries turned red, he had an unexpected visitor. He saw him approaching slowly in Gruber's boat, like a man who had plenty of time. Now and then he turned to watch for the reappearance of a grebe which had just dived into the water. Thomas recognised his over-thin figure with its slightly bent shoulders, his dark hair just turning grey and his way of moving as if he were walking in his sleep.

It was the 'young Graf'. He was older than Thomas, but as he was the last of six sons – five had fallen in the war – he was so called in the district in memory of times gone by and perhaps with the unconscious wish to keep death away from him at least for a few decades. At the duck shoot Thomas had sat in the same boat with him, they had not spoken much, but they liked to look at each other, and they both thought it would be good to sit by the fire together. His name was Pernein and his Christian name Natango, an old Prussian name. Thomas did not know anything about him, except that he was an excellent shot, in spite of his easygoing manner.

Thomas was pleased and got up to put some more wood on the fire. The air was grey and calm, and one could hear the threshing machine at the castle groaning like an animal as it worked.

Thomas went down to the shore to wait for his guest and waved his hand. When the young Graf had clambered out and shaken hands with Thomas, he said that he had intended coming to see him for a long time. However, it had always been sunny, and he wanted to see the island in this light. All things in this autumn atmosphere had voices, but their faces were silent, and that was what he liked best.

Thomas replied that he himself had to be satisfied with any light or any atmosphere – and so he was – but the young Graf was right, sometimes there was far too much light in this world.

'So you think so, too?' asked Pernein. 'I have always wanted to spend some years in Spitzbergen, because it is so beautifully dark there and for such a long time. Only the aurora borealis flares up, a grand illumination – and then all is dead silent; I saw it once. But then the World War came, and now they look at us with wry faces everywhere in the world, and so it has remained a dream. All these dreams, dear Orla, don't you agree? Yours, too: in the sweat of your brow and so on. All these are dreams, however your dream is not so bad.' He looked at the house with sad eyes, at the hill, the shoreline, as if he had grown up here and had come home for a little while, but was thinking already of the continuation of his journey, though he did not know where it might lead him.

He was the first not to show surprise on seeing Thomas's room, and while Thomas prepared the coffee, the Graf remained standing in front of the globe and let the countries and oceans pass by slowly without pause.

'Pretty,' he said, when Thomas came in again. 'One of the few toys for people with grey hair at their temples. One needs neither ship nor railway nor aeroplane. One makes the world rotate and sits in front of it like its creator. But would you have said on the seventh day that all was good, Orla? There–and there–and there?' With his finger he pointed lightly to some places on the globe. 'There they kill each other in the most up-to-date way, also women and children and animals, also trees and flowers, and they have the most glorious words for it and paper on which to print them. Others look at them and wait to see what it will lead to.'

'It has never been any different, Graf.'

'That's just it, that's just it. It always has been like that.' Pointing to the rows of books: 'There it was different and will always remain different. Or with Schubert or Chopin. Do you like music? Yes? Then you must come to see me soon. Music is the only thing that man has written that is without sin.'

They were sitting now in front of the fire smoking. 'It is curious,' said the Graf, 'how you resemble your father.'

Thomas held the burning brand in his hand, as he had taken it from the hearth.

'Yes, I knew you at once, even before I heard your name. You know that my five brothers fell in the war, and the War Office asked my mother if she would like them to send me home. Now my mother is a great woman, and she replied that she refused to tolerate such proposals. She had not borne her sons for her home but for the country. Yes, she is a great woman. Well, they did not send me home, but transferred me to a regiment that was a little behind the front. It was a regiment of dragoons, and your father was the commander of my squadron. You see, the world is small.' And he touched the globe with his finger and made it rotate a little.

'So it was you whom my father mentioned in his letters?'

The Graf laughed. 'Yes, quite a lot has been written about me. It was not my fault. I was just the same in the war, as I had always been, and people were surprised. Once a general came to inspect the regiment, and when he had already begun on the front rank of the horses, they fetched me from the piano where I had been playing Schubert. He took offence at my late arrival but I told him that an inspection might take half an hour or an hour, but Schubert was not to be mastered in a lifetime. He became more ill humoured and your father tried to talk him over. I think I gave him a headache or two. Your father was a good man; they all loved him, but he took the whole thing too much to heart. Later I heard that he died soon after the war. You are like him, even in the way you hold your pipe, and probably in other things, too.'

He looked kindly at Thomas always with that slight melancholy in his eyes, as if all this was scarcely worthwhile – neither talking to nor looking at him.

'And you yourself?' asked Thomas.

'Oh, I myself! There is not much to tell. I renounced the inheritance and asked for the house next to the home farm. It's a curious house which one of our old family bachelors built two hundred years ago. None of us liked to marry. The house lies in a beautiful position, quite by itself, on the other side of the river. There I live with a few servants, maids and gardeners, and sometimes my mother stays with me for a while. A cousin got the inheritance, a very capable man with lots of children and honours.'

'And what are you doing?'

'Oh, not much. I collect a little: etchings, drawings and some sculpture. Above all, idols of all nations. They are astonishing. Goethe once said: *As you are so is your god.* If that is true, and if that includes pictures, then man is a peculiar being. Yes, very peculiar. Well, I am also very fond of plants, especially of flowers. I am experimenting a little in my garden. The vegetable kingdom is such a quiet realm, marvellously arranged, full of law and symmetry and overflowing with beauty. But mainly quiet. Compared with it animals are monsters, and what shall one say of man? The mineral kindgom is probably the quietest of all. Then I play music a great deal. I had travelled round the whole world before the war, but now I don't want to go away any more. But I would like to come here now and again, if you will allow me to, and in the autumn I shall bring you perennials to plant round your house. Dahlias and larkspur, aconite and foxglove, and so on. They will grow quite wild, and people will think that a magician lives here.

Thomas thanked him and asked him whether he believed that he had found the right way of life now.

'You mean, whether I think I am a drone,' replied the Graf. 'No, I certainly don't think so. Look here,' he said, 'I believe that those of ancient lineage have the right to produce a playboy in every generation. Do you understand? They have done so much: worked, ruled, served, fought and bled, so that every fifty or hundred years one of them is entitled to play or simply to look on, to lead a real life of meditation. After five have fallen in the war, don't you think that it is permissible for the sixth to play music or grow flowers? During the great visitation? I believe it is. The blood is resting again and they owe that to us, I think. They didn't treat the old Prussians very gently; it's a miracle that some of us are still alive.'

'I would only like to know,' said Thomas, 'whether you go to bed every night with a happy heart?'

The other let his match go out. 'Good gracious, Orla,' he said, 'what curious things you do say! A happy heart – if I only knew what that is. That is certainly one of Ibsen's ideal demands. Perhaps my brothers knew what a happy heart was, though at times they had a very strange look in their eyes. But I, no, I don't know it, not even as a memory. A happy heart – good gracious, does such a wonderful thing exist?'

'But tell me,' Thomas persevered, 'if your heart is not happy what is it like then?'

'Of course, Orla, my heart is heavy – like a stone in my chest. Did you not know that? Everything is a dream, my dear man, not only your motto: *By the sweat of your brow* – everything else too, even Schubert and Chopin. In the evening when you stop reading or playing music you only need to look out of the window into the mist outside or up to the stars beyond which a 'benevolent Father' is supposed to live. Then you know all that you want to know. Have you ever looked into the eyes of the forester's wife from close to? And you still want to have a happy heart? My dear Orla, only those people have a happy heart who can shut their eyes to reality and say: come sweet dreams and close round me. How many things has man not invented to relieve him of awareness? Gods and art, war and work, dolls and machines. But nothing is of any use whatsoever. The clock ticks, the hands advance, and that dreamless land comes nearer and nearer. For death has no dreams, dear Orla.'

For a moment his face looked as it might look when he was asleep, naked to the world, bereaved as that of an outcast and filled with horror. Then slowly his expression seemed to come back to life, he began to smile as if at home again in space and time and looked at Thomas. 'No, dear Orla, I am not a drone. Drones do not think but I do think sometimes – carrying my thoughts to a logical conclusion. To be able to do that is a hard fate.'

They went out again. It was already twilight and mist was in the air. The threshing machine was silent, only the divers called from the water. A withered leaf fell slowly into the grass from the birch at the gable.

'Yet I love it,' said the Graf softly. 'I love the autumn and my river which flows under the poplars. I love the light that shines out of my windows, and that melody from Chopin's study in double thirds which the prisoners sing on their way into exile. And I like to see a squadron riding along a road through the wood while the pennants flutter from the ends of their lances. And I love my mother when she stands at the head of the stairs and looks over the empty fields, below which her sons sleep and those of past generations – back to the time when the gods wore amber crowns; I love it all, but with a heavy heart.'

He stood there with his hands behind him, his shoulders bent and his eyes travelling over the objects, growing more and more indistinct in the dark, with a melancholy affection – from the birch tree at the gable, over the island and the grey water to the woods where the mist rose. It was as if he were ageless, as if he had been standing there already a thousand years ago leaning on his bow or on his sword and had looked over woods and swamps to the country where the mountain of the gods rose near the large river, and where he saw the amber crowns sparkling on their stern foreheads. He might have asked the same question already then and might have listened for an answer. But there had been no answer. And now he was still listening, although his speech and his dress were different, his eyes had remained the same as well as his transparent temples and his intelligent mouth which no longer asked questions.

The sun was setting invisibly somewhere. A cool breeze came from the water and touched them both. The eyes of the Graf returned to reality and he looked at Thomas. 'I love it all,' he repeated softly, 'and I love you, too, with your brave dream.'

They walked round the island along the shore. They heard the clock at the castle strike and they stood still until it had finished. It sounded as if it were on a ship slowly gliding into darkness through the mist.

'He also dreams,' said Pernein, lifting his hand in the direction of the sound, 'the Prussian dream.'

Thomas saw the vast hall and the glow of the fire on the muzzles of the cannons, the lonely man holding his glass of wine, the child coming downstairs, the pictures silent in their gilt frames, the eagles, the harvest wreaths with bright coloured ribbons, the swords from the battles of Frederick the Great: no, this was not a dream. Beams did not become blackened by dreams, nor stone steps worn. Swords and wreaths did not fall to dust. One nation perished and another rose. This one would perish, too, but its fields remained and so did the golden crown which it had forged for the delicate foreheads of its grandchildren, the crown of duty, obedience and devotion to a law which only existed in their imagination. They had changed the dream into something immortal. He shook his head and looked over the country which grew darker and darker. Nothing would drive him away from here any more, no ghost and no fear. And the man who had wrung his hands in sorrow at his country's plight had said the right word when he mentioned work. God might exist or he might be a dream, but the sweat of one's brow was not a dream.

Thomas clenched his fists and felt his horny palms with his fingers, the result of this summer's work. He was neither frightened of the mist nor of the night nor of autumn. Soon the nets would dry and the fish would go into the depths. Then he, too, would rest for a while, as all living beings were destined to do – and would then talk to himself like the great birds – and take up his routine work again with the turn of the year. He knew that the angel was looking at him.

He followed the boat with his eyes, as it glided slowly into the mist over the water driven by the oars, like two thin legs of a waterbeetle. Then the wall of mist closed, as if it were the gate of the realm of the dead. A chain still clanked for a little while and then everything was quiet. Only when Thomas stepped again over the threshold of his house did he know that the whole thing had been real.

This evening when he had washed his plates and put them back on the shelf over the hearth, he planned to write something – ideas and fragments of which had now and again been in his mind. It was something about the moral education of the sailor. It might help a lot of people or only Joachim or even only himself. Now he could see his former life in perspective. He understood how he had grown up, where weakness, error, mistakes and guilt lay and also the great idea which had upheld them all. He also saw the fissure which had been the cause of the disaster. He felt so far away from all controversy that he was able to start writing quite calmly and objectively. Besides, he thought that morals were everybody's concern at such a time.

Meanwhile the month approached its end: every day brought gay as well as serious hours, and in September he only caught fish for the castle and for himself. He broke up the soil round the house with a spade to prepare it for the promised magic garden; he spent long hours in the woods looking for mushrooms, put his nets in order and hung them up for the winter, built mousetraps and slowly prepared everything for the quiet time which would come to him in the dark months, but which he was awaiting quite cheerfully, like a hermit whose God is no further away in winter than in the time of light.

September brought some warmth, a last afterglow of the earth. The leaves turned yellow and brown; birds gathered in flocks and disappeared overnight, the jays were noisy in the tops of the oak trees, and the path of the sun grew shorter from day to day. The child in the castle wore different frocks because she outgrew the old ones so quickly; the general dined on partridges with Thomas, and blessed the earth because these birds did not take part in the revolution, and the forester's wife stood at the garden fence, put her hands round the high mallows and kept bending them up and down while she sang the marching tune softly. It could scarcely be heard in the yard, for the shadows of the high pine trees covered it and the rustling of the treetops drowned its weak sound.

On one such autumn day Thomas knocked at the Graf's door on the other side of the river, was admitted and found him in his library bent over a microscope looking at the petals of a dahlia, whole beds of which stood like a radiant wall round the house.

He showed no surprise at Thomas's visit. 'Come here, Orla,' he said, 'and have a look at beauty, pure, purposeless beauty.'

He stood beside Orla while he looked through the microscope and noticed how a reflection of the miracle he saw passed over Thomas's face – a miracle of colours, lines and shapes which formed a mysterious picture. He only nodded when his guest said that the dissection of nature may fill a person with deeper awe than its appearance to the naked eye. 'Perhaps we ought not to call it dissection,' he said, 'but rather, revelation. It is characteristic of the greatness of this silent vegetable kingdom that every lifting of a curtain brings us nearer to a holy temple. One cannot claim this of humanity.' He smiled in his absent-minded way, took his guest's arm and went with him through the door on to the terrace, after he had ordered tea to be brought to them there.

On the terrace which was raised above the level of the ground the view was much more extensive than the one Thomas had admired on his arrival. The garden bordered by old trees had broad long flower beds and was divided into several parts by small walls and steps leading down to the river. It was not very wide, and it was made narrower by reeds growing close to both sides. It wound its way among meadows and fields and soon disappeared into a small wood. Its banks varied in height, and light and shade played over it in the bright sun. In the distance the fields of the home farm could be seen but the castle itself was hidden by trees. A white road bordered by rowans lay under the cloudless September sky.

'If I didn't know,' said Thomas, 'that all this is only two hours from my island, I would think myself in some southern part of the country, and that this river were a tributary of the Rhine or the Danube.'

The master of the house agreed, obviously pleased. While the table was being laid for tea, he led Thomas down the broad garden path, where the colours of the flowers almost clashed, and where the last butterflies, Peacocks, Camberwell Beauties and Red Admirals with large wings, swarmed, before the autumn winds would drive them away. They stood for a little while on the river bank and saw stones and floating plants in the river bed. Gnats swarmed above the surface, small eddies swirled into the depths like dark rings. When they went back, Thomas was not surprised to hear the Graf say that the river seemed to him one of the deepest symbols of life, and that it tied him more to this landscape than his possessions or his memories.

'I am sure it is dangerous,' said Thomas, 'to have the symbols of life always before your eyes and especially this one which continually wanders and flows past.'

'My dear Orla,' said the Graf, 'what is without danger? We connect everything with death, and perhaps we are right. I only consider as dangerous things foreign to me which intrude into my life and deflect it from its normal course to stop its even flow, thus preventing growth and decline according to my inner law. But the river? No, it is not an impediment. We both know how transient our life is.'

From the garden there was a clear view of the house with its over-high windows and its irregular roof covering quite a simple ground-plan.

'My ancestor did not aim very high,' said the Graf, 'he only wanted to be original.'

They spoke little, even when they went over the house after tea, the Graf only made an occasional explanatory remark, as if his guest knew as much as he did about all the sculpture, the idols and saints, paintings and tapestries, and as if he only desired to point out those things which were especially dear and familiar to him.

Although Thomas did not come up to those expectations, he was fully aware of the beauty which had been brought together in this house, and that normal life elsewhere must appear strange and cold to eyes used to such surroundings. At the end of the corridor he asked if he might again go back to the long, wide passage which led past the three main rooms, and which received a quiet, greenish light from high north windows facing the forest.

On the walls, which were panelled with grey silk, hung a number of death-masks made of a material like ivory. They looked down upon the spectator in silence. There were faces which seemed to have been torn apart by suffering or passion and looked as if the hand of Death had put them together again for their final destination. There were faces which had probably already been marked by eternity during life, and Death could keep them unchanged as he had found them. Finally there were faces of those who had gone into the great darkness like children, and Death had surprised on them an expression of astonishment, their eyes were wide open, without fear and quite empty, and God had entered into this emptiness, or silence or whatever else they might have seen.

It was neither a museum nor a cemetery. It was a community of dead things, but a tranquil stream of life flowed along among these faces. Light softened by the trees outside threw shadows on those foreheads which were as if turned to stone. They gave the impression not of cold or horror, but of a cool peace, and even this coolness contained nothing strange, nothing from beyond the grave, but only a gentle distance, something far removed from passion or pain or happiness, a great loneliness which seemed to penetrate everything, and which is the attribute of one's own death.

At the end of the passage a high bluish vase filled with flaming red dahlias stood on a low pedestal. It looked like a fire burning with a motionless flame in honour of the dead.

Thomas was silent, and later when they sat on the terrace warming themselves in the last rays of the sun, he only looked thoughtfully over the garden.

'Only music can express something similar,' said the Graf

at last, 'because nothing decays or crumbles to pieces in that art.'

'And when your mother is here,' asked Thomas, 'don't you think it is hard for her to walk along there?'

The Graf was smiling again. 'My mother is a great woman,' he replied, 'greater than all of us. The last time we went along there together, she said: "I expect, Natango, that you won't look much worse!" and I replied that I would do my best, of course.'

'I believe you will smile,' said Thomas, but he shivered a little.

'Yes, that's possible, if He comes at the right moment. But it is difficult to know beforehand. Few of us die in our beds.'

When twilight fell, Pernein began to play the piano. Thomas sat by the fireplace and listened. When he raised his eyes, he could see the Graf's face with the reflection of the fire on it; his expression showed that he was far removed from his surroundings, and that he had no thought either for his guest or his home. His eyes were like those of the death-masks in the grey passage, but they were wide open, entranced by the music – without any emotion; they were humble wells letting the other light enter into their twilight.

While he listened Thomas felt more and more certain that music alone had meaning in the life of the Graf. It was the only language in which he neither smiled nor mocked, the only reality in this world which he recognised. Here was no untruthfulness and it was not shameful to show yourself. Water was not his element nor earth but only sound, the single note that was struck gently, that rose and died away, that which intermingled with other notes, with series of notes, separated again, and in the end remained quite alone – the primeval element, which was denied all union when the last was said; and now nothing remained but the series of questioning notes, and then the last single note for whose sake the whole seemed written.

The music ended softly with an old song, a marching tune, in which there lived a modest bravery and some wistfulness – semitones which held each other up and seemed to be carried towards the distance which enveloped and obscured them.

The last chord vibrated for a long time. The Graf joined Thomas at the fireside and began to smoke. His face looked cheerful, cleaned as after rain, and he began to talk about the plants which he intended to take to the island and of the colours he suggested. He said that he liked the English because of the wisdom and modesty which made so many of them fill the evening of their life by becoming gardeners – statesmen, philosophers, generals and politicians turning into nothing but gardeners. A long and glorious life did not spoil them, but allowed them to return to beauty and to the faithful nursing of plants – those helpless messengers from another world.

He was looking forward to the time when Thomas would imitate them and to the first great step which he had taken out of the noisy world would add the second small one into the vegetable kingdom.

'Are you sure,' asked Thomas, 'that the first was a great step?'

'Let us say a long one,' replied the Graf, 'so as not to make an overstatement. I myself see in the voluntary adoption of a hermit's life something akin to greatness. For resignation – the essence of loneliness – is also present in the greatest we can expect on earth: in wisdom and in love.'

Thomas said that he was glad that the Graf recognised these.

'Why, of course! I recognise a lot of things, but what is the good of it? It is a long way from that to striving after them; this path is too difficult for me, perhaps also too crowded. I only look along it with sympathy, that's all I can do.'

'Perhaps,' said Thomas, 'there are people who achieve this without much effort, by some happy talent. Some of the masks outside in the passage seem to have possessed it.'

'That may be,' replied the Graf, 'but I would like it applied to me. I do not think anything is worthwhile, except music. I do not like to work in the sweat of my brow, that is my whole secret, and that's why I have such deep respect for you who have gone out to seek satisfaction in physical work. You appear to me like a man who immediately on rising starts work with a giant swing, and who in the evening jumps into bed with a breakneck leap. I admire that very much, for I myself could never do such a thing.'

'You are not afraid of death, Graf?' asked Thomas after a while.

'Oh no, why should I be? Perhaps I am a little afraid of the manner it may take, which we cannot foresee. There are many ugly forms of death, I am sorry to hear – but we have to wait for death with good spirits. However, this is probably the concern of the mourners. Everything that makes death hard is the concern of others, not of ourselves.'

'You have killed in the war?'

'Yes, certainly, that's what it's for, I suppose. And I did so without worrying about it, as if it were a game in which we beat the king with the ace. In the next deal the other fellow may have the ace.'

'But you haven't killed in a skirmish with the bayonet or spade?'

'No, I haven't; but of course I would have done it if necessary, but I'm glad to have been spared that. You ask with a purpose, Orla?'

'Yes, of course, your house has such a beautiful deep resonance. I have never discussed it before.'

'Talk if you like, one is generally sorry afterwards, but people who live on an island really ought to speak sometimes, otherwise they may lose their sense of feeling for others.'

'Yes,' said Thomas, 'most people would probably not understand, but it is different with you. One never knows what you think. Well, it was on my last ship when the end drew near. They hauled down the flag and I came along at that moment. There were wicked faces, and I aimed my revolver at one in front. Probably there was only a second to spare, for they were already crowding behind me, too, but it was my fault that I looked into that face. It was not a momentary fault, you know, but an inborn one, a permanent fault. I didn't shoot like an automaton, but I thought first, or I only saw – just a face – not a distorted one and not the evil itself. And what I saw was a face, perhaps not the image of God (I certainly didn't think of it as such) but something alive, full of breath, blood, passion, something which it was in my power to kill and destroy.

'I don't know whether you understand me. I was not afraid, not at all. I only saw and perhaps I meditated, if that can be done in a second. I am convinced that I would have shot – in spite of everything, but I had missed that second, the blind second, as it were, perhaps only the fraction of a second. For when the gun misfired, they felled me from behind. I didn't even know whether a shot was heard. In falling I seized the flag, and they threw me overboard. I lost consciousness, but my man jumped after me and saved me.'

His face had turned pale, and he looked as if tormented by the memory.

'You must not take it too much to heart, Orla,' said the Graf. 'I presume you know that you would not have been able to save the ship. But that really is of very little importance. In your opinion this is a hidden blot on your honour. I do not agree with you. If you had closed the door of your cabin and had pretended not to see anything, that would have been different. But what you call "the seeing", that is another matter. To be able to kill without seeing or thinking, to kill blindly, one must have a certain contempt for life, for one's own life as well as that of others. But he who has once recognised that all life is a miracle, the life of the plant as well as that of man, well such a person is reluctant to kill, or let us say: life fills him with awe and he is not a born soldier. Whether the reluctance is right or wrong is a different question on which I will not express an opinion. Besides, it is beyond our willpower, it only happens when put to the test – and then it is too late. Then only can we understand that we chose the wrong profession.

'By the way, I admire you for having told me this. Very few would have done so. And only now do I understand why you went to the island.'

'It wasn't only that,' said Thomas. 'I didn't have the world which is at your disposal and to which you can devote your time. I had practically nothing, and I recognised that one must have something – if it is only a fishing net.'

'Yes,' nodded Pernein, 'even with a fishing net one can find a happy heart – more easily probably than when I devote my time to my world. I have never succeeded in acquiring that happy heart.'

'But your face looked different after you had been playing the piano; it looked purified, if you will not misunderstand me.'

'No, I understand you perfectly, and besides you are right. I even have a pure heart when I am playing, but a pure heart need not be a happy heart. Well, let us leave that. I always have the feeling as if we were not entitled to think or speak of such things. For none of us is J.S. Bach, for example. He was entitled to search for it with each note and to proclaim it with nearly each note. That's why I never play Bach, I am afraid of him.'

'Are you capable of fear?'

'Oh certainly. I can be very much afraid, of crayfish, for instance, of scorpions and of crickets, when I work in the garden. I would also be afraid of angels, if I believed in them and of their images on earth. Some are said to exist and that may be true. I would feel them too pure, do you understand? On the other hand I am not afraid of ghosts, not even of the ghost of this house. Yes, they say there is one, and when it appears it is supposed to prophesy the death of the master of the house.'

He bent towards the fire, his elbows on his knees, to warm his hands. He smiled, but yet his face looked very, very old – like the face of one of his ancestors a thousand years ago, and that mouth mute and decayed for ages might have said what he had just said.

'There are certainly family traditions,' he went on after a while, 'supposed conversations of ancestors and also of servants – however, one does not know what to think of them. But there are also notes by the first who saw the ghost. He wrote quite a lot, most of it is missing, but a sort of diary is still in existence. He wrote about this ghost: "It was sitting on a small couch in front of the fireplace when I entered – looking into the fire as if meditating. Its hands supported and half covered its face, so that I could not see its expression. It was clad in a colourless gown and seemed surrounded by a mist, though the fire illuminated all other objects sufficiently. It didn't take much notice of my entrance, and we both remained motionless, until the clock on the mantelpiece struck the half hour. Then it became indistinct in its outline, it gradually faded and seemed to evaporate like some liquid on the floor, and no trace of it was left. My hair didn't stand on end–as one used to say–but I felt a chill between my shoulders and I knew that the Lord had looked at me!"

'I have told you this word for word, as it is written, because one must not add nor leave out anything. I have always thought the end magnificent in its simplicity: "And I knew that the LORD had looked at me" . . . the Lord . . . and he wrote it with capital letters . . . but I have not yet seen him, the meditating one.'

Then he got up, took a slip of paper from the table between the windows, read the names of the shrubs which he intended to bring to the island and asked Thomas what colours he would like to have.

Outside Thomas lit his bicycle lamp, and its white light fell on one of the dahlias which grew near the steps. The Graf lifted the flower cautiously with his hand. It as already heavy with dew, and he looked at it attentively. 'No,' he said at last, 'it wouldn't be good, Orla, if we forgot that the destruction of beauty may be a deadly sin, would it?'

Then he thanked him for his visit and wished him a good ride home.

From the road Thomas could see the house once more. A dim, reddish moon hung over the angular roof and over the windows of the library with their subdued light. It looked as if the moon were something near and real, and as if all that belonged to the house were far away and only illuminated by a borrowed light. The roof hung over the dim squares of the windows, and Thomas thought he ought to suggest to the Graf that he have a newly timbered roof put on the house, steep and simple like that on the castle at the lake.

CHAPTER SEVEN

A MAN in a shabby naval uniform is walking along the white road towards the east. The rain has washed the skin of his face, and the sun has dried and bronzed it. His eyes are grey and calm. They do not beam with pleasure when a rainbow spans the heavens and the vast expanse of the earth lies steaming under the seven colours of its light. He does not look disheartened when mist hangs from his eyebrows, when the mud of the road soaks into his shoes, nor when the storms of the equinox blow the dry birch leaves into his face. He looks straight ahead, calm and cool, always alert and never surprised. He reads the figures on the milestones and every morning and evening he consults a large, old map which he carries in his tunic.

He observes the homes of the rich, where façades give a false impression of well-being; he also notices slight signs of decay on either side of the road, among houses, fields and human beings. He sees large estates where people work or are idle, and empty barges on the river with rotting planks. He hears the screaming of gramophones as he passes inns and the harsh sound of automatic pianos; the dancers have a breathless and hunted look, as if they felt themselves observed by a face from behind the blind and broken window panes; a face from a faraway grave with earth on its forehead and an expression of melancholy surprise at the changed world it beholds.

He gazes calmly at all the wanderers he meets. They come from the emptiness of the east, as if driven towards a land where men and houses are nearer to each other, where perhaps there will be more light and more warmth where the sky is not so dark and depressing with torn clouds and menacing sunsets, where the many-coloured lights shine over the houses forming circles and letters, and where they imagine the terrible penury of everyday life will change into a fairyland of splendour, wealth and power.

He looks at all who pass him, at young and old, at faces which are pure as well as at those which show the stamp of vice. He exchanges words with them when they ask him a question, but he does not tell them what is waiting for them; at the most he says that in the west they still bake bread with rye or on rare occasions with wheat, or that the rivers still run down into the valleys and not uphill. Then he nods and the long black ribbons of his cap stream over his shoulders in the west wind.

His papers are in order but it seems that his uniform attracts the attention of all kinds of people, those with caps pushed back from their foreheads as well as those with shining helmets and service revolvers in their belts. He gets rid of the former quickly enough, but the latter are more persistent and ask every question a man on the road can be expected to answer. He gives full particulars patiently, while his eyes glide over the brightly polished buttons – indifferently. But the officials do not interpret this indifference in his favour, and now and again he has to produce the money he has hidden in his tunic, to prove to them that he is not a beggar. 'Honestly earned,' he says, emphasising the first word in a way which greatly displeases those who ask.

When he is in high spirits, which happens sometimes, he

answers the inquiry as to what he is doing or seeking by saying:

'On Friedrich Wilhelm Bildermann, now listen well,
There lies a soft, but magic spell.'

And his eyes look thoughtfully at the helmets of the military police.

Those who enjoy a joke smile and pass on. However, there is not much sense of humour in these times. The low-hanging clouds depress the heart of man, the broken window panes of the factories are like the eyes of the dead staring down upon the road. From time to time he sees ploughs without horses standing idle in partly ploughed fields, and young fellows with their hands in their pockets standing at the entrances of the villages or at the gates of estates staring at the wanderer gloomily and suspiciously.

However, the sailor does not care. Like a homeless knight he walks along between death and the devil, his eyes turned eastward, as if he were looking for the towers of a promised land on a cold horizon. A week ago when the first heavy rain of autumn fell on the roof of his hut, when the wires between the telegraph poles sang in the gale and his small iron stove smoked until tears poured from his eyes, he realised that the captain would need him now. He would want neither his wife with her red lips and her sparkling car nor his young son cycling through the quiet streets of the suburb, his arms crossed on his chest, but only him, Friedrich Wilhelm Bildermann, first mate, out of a job, who can stoke any sort of stove, who can wash the crockery and scrub the floors, who can be silent for a month, if that is the order, who can play the accordion and is a match for everybody in wrestling, who has lived through good and evil years, has been shipwrecked and a prisoner-of-war. He knows the barbed wire and the consequences of flight, but his eyes have always remained the same: grey, cool and alert, though sometimes they, too, can sparkle like a warm, beautiful flame when a word or a gaze penetrates to his heart. So he packed his box and carried it to the station, rolled up a blanket and strapped it on his back, put his haversack on top, cut a stick in the first wood he came to and now walks towards a country which he knows only by hearsay as a frozen land where men do not speak but bark.

He sleeps in barns and stables, and often enough in haystacks in the meadows. His table is quickly laid, for beyond the chalk cliffs he also learnt to go hungry. He is a good walker and needs no other comfort but his short pipe. He knows a lot of songs which he hums whilst walking, English and American ones, with half-remembered words – shanties – from his time on a sailing boat, and slow, melancholy tunes from the time when he was a prisoner. When the rain runs down his neck and out of his shoes, he only spits into the road, saying: 'Blast!' – and no resentment is left in him.

On the frontier of the foreign country which projects into the German empire, he considers for a while whether to spend some money on a railway ticket; but then he remembers how he left the chalk cliffs of England. What was possible with the Tommies ought to be possible here, so he walks into the thin pine woods, sleeps by day and wanders by night, always alert, always on the look-out. After a time he finds a leaky boat on the bank of a large river and is carried away by the wild current, but in the end arrives somewhere. His bread is soaked and his tobacco wet. He dries himself at a potato-fire and treats himself to some brandy out of a tumbler, thus spending the money he saved by not taking the train. In spite of the mist and the loneliness he does not think the country bad at all. One evening in October he arrives in the yard of a castle and takes a deep breath. A little lady who comes from the stables confirms that this is the castle he is looking for. Only important residences are marked on the map which he had spread out like a sail – no foresters' houses nor any islands. Young Master Joachim had told him that it was easiest to cross to the island from here, so he had come here, and he thought that now he could manage the rest.

'Joachim?' asks the young lady, looking at him kindly, as she would have looked at a new St Bernard's dog. 'What Joachim?'

'Joachim von – Joachim Orla, yes, certainly.' And he was looking for his father, the retired helmsman, Thomas Orla.

The young lady knits her brows and then smiles. Her face looks quite different and the first mate who has travelled far and wide and experienced much, and who is cold and tired, all of a sudden feels warm and safe when this child smiles at him and putting her hand on his coarse sleeve, says: 'So you are Bildermann?'

'Certainly,' he says in high spirits. 'On Friedrich Wilhelm Bildermann, now listen well, there lies a soft, but magic spell.'

She listens as if to music, then her face beams, and she asks him to say that once more.

He would have repeated it a hundred times for her, but she is satisfied with one repetition. She takes his hand which is not very clean, and which he tries in vain to wipe, and leads him past the house through the park to the shore of the lake, where the boats lie. She points to the edge of the forest to the left and says: 'From there you can see it. North-north west. At this hour the light is shining from his windows.'

'North-north west,' Bildermann repeats, full of admiration.

'He is very lonely,' she says, looking into the twilight.

'The captain was always lonely,' he replies, 'the helmsman, I mean . . .'

'It doesn't matter, you might just as well say captain.'

'Yes, always alone, even on a ship with a crew of a thousand. At home too. He was like a board drifting on the ocean.'

'Oh, that's why you have come?'

'To be sure, in autumn it always gets a little difficult. I know that – having been a prisoner-of-war – little lady; Bildermann knows the ins and outs.'

'And how did you come here?'

'I walked, little lady – it's a long way to Tipperary – but now we are here.'

'Yes, now we are here,' she repeats, 'and now we will stay here, Bildermann, won't we?'

'For ever, little lady,' says he.

She puts her small hand into his and they feel that they have entered into a pact. He feels as if he were in a dream in this landscape and with his child. His eyes still see the white road leading up the hills and down to the valleys and his feet are sore. But here is the water, iron-grey, with bright, cold streaks of light and in the distance a black forest in which the owls hoot, and above which the glow of the sunset is reflected. Flocks of wild geese sail above him with high-pitched screams, and at his side stands this child, like a noble lady looking thoughtfully towards the north-north west, where she says the light can be seen above the water.

Then he gets into the boat and leaves. The oars are light, and for a while he can still see the dark figure standing motionless in front of the yellow trees of the park. She fades away and is lost in the twilight before he reaches the edge of the forest. But he seems to know that she will be there as long as his boat is visible.

Beyond the forest he unships the oars, lay one down and sits in the stern with the other on his knees. Suddenly everything is vast and wide, the sky, the lake, the glow of the setting sun. The edge of the forest fades away in darkness, and in the distance over the grey surface appears a dark hill from which a light shines through the night. It is the light from a ship which lies at anchor there, all alone in the grey evening, and only one man will be standing at the mast waiting to see whether the evening will send him a gift.

Suddenly Bildermann's heart grows heavy. He is not depressed by the vast silence nor by the melancholy of the night. There has been silence enough in his life, and he knows what it is like when one looks into a strange evening sky through barbed wire. He also knows how it feels when the rain falls on a thin roof of leaves or on the slanting thatch of a haystack, and how the heart throbs heavily and slowly all alone and there is nobody to ask whether you feel happy in all this solitude. He did not call it the melancholy of the evening when he heard the footfalls of the sentry on the grass or the sound of an accordion in the distance above the narrow paths of the allotments. He did not give it a name, but he knew what it felt like. Hunger always present and gnawing like a dull pain, the chill that runs over one's back, even if one puts one's hands on the stove which is growing cold. His heart was heavy without any special reason, perhaps only because a grey morning would dawn and a grey evening would follow, and his idle hands had nothing more to occupy them than a piece of wood to carve – no cable to haul, no gun breech to close, no helping hand of a friend.

The dreariness of a life, the beginning and end of which are lost in horror; no order, no stand-to, no laughter, no turns at the wheel which moves noiselessly without beginning or end.

He does not know whether he is thinking of the captain or of himself. His journey has come to an end – the spring has run down; he has gone forward blindly for days and nights and now he sees a light shining over the water, and he does not even know whether it is his light.

Friedrich Wilhelm Bildermann, imperturbable in war or peace, holds the wet oar on his knees and looks to the right and left, in doubt whether to turn back and disappear in the forest.

'And now we will stay here, Bildermann, won't we?'

'For ever, little lady!'

'Damn me!' he spits into the black water and thrashes it with his oar, so that the keel turns aside. He has not noticed that men bark here, but that this country is haunted seems to him as clear as crystal.

The light grows clearer as he approaches, so that the windowbars look like threads – the calm yellow light shines in the darkness, a clear light coming from a room where there are no cares, where it shines on the pages of a book or on a sheet of paper addressed to the first mate Bildermann, or on two hands on the knees of a man tired after a good day's work.

Bildermann scents the withered oak leaves, the sweet smell of newly sawn wood. He finds the landing stage, fastens his boat without making a noise, takes out the oars, his blanket and haversack and knocks at the door.

'Yes,' says a quiet voice which seems to come from the bowels of a ship.

Bildermann must have staggered with fatigue on the bright floorboards in front of the lamp and the fire; otherwise it could not have happened that the captain was holding him tight with both arms shaking the sailor's shoulders slightly and saying over and over again: 'Bildermann, is it you, Bildermann?' in a voice that seemed to come from far, far away.

He cannot but answer yes, but it is by no means easy for him to do so. He has spoken very little on his journey, scarcely at all, his voice does not obey, and there is a slight mist in front of his grey, cool eyes before which the rows of books, the globe, the firing cruiser and the face of the captain float like unreal things, like things seen below the water drifting by indistinctly.

'Yes, sir,' he says in a hoarse voice. 'And if you want me to go away again, then say so right away, captain.'

He hears the captain laugh (and thinks that he has not heard that sound for a long time) and then suddenly he finds himself sitting in a deep chair, so deep that he fancies he were going overboard. In his mouth there is the sharp taste of rum, and the fire warms his dirty hands, the wet drops on his blue tunic shine in all the colours of the rainbow.

'This is a dream,' he thinks. The rain does not fall on a leaky roof, the wind does not hum in the wire; everything is all right again, the books, the globe, the cabinet with the masks. The beams of the ceiling are dark brown, like the skin of a smoked eel, slightly greasy too; the walls are dark and so are the tiles on the hearth. There ought to be a skylight at the top through which the stars could twinkle, and water ought to glide past the walls lapping them with a warning sound.

'Is all this real, captain?' he asks, rapping the tiles with his knuckles.

'All right, Bildermann, you need not hold on tight, we shall not fly away.'

'Funny,' said the sailor. 'It is as if all this has been standing for a thousand years–such a reliable country.'

'Isn't it, Bildermann? Let's stay here, shall we?'

'For ever, captain! Oh, that reminds me –' It occurred to him that he had said so already once, but it seemed a long time ago, many evenings, many fires in the hearth, and he turns his face towards the window. 'There was a little lady in the west. And she said: "Now we are here, Bildermann, and we shall stay here, shall we not?" And I answered: "For ever, little lady." I am sometimes a little quick with my tongue, captain.'

Thomas looked at him thoughtfully. 'That was Miss von Platen, Bildermann, Marianne von Platen, the grandchild of the general to whom all this belongs. She has been a good guide to us, hasn't she?'

'Certainly, captain.'

'And now we shall stay here, Bildermann, both of us, as she said, or all three. Let's get that clear at once, so that you can sleep well. This is the island of the veterans, Bildermann. For now and again I happen to think that I wouldn't be sitting here if you had not been –'

'That's a silly idea, captain, with due respect. For I wouldn't be sitting here either if you hadn't been. So the one cancels out the other. Anyhow, it was never worth mentioning. But if it must be – then – rolling home my boys – then Bildermann will show what he can do.'

'We know that, Bildermann, don't worry. There's work in plenty here, although not exactly in winter. And you know, a man must speak sometimes, even if only a few words during the day.'

'All that I have thought of, captain. I know it is difficult at this time of the year. I didn't even ask madam or the young gentleman. When the wind begins to howl so peculiarly, before it veers, wailing all night long, then the time has come for old sailors to sit together for a while, captain. I don't mean here at his damned good fire, that's exceptional, captain. I only mean in the same house, in the next room or in the attic, or only on the threshold. "Bildermann, are you there?" "To be sure, captain." "All right, I thought I was all alone under the clouds." That's the main thing, captain, to know that somebody is there. He may be as quiet as a mouse in socks, sometimes he should be, but he must be there. "Is there nobody in all the world?" "Yes, captain, Bildermann is here, don't worry, he is always at hand. With Bildermann there is no empty space."'

Thomas nodded and looked into the fire. 'You are quite right, Bildermann, no empty space. You know in spring and summer it was quite easy, much too easy. Long days full of work and bright nights with many stars. But now the land here shows its real character. It is a grand country, I can tell you, nearly as grand as the ocean. Not a sound all day long, and still as death at night. People grow odd here, but I don't want to grow odd, Bildermann. My predecessor started drinking brandy and wrapped a red flag round his body, and he prophesied that I would do the same – the brandy, I mean. I am glad that you have come, very glad. I suppose it will take a little time, before one can become like a stone at the bottom of the lake. My last discovery is that it does not fall into one's lap nor into one's outstretched hands; it costs just as much sweat as other things. Anyone can make a man silent, but to grow quiet of one's own free will, slowly and on purpose and without bitterness that is, I believe, nearly as difficult as to get out of a net without touching it. I wonder, if you understand me?'

'I hope to understand everything which you say is happening to us. I have sailed a few knots in my life. I sat in my hut and listened to the falling rain. No human being, not even a mouse, nothing but rain. I might just as well have lain in my coffin or in the Atlantic. There was no need for the sun to rise. Why should the sun rise? I was like a board drifting on the ocean. That's what it was like, captain.'

'And no letters, Bildermann?'

'Madam took the wind out of my sails a little, captain. She said that you wished to be all alone.'

'Indeed – and how is everybody at home, Bildermann?'

'Oh, I think all right, captain. The young gentleman is very smart. He goes straight towards his goal – a naval commander – looking neither right nor left, only straight ahead. Bildermann was a calf when he was his age, but the young gentleman is a racehorse – first-rate, captain.'

Thomas nodded. 'In ten years, Bildermann, they will have got ahead of us. They will still throw wreaths on to the North Sea, but afterwards in the mess they will say: "They hadn't got enough pluck, the old boys! We should have gone about it in a different way!" Am I right, Bildermann?'

'Certainly, captain. They'll get a free dinner and places of honour at the parades. Such is life. It was just the same in 1870. Youth is always right, captain. We were just the same.'

Thomas nodded again. 'And my wife, Bildermann?'

'Oh, I think she's all right, captain. I only spoke to Madam once in the garden; no twice. I sometimes opened the doors of cars at the theatres when tobacco became scarce. Once it happened to be her car. Madam is very grand, captain, only a little thin. I suppose she has set too many sails.'

'Yes, isn't it strange, Bildermann, *we* do not want to make up for anything we have missed, it is only the others who stayed at home who wanted to do that.'

Bildermann put his big hand hesitatingly on Thomas's sleeve and said: 'Don't worry, captain, we also want to make up for many things – only for different ones.'

Thomas looked at him doubtfully, but Bildermann's face was serene. 'You think so, Bildermann?'

'Yes, captain, I do.'

Their new life soon settled to the same course as Thomas's old one, but Thomas soon realised that things were easier. There were now two horses to the plough. Bildermann took a look round for a whole day, his hands in his pockets without saying a word. Then he took the boat and sailed away. 'Will you give me full authority, captain?' he asked, departing.

'Certainly,' said Thomas.

His boat came home from all points of the compass; and it was never empty. It was loaded with boards, with brushwood, horse manure, with buckets full of chalk and oil paint, with an old anvil and torn bellows. It looked as if he was going to build a wharf, or at least to open a second-hand shop. But he proceeded slowly, one thing at a time.

He made a new floor for the smaller room and painted the walls. He fixed a double door in the main room to keep out the east wind. The house was whitewashed, the frames of the windows were painted and the plants were covered with straw. He made a new surround for the well and built a 'wharf'. He erected a mast with a flag behind the house to test the wind, and at the other side of the hill he started building a hut with a small forge. The boats were drawn up to the shore, were caulked and pitched, and he began making a ship in a bottle for the 'little lady'.

All this he did in silence, or while he hummed or smoked a pipe. The ends of his woollen scarf and the ribbons of his cap floated in the wind. The waves of the lake were covered with white foam, and black clouds sailed over the bare tops of the oaks. Bildermann lowered his axe, straightened himself and looked over the water. There he stood with legs wide apart in his faded and worn-out uniform, and the sharp wind brought tears to his eyes. He had no ship, no home, no wife nor child – but like a tower of strength in the quiet battle of their lives, he stood at the oars. The ribbons of his cap fluttered in the storm, water splashed on to his forehead, and there was a whistling in the reeds like the sound of wind in the rigging. Behind the window the captain sat writing, a silent man, but who wanted noise in this country? Hadn't they had noise enough in those years which had passed and of which nobody wished to speak?

He knew all the villages in the neighbourhood, all the craftsmen, all the foresters. Only a vague rumour about the captain had penetrated the district, but Bildermann walked through the streets of the villages with a nautical gait, his hands in his pockets, the ribbons of his cap flying like two streamers behind his head, his eyes wide open looking attentively for the things he needed. 'To be sure,' he said, 'both of us were nearly drowned at the Skagerrak – together in all eternity – I am sure you don't need this plane any more, I will give you some fish instead next summer – you old land shark – goodbye, my darling.' They did not know what to think of him – whether he was a worker like themselves or the valet of an aristocrat, but he looked at them in such a peculiar way that it seemed wise not to ask too many questions. He was like a man in a strange boat, with an unknown cargo, but as long as he and Thomas did not build gun emplacements on the island, the villagers did not bother. Times were hard, and each carried his own load. Besides, the castle was behind those two, and although the owner was a reactionary, a militarist and a bloodsucker, he was, after all, a general, and not many districts around the lakes could boast of a general.

The forester's wife knew Bildermann too. When he came for the first time, she stood at the garden fence singing the marching tune. But he did not stop in embarrassment as others had done. He leant over the fence opposite her, listened attentively with a smile, and then in a low voice sang the second part: 'Proudly floats our flag, black, white and red, from the mast of our ship.' He knew all the three verses by heart, and when he had finished he doffed his cap with the ribbons and waved it above his head. 'Cheer up, mother,' he said, 'they died a good death. God knows, how the devil will catch us.'

'Fire,' she murmured, 'nothing but fire!'

'Fire is clean,' he said, 'better than water, where the fish eat them and the gulls pick out their eyes. Come along, mother, let's sing another song! "Rolling home, my boys, rolling home. . . ." '

'Rolling home, our cable is all clear . . .', he sang the tune slowly sustaining the notes, his left hand on the fence and his right lifted towards the wood, as if he saw a distant coast or the banks of the Sacramento behind it.

She listened, her eyes on his lips, as if she were a deaf-mute, and as if he were singing a psalm or announcing a new gospel, more trustworthy than the old one, to be sung in flood and fire. Her lips silently moved with the unknown melody, a lost tune which came from far away, just as Bildermann seemed to be like a lost picture, blue with floating ribbons, once known so well, but now faded and cracked in the ordeal of fire. 'Rolling home . . . sing it again.'

He held her fragile hand in his and sang merrily, a comforter from the far oceans, a spirit with a message – but the tune remained – different from the eternal rustling of the trees, a happy tune as if sounding over the crests of the waves in the wind.

'You are a magician, Bildermann,' said Gruber, 'a real magician.'

He waved his hand. 'You learn all that beyond the white cliffs of Dover, old gentleman,' he said, 'where the prisoners-of-war stand and stare at the horizon. They see a house, but there is no house; they see a child, but there is no child. They see everything that does not exist and nothing that is in front of their eyes. All prisoners-of-war are long-sighted. Sometimes they are so long-sighted that the knife with which they are peeling potatoes goes into an artery. Every mother's son learns a lot when he has to look after such people. For better, for worse, for richer, for poorer. That's the English marriage ritual, sir. We buried many a man for whom God was too far away. He was too far away, even for the long-sighted ones, sir, and that does mean something.'

Bildermann also got to know the Nabob, and their acquaintanceship did not seem bad to either of them. Thomas had said: 'You must present yourself to the general; you can't just annex the island.' So Bildermann shaved, pressed the ribbons of his cap, and sailed across the lake. It always looked as if he were trying to sail the boat upside down.

However he got there all right, rang the bell, and the grenadier in his uniform of the time of Frederick the Great opened the door. 'Hullo,' he said in surprise, 'have they forgotten you, boy? Wait until I come back, will you? We have the same sort of job – and now to see His Excellency. I have got a message from Herr von Orla. Which door? Thank you! Think a little quicker, ducks.'

Bildermann clicked his heels. 'First mate, Friedrich Wilhelm Bildermann, asks to be allowed to enter as a fisherman's mate at Captain von Orla's fishery.'

The general had a threatening expression as if he were gazing at a whole platoon of rankers. 'You are Bildermann?'

'Yes, sir.'

'You saved his life?'

'Yes, sir.'

'You would go through life and death for the captain?'

'I'll be roasted on a red-hot grate for him, sir.'

The white moustache quivered slightly. 'I am told that you said "for ever" to the child. That's a very precise way of expressing yourself. You are engaged and so belong to the household; leave your papers here. I will come to the island one day and see how it works. Why did Johann not announce you?'

'Johann was flabbergasted, sir. He is slow on the uptake, but probably thorough.'

'He was a soldier for too short a time. Only four years. It would take eight to make him one.'

'Yes, sir, a year for each button.'

'True! You have good eyes. My regards to the captain. Good morning.'

They shook hands. Bildermann clicked his heels and left the room.

Johann was leaning against the cannon. 'Boy, if that goes off!' said Bildermann. 'We had such cases at sea, when the big gun fired. A signal rating was shot right through his stomach. They had to line the hole with aluminium and put a bucket in. He is still alive today, and every morning he takes the bucket out to disinfect it.' Johann stares at him with wide-open eyes.

'Come and see me sometimes,' says Bildermann. 'There is always a drop of rum for old soldiers on the veterans' island. Goodbye, sweetheart.'

So Bildermann became a sort of bridge to the world, a happy bridge where many a person stopped to take a look at the island. But for all who stood on uncertain feet in those changing times he remained a suspicious character, a man without respect and with doubtful friends, a man who never dropped his eyes and his gaze seemed to strip the veils from what one preferred to hide. The general beckoned with his stick when he saw him and talked with him for a quarter of an hour, listening 'to the wisdom of the simple man'. ('He is a German oak, dear Orla, there is not one rotten spot in the man.') The little lady gave him serious advice how to divert and cheer up the captain, should he forget again how to laugh. The silent woman at the garden fence wanted to hear his songs, and from time to time he met Johann 'on the high seas', when the Nabob passed from man to man, and nobody in the whole district was so astonished as the slow-witted Johann at some of Bildermann's remarks.

So Bildermann, without any special effort, became part of the daily life of many, and he hardly realised that he had 'the contented mind' for which his master longed, and that all hands were stretched out towards it because it was the only permanent thing in these changing times.

When he looked back on his life, he realised that he had been a wine press rather than wine, that many men's feet had trampled on him, but he did not realise that he was able to give comfort and security to others; for he did not feel quite certain yet whether some day all this might not disappear: the island, the house, the narrow bed in his room and the grandeur of the dawn above the forest. He did not accept a new belief easily; he had become a little 'far-sighted'–on water and on land, he knew what fate could do to a man–even without a war.

Though he felt satisfied with his cruises on the lake, he started to dig up the overgrown soil of the forest behind the house, for he thought that a potato patch would be useful and also would look pretty when the young plants showed their bluish flowers.

'For sure, captain,' he said when Thomas questioned him, 'the greatest men have grown fat on potatoes and salt, perhaps even Horatio Nelson, and I think the little lady will be pleased to sit here by the fire and eat a supper cooked in hot ashes.'

Thomas thought so too, and so they dug until dusk, until the curlew called from the cold, high clouds and the lamp from the forester's house began to shine into the darkness.

After Bildermann had washed the crockery and fetched wood and water for the next day, he sat on a stool near the fire, splitting pinewood or making a new oar, or with *The History of the Conquest of India* open before him. His brows were knitted and he supported his head in both his hands. His bright eyebrows often twitched and now and again he said in a low voice, 'Damn it all.'

From time to time he looked furtively at Thomas, who was making notes on white sheets of paper or reading or only looking at the globe through the smoke of his pipe. The birch-wood crackled in the fireplace, the clock measured the time, and a night bird called across the water.

Then they both raised their eyes towards the window and listened to the wind as it rustled through the high reeds.

'A dream, captain,' said Bildermann in a low voice, 'it's still like a dream.'

Thomas nodded and slowly turned the globe. They both looked at the continents as they glided past and the bluish oceans where they had been at home all their lives. Oceans which were now far away–coloured patches on a globe spanned by the circle of the equator. In their mind's eye they saw the ships on which they had lived and those which they had met. They saw how storms rose over the waters; they saw the blue waves breaking over their own ship and over others. They saw the signs of the zodiac rise and set, a thin line of palms over the horizon; they heard the stroke of the bell and the lonely step on the bridge. They saw fire breaking from the long tubes and the white fountains thundering on the glowing iron of the deck. They saw the grey keels, like monsters of the deep, dive down into the foaming abyss; they saw white faces drifting in the water and hoarse birds screaming above them. Hours, months and years glided past with the globe; they imagined that they could also see the island on which they were living now, rising above the horizon and disappearing again, a dizzy game played by the hand of man and ending as and when he wished.

'A dream, Bildermann,' repeated Thomas, 'but a good, solid dream, which will still be there tomorrow and in a year's time – provided we do our duty and hold it fast.'

'Let's hold it as tight, captain,' said Bildermann, 'as the poor man holds his bread.'

When they lay in their narrow beds, the door open between their rooms, they saw the reflection of the slow-burning fire playing above the row of books and on the dark beams of the ceiling. Rain poured down on the roof and from time to time flapped like a wet sail against the window. The wind howled monotonously down the chimney.

'Are you asleep, Bildermann?'

'No, captain.'

'I wonder whether you notice how alone we are?'

'You're damn well right, captain – beautifully alone!'

CHAPTER EIGHT

MARIANNE USED to wake up in the morning when Frau von Sperber, in the next room, began to gargle as the doctor had advised her. She had been in the family as long as Marianne could remember, at least since Death began to roam the castle. Perhaps he had brought her as a substitute for all those he had taken. It must have been when Marianne's mother died that Frau von Sperber arrived from the small garrison town to stay with her grandfather. Then war had come, and she remembered that of the many who had gone away, some had not come home. They had gone on a long journey, she was told. Uncle Jochen in the light blue uniform of a dragoon who had always given her a ride when he was on horseback, and the valet Fritz who smelt so nicely of soap. The inspector Mertineit with his big head and loud voice whom the people called 'Boisterous Johann', and Michel, the assistant gardener, who risked losing his job by stealing yellow plums and carrots for her, which he scraped with a huge penknife before he pushed them into her mouth.

And at last her father with his black helmet and high shield, behind which one could not see his hands, had gone, and now only visited her in her dreams. She hardly felt any pain at the thought of him, only a constantly increasing emptiness. It was like the park in autumn when the birds fly away and the leaves fall, and when you can see the paths and the railings which you have not seen for a long time, or when a house empties of many noisy visitors after bright, cheerful days, and you stand at the top of the stairs and see them drive away. They all say that they will come again soon, for a long stay, but you never know whether grown ups tell a child what they really mean. Death had brought Frau von Sperber to the house and had left her there. She had worn black clothes and had short grey hair, so that Marianne thought for quite a long time that she was a man, disguised because she did not want to go to the war. She was tall and strong and had a deep, hoarse voice, and Marianne expected her to appear on the stairs with a spear in her hand like Pallas Athene whose picture she had seen in books. Marianne had been rather afraid of her, until she had found her one afternoon in front of the picture of 'the handsome man', which hung above her writing desk, a cuirassier with a silver helmet that reached to his shoulders, wearing an eye-glass and a bold smile about his lips. Tears had been running down Frau von Sperber's red cheeks, all hint of spear and armour had disappeared, and she had looked like one deserted, because her dear ones had gone on a long journey. 'He was a good man, darling,' she had said, 'only like a feather and he could be blown wherever the wind sent him.' And she blew across her hand, as if she were sending 'the handsome man' flying into the park through the open window.

Marianne did not understand how somebody with a helmet could be as light as the mysterious flowers in the meadow, the tops of which you blew off to know how long you were going to live. But she understood that Frau von Sperber had a heavy heart, and that she need not be afraid of her, but must comfort her, and this she tried to do shyly and awkwardly.

Frau von Sperber's tears flowed again, but she apparently felt better, and then the two sat hand in hand on the low sofa near the round stove, the tiles of which pictured the homecoming of the Prodigal Son, and the child listened seriously to the story of 'the handsome man', in which a lot was said about money, more of women and still more of horses. It appeared that the tall, strong woman with the spear had always been in his way and had been ridden down, and finally 'the handsome man' had not come back like the Prodigal Son, but had gone on the long journey soon after the beginning of the war. Now he lay buried in Poland, 'the handsome man', who had been Frau von Sperber's husband.

'Your husband, Auntie Mary?' Marianne had asked. 'Don't you think you are mistaken?'

But it was no mistake, for Frau von Sperber took the marriage certificate out of a small ebony casket, and though Marianne could scarcely read, she had to believe it. She caressed the strange widow once more and then went into the park, where she picked one of the white balls in order to blow at it. However, she was suddenly frightened to do so because she remembered that 'the handsome man' had been just as light as a puffball, and now he lived perhaps in this flower after some mysterious metamorphosis.

From that day on a silent friendship existed between those two, whom Death had refused to take along on the great journey, even if in some things the widow of 'the handsome man' seemed to be peculiar, and the child did not consider his frivolity such a bad fault. The aunt with the soft name and the gruff voice had been told that her hoarseness would disappear, if she fought inexorably against 'the parasites' on her vocal chords. They could be killed with cooking salt, a tablespoonful in a small glass of hot water. With this deadly mixture she was to attack them every two hours, which meant that she had to gargle. The very word frightened

Marianne, and she thought of someone being strangled and buried in the ground.

'Don't worry, darling,' said Aunt Mary, 'salt was mentioned in the Sermon on the Mount, and if my husband had been given salt as a child, he might not have become so frivolous.'

The joiner had made a support for her head on one of the armchairs like that on a dentist's chair, and there her white-haired head rested every two hours, while the noises so feared by Marianne came from her throat. It sounded as if somebody were drowning and as if the last note were sucked down to the fish by a whirlpool. She also feared that Auntie Mary might turn to salt in time like the Dead Sea of which she had heard amazing stories.

At dusk when they were sitting near the stove, Aunt Mary would sometimes say: 'Darling, you are a funny creature. You live like an oyster in its shell.'

As the war had not made the castle rich, Marianne did not know how oysters lived, and when she had learnt, she looked thoughtfully at Aunt Mary's garnet brooch which sparkled over the breeding place of the germs. Then she considered what might become of an oyster, if it were born without a shell. She pondered for a long time over this comparison, and whether Aunt Mary had thought that a pearl might be inside her, too. At last she decided that salt made people talkative, and that her father under his dark helmet had certainly been a silent man, as silent as the pictures in the hall or as her grandfather or her friend Thomas Orla.

She sat up in bed and saw the golden glow of the dawn on the treetops in the park through the parted curtains. It was quiet in the next room, Frau von Sperber was reading her Bible. That was the time when she could think of beautiful things, before the duties of the day began: of her fourteenth birthday, for instance, which fell in the summer holidays and when she would be allowed to spend the afternoon on the island. Joachim would be there and give away the whole world. Bildermann would tell marvellous stories and smoke eels over fir cones, and Thomas – there was nobody who could listen as well as he could, so seriously, as if only admirals and princesses were sitting around.

'We two old people,' he had said last year. All the others said 'I' or 'you', but he said 'we'.

She curled her hair between her fingers and felt how soft it was. If she cut off a curl and gave it to Thomas, where would he keep it? In the cabinet with the masks or in one of his books? Or would he wear it on his heart? She pulled out the locket which she wore on a thin gold chain under her nightgown and opened it. There was a faded picture of her father in it and a tiny thyme blossom. Thomas had given it to her last summer after they had been swimming and had asked her to look at it attentively. A poor flower growing in the sand, but it was so beautiful, and there was nothing on the island he liked so much as its scent, strong and pure. She had hidden it in her hand until she had got home. At that time she did not yet know that he was Thomas von Orla.

She closed the golden case and felt her heart throb under her hand. The blossom lay in the thin locket like the pearl in the oyster. So far Aunt Mary was right. But why did he not have a picture of his wife in his house? Even if he did not wear it on his heart, why did it not stand in front of his books or hang on the wall? And why was she not with him, not even for a few days? Last year Marianne had once asked whether she would come for Christmas. But he had put his hand on her shoulder, as they were standing on the shore, had looked over the ice and had said: 'We are on the ocean, little princess, nobody comes to us.' Probably he had meant

Bildermann and himself. He had not looked specially sad, but the lines round his mouth had been deep.

'But I come, Thomas,' she had said.

'Yes, child,' he had replied, 'you come to see us also on the ocean.'

Everything he said was like this. You could understand it as you could understand the others, but behind it there was something you did not understand–something vast and unlimited that made your heart throb.

She sighed, threw off the blanket and put her feet on the floor. Aunt Mary thought that she was too thin, because she took so little salt and made life too easy for the 'parasites'. But she saw no parasites on her tanned skin, only a few scratches from the shrubs on the island and a blue bruise where she had knocked against the seat in the boat.

Joachim . . . oh yes.

She smiled and went to the windows to draw the blinds. It was good when someone knew everything, could do everything and was never embarrassed. But was he 'on the ocean'? She thought while she held the cord of the curtain in her hand. Probably he was on a captain's bridge high above the sea, but only Thomas was on the ocean. And perhaps her grandfather, too, when he sat in the evening in front of the fire in the hall lifting his glass towards the flames. Sometimes she crept out of her bed late at night, went to the stairs and peeped through the bars of the banister down to where he was sitting at the fireplace, moving his lips and lifting his glass as if he were drinking somebody's health. He was so lonely in the vast, dark hall with the dead birds and the antlers which threw wild shadows, and the dead men and women who looked down from their gilt frames. He was so terribly alone that once she had run down in her long nightgown which covered her feet and had leant against his shoulder like a young, strong shield. He had neither asked why she came nor had he scolded her; he had only pressed her to him without looking at her. 'I am an old man,' he had said, 'I have many visitors in the night – you must not worry – they are quiet people.'

That's what he said. Who were those quiet people that came to see him at night and whom she could not see? Did the magic cap still exist or were they brownies from under the roots of the oak trees in the park – or were they the dead?, And did the dead return except in a dream? 'Oh, darling,' said Aunt Mary, 'you think too much. Those are memories and they come to me too when I lie awake at night. He is so still now, he has no saddle any more, no glass in his hand, no flower in his helmet. After all, he was a good man, darling.'

But Marianne did not believe that 'quiet people' came to see Aunt Mary. Certainly they did not come to those who before going to bed sat in a dentist's chair and made a noise as if they were drowning. She tried to get some information from Johann, as he leant against the muzzle of the cannon, but he only wrinkled his eyebrows and said that they were probably deaf and dumb. 'Oh, Johann,' she sighed, looking up to him, 'it is so difficult with you, because you are so tall.' Whereupon he fell into a brown study. Bildermann sucked at his pipe and looked into the water.

'Little lady,' he said, 'it may be those who sit behind bars.' And he did not want to say anything else about it.

Only Thomas did not evade her questions. 'Today, my child,' he said, 'there are only two kinds of people: the soldiers and the dead.'

'But do they come back, Thomas, as visitors?'

'All come back to those who love them, child, even the dead.'

'To those who love them,' she repeated to herself. That

must be the great thing, so that nobody was afraid of them. She sighed once more and then at last she drew the blinds. The dew sparkled, the tops of the trees looked like beaten gold, and when she leant out of the window far enough she could see the blue water in which the trees were mirrored. They had already come home with the nets, and Bildermann was sitting on the doorstep grinding coffee beans.

The cuckoo called and she started counting. She did not wish to live so terribly long, until her hair grew white and germs grew in her throat and in other places. She only wanted to live as long as her grandfather. Or Thomas. She did not want to be left alone with the others. Fifteen minutes . . . twenty minutes . . . twenty-two times. That was long. Thirty-five years was a good age at which to die, if the others were still living. Then the children of the cottagers would come with flowers, and Bergengruen, who would have been a vicar for a long time, would preach the funeral sermon. And she would like the schoolchildren to sing the beautiful song of Loewe: 'Shepherdess, how sweetly have they buried you. . . .'

She began singing it softly, swallowed her tears bravely and saw in her mind's eye Thomas and Bildermann walking behind the open coffin, and then she would become one of 'the quiet people', who returned by night, when the man 'on the ocean' was sitting by the fire. But that was so far away . . . twenty-two years . . . my goodness!

'Darling, darling,' said Aunt Mary, standing in the doorway, 'must you sing songs of the dead early in the morning? I wonder what sort of a house this is?'

But Marianne smiled, waved her hand and disappeared into the bathroom; however, she put her head round the door again and said: 'The house of the king's children, Aunt Mary.'

Grandfather had already come home from his morning ride, and they had breakfast together on the terrace. The cuckoo was still calling and Bergengruen should count how many years he would still have to live, but he refused to do so, saying that even a funny superstition reminded one of heathenish times. The general looked at him menacingly. 'Only heathens could look upon death as a joke. The clergy invented the skeleton – a very bad invention. He would not like to be fetched by the skeleton. "To die is the most beautiful death!" Have you heard that before?'

Bergengruen was stupefied. 'Pardon, sir, to die . . .?'

'Yes, to die is the most beautiful death . . . that was a music-hall song in the war. . . .' And then grandfather and grandchild laughed until the tears came into their eyes.

'But that really is . . . a matter of course,' said Bergengruen after a while.

Now Aunt Mary laughed too, and Marianne put her hand on Bergengruen's arm: 'We are only joking,' she said consolingly. But he shook his head for quite a long time and looked at the general furtively. He was a respectable man, a very respectable man, but a rough soldier. Just like those of the Thirty Years' War.

They talked about the fields and stables, the poultry farm and the fishery, the cottagers and their children, weddings and death. Every morning the life of the estate began its routine from this place according to ancient laws, with the sun as its guiding star. They were all industrious and obedient servants, but every cloud was more powerful than their will. They knew that the earth was full of goodwill, more so than men, and the next year could make up for the shortcomings of this. The waves of modern times washed their shores, and sometimes inundated them. Property changed fast, but the earth quickly got rid of what was not made of earth. The steep roof stood high and safe over their lives.

'To work!' said the general, getting up. The schoolroom was filled with a greenish light reflected from the trees in front of the windows. Bergengruen said a prayer as he did every morning and then they began. The child never gave him any trouble. She was not too eager to learn, but she knew what her grandfather meant when he spoke of the sense of duty and of the Prussian soldier and his children. She was neither negligent nor careless, and strictly honest. The portraits in the hall looked down on her; and she did not like to cast down her eyes. She did not work for any examination.

Daydreams were far more difficult: when her grey eyes could not keep open, and when her guests of the night were still under her eyelids. When her fingers played absent-mindedly with her thin golden necklace and when she said Tobias instead of Herr Bergengruen. He felt then as if her familiar voice were coming from far away, perhaps from a well in the Holy Land around which sheep, cattle and camels crowded on the reddish sand of the desert, and the angel of the Annunciation had just left to open his silver wings behind the olive trees.

Then Bergengruen stopped on his regular walk between the window and the bookshelf, put his hands behind his back and looked at her furtively. He was fond of this child, as he was fond of the whole house in an awkward and altogether devoted way, for it was an island in the grey ocean of his life. But what would become of her? Was he the right guide for her youthful steps, which wandered in such odd directions – whilst he had nothing to guide him but the word of the Lord? He was a poor student, an orphan, who had spent his holidays working in factories and mines, not very popular and often made fun of, always a little dazzled and even a little blind behind his glasses. Should he go to the general and tell him that his hands were too rough for a dreamer? That he was not a mother, and that there were children who should not grow up without a mother? Probably the general would answer that the Platens could even grow up without clothes–if necessary.

Then he could only push the grammar and the geometry book on one side, sit down opposite the child, his head supported in one hand and start telling her one of his quiet stories. This he was able to do without any preparation and with a certain talent of which he himself was quite unconscious.

'Once a very long time ago a child grew up in a poor house. . . .'

'Oh, Tobias, was it a real child?'

'Yes, a real child, and he could sing like an angel.'

'What was his name?'

'His name was Franz Schubert.'

'Oh, Tobias, tell me all that you know about him.'

And Bergengruen told his story. He knew so much about these men and their times, for once he had wanted to become a musician, and in the end he sat down at the piano, and the girl stood near him with her hand on his shoulder and sang in her thin, high-pitched, but quite pure voice: '*Trinkt noch Glut . . . und schlürft noch Licht. . . .*'

They both listened to the last note, as it faded away, just like two children looking at a shining cloud, and neither knew what blessing had been vouchsafed to them.

'You are so good, Tobias,' said the child. 'Tomorrow everything will be better. Last night the quiet people visited me.'

He did not ask a question. He only nodded. He knew that even children can live hidden lives.

Then there were days when she liked to 'sidetrack him'. Not because she did not want to work, but because she liked to see how 'his wings grew'. At the glorifications, for instance, or when he told her of the life of Anton Bruckner or of that of the great organist who gave up everything to look after the sick in the tropical forests of Africa. Then she saw his plain face behind his glasses become almost beautiful, a glow seemed to spread over his features, and in her eyes he appeared like a soldier in the service of humanity, imbued with love. She looked at his hands usually covered with ink spots which now looked beautiful as if inspired by devotion to the greatness of human ability. She looked at his lips which were often tired and uncertain and which now pronounced the sayings of those men whose disciple he was and whom he admired. In that admiration he forgot completely that a man called Bergengruen lived on this earth and tried to walk in their footsteps.

And again a cloud sailed above them and they did not know how much blessing fell from it on them.

Sometimes the general passed under the window and heard the voice which seemed oblivious of its surroundings. He did not always know what they were talking about, but he felt that it was beautiful and 'over the head', the great picture the tutor was creating for the child without thinking of himself. Then he went on softly, lost in thought, pausing a little in front of the lilies whose scent dulled his senses. After dinner before he went out of the room, he would say to the surprised Bergengruen: 'You are a good man, Bergengruen. I have always known it. I am grateful for the child's sake. Go in for your examination and be a vicar here. I shall see to it–you understand?'

At eleven o'clock Bergengruen sat down to study Christian dogma, whilst the general rode over the fields with his grandchild. It was his favourite hour, when he forgot the war, the misery of his people and the loss of his two sons. Perhaps he did not forget them, but his love for them had been transferred to the bright shape of this child who rode straight and attentive at his side. Men had always given their sons to their country, but the line was preserved through the daughters. Destiny did not only fertilise the soil of the country with blood, it also ensured the continuation of the race.

He let the child grow up naturally. He did not want her to be like himself. He would have wished soldiers to be like himself, probably they would have been. But the child was different, though she was his own flesh and blood, in her he recognised his race. All he demanded was that she should be truthful and obedient, not to him but to the soil which would one day be hers. Without being present at her lessons, he knew that she lived in a dream world of her own sometimes. But without an ideal one could devote onself neither to the king nor to the soil. There are hours in a man's life when he has to believe in something. When his faith is shaken, the dream alone remains.

'When times are better, you should plant a wood here, my child,' he said, pointing with the handle of his riding crop to the bare side of a hill.

'Yes, grandfather, pines, birches and juniper.'

He nodded and they rode on. The rye fields moved in the wind, and in the distance the blades of the mower went through the meadows which were covered with blossoms.

'Can one sing songs, grandfather, and ride here and always be good?' asked the child. 'Can one do all three things at the same time?'

'Not always,' he replied. 'Sometimes one after the other –

sometimes simultaneously. One must have a big heart, my child. A big heart has room for the whole world.'

' "*Trinkt noch Glut und schlürft noch Licht*", can one always sing that, grandfather?'

'Always,' he said, stealing a glance at her sideways.

At lunch the general was silent but he listened attentively.

'Are you going to the island?' he asked when Johann brought in the cigars.

'Yes, grandfather.'

'Give him my regards and bring him back if you can. There is room for two at the fireside.'

'Yes, grandfather.'

She ran upstairs to her room.

'Are you going to work, Bergengruen?'

'Yes, sir.'

After a while he said with menacing eyes: 'Mind you look after the child, Sperber, Bergengruen, you understand?'

'But, Herr von Platen . . .'

'Oh yes, I know – but salt alone is not enough. I know you mean well, both of you! No harm must come to her, you understand? Suffering comes of its own accord.' He pushed back his chair, nodded, and went to his room.

The lake was like glass, and as in a glass her reflection glided along with her, slightly disturbed by the ripples. The birds were silent, only the woodpeckers hammered indefatigably in the forest. They were as busy as Bergengruen, whose weak eyes travelled up and down the pages of his old books, to find the salt of the earth. There were so many mysterious questions which had to be answered by all of us, even by himself.

One day he would be the vicar here, Grandfather had promised, and they would all stay together. In the outside world the ever-changing years passed over the land and the whole earth, just as the light did over the big globe when Thomas moved it. But here everything remained as it had been. The fields grew, the young forest grew, and the children of the cottagers grew. When the old coachman died, his son got the job. When the old horse Freya kept in the stable was unable to work any more, its colt was saddled.

She would never go away from here, nor should the others be allowed to go. They would have to stay here for another twenty-three years. Aunt Mary would have become a pillar of salt like Lot's wife, and the deer would come to her in winter and lick her hands softly. But Thomas would never grow old. The reeds and the plantations would grow and eventually hide the island, and the blue larkspur would overshadow the roof and look like a shining southern sea. But he would remain unchanged in his grotto with his dark, smooth hair, his narrow mouth, and his hands which moved more calmly than anybody else's.

She sighed with happiness and let the oars drop. She knew that she was dreaming, but only the pictures were dreams. The soil in which they grew was a reality; her faith in the reliability of life, in obedience to the lastingness of the soil which bore her, and her belief that love was stronger than fate. If one took men and things into one's 'big heart', one could keep them there like a ship in a bottle. They did not go away, they only changed as much as one let them change. They were everlasting.

She heard the bright clang of a hammer coming from the island. That was Bildermann at the anvil of his small smithy. It sounded as if he were shaping a child's scythe. He also would remain here. He had eyes in which the sea seemed reflected and was stronger than death. He had sunk to the bottom of the sea once and yet had come up again. They had dragged him away and kept him like an animal in a cage, but they could not keep him for ever. Thomas had called over the grey ocean, and he had come to save his master. Oh, there were angels, even if one did not see them. When the great invisible ones had accomplished what they were sent out to do, they rose, and one could only hear their silver wings rustling under the stars like the wings of the great birds on the island.

The perennials which the young Graf had given Thomas were in full bloom. The mallows reached to the roof and laid their white and purple calyxes on the grey reeds. Below stood the larkspur and the blue helmets of the aconite. The wall of dahlias was still green, but the phlox in front of them showed its first blossoms, and their sweet scent wafted across the lake. All colours stood motionless in the heat of the noon as in a picture, only the air above them vibrated, as if the whole were made of glowing metal; now and again a butterfly – a Red Admiral or a Purple Emperor – rose drunkenly and dropped again.

Slowly, under the impulse of the last stroke of the oar, the boat drifted to the shore. The girl hardly knew whether all this was a dream at noon, a magic garden reflected in the water with all the glowing colours, its blossoms and blades of grass. The magician was invisible, only the bright sound of the hammer which beat on some jewellery still filled the air. An oriole called from the oaks, also a magic bird, trying to find the release of a song and never finding it.

As the keel scraped the sand and the reflection of the house and the garden quivered in the water, Thomas was standing on his doorstep. He saw the girl step on to the sand and wave to him, then she faltered and leant against the pole to which the ends of the nets were fastened and slowly sank to the ground. He lifted her up and saw how she opened her eyes in surprise. Moisture stood on her forehead, and she was pale to the lips.

She smiled hardly conscious. 'Oh, Thomas,' she whispered, 'was somebody standing there?'

He held her in his arms and looked into her eyes. He was frightened. 'You must not row over the lake at this time of the day, child,' he said quietly, and carried her to the house.

She had put her arms round his neck and was looking back over the lake. Close to her eyes she saw some grey strands in his dark hair.

'Is there something special about this time?' she asked.

'The ancients say that Pan is asleep,' he replied.

The curtains of the room were drawn, making it cool and dim. He laid her on his narrow bed carefully, knelt down in front of the cabinet containing the masks and came back to her with a light-blue silk shawl embroidered with golden birds with slim, delicate bodies and outspread wings looking like purple mist. A strange scent came from it as he covered her. She did not dare to put her hands on the golden birds.

'You need not be afraid,' he said, smiling again. 'A princess wore it once, and it is just made for you.'

'What princess, Thomas?'

'On the island of Bali, my child, far from here. They call it a sarong, and they wear it wrapped round their hips.'

He felt her pulse and she had the sensation of her blood throbbing against his fingers. 'It was only the midday heat, little princess,' he said, putting her hand under the blue silk. 'Lie quite still.'

He went into the next room. The handle of a pail clanked, and she heard the chain of the well going down with the familiar groaning sound. 'Now he is drawing water,' she thought.

An infinite happiness filled her heart so that she had to take a deep breath to give it space. She saw the wall of books in the dim light, the immortal wall, as Bergengruen called it, and at her side, so that she could reach it with her hands, stood the globe. She took her hand from under the cover and cautiously put the tips of her fingers on the Rocky Mountains of North America. Robinson Island floated noiselessly past, Salas y Gomez, about which she remembered the beautiful, sad verses, the Paumotu Island with the red line of the ecliptic passing through it and sinking into the Pacific (how solemn was this name), and new islands rose, palm trees and coral reefs, the broken shore of the Sunda Sea. And there was Bali, where his shawl had been woven and worn, lost in the blue ocean, and only the threatening mountains of New Guinea sparkled over the horizon.

She let her hand drop, while her eyes still gazed at the world on which she saw the shadow of the shining circle of the equator. 'So far away,' she thought, 'so far away – and now he catches fish here as Christoph did – but his eyes are still on the ocean, his eyes and Bildermann's sea-eyes unlike any others in the district.'

Thomas came back with a bowl, dipped a cloth into the cold water and put it on her forehead. Then he drew a stool up to the bed and sat down and supported his chin on his folded hands. He changed the cloth from time to time and saw how the colour came back into her cheeks.

At first she kept her eyes closed. A fly buzzed round the room, knocked against the globe and disappeared into the next room. Then the only sound was that of the small hammer beating some jewellery.

'Would you like him to stop?' asked Thomas.

She shook her head and opened her eyes. 'Will you go there again?' she asked, lifting her hand towards the distant island.

He bent forward to see what she was pointing at. 'No,' he said, 'I shall stay here now.'

'Always?'

'Yes, always, if nobody sends me away.'

She looked at a gap in the curtains through which a single sunbeam penetrated and ran like a golden thread over the black beams. When he took the cloth from her forehead, he saw two tears slowly running down her cheeks. 'What is the matter, dear child?' he asked in perplexity.

She smiled. 'You must not ask me, Thomas,' she replied. After a while she fell asleep. He looked at her for a long time. The sarong covered her to the chin, and one of the golden birds seemed to spread its wings over her chest, as if about to fly over her forehead out of the room. Her body was hardly noticeable under the cover, only her face shone in the dim light. She was like a dead page carried from a battlefield on a stretcher and put down here in the twilight.

He stopped the clock, listened once more to her quiet breathing and left the house through the adjoining room. He spoke to Bildermann and asked him not to stop hammering, as it had sent her to sleep. Then he sat down in the shade next to the house where a cool breeze blew round the gable. He filled his pipe slowly and meditated. He was rather embarrassed, for he knew so little about these years, when a child grows into adolescence. Everything was so much easier with Joachim, and he had never had sisters. However, it was probably not a matter of thinking or knowing. They had to be protected, and one had to watch where they were going and always be prepared to catch them should they stumble. She was like a child on a golden thread.

The other thing which was like a breath on a mirror would pass by when Joachim would come again. There were too many old people round the child.

Now and again he got up and looked through the door without making a sound. She was still asleep, her right arm had slipped from under the cover and hung down. She was breathing deeply and quietly.

He got some milk ready to make a cup of chocolate, lit a fire in the hearth, put the kettle on it and went out again to smoke his pipe. A greyish wall of cloud hung over the forest in the south-west and the orioles called for rain. It might have been due to the heavy air before the storm, he thought, then sleep closed his eyes too. The scent of the phlox filled the air, and Bildermann's small hammer still beat on the anvil. 'So many years,' he thought, 'and only now peace had come. But why tears? Even little women can be problems.'

He woke up when he heard somebody clattering with the fire-irons and the sides of the boats knocking against each other as Bildermann drew in the nets, 'All right, captain,' he shouted up to him, 'the little lady has come round all right.'

She met him in the doorway, still a little pale, but pleased that he, too, had slept. Bildermann drank his cup standing as the storm approached. He wanted Thomas to stay in the house. He wished to try his luck single-handed, and the little lady still needed a protecting hand.

Thomas brought the armchair into the open, put the blue garment round her shoulders and begged her to be obedient. She had frightened him and he was still worried.

She received her chocolate with surprise and asked whether they had captured a boat. Then they watched Bildermann as he rowed across the lake to the bay. The grey nets reached well above his head.

The clouds had darkened and hid the sun completely. Their edges were still white but a different light illuminated the lake, and the swallows flew over the reeds. They decided to wait until the storm was over before going to the castle, where the general expected Thomas that night.

They saw the nets gliding over the side of the boat on the opposite shore. From this distance they looked like grey ribbons. Then Bildermann collected the other nets which had been left on the grass to dry, and they, too, slid down into the black water. He worked so quietly that they did not hear a sound, and the whole thing seemed to be a vision.

'Now the fish are migrating,' said Thomas. 'There will be a big catch tomorrow.'

'Why do they migrate?'

'I don't know. Animals sense the future which is hidden from men. Probably we know too much that we can understand with our brains, and we have lost the gift of divining the future. Only old nations and old races have kept this faculty.'

'Are the Orlas an old race?'

'Fairly,' he replied with a smile. 'They certainly go back to the Middle Ages, and the catalogue of their sins must be quite extensive. But I was just thinking of the Perneins, and when you are a little older, I will take you to the young Graf. His garden is like a piece of magic.'

She shook her head. She was afraid of him. 'He is always smiling, but he is not happy.'

'That is not a reason to be afraid of him.'

The first low rumbling of the storm behind the wood was heard; the high stalks of the mallows knocked against each other on the dry reeds of the roof. A grey glimmer of light passed over the lake, a narrow strip with bright edges, and disappeared before it had reached the opposite shore. He asked her whether she was afraid. Not when she was with him.

An eagle came over the wood from the east. Its wings

sparkled like bright metal. It pounced down close to Bildermann, who looked up at it; his face was a pale oval against the black background of the forest. The scream of the big bird from above seemed to fall into space.

'So much happens here,' said the child.

It grew dark quickly, and they carried the chair and the crockery indoors. The lightning flickered over the wood like a golden whip, and Bildermann encountered a heavy gust of wind just before he reached land. It rushed over the water so fast that it lashed it to foam before they realised what was happening. The forest roared, sand whipped against the windows, and the reeds were flattened on the water. As the storm veered towards the eastern shore, it had become calm on the island, only the lake roared menacingly for quite a long time.

They saw how Bildermann scanned the sky. Then he drew Marianne's and Joachim's boats up to the land and turned them over. Under his hands they looked as if they were made of brown paper. As soon as he got into the house the rain began to pour straight down.

Thomas and Marianne stood at the open window.

The rain pattered on the roof noisily, and the water ran down to the shore in small gullies. The lake became calm, only its surface was spattered by the fall of the raindrops and looked like a huge bowl of boiling grey-blue metal. The wood on the other side appeared to be nearly white, and they thought they could see it split by the lightning.

They stood quite still and breathed in the clean air. The perennials had been pressed flat, but their scent wafted over the earth. Now they really seemed to be on the ocean; it was as if they were drifting along slowly under heavy sails. When a rent in the clouds appeared, the rainbow would not stretch from forest to forest, but would seem to rise out of and sink into boundless waters. And all land would seem to be far beyond the earth.

But when the wall of rain shifted to the east and only fell on the woods, when blue gaps appeared in the clouds, when the wind which had veered round, swept the sky clear, then the bridge of the rainbow stood behind the last veils as if it had always been there. It even had a pale reflection at its side. The swallows left the roof of reeds shaking their feathers and flew over the island with a high-pitched scream. Then the land appeared once more as a reality, familiar in the smallest details of its bays, loved in times of work and of rest. When they stood on the doorstep inhaling the scent of the birch leaves and saw the columns of white mist rising from the woods, then Thomas knew that he did not need a ship to gain a happy heart. They walked slowly along the shore round the whole island, so as to make sure that it was still there, and sometimes they turned round to see how close their footprints were to each other in the soft sand.

'Do not tell anybody, Thomas,' begged Marianne as they sat side by side at the helm and the white sail drew them through the evening.

He thought for a moment. 'Not if you promise to tell me, if it happens again, and if you will promise not to disturb he who sleeps at noon, then only we two shall know about it.'

'I promise, Thomas . . . but why must one not disturb him?'

'Because he is a god and embraces all: wood and water, bird and animal, bush and flower. And at noon they sleep, and sleep is sacred and the brother of death. That's what the ancients say.'

'Shall I ever know as much as you, Thomas?'

'Probably more, but knowledge is our least possession.'

'And which is the greatest?'

'Love is the greatest possession.'

'Once you said that it is present when one has no desires.'

'No, I only said that it is purest when one does not want anything for oneself.'

She thought for a long time. 'Is it what we find in St Paul's letter to the Corinthians: "She seeketh not her own"?'

'Is that there? I had quite forgotten. Yes, that must be it.'

'And what Grandfather calls a great heart?'

'Yes, that is probably the same thing.'

'I will always obey you, Thomas,' she said after a while.

The evening grew cool, and after dinner a fire was burning in the hall. The child walked slowly past the row of portraits of her ancestors, stopping here and there and looking up at them, her hands behind her back.

'Some of them look quite old, Thomas,' she said when she sat on the arm of his chair.

He only smiled and nodded. When she said good-night, he got up.

'You are too polite, Orla,' said the general. 'Old-fashioned . . .'

'There are children,' said Thomas, 'for whom one must get up sometimes.'

Before Marianne went to bed she put a note on Bergengruen's table. 'Dear Tobias, tomorrow I would like to learn something about the island of Bali, Pan and the first letter of Paul to the Corinthians (13th chapter). Marianne.'

Then she leant out of the window, listened to the nightingales singing on the shore and saw the familiar stars rising above the tops of the oaks and the reflection of the distant lightning on the lake. When she cuddled into her bedclothes she tried to recall the perfume of the blue shawl, but could not do so, she only saw with closed eyes the golden birds in the darkness. They flew noiselessly over a blue island, and the slight stroke of a hammer seemed to make their wings lift and drop, regularly like clockwork. 'That's Pan,' she thought, already half asleep, 'shoeing the hoofs of his goats.' Then she fell asleep.

Bergengruen shook his head when he found the note, and went into the library to read about the island of Bali in a book of geography. The other things he knew.

'They are rare in our race,' said the general to Thomas as they sat by the fire. 'Our women were generally clear-headed, the daughters of soldiers and landowners. They rode on horseback and looked after the poultry farm – brave, decent, reliable. It was rare for one to like music, religion, poetry; they had a hard life in our climate; they strode about in high boots, smelt of the stable. Look after her, Orla, you, too. I am an old man, have worries enough, am very lonely – some drain away your lifeblood.'

Thomas looked into the fire. 'She is very fond of you, sir,' he said slowly. 'Of the grandfather and his great heart.'

The old man looked menacingly up at the portraits of his ancestors and passed his hand over his white eyebrows. 'She is a good child,' he said hoarsely, 'too good for these times. You know, Orla, one ought to build walls round her, walls and a shield.'

'Yes, sir.'

They stood on the steps for a while, before Thomas left. Beyond the roofs one still could see the lightning flashes. 'Bread grows,' said the general. 'But the little one – man does not live by bread alone – always think of it, Orla. Do not leave us, Orla.'

'No, sir.'

He felt his hand held fast. The old eyes travelled over him. *Trinkt noch Glut und schlürft noch Licht* . . . he said absent-mindedly. 'Good-night, dear Orla.'

'Good-night, general.'

CHAPTER NINE

THE PRESENT that Joachim wanted for his birthday in the spring was neither a uniform nor a racing yacht – but a hut on the island made of reeds, 'In a secret spot and only half finished, please,' he wrote. He intended to complete it himself. It was his last summer at school, as he was due to sit for his matriculation next spring when he would be seventeen.

Thomas was surprised that the future admiral wanted to play at Robinson Crusoe, which he had never done as a child, but he made no comment and began to build the hut with Bildermann's help.

The past year had been a good one. Both the fields and lake yielded rich harvests. The general sat straighter than ever in his saddle. In the evening, when he had entered the last figure in his books and had closed them for the day, he said to Johann that he 'would show the fellows up there how to do things'. This set Johann wondering which rascals in the village his master meant.

Ethics of Life at Sea was published at Christmas and sold well; but the professional critics did not accept it. They considered it a record of the peculiar ideas of a peculiar fellow, whilst admitting that those ideas originated from a feeling of high responsibility. They claimed that stern discipline had always been the backbone of the navy, and that's a rope's end was not the worst beginning for a seaman's career. The ideas concerning the origin of the mutiny were not considered valid and were thought to be only the product of the writer's personal experience, which ought not to be generalised.

However, Thomas received letters from seafaring men of all ranks, in which those who had obviously thought about their profession, expressed their gratitude, often in simple words. They thought it was not always necessary to do everything in just the same old-fashioned way, or as they put it, 'the deck can be scrubbed from fore to aft as well as the other way round'.

The 'peculiar fellow' put the letters and newspapers carefully away in a blue file, which he kept on one of his bookshelves. He wound a muffler, which the child had knitted for him as a Christmas present, round his neck and went down to the ice to cut reeds for his son's hut. He knew that he had done his best, but he appreciated that the critics had a right to believe that it should have been done in another way. However, he liked to see his book on the table, where Bildermann put it in a different position every day. He looked at it with pleasure, not from a desire for fame, but because the brown binding seemed to contain and keep the memory of all the lonely hours he had spent on his task. He alone knew that it was this book which had enabled him to build a new life out of the ruins of the old one, to earn his bread and to find sleep again.

Bildermann was proud of his master ('my master, the great writer Orla,' he used to say), but he also felt the gratitude of a simple man, whose soul was described in the book as a powerful influence and a precious possession in the life of all sea-faring nations.

'I've been trampled on by many men in the course of forty years or more. But few have said to me what is printed here.

If one day a tombstone is put up for Bildermann, even if it is only a plain cement one, then I hope the inscription will be what is written here.'

Now that he had an iron, he no longer pressed the ribbons of his cap by putting them under the anvil. He heated it carefully and ironed the ribbons, before going to the village or the castle, where he gave Johann a lecture explaining how Captain von Orla 'sounded' the soul of the simple man. After that Johann became convinced that the sea air made people very peculiar. But their run seemed to be good in all longitudes and latitudes.

After he had read the book, the general showed Thomas a sort of bewildered respect. Never since the island had been in his family, he said, had it given a home to such a peculiar fisherman. One evening, many weeks later, he took hold of a button of Thomas's coat and said: 'I have been thinking a great deal. The German Empire and the Kingdom of Prussia were always two different things. The army was Prussian, but the navy felt that it belonged to the empire. The two never went together. There was no tradition for it. A man in the army is different from a man in the navy. I often think of my men at night. I made many mistakes, but they always liked me; called me "Old Bulldog", but meant it as a compliment. What you have written is right. One must learn, and not only exonerate oneself. We are all proud of you, Orla, especially the child. She keeps your book under her pillow and thinks you are a second Nelson. Grandfather plays second fiddle now. No complaints.'

The child did not speak for a quite a time. She often sat in Bildermann's little smithy and watched him at work. She asked him how lonely the captain had been. 'Was he sad as well, Bildermann?' He dropped the bellows and looked fixedly into the fire.

'Well, little Missy,' he said, 'certainly I didn't see him skipping from one mast to the other. He seemed to look through you, as if he saw what was going to happen. Some old seamen do that. They have no more will-power and are quite ready to capsize and sink to the bottom of the ocean.

He filled his pipe thoughtfully and lit it with a live coal, which he took with his fingers. 'He thinks too much, while his son doesn't think enough.'

'But he's better now, Bildermann, isn't he?'

'True, little lady. He's out of the doldrums now and sailing before the wind again. Rolling home, my boys. . . .' The bellows started to roar again and the iron in the fire turned white.

When Marianne met Thomas in front of the house, she said to him: 'You ought to have been King of Prussia long ago.'

He drew himself up and looked at her quite seriously. 'Of course, my dear, but up to now they seem to have forgotten me.'

Only Joachim's voice seemed to have changed. It appeared sometimes to use the highest, sometimes the lowest notes. But it soon became clear that he was already living in the future and was observing the island in the same way as a man takes a last look at his hotel bedroom before boarding a liner which is to take him round the world. He does not want to take anything away which is not his, but he wants to make quite sure that he has forgotten nothing.

Joachim eagerly went to work on the hut and refused all help. However, when the water dripped into his eyes the first night it rained, he said to Bildermann that perhaps there was something they had not done quite right.

Bildermann had a look at the roof he had made and began to take it off, remarking at the same time good-humouredly that one couldn't expect a public school to teach its pupils how to build a roof of reeds. But he added that it would be quite a good idea if the young gentleman did not rely entirely on himself 'out there'–this with a vague movement of his hand over the water. Nelson was a great sailor, but he had heard that some people played the piano better than he.

When the hut was weatherproof, Joachim insisted on spending the nights there and cooking his porridge in the morning over two flat stones.

He told Thomas, who was watching him with interest, that he had remembered in time that he had neglected the practical part of his education. If his training ship happened to be wrecked on a desert island, he would have to know how to do such things himself and couldn't always rely on the captain.

'Sometimes,' said Thomas, 'it's not a bad idea to rely on the captain. There's no loss of face for the man who does that.'

Joachim swallowed his porridge bravely, although it seemed to be burnt. 'Nowadays,' he said, 'we don't like to rely on the old gentlemen exclusively.'

'That was always the case,' replied Thomas. 'It's right that each should pay for his apprenticeship.' He rowed away with his nets, very slowly and thoughtfully.

Later Joachim told him that his mother had been in a sanatorium in Switzerland in the previous spring, that she coughed a lot, and became impatient if anyone asked after her health. She was often out in the evenings, and she had told him to say that she was very well.

It was quite impossible to know what Joachim thought of this. He told his father about it–almost in an aside–between tales of his life at school. He might have been speaking of a boat which had been wrecked.

Sometimes Thomas felt downhearted. They were happy

together, but Joachim no longer said: 'You are the cleverest man in the world, Daddy.' How quickly they grew up, and how soon they went out into life. His thoughts went back to the time of his boyhood, and he tried to remember whether it had been like that with his father. Even then poets sang of a new earth and iconoclasts shattered the windows of old tradition with the stones of new ideas. He also had been quick to praise and blame in a loud voice. But when he sat with his father in front of the fire all that had faded away. Only his father's kind face, wrinkled with age, remained. The old man had told him that if only a small part of the paradise dreamed of by successive generations of youth had become a reality, we should all have been angels and master and servant would have embraced in brotherly love.

On the other hand his father had never found it necessary to go to an island to gain a contented mind. So there may, after all, be some justification for Joachim and his generation not to rely fully on the old men.

This however did not worry him. Life and duty would soon prove to the young how much they needed the old in their quest for the ideal. He found it much more difficult to accept the fact that every hour in Joachim's life, even in his holidays, was filled with the desire to learn something practical. Bildermann said one day: 'The young gentleman is thinking of being a commander even when he is eating his porridge.' He rarely laughed, seldom played and never did anything silly. Beneath his knitted brows, his eyes stared fixedly at the goal he had set himself.

'Most fathers,' said Thomas to himself, 'would be happy about this, especially nowadays, when concentrated effort is so rare. But I am not happy because I know that there will be something missing one day, and there is nothing I can do to alter it. He will never need an island to save his soul; he will never need saving. He is so sure of himself.'

He was often tempted to believe that Joachim was like a motherless child, robbed of tenderness and much too old for his age. Yet at the same time he realised that it was his, Thomas's, fault and that he could do nothing but wait ready to help, should help be needed. He himself did not know anybody who had not needed help now and again in his life.

In the course of conversation Thomas learnt that Joachim had taken riding lessons with his mother's consent. 'If ever we have an emperor again,' said Joachim, 'to hold reviews, naval officers will no doubt have to take part, and I should be in a difficult position if I couldn't ride. Anyhow, I don't want to be caught out.'

Bildermann raised his eyebrows in astonishment. But Thomas was less surprised at these ideas of the future than at the boy's manner of expressing himself. Up to now he had not paid much attention to this. In his book he had taken great trouble to express himself in such a way that ordinary people could understand. So it was all the more surprising to hear this boy talk about 'being in a difficult position'. However, he only said that the castle people would be pleased, although they rode for quite different reasons.

Marianne had passed her childhood surrounded by adults and probably thought that all the boys in large towns were like Joachim, serious and dignified, always thinking of the future. She came to the conclusion that living for the pleasure of the moment and forgetting everything else in that pleasure, was either an attribute of country folk or of the female sex. She was happy in his society, and noticed every new blossom on the young tree in silent surprise. Sometimes she looked at him for quite a time, as the question arose in her mind, 'Why is this boy so different from his father in so many ways?'

She accepted without question that a future naval officer should know as much about riding as about navigation, and very generously lent him her horse, because he was the guest of the island and would soon be the guest of the ocean. She observed some of his equestrian habits with a certain surprise and pointed out with great tact that her grandfather did not do such things. Joachim replied that her grandfather probably belonged to the old school and that, no doubt, with time even riding had progressed.

She frowned at this but said nothing – she had been brought up to accept things in silence – but when she saw that the horse's chest and flanks were covered in sweat, she had the saddles exchanged next time and said innocently, that she was convinced by now, that he could ride any horse.

'Of course,' said Joachim, 'any midshipman can.' When, however, his new horse refused the first fence after several attempts and threw him quite easily, he became silent.

'Hurt, Joachim?'

'Of course not. You seem to have given me an obstinate brute.'

'You must help him a bit more.'

'I'll help him,' growled Joachim, and after a few more abortive atttempts he managed to clear the fence. It was however apparent that horse and rider were not on the best of terms, and for the rest of their outing Marianne stuck to the forest paths.

'You mustn't try to force it,' she said a few days later. 'A horse is not a boat, and riding can't be learnt in six months.'

'God bless your grandfather,' he thought, but aloud he only asked her whether she thought that she could ride better than he. 'Of course,' she said with a smile.

Instead of answering he suggested that they should ride as far as the village where he wanted to get some fishhooks.

'All right,' she said, 'but we shall have to ride hard, if we are to be back in time this evening.'

On the way she explained to him that on a long ride one ought to trot, gallop or walk one's horse alternately, so as to save the strength of both rider and mount as much as possible. He nodded absent-mindedly and was soon far ahead of her and did not turn round, whilst she continued to ride as she had been taught. Soon she lost sight of him and smiled when she realised that he was trying to show her his superiority. She foresaw, not without a certain satisfaction, that the day would not end without a severe shock to his self-confidence.

She found his horse tethered to a pole in front of the shop. It was hanging its head and it was covered with flecks of foam. She led hers to the windward. When Joachim came downstairs with the roll of an old cavalryman, she looked at him earnestly and exchanged a few words with the shop-keeper, who had come to the door. When Joachim had remounted, she pointed with the stock of her whip to the flecks and said: 'Three days' solitary confinement.'

'Wait and see,' he said.

Already in the first wood he began to drop behind, whilst she continued to ride as was her custom, changing every now and then from trot to walking pace. From time to time she looked round to see whether he was following, but she never waited for him to catch up with her. In her imagination she saw Thomas's serious eyes looking from one rider to the other and nodding to her approvingly, as if he were satisfied with her, but not very happy about the whole matter.

Only when they reached the beginning of the lime avenue did she wait for him. He approached with a stony expression on his face. They arrived at the stables without meeting anybody. Marianne told the stableboy to rub the horse dry and not to give it water for half an hour.

Joachim said he wanted to go straight back to the island. She gave him her hand and sent her love to his father. 'Don't be angry, Joachim,' she said, 'it was only the old school methods.'

He only waved his riding-whip carelessly in reply.

Back on the island he hardly spoke and went to his hut immediately after supper. Bildermann raised his eyebrows. He rummaged about in his seaman's chest for quite a time and finally found an old, badly dented tin. He pushed it through the low doorway of the hut and said with sympathy, and consolingly: 'Stag's fat, young man. It's still the best.'

The events of this day were never referred to again. Next time Marianne came, she said that they must now live on the water, as all the horses were needed for the harvest. Joachim nodded without saying a word.

In the evening, however, when he was resting in front of the hut and was smoking a short pipe with little pleasure, he said to himself quite seriously, 'Now I shall never be able to marry her.'

Thomas never heard about this ride. In the previous autumn and again in early spring he had been to see the old fisherman on the neighbouring lake, the man whom people called St Peter and who, they said, was over a hundred years old. On each occasion he had stayed for an hour, had asked a few questions, but had preferred to listen to the rare words, which fell from those withered lips. They spoke of the wind and the water, of the fish and the events of Peter's life, which spread over several generations. He had lived through four wars and the revolution at the time of Wrangel. The water which flowed around his peninsula was older than all the wars the world had ever seen. He thought that some of the pike he caught were older than Father Wrangel. At last he gave Thomas a straight look with his piercing eyes. 'Your eyes are right, captain. Keep them so.'

Thomas wanted the two children to see the fisherman. Even centenarians must die, and he wanted to know what the children thought of him. On Thomas he made the impression of one of the wooden idols which the Graf kept in his showcase. When you looked at it, you did not think of a god, but of the many generations which had an image of their earth and a pointer to the heaven of their dreams.

'Those old boys,' said Joachim. However, he did not object, for they would have to pass through the stream into the other lake where the wind was more favourable for sailing. Marianne always agreed to anything Thomas suggested.

It was a lovely trip. The narrow stream was nearly black and the brown swamp sparkled in the July sun. The landscape seemed dead, different from any they had ever seen. Heavy clouds hung on the horizon and a smell of mould and decay surrounded them. During the whole trip a bird of prey circled over the rush-covered pools. From time to time they looked up to see if it would dive down and bring some life to the dead landscape. 'He is watching us,' said Marianne.

When they passed beyond the sheltering roads, the lake opened out – a blue expanse framed by the sandy hills of the shore and by the wood in the distance. The boat shot forward as the sail took the wind. The green spit of land pointed at them like a long finger.

'Two strokes with the oars,' said Joachim. Marianne nodded. It was always easy to get on with him when they were on the water.

The fisherman was sitting in front of his hut on a mat of rushes. His back was turned to the wall and his feet were tucked under him. He was making a bow net with his bent fingers, and his bright eyes watched their approach. His white hair was still thick and so long that it fell over his coat collar. He wore large yellow earrings. The skin of his face was wrinkled and dark and he was so still that he looked like an old Red Indian chief in communion with the Great Manitou.

Marianne stayed at the bottom of the slope because her heart began to throb. But Joachim went up calmly and said: 'Good day, fisherman Peter.' He handed him a basket containing some tobacco, a short pipe and a bottle of rum, which Thomas had sent him. Then only did he look at Joachim, motioned him to put the present down and with a second gesture invited them to sit on the ground.

'You are the son,' he said, 'and you are the granddaughter from the castle.'

'We bring you the captain's greetings,' said the child shyly.

He leant the back of his head against the wall of the hut and looked past them over the blue water. 'When my mother was still carrying me,' he said, 'she saw him on horseback carrying a stick. He always rode over the fields and when he swore he did so in French. He had been to Russia with Napoleon. He was the second son and had taken service with the Wuerttemberg forces. He saw Moscow burning. He died early. The women who prepared him for the grave said that he had twenty-four wounds. He was a strict master, but the people loved him. The king wrote to his widow.'

'That was Friedrich Christian Ehrenreich,' whispered the child.

He nodded: 'His son was born in the night when the master crossed the Beresina. The mother bled to death. There was no doctor in the whole district, and the snow lay high over the fences. The master stood at the grave and shook his fist towards Heaven. He brought the cannon back with him. The son was sad. The old women said that he must have drunk blood at his birth and that it was bitter. In 1848 he stood by his king and was shot through the thigh. His sons used to spear the pike in this lake. One fell through the ice and was drowned where the stream runs into the lake. They heard him call out, but when they got to him, it was too late. The second son was killed at Koeniggraetz. The father who had been shot through the thigh died a month after the wedding. People said that his son had called to him from under the ice. His face in the coffin was peaceful. I saw him and I thought that one should not fear death. . . .'

'That was Friedrich Wilhelm Fuerchtegott,' whispered the child.

He nodded. 'The one with the crutches. He had three sons and a daughter. They all seemed as wild as wolves, but were really as kind as lambs. They all used my boat, and they all ate fish cooked with salt and onions in my hut. The eldest served with the guards and fought in South West Africa before he inherited the castle. He has sacrificed two sons and his wife for his emperor.'

'That's my grandfather,' said the child.

He nodded. 'The second stayed in China, where dragons are set on the roofs. The third is buried on the Oranje River. The emperor took the daughter into his house. The man with crutches lived as is written in the Ninetieth Psalm; he stood on the castle steps when the Russians came. He was dressed in uniform and took the officer into the hall. There the countess was lying in her coffin and we all knelt before it. We all had white hair. Johannes, the shepherd, was the youngest, and he was seventy. The officer took off his cap and crossed himself. Then he rode away with his cossacks. The man with the crutches sat by the hearth and looked at the countess. He survived his grandchildren. He was over seventy. He had sat on my knees as a child at the time I put on my earrings. . . .'

'That was Friedrich Christoph Leberecht,' said the child.

He nodded and began to fill his short pipe. 'They were like fish, and the nets were already spread for them. They began, when the wind was in the east, and when it turned to the south the first ones went into the nets. We throw the small ones back, but He keeps what He has got. Man is like a fish or like the reed under which it lives–you must walk more slowly, young man, like your father–the ice appears strong to quick eyes, but only the slow ones notice, when a hand reaches up from below through the thin crust.'

Joachim smiled in embarrassment. 'Perhaps we have to live faster today,' he said with a vague movement of his hand.

The fisherman lit his pipe. He had a flint and tinder, on which the spark fell. 'He who lives quickly, dies suddenly. Your father came to gain a happy heart, he said, and they will bring him a golden crown out of the depths.'

Joachim looked at the girl and raised his eyebrows, but she did not take her eyes off the old man. 'You will protect him, won't you? Against mist and storm, against the water sprites and the thin ice?' She put her hands together as if pleading with him.

'They obey me,' he whispered. 'I have served them and they obey me. Be not afraid, he will be here a long time, long after I am gone. He will serve them and his grave will be on the island. His psalm will be read over it. Be not afraid little Gräfin. None of those who have gone before you were ever afraid.'

He closed his eyes as old people do who sleep between words. The children sat without stirring and watched his face. In spite of the heat of the sun Joachim shivered, but he only knitted his brows.

Then the old man waved his hand and they got up. 'I should like to row you over the lake, little Gräfin, but I am tired. Greet your grandfather from me; he has always been a good master. Tell him the bird has called, and Peter does not hide. God bless you, little Gräfin.' He made the sign of the cross over her brow and nodded to Joachim. Then he folded his hands and closed his eyes. He did not see them leave.

On the way back Marianne sat under the sail, looked ahead over the water and did not speak. Joachim had tried to start a conversation by calling the fisherman a 'funny fellow', but the child turned round in anger and said: 'Be quiet.' He shrugged his shoulders and attended to the boat. It was time for him to go home again. Life with children and centenarians was no life for him. But before they got into the stream where one of the sons had been drowned, he turned his eyes once more to the spit of land. The hut appeared like a small brown dot under the trees. No smoke rose from the chimney. Perhaps the old man was already dead and was following them with sightless eyes. Again he shivered in the sun and the black water lapped the sides of the boat. A heron rose from the reeds and screamed hoarsely; its shadow passed over the boat. No, there was only one kind of really clear water and that was the ocean.

'Thomas,' said the child, 'he was like one of the old Prussian gods in the books. His name must be Perkunos, and his earrings are made of amber.' He felt her hands and found they were cold. He looked at her with concern.

'Was it too much for you? Sometimes he does not know what he is saying.'

'He is a regular historian,' said Joachim. 'He knew all the Platens from 1812 on.'

'It is good, Joachim, when they speak of the old families in the fishermen's huts.'

'True, but he said such funny things about you, and he sat on a mat with bare feet like a Buddha.'

Thomas looked from one to the other carefully, but he only said: 'Nowadays it is easy to pass judgement.'

They did not understand him. Marianne wanted to row home alone. 'Tomorrow I will tell you everything,' she said. Nevertheless she drew him towards the boat, turned to see whether anybody could hear and whispered: 'You will stay with us a long time, he said. Nobody will hurt you. Neither mist nor ice nor water sprite. Nobody, Thomas, and it will be for a long time.'

'What would hurt me, child?' he asked with a smile.

She looked at him fixedly and her eyes betrayed fear. 'But it is good to know, Thomas. He sees into eternity.'

He watched her for a little time as she rowed away; and he said nothing to Joachim about the day's excursion.

On the last day of the holidays Joachim went to the castle to say goodbye to the general. The latter, to his great delight, gave him an old pipe with silver bands. Then he went back with Marianne to the shore where he had made his boat fast. The future seemed to have come quite close to him, and the world of ships, of sails, of shipmates, which he had longed for so ardently, appeared in white dreamless light before his eyes. He was not afraid, he did not even hesitate, but everything he was about to leave seemed to him more attractive and more familiar than ever before. It was as if he had suddenly realised that he had lived through these years too quickly. It was unlikely that he would return; for he would soon be in uniform, and midshipmen who remained children under their uniforms he despised thoroughly.

He took more time than usual getting into his boat and hoisting the sail which had been flapping in the wind against a loose spar. Then he got out again and came towards

Marianne. She stood there without paying attention to what he was doing, fingering the wooden beads of her necklace; she was watching the sun sink behind the forest at the end of the bay. The birds were less noisy than usual; through the trees on the left one could catch a glimpse of the bound sheaves of corn on a carpet of yellow stubble.

After a time she looked at him and said: 'All the best, Joachim. And, please, never hurt your father's feelings.'

'What on earth do you mean? Surely you know that we get on splendidly.'

She looked him straight in the eye. 'It wouldn't satisfy me, if I only got on splendidly with Grandfather. For him also that wouldn't be enough. You must never forget that your father is more than we all are.'

'Indeed?' he replied in some surprise. 'However, you needn't worry, and when we're married, we shall be a magnificent family. Depend on that.' The blood mounted to his cheeks, but he looked at her with his usual self-assurance. If she reminds me of the ride now, he thought, I shall throw her into the water.

But she did not dream of referring to that. She dropped her eyes for a moment and then looked straight at him again. 'If that was supposed to be a proposal, it will be best if you never mention it again.'

He stared at her. She was only a year younger than he was; why did she suddenly look like one of those women in the hall who looked out of their picture frames as if they had been hanging there for half a thousand years.

'Yes,' he said, 'but isn't it understood? In a few years' time, of course.'

She looked at the flapping sail. 'You always take everything for granted, Joachim. Do you remember what the old fisherman said? You must walk more slowly, young man.

You always think that everything is yours. Others want something too.'

'Which others?'

'I was only speaking in a general way. Well, goodbye, Joachim, and don't become an admiral right away.'

She gave him her hand, which he took absent-mindedly, nodded and went back to the castle.

Only when the sail had filled, and the boat was driving before the wind, did he realise what had happened. He caught sight of her crossing the lawn in front of the terrace. 'Like a mother who has seen her child off to school.' He was furious.

Bildermann had prepared a farewell dinner with splendid crayfish. Joachim ate with a good appetite and spoke of his first intended trip round the world, but now and again he was silent and looked at the globe, which shone in the half light.

Later on when Joachim and his father were sitting in front of the fire, the boy said that he would like to ask Thomas a question. It appeared that he had read quite a number of criticisms of the *Ethics of Life at Sea*, and he feared that the book might harm his career, for its critics might take it out on him when they could not reach his father.

'And what do you suggest?' asked Thomas, and watched him carefully.

Joachim seemed somewhat embarrassed. He could not rightly say, but perhaps in the second edition, which no doubt would be required soon, some passages could be altered or toned down. Some of the critics were highly placed naval officers.

'Do you think those passages are wrong?'

'That I can't judge.' Joachim was quite embarrassed and his fingers kept turning a piece of firewood round and round. He felt very uncomfortable at having broached the subject.

Thomas went on smoking without saying anything and did not notice that the end of his stick was becoming completely charred by the fire. Then he leant back and looked at his son.

'I don't know,' he began, 'whether you realise that you belong to a different generation from mine. We didn't have to go through a war in our childhood, nor experience revolution and inflation, to give events their labels. It is natural that in many respects you should think and feel differently. Whether that is an improvement or not, we won't discuss. You believe that *we* have lost the war, our money and our reputation, and you think that *you* can restore all that.

'When you came here for your first holidays, you received at once a painful impression of my life here. Let me finish, Joachim. You thought I was the king of a dozen lakes, when in fact I am only the servant of a master. I have never been anything else and have never wanted to be anything else. You didn't like my renouncing my old name and rank. You were and still are too young to understand. You can't imagine why one should take off gloves and work with one's hands if one doesn't have to. But I am your father and am nearly fifty and so you must accept this.

'However, I will tell you one more thing: I consider it honourable to do some simple work, to look after part of the land or the water, to give a comrade bread and a bed and–However, that will suffice. I consider it just as honourable as commanding a squadron.

'One thing more: when you have come to the conclusion that you are better at laying nets than at commanding squadrons, it is your duty to do what you are best at.

'I've thought a lot about you these few years when I had plenty of time. I'm happy that you have chosen a profession for which you feel a call. Not all are so fortunate. But I am troubled when I see the road you are taking. I was in charge of a corvette; you want to be commander of a squadron right away. *We* have made mistakes, not only with inanimate objects but also with human lives. *You* think you're not going to make any mistakes. If events and even your fellowmen turn against you, you still expect to come out on top. You have not yet learned the lesson of the last war. You don't realise that it was more than a sequence of battles.

'I'm not anxious that your path should be easy, easier than mine. But I do not want to see them hauling the flag down above your head and throwing you overboard. Nor do I want this to happen to your comrades in arms. See to it that every man on your ship is like Bildermann. He will not be like Bildermann when he joins. But it is your job to see that he becomes a Bildermann within two or three years. Those who cannot change in this way should be dismissed – or those who could not make them change, dismissed!

'This requires a new generation, not merely a young one. A generation that has those characteristics in which we were lacking. A commander who hauls down his flag should be court-martialled, stood against a wall and shot, regardless of his rank. We ought to have been court-martialled, all of us except those who were killed.

'What I am saying is, however, of no great help to you; for you no longer believe in us – that may be our fault more than yours. You don't believe in us, because you have over-confidence in yourselves. A sailor must believe in more than just himself, Joachim. Every human being must. The war has cost us more than our ships, and we cannot get back to normal conditions just by replacing these ships.

'You think that your father was never a soldier and you are not altogether wrong. I was never what is called a born soldier, and that is the reason why I am now trying to do something else, something simpler. I've been criticised and you fear that you also will be criticised solely because you are the son of your father. Well, all you must do to counteract this is to show that you are a better soldier than your father was. I cannot, of course, tell whether after thirty or forty years you may not want to change your profession. But today it does not seem to me to be a good thing to ask your father to haul down his flag, so that your start should be easier.'

Thomas knocked out his pipe and got up. For a moment his eyes fell on that world which is every seaman's home. Then he took Joachim's hand. 'Dear boy,' he said, 'we are all beginners, and you must have a little patience with me.'

Joachim had turned pale. One could imagine all these new ideas being pondered behind the wrinkles of his frown. However, he only pressed Thomas's hand and said: 'Good-night, father.'

Then he went to his hut for the last time.

Bildermann took him to the station.

'It will be better if we don't mention these matters again before you leave. So I will say goodbye to you here. Don't forget us, Joachim.'

Joachim nodded. His heart was much heavier than he had thought possible.

Thomas stood on the shore and looked after them. Bildermann's ribbons fluttered in the wind, and Joachim steered. The white sail shone in the sun. When they had hauled it down, they waved back once more. Then the wood swallowed them up. Bildermann carried the trunk on his broad shoulders.

He went up to the hut and sat in front of the cold hearth. He smoked his pipe and looked at the blackened stones. The sky was blue and a gentle wind stirred. Complete peace reigned. The island seemed big and empty. His mind ran on the chances one missed, and he could not but wonder at how much a man could miss or do wrong in fifty years without getting discouraged. He saw a fish hook lying in the ashes; no doubt Joachim had lost it. He picked it up and pressed its points with the tips of his fingers. It was strong, a three-barbed one, as used for catching pike. He made up his mind to write to Nurse Beate and ask her to send him the wooden boat which Joachim had taken to bed with him once. He had nothing belonging to the boy which he could finger and look at from time to time.

Then it was time to fetch in the nets, but he went back to the house first and put the fish hook in the cabinet with the masks.

Joachim had to travel two hours on a branch line to get to the station where the express stopped. A quarter of an hour before his train was due, the night express from the other direction arrived. He liked to watch the signals move on their high masts, to see the white smoke appear over the wood and to follow the engine as its squat black shape grew, until the whole moving giant came to a sudden stop on the quivering rails. The faces at the windows interested him, also the few people who got out. He liked to see the guard with his red satchel and the huge wheels dripping oil, every part of the train awaiting the signal to move, just as if it were part of a ship.

A lady with piercing blue eyes passed him and dropped a brown scarf which had been hanging over her arm. He picked it up, ran after her and handed it back with a few polite words. She looked at him as if she wished to impress his young face indelibly on her memory and thanked him.

'Please, do not mention it,' he said, clicking his heels.

She was the general's sister whom 'the emperor had taken

into his house,' and she was on her way to the castle to visit her godchild.

She was one of the Platens of whom the fisherman had said that they appeared as wild as wolves, but really were as kind as lambs. She was quite a pugnacious lamb. That evening she sat with her brother in front of the fireplace in the great hall and played patience. She wore simple steel-rimmed spectacles and put each card down as carefully and exactly as a builder laying bricks. 'It's coming out, Christian,' she said. 'Of course, it's coming out!'

She looked at the little piles of cards again, took off her spectacles and looked up to her brother, who nodded good-humouredly.

'You nod, Christian,' she said, 'but you must do more. I will not say that you live like heathens, for you keep a chaplain, but I do say that you live like savages, and Gabriele von Platen knows what she is talking about.'

The general put down his wine glass and looked at her thoughtfully. 'You were always given to speaking your mind, Gabriele,' he said. 'I remember once you maintained that every other milker in Prussia ought to be shot. Do you remember? We argued about it for a whole week. But now you really surprise me. Was the girl who waited on you dressed in a loin cloth? Or did Johann wear a nose-ring?'

She waved her hand. 'Not bad, Christian, but I want to talk about more important things than nose-rings. Do you really think that the last of the Platens ought to find her life's fulfilment in the breeding of cattle and eventually in inheriting your boots and your wine?'

'But, Gabriele–'

'Don't "but, Gabriele" me. Do you realise that your granddaughter has never been to a concert or a theatre? That she speaks no foreign language with the exception of a little bit of English picked up from seamen? That she doesn't know what a waltz is, let alone a figure dance, that the outside world may be – as far as she is concerned – on another planet? That, for example, she doesn't know on which side you get into a tram and a thousand things like that. Do you realise this, Christian?'

'She has a wonderfully good heart.'

'I need spectacles to read with,' she answered affectionately, 'but I'm not blind. Old people always think of themselves and at the same time imagine that they are doing good to others. No princess will ever lose her heart to you any more than a prince will lose his to me. Her two eyes are all that are left to us, and they should be opened to what she should know of this world, before she takes root in this place and chooses a husband who will inherit and pass on our name to those who will come after. Isn't that so?'

He nodded in some concern.

'Well, I'll give you until the autumn. Then I shall want two years. That's not much to ask, but in two years Gabriele von Platen can do quite a lot. My dear Platen, her Royal Highness used to say, you are not a Venus, but you have the strong hands of a rider. She had a good heart, Her Royal Highness, but she was not always very tactful. You will get your child back, as God made her, with her "marvellous heart" unspoilt. But she will have altered considerably in deportment, knowledge and so on. The last of the Platens must be able to do more than ride, sail a boat or fish. You know well that if Johann Friedrich had remained alive, it would have happened as a matter of course. Quite a few important people call on me still, although I am not a Venus.'

'They used to be called Parcae, those sisters who cut one's life thread.'

'Oh brother,' she replied, 'that thread is stronger than we

think.' She turned to Johann who was clearing up. 'Stop messing about here and fetch me a bottle of beer.'

Johann obeyed as quickly as his gaiter-encased legs permitted. It seemed to him that it was not only the sea that made people a little crazy.

'Let's consult the child,' said the general at last. 'Nothing must be done against her wishes.'

'I agree, although these women were never asked what they wanted.' She waved her hand towards the ancestral portraits on the wall. 'Otherwise you and I, Christian, would probably not be sitting here now. But even Prussians have soft spots in their hearts. By the way, if you could get rid of Johann, that target of a shooting booth, you and I might be able to smoke a cigar in peace. I hope you know that I am very fond of the child, perhaps more than I ought to be.'

He had no doubt about that.

When the matter was broached to the child, she turned pale, but listened bravely. 'I am not thinking of myself, Grandfather,' she said, 'but who will go riding with you and sit with you in the evening while I am away?'

'Well, well, there are plenty of quiet people, my child. I will think of you – and count the days,' he said hoarsely. 'That man on the island is still more lonely than I shall be.'

'Might I ask Thomas for his opinion?'

'A good idea,' said the general. 'We will abide by his decision.'

They were sitting on the bottom of an upturned boat, which Bildermann had brought to land, so that he could pitch the seams. A thin mist lay over the lake and moistened her hair. The leaves of the wild pear trees had begun to turn yellow and the jays were already carrying the old fruit to their winter hideouts. It looked as if the autumn would be short.

'You know, my child, that it will be hard for all of us,' said Thomas, 'but of course you must go. One has no right to settle down on a lonely island, until you have learnt what the world outside is like.'

'Must one learn that?'

'Yes, of course. They all had to learn, those on the wall in your hall, and they had much further to go than you. It is a long way to the Oranje River. You would not want to be less than they were.'

She shook her head.

'At your age two years do not count. It is only later in life that time begins to slow down, and even then we cannot catch up. . . .'

'You will forget me, Thomas.'

'Do you really think so?' He smiled absent-mindedly and got up. 'We shall be on the ocean again, Bildermann and I, but we shall both be on the look-out. Do you understand what I mean?'

'Yes, Thomas.'

Before she left she asked Thomas to invite Bergengruen and herself to a potato roasting. The former was also leaving to sit for his examination. Thomas had been working in the small field all day and his back ached; but it had been a pleasure to hold the sandy potatoes in his hands and to throw them into the basket which stood in the furrow in front of him. It was forty years since he had done such work. When he leant back on his hoe to rest, he looked over the calm water and the silent wood and had the impression that he had never done anything else in the decades in between. He felt as if he had grown up on the island with no other object in life than to gather his crop and get it into the cellars before winter came.

After the midday meal Thomas sent Bildermann into the

woods to find some mushrooms which they could cook over the fire.

They waited until the sun began to go down before lighting the fire. The white smoke rose straight up and gradually disappeared between the brown oaks. Bildermann put the potatoes into the hot ashes and peeled the mushrooms. Their hearts were heavy and Thomas said that this was for all of them the end of youth. If in two years' time they met again round the fire, after having got to know the world outside, they would have to find out whether it still gave them satisfaction to sit by a camp fire and to eat the simple fruits of the earth.

Of the three, Bergengruen seemed most in need of consolation. Bildermann tried to teach him how to cook mushrooms and how to squeeze them in a cloth before salting them. Bergengruen thought that this knowledge would be of little use to him, and that he could hardly expect the high Consistory to ask him such questions. Indeed, he did not seem hopeful as to the result of the examination.

'What do you expect of these two,' asked the child, 'who must stay here alone, as if they were on Salas Y Gomez, if you lose your courage at the outset?'

'Don't bother your head about that, little lady,' said Bildermann. My master and I have got over many a deserted island. When we sit in front of the fire in the evening, we shall turn to the globe and find the place where you are putting on your pearls. Each pearl will remind you of a day on this island, and the biggest and last pearl will remind you of this day. No man is lonely until he has thrown away his compass.'

'You are wiser than all of us, Bildermann,' said Thomas.

The twilight crept over the trees in the east. The wild geese flew so high that they looked like shadows in the sky.

Their cries could be heard for quite a time in the stillness of the air. Mist began to rise over the meadows, and the evening star twinkled through the oaks.

They got up and went down to the shore. The fire threw a red glow on the darkening bank.

Marianne went back to the house to fetch her coat. The birch logs were glowing in the hearth and shed a dull light over the room. Thomas fetched a small wooden box from between his books. He opened it and took out a thin chain of garnets from which hung a small cross. He looked at it as it lay in his palm before giving it to the child. 'It was my mother's and I should like you have it. She was a brave woman and she had a happy heart.'

He shook his head when she was about to speak and helped her into her coat. 'Thank you for all these years,' he said on the doorstep.

As they went down to the shore, she was as erect as if she were on horseback, but she said no more.

The boat remained visible for a little while, then its shape melted into that of the water and the wood, but the sound of Bergengruen's oars could be heard for a long time. He was rowing as jerkily as on the first day.

'Now the sun has set, captain,' said Bildermann.

'Yes, Bildermann, and we must steer by the stars,' replied Thomas.

Then he went back to the field to keep the fire going. Until the rowers reached the bay, they could steer by its light.

CHAPTER TEN

THE FIRST SNOW fell in November, and as the wind was in the east, it remained on the ground. The cockchafer grubs had dug deep into the earth; the bullfinches and waxwings kept to the tops of the pine trees; everything pointed to a hard winter.

Thomas and Bildermann had been at work on their skates for quite a time, cutting holes in the ice and marking the way to the castle and the forester's house with young pine trees. In the first week of Advent they used the large net for a whole day. The people from the castle helped them, as it was customary not to ask strangers to lend a hand.

Then they put away their skates, and Bildermann fetched the skis from the loft. They were of birchwood and quite light, and Bildermann, who had made them, was very proud of his handiwork. The general had discharged the game keeper because he had too many friends in the neighbouring villages, and had asked Thomas to keep an eye on the large forest. He himself saw to it that the deer were fed; however, because of the hard times, it was advisable that watchers should guard the woods and that their criss-cross tracks should be seen. Bildermann was given a second rifle and carried a hunting licence in his pocket. On calm days when the snow fell early, he would appear at Thomas's bedside in the morning twilight and ask for leave of absence. 'This is the right time for those who want to remain unseen. I remember that the elk and bear hunters in Finland and Lapland used to set out at this time of the day, when the breaking of a branch can be heard almost for miles. I have put the kettle on the fire for your morning coffee, and you can sleep for another couple of hours if you like.'

He lit his first pipe of the day with a live coal and closed the door gently. As he glided away from the house down to the shore and over the plains, round which the woods stood silently in the dim light, he felt like one of those lonely hunters beyond the Arctic Circle, for whom no life exists other than the game they hunt, and whose eyes see no sign of life except the tracks of their prey, tracing grey lines on the infinite snowfields. When the first rays of dawn appeared with their crimson light, the shadows they cast were a delicate blue.

He never tired. His eyes learned to read the tracks in the snow and to know whether they were caused by man or beast. Soon he was able to distinguish those signs which it was better to leave the general or his bailiff to deal with. He saw the pad marks of a wild dog, at which he looked angrily; otherwise he saw nothing dangerous. The people in the villages soon realised that the man with the ribbons on his cap was on the road day and night, roaming the woods on his narrow skis; they remembered that often when he looked at them with his piercing eyes they felt uncomfortable. So they preferred to do their poaching in the State forests, where the officials did not wear magic boards under their feet, and where the habits which Bildermann seemed to have brought with him from polar regions were unusual.

When Thomas left the house a few hours later he paid due attention to the tracks, just as Bildermann had done; but he also noticed other things, which Bildermann had not seen, and sometimes he stopped and became lost in contemplation.

He observed the long shadows thrown by the tall pine trees on the side of the hill on which shorter larches also grew, the beautiful network formed by the branches of a hazel bush, lightly covered with snow, silhouetted against the crimson sky of the early morning. He saw the blue line of distant woods and in front of them a house with a high gable, from the chimney of which smoke rose slowly straight into the air high over the treetops, where it glowed in the light of the sun.

For the first time he realised what true serenity really meant; the deep breath of an existence free from all desire, without stirring and without regret, indeed without any recollection of the past, an existence which was neither joyful nor sad like that of a human being, but which passed with the same inevitability as the stars traversed the heavens, obedient to an unalterable law. Peace pervaded it, as it pervades everything which is perfect. Here was a clearer perception than in the world of man that death and life are inextricably intertwined, and here the horizon does not signify the end, but only the everchanging frontier between light and darkness.

Thomas ventured more frequently now into territory hitherto unknown to him. The uniformity of the white covering induced him to venture into fresh country. When hills and woods barred his way, he glided down to one of the innumerable lakes, whose frozen surface lay almost imperceptible in the white landscape. Thus it happened that sometimes he put up at villages where he had not been before, that he conversed with strangers, listened to their opinions and ideas of current events and thought them over when he returned to the solitude of his home. Nothing had changed; there was still no joy and no peace in the world. The ravens still flew over the land; the faces of men were still without hope and life drifted like a rudderless boat at the mercy of the winds while the shore was hidden in deep mist. Prophets stood on the bridge and foretold the future, but on deck stood others who predicted the end of the world and of these prophets, and children ran from the one to the other seeking bread. But they found only fanaticism and hatred.

He often returned home at dusk. When he saw the light of the lamp shining upon the snow, he realised that he could only find peace in the small space of his home. He understood that before the world as a whole could achieve peace, each individual would have to find peace in his own life, and that only a small devoted group would have the initiative to do this, and that they must take infinite pains.

Bildermann had laid the table and lit the fire. The lamp was alight, the globe seemed to hang in an empty space, the books on their shelves were a serious and continuous reminder that humanity had striven for thousands of years, but that all its efforts could not prevent death from roaming the world: death, discord, hatred and despair. Yet humanity had continued to strive as if it were only necessary to find a magic spell, that one day would be found–perhaps tomorrow, perhaps on a day in the far-distant future.

After Bildermann had washed up, he sat down in front of the fire working at something mysterious: a large frame criss-crossed with wires, spools round which he wound other wires, curious bulbs, which he held in his hand meditating where he should fix them. He begged the captain not to ask him what he was trying to make, until either he had succeeded or given it up and thrown the result of his efforts into the lake. Now and then he would look up with those eyes of his which reflected the sea, and they would rest either on the globe or on his master, who sat over his book, his head supported in both his hands, or sometimes merely gazed into the fire, where the burning wood sang a gentle melody, rising at times to quite a high pitch and then again almost dying to whisper. The wind moaned in the chimney, and the snow was driven against the windowpanes; from the distance came the sound of a tree splitting in the frost or the sharp crack of breaking ice from the lake.

Then they would both look up and listen. But the island remained firm under their feet, the roof did not sway to and fro, the dark beams of the ceiling did not move, and the pendulum of the clock went its monotonous way measuring the hours which its hands recorded, and what they had put behind them could never return.

Thomas put down his book, leant his head against the top of his armchair and looked up to the ceiling. Where were those now who had walked at his side for so long? His wife was silent; he knew as little of her life as he knew of the chatterers which perched on the boughs of the oak trees in the early morning and had disappeared by noon. Joachim wrote that he was well, that the written examination would soon start and that he was not afraid of the result. The headmaster was well disposed towards him and was more likely to fail one of the crammers than to fail him. He always signed: 'Your obedient son, Joachim von Orla.'

Thomas smiled and emptied his pipe. It sounded very charming, but obedient sons existed nowadays only in letters. Time had passed them by.

The child wrote often, once a week. She sent a full report of her doings, of what she learnt, saw and heard, but not one word of her thoughts. It was left to Thomas to read what he could between the lines of her straight handwriting. She told him that she had learnt by now how to order something in a shop, how to refuse to take it if it did not suit her, how to hail a taxi, how to talk to a visitor calling on her great-aunt. She had also experienced at a concert that wonderful feeling when the bows of all the violins are poised ready to produce the tone which one knows will make one's heart vibrate.

She mentioned fresh knowledge and new experiences every week, but of what Thomas really wanted to know, there was little. Sometimes there was a note at the bottom of the page: 'I am obedient' or 'I have been dreaming of the island' or 'Do not leave Grandfather alone too much.' She also mentioned that the grown ups had decided that she was not to go home during the two years' visit, because the subsequent leavetaking might be too hard for her. She added: 'In that I think they are right.'

Thomas answered regularly. He had to write so few letters. His life was so uneventful that he had little to write about, but he described that little to her lovingly and in detail. He mentioned a very beautiful sunset and all those little stories which Bildermann brought out of the sea-chest of his experience. He remembered to tell her what he was reading, and that they had set twelve mousetraps because the mice used to gnaw the nets. Judging by his letters they were living in a snowbound Garden of Eden, in which they fed bullfinches, titmice and hares, and broke off the icicles which the cold had formed on the hair. And all the time an angel with a flaming sword stood at the gate and prevented others from entering. He did not know that she always kept his last letter next to her heart and that her aunt used to stroke her cheek now and again and say: 'Well, my dear, is it Thomas day today?'

Perhaps he would not have believed that, for the last ten years had dealt hard with his beliefs, not only in human beings, but also in a divinity ruling the world. He had seen too much, yet his eyes still saw clearly. The logic of his thoughts had become keener and more fearless; he now felt an almost bitter urge to think a thing out to its logical conclusion, disregarding the limitations set by religion and tradition, and letting his thoughts roam as far as thought could reach to the limits set by human reasoning.

In the world of his imagination man had a different appearance from that which he had been taught in his youth. God also seemed to have changed from the form in which he had been taught to see Him. God seemed to withdraw more and more from this planet bathed in blood, to become harder and more unapproachable, indeed almost to merge in the infinite distance with the inexorable forces of nature: in the silent battles of the ocean's depths and the perils of the tropical jungles. He seemed to keep aloof from the devious paths that not only the individual but humanity as a whole were taking. He seemed to view without compassion the torn and tortured bodies behind barbed wire and the wide-open eyes of those who drifted lifeless on the waters or had sunk to the depth, and also the long, silent processions of starving children.

To Thomas this God appeared to be standing as stern and cold as an idol of brass of Moloch, with a mouth that could not smile, eyes that could not weep and ears that could not hear. His face seemed to be nothing but the pale shape of an inexorable law, to which a tear meant no more than a raindrop, a scream no more than the pounding of the waves, the agony of whole towns and empires no more than the fleeting sound of the wind, as it passed over the surface of thousands of stars.

Little was left to Thomas and Bildermann of the beautiful time when they had asked the Lord to bless their wooden swords, nor of the time when the priests of all religions had prayed to the Lord to bless their swords of steel and the muzzles of their cannon. Nothing remained to them but bitter dregs. They knew that blood tasted different from wine and that the eyes of the dead grew dim. They had seen ships under fire being blown piecemeal to the stars. They had seen men behind barbed wire fighting for scraps that would be spurned by the very beasts. They recognised an order and a law in this, but they refused to consider them divine.

This was not a cause for satisfaction for them; on the contrary, they felt that they had lost something, something dear to them, with which they had set out to conquer the world: a good comrade, sparing of words, but always reliable, who never asked questions, but whom one could always ask, even if His answers were laconic. They had overcome many difficulties only because He was present, and some things they had only been able to do because they forgot His presence. Now they were alone after the great shipwreck, for the time being the two of them, but one day one of them would be alone relying only on himself. They observed others who still saw Him walking at their side sadly but without cynicism; their calm eyes foresaw what would become of them when the Silent One would no longer be with them.

They had accepted the years as they had come and had turned a deaf ear to the speeches and explanations that accompanied them. They had tried to interpret them in their own way, which was different from the popular interpretation, shorter and more reasoned; however they knew that this must suffice and therefore it did suffice.

Christmas Eve found the island as quiet as if it were a lighthouse. The general had gone to see his grandchild; he had even asked Thomas whether he would like to accompany him. But Thomas shook his head. In the morning a large basket arrived from the castle, a large case from Frau von

Orla and a small parcel from Marianne. Johann and Bildermann carried the case into the house and drank some of the mulled wine which was keeping hot on the fire. 'What shall we do with a tree?' said Johann sadly. 'They have taken the young mistress from the castle and now we are left like apes in a tree.'

Bildermann consoled him. 'Two years is not a long time, and I have been told that some apes grow very old.' But Johann kept on shaking his head. After the third glass he wound his scarf round his neck and stamped off through the snow. The sledge which he pulled after him looked like a child's toy.

As twilight fell Thomas went to the forester's house and put some small gifts on the table. Overhead the restless step went to and fro, and the floorboard creaked again. The old man stood near the stove and looked at the ice on the window panes. 'Well, dear sir,' he said, 'people think nowadays that the Star of Bethlehem only shines for the foolish or that it has set or even that it never appeared at all. It seems to me that much has perished or is about to perish, but the Star, dear sir, the star still stands over all the dark houses – and the wise men from the East, what would they do without their star? And the dead who rise tonight to pass an hour with their mothers, how should they find their way without the star?'

He was tall but bent with age; his hair had grown white over the temples, yet his eyes shone like a child's on Christmas Eve, notwithstanding that the sound of the steps overhead did not encourage the Christmas spirit.

'Yes, I would like to come and see you soon. Only tombs and prisons are as quiet as my house.'

Thomas walked home slowly. It was still snowing; when he got on the ice he could not see the woods any longer; nothing was visible but the white dome of Heaven. Halfway down the narrow path its beginning and end were invisible; they seemed to have melted into the white wall, the end of the world. Suddenly a light on the island became visible, like a star above the horizon; at first it flickered a little, but then it burnt with a bright flame becoming bigger and bigger as he drew nearer.

Bildermann had decorated the tree and opened the cases. Now he lit the candles and they both sat near the fire and watched the threads of tinsel sparkle in its light. They did not sing nor did they read the Christmas gospel. They were silent and a vision of the Holy Child may well have touched their eyes. In both their lives there was much they wished to remember today.

Then Thomas began to unpack the presents, and they were surprised to see how much had been spent on two lonely men. 'For ever, little lady,' said Bildermann, 'you must believe that now –'

Thomas stood in front of the model, which they had lifted on to the table, and looked down on the island which rose between land and water. The water was blue, and the woods an inch high framed it with a soft green, the sand of the shore sparkled, and the grey roof came low over the windows, and a bright golden star stood on a mast as thin as a needle. It shone down upon this work of a young, shy love, and on the narrow landing-stage Thomas fancied he could see her sitting with her bright eyes looking up to the house from where the light was shining for her.

'And if nothing were left to us but to look after her, would we not be rich, Bildermann?'

Snow fell on the roof, and the old beams cracked and mice rustled in the reeds. Bildermann had caught the bells out of space with his mysterious apparatus, and they had become silent again. They had sounded a little hoarse, and now and again a scream had run like lightning through the sounds, however for both of them it had been like a miracle. The globe at their side seemed to be filled with life, life far away, which they could capture with the wires and the shining valves in their snowbound solitude. A human voice was heard from afar, almost from beyond the ocean, bells rang in honour of the Child Jesus, and a voice sounded loud and solemn at their hearth: 'For unto you is born this day, in the city of David, a Saviour, which is Christ the Lord . . . and this shall be. . . .' Then the voice faded away in infinite space and came back no more.

Bildermann gave it as his opinion that this was the most marvellous theatre imaginable. For if you did not like the performance, you only had to turn a knob–like this–with one finger, and everything went dead, as if the performers had all been executed suddenly. In its place another voice could emerge, from another country, and if you did not like either the voice or the country, you could simply cut them off, and they disappeared like a boat that capsizes and goes to the bottom.

But if they had a mind to be where the little lady was at the moment, they simply went there too, and if it was to a concert, they knew when the people applauded, that the little lady was applauding also, she who had given them that marvellous Christmas present.

'You are a magician, Bildermann,' said Thomas.

They were highly pleased with this Christmas Eve. They let the candles burn down and drank to all the Platens, from the ancestor who had gone over the Beresina to the young girl who would be the last of that name. Their conversation was a little more thoughtful than it usually was and their eyes more serious, for so many 'quiet people' called on them. They could cope with those quiet visitors, as they had been able to cope with the war and all that followed. The candles went out and the fire died down, but the golden star on the thin flag mast still sparkled. When Thomas woke in the night, he could see it floating in the dark room illuminated by the dying glow of the fire.

A telegram from Nurse Beate arrived on New Year's Day. The thin strip of paper told them that Frau von Orla was seriously ill and wanted to come to the island. Thomas was asked to telegraph his consent.

He did so immediately. Then they fetched a bed and bedding from the castle, and many other things Frau Sperber had packed on their sledge. Thomas and Bildermann drove to the station where the express stopped, and the general had put the old, closed sleigh at their disposal in which Friedrich Ehrenreich might well have crossed the Beresina. Frau von Sperber had put fur rugs and hot water bottles into it, and in this they drove through snowbound forests which glided past the windows noiselessly, past the forester's house, where the woman dressed in black was leaning against the fence and over the ice of the lake, invisible under the cover of the snow, along a narrow path – marked by small pine trees.

She lay almost at full length on the low seat, supported by cushions, a fur cap with a bunch of violets on her damp hair. Her lips were still a bright red and her big, dark eyes looked in surprise at this silent white world.

Thomas and Nurse Beate sat next to her. He held her hand, and when she asked whether the seven dwarfs lived in these woods, he smiled and said that it might well be so, that they often met queer people under these pine trees. Bildermann sat next to the driver and Thomas's eyes were fixed on the ribbons of his cap. He did not understand why they streamed so merrily, and all the time he thought: 'Three years . . . how can a human being come so low in three years – and I knew nothing about it? And did not want to know? Now she has become much more silent than I have, and it was I who went away to seek quiet.'

The broad gilt bedstead which they had put up near the fire might well have been made at the time of the Beresina, but Frau von Orla thought it splendid. She smiled as she saw the rafters blackened by soot and then her gaze travelled to the gilt cupids which leant tenderly against each other at the foot of the bed. With this smile she tried perhaps to understand the two worlds: the one she had left and the other in which he who sat at the foot of her bed might well feel at home.

She was exhausted now. Her cough was harrowing and towards evening the fever confused her thoughts. Then she fell asleep, and Nurse Beate, standing in front of the hearth in the adjoining room, told Thomas how all this had happened. Her eyes were full of tears, but she did not know whether it was because she saw the shadow of death looming over the snowbound lake, or because she saw the small, modest room with pails of water and oars in the corner, Bildermann's poor bed, and the two men who once had sailed far and wide over all the oceans and were now living in this great solitude like two animals in the thickets of the forest. Their eyes had a faraway look, as if this world no longer existed for them.

Thomas asked whether she knew how all this had happened to Frau von Orla. She had lived a hectic life as always, as patients do who know more about themselves than healthy people. She started to cough, at first only in the morning. She enjoyed her meals no longer. She smoked without stopping and . . . (there are no secrets from Bildermann, said Thomas) . . . well, she liked a glass of champagne and strong mixed drinks. She got up very late and came home very late. She tried to force her body to allow her every pleasure, but it began to rebel and sent out warnings. Her sheets were damp in the morning and she lost weight. There was something else. Although Frau von Orla had many friends, she knew that she was alone, quite alone. Sometimes nurse had found her standing at the window in the evening looking out like a bird from a cage. 'It is so quiet, Beate,' she said, 'so terribly quiet. . . .' About that time she probably started giving herself injections which made her eyes bright, and after which she sang and fascinated people. But gradually her body, which did not want poison, but sleep, fresh air and good food, began to take its revenge. Nurse Beate had noticed it very early. At first she said nothing, but then she begged, implored, threatened – all in vain.

At last Frau von Orla had gone to see her doctor. She knew him well and perhaps he told her the truth, for he sent her to Switzerland, and for a while the deadly syringe disappeared. When however she came back, she started to cough again. She danced the nights through, until suddenly like a wall undermined by water she collapsed. There had been bloodstains on her lace handkerchiefs, and her eyes looked as if she were seeing ghosts. Then in her imagination the thought of the island began to take shape and gradually overruled everything else. Then it occurred to her that she might get well in her husband's house among the woods and lakes of which Joachim had spoken with joy. Her only wish was to go to him, even if it meant sleeping on straw.

'Put on your skis, Bildermann, and go to the castle. Ask them to send for the doctor first thing in the morning. Ask them to tell him that he can drive in his sledge right up to the island.'

Then he sat beside the gilt bedstead, listening to her fast breathing, the sound of which filled the room like the flapping of a bird's wing. The fire burnt as usual and shone on the rows of books and the globe; the golden star glistened in a dark corner above the table. Through the windows the night looked blue and white, no sound was heard, only the worm moved, boring into the old beams. In her waking moments the patient talked to herself in a low hurried voice. She showed neither fear nor pain, but she was like someone in haste, who has lost something when about to set out on a long journey and cannot leave before she has found it.

One could understand but little of what she said, the few things that one could grasp flowed restlessly above the ocean of memory. They were mostly recollections of her youth spent in a big house with many brothers and sisters and parents who built castles in Spain, and in whose hands everything melted away that should have been retained. The dull years of the war went past and the wild, noisy nights of dancing which followed. All that passed like a rushing stream only recognisable by the debris it left behind.

But behind all this the thought of Thomas was always there. A shadow not to be grasped, a phantom changing and losing its shape in which only the eyes remained unchanged, 'the warning quiet gaze, without a word of reproach'.

He saw the corners of her mouth tremble, and he realised now that she must always have been nearer to crying than laughing. Now that it was too late, he understood much. One day he would have time to think it all out. It was not as easy as he had thought to leave a human being and go away. Right and wrong could not be separated from one another, as children will separate them, and the person who fled was not always the one who was wronged. You could become guilty merely by touching another life with your hand, by cheering and comforting with a loving word. It tied the two lives and made them grow together. Each severing meant a loss of blood which could never be replaced, and which weakened that other life. It abandoned it to that danger which was always lying in ambush: that dark power for which there are so many names, but which is nothing but the law which demands that the wheel of life must break at its weakest point.

Nurse Beate slept on the floor near the gilt bedstead. Bildermann had put Thomas's bed into the adjoining room. The door was ajar, and from time to time they heard a soft, low voice through the darkness, as if it were seeking for something.

'We have been too sure of ourselves, captain,' said Bildermann gently. 'We did not take soundings, and now we have run aground.'

'Yes, Bildermann,' replied Thomas.

The doctor came early in the morning. He walked up from the shore in his fur coat which reached to his feet–a tall, heavy man with an unsmiling mouth. He looked as if he carried on his shoulders the fates of all those who had passed through his hands in a long lifetime.

Halfway up the slope he stopped and looked round in the vast silence, as if he wanted to see whether this was a suitable place for death, this island which looked so dead, and yet he saw tracks in the snow leading to the house, and smoke rose from the chimney straight into the air. Some boats lay on the shore of the lake, bottoms up like coffins.

Thomas led him first into the small room where he took off his fur coat and warmed his hands at the fire. He nodded as Thomas gave him a short report, looked at him attentively and asked him whether he intended to stay here always. 'Indeed,' was all he said. 'Such things do happen sometimes. I call it the monkish impulse in man, and it is not the worst of human impulses.'

Then he asked to be taken to the patient.

She had touched up her lips with the lipstick and had put a small pearl necklace round her neck. She smiled as if she had just had a child and was receiving her first visitor. But something like horror lurked behind that smile, and the pearl necklace looked as if it were gracing a dead child. Thomas turned away and went to the window. After a series of grey days the sun was shining over the forest in all its glory.

The doctor sat at the side of the gilt bed and looked at the patient in silence. She was still smiling, but in her eyes there was a slight, hardly visible, expression of mockery. It seemed to be there only for the doctor, a sort of secret language which said everything without words, and which only doctor and patient understood. The doctor saw it; he seemed to nod slightly, as if to indicate that she was right, and that he was willing to play the last act of this comedy with her – two adult actors before childish spectators.

Then he asked her to tell him about her symptoms, which she did smilingly and obediently, while he felt her pulse almost negligently until, all of a sudden, he pushed the left sleeve of her nightgown back and passed his forefinger over the delicate scars. She made a movement as if to pull her arm away, and the place of the smile was taken suddenly by an expression of fear. He only nodded, and in the corners of his eyes also a gentle, almost contemptuous look of mockery became visible, betraying knowledge of the foolish, devious ways of men. 'How long?' he asked, then he nodded and told her to let him know when she wanted more.

Then only did he begin his examination. 'As soon as we have got you over this,' he said, while she lay back on her pillows exhausted, 'you must go to Switzerland. Patients who were much worse than you have been cured there.'

She looked at him with beaming eyes while he wrote two

prescriptions, but when he got up and said goodbye, that peculiar expression was in her eyes again. It followed him to the door, which Thomas opened for him, and he had to look back and answer it in silence once more.

'Brave,' he said in the adjoining room, where he warmed his hands again over the fire, 'very brave. . . .'

Thomas asked whether there was any hope.

'No,' said the doctor, 'I am afraid none. We must make it as easy for her as we can. How many injections have you got?' Nurse Beate said that there would be sufficient for a fortnight. The doctor thought and nodded. 'That will do,' he said, and looked at Thomas again. 'One must make the last road as easy as possible,' he added. 'Life is hard enough for most human beings, we do not know where the last road leads to. Or do you know anything about it?'

'No, I don't.'

Then they helped him to put on his heavy fur coat and Thomas accompanied him to his sledge. The sun was still low above the wood and its crimson light flowed over the white snow. It was cold and the two horses were covered with hoar frost.

The doctor wrapped himself in his fur rug and shook hands with Thomas. 'If it's true that man is the crown of creation,' he said, 'then I don't think much of the world. It could have been much better made. I will come again the day after tomorrow in the evening.'

Gloria's condition became rapidly worse, so much so that it seemed as if death had already done its work, but had not stayed to cut the last threads. After the injections, however, she sometimes had a bright, clear hour, full of childish happiness, as if the whole thing were only a joke, a little comedy to frighten people, but now those who had been afraid could be reassured.

In one of those bright intervals Bildermann took her all round the island. She sat, wrapped in furs and rugs, in a small hand-sledge to which they had put a back, and Bildermann pushed the sledge across the virgin snow. It was noon; the sun was shining, and melting snow dripped from all the trees. She asked him about everything: where the castle was, where he put out his nets, and where the herons perched in the evening. She was as light as a bird, and her voice was also like a bird's, which could sing no longer, but could only twitter forlorn and tired, in the vast solitude like the thin voice of the waxwings, which sometimes came here for a few hours, probably from the north, and disappeared again, nobody knew where.

'Bildermann,' she said, when the house was no longer in sight, 'Thomas may think that I would like to be buried here. But you must tell him that I don't want that. This island belongs to the living, to you two, and a tombstone is something one always trips over. Like a runner who has not fastened his sandals properly. You will find a good place over there where the woman stands. There I shall not be too near nor too far. Will you promise, Bildermann?'

'Yes,' he promised.

'And one more thing, Bildermann. I have made a will. I have saved a lot in those stupid years. I think that he is going to stay here, and you must stay with him, Bildermann, will you? He is so quiet that it is better for him to be alone. It was different with me; I wasn't the right person for him, but I know that you will look after him. I have left you a small legacy, Bildermann. No, no don't answer – you have stayed at home so that I could dance, I know that very well, and I shall die happy if I know that you will stay with him. Will you promise me that, Bildermann?'

He gave this promise, too, and then he carried her indoors.

He remembered how she had stood in front of him under the pine trees in the garden, fumbling in her handbag for some money for him, while her shining car waited in front of the gate. He saw close to his eyes her moist forehead where the delicate blue veins crossed, and he ground his teeth. 'Never mind, madam,' he said softly, 'I'm sure we shall continue to sail before the wind.'

Gloria let her head drop sideways so that her cheek rested on his shoulder and smiled. Her eyes were close below his own, and he held his breath, so that their moist mirror might not be dulled.

In such an hour when evening drew near, she asked Thomas where the golden star above the model of the island came from.

'The child came to see me,' she said, when he had told her. 'Shortly before I came here. I think she wondered what a wife who lets her husband live alone looked like. She was very shy, but at the door she turned back and said: "Please, do go and see him – they are on the ocean both of them." She kissed my hand and left quickly – a peculiar, beautiful child – and now I have come, you see.'

She closed her eyes and stroked the blanket with her right hand. 'On the ocean . . .' she repeated softly. Then she fell asleep.

One afternoon the general came over the ice, on foot, in his long, grey coat from which the red facings had been removed. He entered gently by the backdoor with menacing eyes under eyebrows covered with hoar frost.

Yes, Frau von Orla would like to see him if he was not afraid. He sat at the side of her bed, trying to soften his voice, until it sounded quite hoarse – and read every question in her eyes. 'It's nice that you have seen my grandchild. She is already a little woman; the only light in this dull world –

what all women were born to be. You needn't worry. The island belongs to Herr von Orla for life. He is an officer and a gentleman of whom the great king would have been proud. He is a comfort to my old age – he and the child, and when you are well again, madam, we will decorate the big boat with roses and row you over the lake to the castle.'

'A knight, Herr von Platen,' said the patient with a smile as he took his leave. 'It is nice to have seen a knight with shield and helmet, before setting out on the last journey.'

'The Lord has forgotten us, Orla,' the general said on the shore. 'That was not necessary. So young – an error is possible even up there.'

'No, sir,' replied Thomas in a low voice, 'there is no error. There is nothing but the law; the law is blind. It makes no distinction of persons. That's how it must be.'

'Perhaps, Orla.' He looked over the ice. The sun stood behind the island; the roof cast its shadow far over the lake. In the distance some woodcutters crossed the bay on their way back to the village. They walked in single file with their saws and axes on their shoulders like rifles.

They both looked at them. War was not dead yet. The moment one saw men with something narrow on their shoulders, the thought of it came back. The earth was asleep, but death did not sleep.

Thomas waited until the men had disappeared into the wood. Now one could only see the general on the ice. He grew smaller and smaller like a man going away never to return and his shadow marched at his side.

On the twelfth day it was clear that the end drew near. At noon Gloria grew restless and wanted to sit by the fire in the armchair. Thomas carried her there and put some more wood on the fire so that she might be warm. He stayed at her side, and once she stroked his hand with her transparent fingers. 'Forgive me, Thomas,' she said.

He kissed her forehead and sat down on the armrest with his arm round her shoulders. She was as thin as a child. She leant her head on his chest and looked past him through the window. It was snowing again, and she watched the flakes as they fell.

That evening, before she became unconscious, she asked for the globe to be put close to her bed. It was dark in the room, only the flames in the fireplace threw a flickering light over the continents and oceans. He sat at the head of her bed and saw her transparent hand touch the globe. It looked as if she dipped the tips of her fingers into the Indian Ocean.

She let the globe rotate slowly, so that the lines of longitude appeared above the horizon one after another at long intervals. The equator cast a dark shadow like a ring on continents and oceans, and the red line of the ecliptic grew and disappeared. Her eyes followed the movement and once she said: 'The world is so large, Thomas, so large.'

It hurt him to see her delicate, frail hand on the image of the world's life, and he put it gently back on the blanket, but her eyes were still fixed with longing on the distant countries which had come to rest now.

'So quiet, Thomas,' she said. 'That was probably my greatest difficulty. At home, you see, we were so many, six brothers and sisters and parents, and we were all noisy and merry. Then with you it was so quiet, even when you were not at sea, yes, especially when you were at home. In my parents' house we were always laughing, perhaps even when it was not right to laugh, and you laughed so little. I was a silly child – I was young and so cold – I wasn't wicked; I even loved you, but it was so quiet, Thomas.'

'Forgive me,' he said, 'it was my fault. I grew old too early, much too early.'

'No, no, Thomas, don't say it was your fault. You have

been living here, you two, so poor and so "on the ocean", while I danced and celebrated. But do you know, Thomas – come close to me – for the end I wanted to be with you, the passing away.'

'Please, don't speak any more now,' he pleaded.

'You are no fool, Thomas,' she said, after a while, 'once I called you so, but it wasn't true. You are not a fool, but we both are, Joachim and I.'

'All of us, Gloria,' he said. 'We have been thinking too much, and the end is always so simple, and no thinking is needed.'

Her eyelids dropped and she began to lose consciousness. 'So simple . . .', she repeated several times, but it was probably the fever that made her speak. After a time there came a long, deep sigh: 'So quiet, Thomas.'

After that she spoke no more. In the evening she began to sink and did not regain consciousness.

She passed away an hour after midnight. Thomas looked at the clock as he stopped the pendulum. Then he went to the door and looked out; it was still snowing.

Bildermann dug a grave not far from the forester's house. He did not want any help, though the earth was frozen to quite a depth. He, too, had had bitter thoughts sometimes, and it was proper that the sweat from his brow should drop into the grave.

From time to time the forester's wife came to look at his work. She was wrapped in a large, black cloak, and as she approached under the snow-covered pine trees, humming softly to herself, Bildermann thought that the Angel of Death might look like that to those who believed in him. She stood at the grave gazing with her lifeless eyes at the crumbling sand. 'Rolling home, my boys, rolling home . . .', she began in a low voice. She sang slowly as old women will do in church and rocked her body to and fro to the tune. Bildermann dropped his spade, took her arm and led her gently back to the house.

The general had seen to everything and Thomas had leisure to sit by his dead wife. Sometimes he got up and put on his skis and roamed the woods for long hours, but as soon as he got back, he sat down again by the side of the coffin and looked at her quiet face. He had seen many dead, but this was different. Now that all colour had disappeared and the light had left her eyes, it had become a poor face, as poor as if it had already squandered everything, even the last penny for the final journey. Its expression was neither sad nor severe nor forbidding, it was only a little hopeless. The pale corners of the mouth drooped a little like a child's. You could not look at her without regretting that you had not taken better care of her, and you felt as if you ought to cover her so that she might not be cold.

Thomas knew well enough that it was too late now. He did not believe in a reunion after death. She would disappear as so many had, and what they considered immortal lived on in tenuous things: in Joachim's blood, in memories, in the soft shadow that was all that remained of her life. Part of it would live in his thoughts, part in Joachim, but the greater part would fade away like the afterglow of the setting sun. One would know that she had lived, men, animals and plants had rejoiced in her presence, but the dawn had enveloped her, and the new day would make people forget.

He realised that one could not take up a life of solitude without wronging others, though sometimes a man had to do this in order to preserve his individuality. Solitary guilt was to be preferred to a joint life of pleasure.

The vicar had lost his left arm in the war, and he spoke to them in their shabby uniforms as to comrades. He spoke of death as of a bitter fruit which they must eat. The flag was still flying above the dead, nay, especially above the dead, and they had to carry it again and go on marching. One did not understand what the goal was, but one had to believe that there was a goal. Man was like a bird, spellbound by a dark wood, but one day the chain would break and the bird go free.

Thomas stood near the coffin, and when he raised his eyes, he could see the globe which had been moved by her hand. The general stood at his side supporting himself on his stick with both hands. He knitted his white brows and looked at the coffin menacingly, as if it were a mistake which God had made. The Graf, in a light-blue uniform which his father had once worn, stood behind them. The same weak, melancholy smile played round his lips as when he had spoken of the grey visitor who sat by the hearth 'meditating' as a warning of the future.

Joachim had not come. He had sent a wreath and had written that he was in the middle of the written examination and could not possibly leave as it would mean not passing.

They walked behind the coffin and the sledges followed. The sun shone behind the island with a crimson light, and long shadows fell in front of them. A gentle east wind blew from the snowbound forests, and made the ribbons of Bildermann's cap stream sideways. The forester's wife stood at the fence singing the flag song softly to herself.

Involuntarily their steps fell into time with the music. During the whole ceremony the sad chirping of the bullfinches was heard from the tops of the pine trees, and the brown pine cones which they dropped were blown by the wind out of the blue air down into the grave.

Thomas wanted to be alone. He thanked the general for all his kindness, and said that he would call at the castle soon.

He went home with Bildermann, set off on his skis and only returned to the island after dark. The lamp was burning, the gilt bedstead was no longer there, everything was as it had been before. They sat by the fire and smoked silently. The scent of the wreaths and flowers was still in the air. The clock was ticking again.

'Have you heard that verse, Bildermann?' asked Thomas. 'The chain is broken, the bird goes free.'

'No, captain.'

'There are beautiful things in the old book.'

'Yes, captain. What he said about the flag too was beautiful. And I am sure, he did not find that in my book.'

'Yes, what was it, Bildermann?'

'"The flag flies above the dead too", captain. That, I think, we can believe, captain.'

Thomas looked at him. 'Yes, let us hold on to that, Bildermann,' he said.

CHAPTER ELEVEN

SOME YEARS PASS by without being in any way notable or remarkable. They are like the thin boards of a fence; but every now and then these thin boards are interrupted by an oak post, which supports the whole and gives it strength. But no fence consists solely of posts, and no life can comprise eventful days only. Such a fence would be terrifically strong and such a life too much for anyone.

Fate produces great years sparingly. A boy who glides a stick along a fence hears a monotonous sound until the stick strikes one of the posts. That produces a more distinct and firmer tone. It is the same with the years of our lives over which fate passes. They clatter monotonously on until a 'post year', is reached. Those quiet years should not be despised; neither should they be stressed too much. Quiet lives are like stones that lie deep in the earth. No one knows of their existence; yet one day they may build cathedrals.

Twice in recent years fate had shown itself to Thomas and Bildermann, had touched them, and disappeared again. The first time they had felt its touch, they had risen and gone away. They broke off their empty lives and wandered eastward. But fate cared little towards which point of the compass they went. It lay in wait for them everywhere.

The second time, a dying woman had come to them, and watched them in silence for a fortnight and had then left them for ever. It would seem that they had been too certain of themselves. The broken threads of fate hung from their arms, but they had brushed them off, as one gets rid of cobwebs after a walk through the woods in the autumn. Feeling so certain of their course, they had not taken soundings; but fate had grounded their keel, the masts trembled and the lamps rocked. It had happened suddenly and had passed; but they heeded the warning. To them it did not seem to come from God, but rather from that sinister power with a face of stone with which they had become familiar in recent years. Though names had no meaning for them, they realised the anonymous challenge.

Then they began to realize that every grip of a hand, every word is enough to bind human beings, those who live in solitude most of all, that a life cannot be jerked out of the past, as a fish is hauled out of water. With every step we take, we trample on life, unless we walk on air, and even then we cannot be certain that we do not cause pain. Both men were more cautious and more industrious than they had ever been before. Work for them was the only safe thing.

For them it was not enough to do their duty daily, to do what they had contracted to do. That would leave them too much time for leisure or thought. They planted more potatoes; they extended the garden to the water's edge; they built a bathing hut. The days were too short for two men who had no ambition to be either good or bad, happy or unhappy, who only wanted to work hard, because life had in some measure lost its meaning for them. There was no need for them to look after the child while she was away. They could only write to her and make her feel that they were invisible companions at her side. Now and again Thomas would sit by the fire with the general and have the satisfaction of reading his pleasure in his eyes. He also called on the Graf occasionally and went to see the forester who believed in the saints. These were silent people, who were visited by the invisible ones. You would sit with them and bring home to them without speaking that the visible world still existed and took an interest in them, and that their battles were not always fought in darkness and solitude.

That however seemed to be the limit set to their activities. Occasionally Bildermann tried to widen the circle. Like the dove from the ark he ventured forth. But from meetings and inns he always returned without the leaf. 'They are still only talking, captain,' he said, 'but there are more children's graves in the cemeteries than ever. When they don't want to work any longer they strike and kill those who are willing to work. If they were to come here, they would kill us, too.'

Thomas looked up from his work. He was tying leaden weights to the nets and now and then he stopped to make a note on a sheet of paper. 'We are not the only ones, Bildermann, who keep quiet and work. Those who are like us will find each other one day. But we must get out of the habit of using the whip.'

The winter was hard and long. Strange birds flew through the air, and strange men, prophets and vagabonds, walked over the land. One morning Christoph appeared in the doorway. His beard still reached down to his waist; his eyes had not become brighter, and his shabby clothes still smelt of fish and smoke.

He closed the door, took a glance at Thomas and Bildermann, who were having breakfast, and shuffled with feet bound up and tied with rags, to where the globe stood. There he stayed for quite a time supported on his heavy stick and contemplating land and sea. At last he raised his hand carefully and set the globe in motion, so that it revolved on its axis. An expression of surprise appeared on his face, mingled with hidden sorrow; he could not stop turning the globe and watching those unattainable lands glide before his eyes.

They looked at him in silence and were moved against their will, as they saw him standing there like a slave in fetters, while the multi-coloured dream of the world passed before his eyes. He did not look like a victor; he seemed more like one who had suffered shipwreck. Yet although beaten he showed all the doggedness of a man who refuses to accept his fate.

Then his glance travelled reflectively over the books and the other contents of the room and he said: 'So you were disguised after all, captain?'

They offered him food, and after a while Thomas asked him how he had fared and whether he thought the flag of victory was any nearer.

He made a gesture of contempt. 'Nobody is surprised when the citizen grows fat. He has never done anything else. But when a member of the proletariat grows fat, it is considered disgusting. I am off now.'

'Where are you going?'

He waved and looked towards the east.

'Would you like to stay?' said Thomas. 'I will ask the general whether he can't find you some work. Even the fruits of Paradise, I fear, have worms.'

'No, I don't want to stay. I have been a fisherman too long. As you know, captain, the fish migrate.'

'Yes, but generally into the net.'

'That may be,' said Christoph, 'but I want to die decently.'

They gave him a glass of rum and a packet of tobacco. Then he picked up his stick. On the threshold he turned: 'What about the golden crown, captain?' he asked, and laughed into his beard.

'It is rising, Christoph; it no longer lies on the bottom.'

'Well, captain, hold on to that,' he said good-naturedly.

They watched him, in his short grey coat, depart over the ice with noiseless steps, leaving broad tracks in the snow.

'Like a wolf,' said Bildermann thoughtfully.

The animals also wandered over the frozen snow, miles and miles in a single night, provided the surface could bear their weight. One morning towards the end of winter Bildermann found a large spoor, which he took at first to be that of a dog. On closer inspection however it seemed so unusual. He skied to the castle where he arrived in a cloud of snow, and would not rest until the general ordered a horse to be harnessed to the sleigh.

It was the spoor of a wolf.

It took them until the afternoon to assemble the guns. The wind had turned and brought warmer air from the south-west to the forest. It did not bring rain, but the snow slipped from the trees, at first like a veil of dust, and later in long white streamers, which were blown through the forest. Still later it began to fall in big lumps, sliding off the boughs and hitting the earth with a dull thud. The branches moved and sometimes broke under the added weight. There was a feeling of disquiet in the thickets, and they feared their prey might escape without a sound.

Thomas and the 'young Graf' stood side by side, until the guns had taken up positions. Pernein wanted Thomas to go back with him, but Thomas thought that it would be too late, as they could not refuse to go back to the castle for a victory toast. 'Such victories do not seem to me to be quite clean,' said the Graf. 'Twenty beaters and ten guns pitted against a single animal, that is nothing to be proud of. On such occasions I am always tempted to turn a blind eye and to let the prey escape. I dislike unequal contests.'

'We think too much,' said Thomas with a smile. 'Look at Bildermann and the others. For them only the wolf exists.'

'Yes, but we see the wolf in the abstract, my dear Orla. That is our secret, not only when hunting–well, we meet later.'

At the end of the path an arm appeared; it was the signal that the beaters were in position. They had been ordered to go forward slowly and quietly. From time to time they beat against the trunk of a tree with their sticks. The only other sound was the wind moaning through the treetops with a hollow tone, a sign of an impending thaw; and the thud of falling snow. Thomas thought of old Christoph, who was probably wandering through just such a wood with his rag-bound feet and the snow falling on his cap. Indeed, faith was a gift of doubtful value to man.

Suddenly a jay started to scream in the copse; it sounded loud and excited. The sound went through the wood like the crack of a whip. Then the loud clamour of the beaters broke out and was cut off suddenly by three shots in quick succession, after which it started again more loudly and urgently than before. Apparently the wolf had tried to break through the cordon of beaters, had been shot at and turned back.

'No, it is not only an abstract idea,' thought Thomas. He could hear the beating of his heart, and the barrel of his gun moved under his hand.

A cluster of small pines about the height of a man stood between him and Pernein. They were covered with a thick layer of snow and obstructed his view. He could only see the copse over a shallow trench, which was covered with snow and bordered by hazel trees.

Now and again he could hear the sharp click of a beater's stick against the trunk of a tree. Suddenly the wolf appeared at the end of the trench, its grey head showing through the branches of a fallen pine. It moved forward under the branches and the snow as silently as a picture on a screen. It looked back to make sure it was not being followed, and then turned and gradually came nearer and nearer under the brushwood. Now and again a lump of snow fell to the ground, and the branch thus freed from weight waved up and down. This was the only indication they had that the animal was approaching them.

Both men had their guns at the ready, butts in the hollow of their shoulders, and eyes in line with the sights. But they could not shoot into the brush; this was just not done. The beaters gradually came nearer and one could hear the old Polish yell of 'Jilk . . . Jilk! Jilk . . . Jilk!' It sounded like an exorcism.

A man covered with snow appeared on the warm scent at the end of the trench; he climbed over the fallen pine, threw up his arms and careless of caution uttered one wild, piercing cry. This seemed to throw the wolf off his balance and make him break cover. He got to the edge of the path with three leaps. A fourth took him well over it, but while he was still in the air the Graf's bullet caught him. Thomas thought he heard the dull thud of the missile and saw the body flinch in mid-air before it collapsed into the powdery snow. After one final convulsive leap it fell to the ground dead.

'What a pity,' said the Graf, as they stood beside the carcass. His eyes looked down reflectively, and when he raised them again, they showed his usual absent-minded, melancholy smile. In his mind's eye, Thomas saw behind this tall man with his stooped shoulders a long row of ancestors who, no doubt, had hunted the wolf in these same forests. They would not have had a word of pity for the fallen prey.

'Why did you not shoot, Orla?'

'He was nearer to you than me. Besides to be as quick on the trigger as that, one must have had more hunting ancestors than I have.'

'I would have liked you to have the satisfaction of killing it,' said the Graf. Later on he reported the shooting to the general exactly as it had happened.

It was late before they left the castle. The Graf did not want the wolfskin; he said he had no use for it, and that it would look well in the hall of the castle. He hoped the general would give him the pleasure of accepting it.

The general offered them hot, mulled claret; he also made a speech. He spoke of it as a symbolic event . . . said that noble blood was stronger than the grey freebooter . . . hoped that a similar thing might happen, when the fatherland was at stake and emptied his first glass to the health of his royal master.

Thomas and Pernein took deep breaths when they went out into the cold, damp air. They drove along the shore of the lake in silence as far as the forester's house. Here the Graf tied the horse to a tree, and for a time they walked up and down together on the ice. Bildermann had already got back to the island; they could see the light shining through the windows.

'It makes you happy to see the light in your home, Orla, doesn't it?' said Pernein.

'It most certainly does. It gladdens my heart every time afresh.'

'That's right and proper. But I, on the other hand, don't look forward to going home. On the contrary, I'm walking up and down with you here, although my feet are cold, just to postpone my return, to that passage with the death-masks, Friedrich, my old valet, who bows so obsequiously, the candles, the fire, and to feel that oppressive silence which fills the whole house. There are houses in which, you might say, only the dead breathe. I seem to live there as if by mistake, a forgotten remnant of life, like a butterfly in a cellar. I can find no satisfaction any longer in my books and music; I dread waking in the morning and having to get up and dress. Every day is like this, I hope vaguely to find the grey, old gentleman sitting at my hearth, waiting for me. It is like a game, like walking over thin ice and watching the plants in the depths as they reach up to the thin layer above.'

'You have no work to do,' said Thomas.

'Yes, I know. The workless disintegrate slowly. Stick to your nets, Orla. I imagine that you were in the same position as I once, but your hands saved you.'

'A hand is only a tool. You must have the wish to live, Graf.'

'Yes, you are quite right. The wish to live. Well, let's try again for a day, or a year, or ten years.'

Pernein went back to where they had left the horse and shortly after Thomas heard the dull thud of its hoofs in the snow.

Spring and summer passed quickly. The days went by as the links of a chain glide through the hands; they began with the sun and ended with it. On some mornings, the lake was calm and they could load the boat with fish, until it rode deep in the water. On other days, the weather was stormy and then the nets were empty, and in the evening their arms ached from the strain of rowing against the wind. A fisherman learns to be more patient than a hunter, for his prey remains invisible day and night and goes its way hidden from the eye of man.

Joachim wrote that he was popular on board, and that occasionally his work received favourable comment. He expected their first voyage to take them far away. There was some talk of the West Indies. Sometimes, however, the captain said that he would rather cross the Pacific with a load of monkeys as crew than sail with them across the bay of Kiel.

The absence of the child taught them patience also. They both felt that they missed her badly. She had been like a flower in their masculine lives. They had been capable of laying aside their oars and putting down their tools only to look at her. She had been associated with their new lives from the very beginning, a quiet companion from the big house who had lost her heart to the seafarers and confided in them as if they knew and understood and could do everything.

Both men realised that Joachim no longer believed in them. He had grown up too quickly, and was about to sail the seas not for the purpose of emulating them, but with the object of outdoing them and of setting them a new example. If he came to see them at all, he would come in uniform. He would see the fish-scales in their hair with some embarrassment and in his innermost self he would think of them as two peculiar men who had found each other because the outside world had been too much for them. He had a house in his home town, which Nurse Beate let out and looked after for him. He did not need either his father's money or his advice. Neither did he require much affection. He was like a young bird of prey which had left the eyrie of its parents. Thomas thought this quite natural, yet it caused him pain.

Bildermann rarely pressed his cap ribbons now, but on Sundays he often went away and came back wrapped in thought. One evening he asked whether the captain would like to take part in an activity which he had discovered and which might be quite a good occupation for the long summer days. A number of decent young men had been got together and were being trained as recruits, being drilled and taught how to shoot. Former officers were in charge, and the whole was loosely connected with the 'Stahlhelm', and of course, absolutely loyalist. He, Bildermann, had been asked already several times in a discreet manner, whether his master would be interested. As the harvest was now well in, and as manoeuvres were planned for next week, he suggested that Thomas might like to see what was being done. 'For,' said Bildermann, 'to talk to fish only is a one-sided affair in the long run.'

Thomas looked at him good naturedly and asked him whether the outside world was calling to him again. However, he promised to think the matter over. When Saturday came round and turned out to be mild and fine, they prepared the sailing boat, put their bicycles, knapsacks and blankets into it, and departed.

They left the boat on the shore near the town and rode away on their bicycles. In the afternoon they arrived at the out-of-the-way district where the young troops were to muster. Bildermann who seemed to be very popular and was greeted by most with pleasure, took his master along the various ranks, introduced him to the platoon commanders and eventually took him to a small hill, where the general staff was assembled with cars, messengers and field kitchens. Thomas was welcomed politely and was given the choice of looking on or of acting as umpire. He preferred the latter and asked a good-natured militia captain to explain the position and to put him wise as to the rules which were to govern the exercise. Then he stood aside, somewhat dazed by the unaccustomed noise and bustle which normally precedes exercises in which both civilians and military take part.

The officer-in-charge was a retired colonel. He had a narrow, red face with a prominent aquiline nose towering over a white moustache. He directed operations from the saddle of a lean, bay horse, and his orders seemed a trifle too loud and too abrupt. After a last 'Hurry up, gentlemen!' which seemed to whistle over the heads of the staff like the sharp blade of a sword, he beckoned to Thomas and asked whether he had received his orders, and whether he intended to keep his somewhat subordinate post with the old fellow.

'Are you referring to General von Platen?'

'Of course; to whom else?'

'Then permit me to point out that I never speak of my employer as an "old fellow"; and, by the way, I see no reason to give up my employment.'

The colonel sniffed and looked as if he wanted to use his sword on Thomas. But he pulled himself together and only said that formerly it had not been the custom for active officers to accept such employment.

'I realised quite some time ago,' replied Thomas, 'that what we have considered as customary, need not necessarily be the model of our present behaviour. Now the war is over, we must understand that it is not always right to take up things at the point where they stood at the outbreak.'

'I know,' said the colonel, 'that Herr von Orla has expressed extrordinary opinions in his book. However, the developments which have occurred in the last few years have surely shown the necessity for all loyal men to stand together against those rascals.'

'Which rascals do you mean? We on the island do not classify a whole group of the population as rascals, even when they do evil or only intend to do evil. If the country is to be saved, which is what we all want, it can only be done if all the people stick together. It can't be done if an abyss remains between those who are masters and those who are "rascals".'

The colonel sniffed again. 'We will discuss that another time,' he said. He dug his spurs into the flanks of his horse, as if he wanted to tear the unsuitable thoughts of this young man to pieces and with one great leap leave those pieces far behind.

'A bad start, Bildermann' said Thomas, as he mounted his bicycle to reach the head of the column. However, this impression was soon effaced by his preoccupation with his new duties and by his observation of the keenness with which the young men sacrificed their spare time to discipline and the common goal.

Only in the evening, when he thought about all this and spoke to some of these young men, he heard that they only repeated opinions and demands which were familiar to him from the newspapers. He was invited to spend the night in one of the local hotels with the staff, but he declined politely. Only then did he realise how different his ideas of and his attitude to life were from those of the others. For him it did not seem sufficient to seek that which was lost, by going back to the starting point and working along the same road again. Especially as that which was lost might not lie along that road.

The good-natured militia captain had also refused the invitation. For a little while he sat with Thomas at the side of the fire. 'No other way is left for us, Herr von Orla,' he said with a deprecatory gesture towards the other groups. Nowadays only old soldiers know what discipline is. The trouble is that this is very often all they know, so that although we have a staff, we have no real general staff. But as we cannot just sit back and do nothing, we must be content with what there is for a start.'

'Laurel is an evergreen,' said Thomas, 'but if you rest on it for too long it fades just like any other plant.'

'In my opinion laurels earned in a lost war are just as imperishable as any others. The hard fact however remains that one cannot live on laurel alone.'

'That's just it,' said Thomas, 'the war was more than a series of battles. You must either describe it with entirely new words or put your pen aside for good. Ten councils of Constance do not make a Reformation.'

'That is all very well, but who is to do the writing? I still keep my fields in order and look after my people, but I'm not much good at writing.'

'That doesn't matter,' said Thomas. 'Personally, rather than help to hammer into the heads of the young generation nothing but the old ideas, as if we had not eleven million dead to mourn and had not seen our old ideas perish, I spend my time mending nets and digging potatoes. One day perhaps people will realise that history doesn't knock at the door just to buy old clothes.'

Next day the exercise began before dawn. The principal engagement took place on the banks of a stream between two lakes and was decided in the early afternoon. The signallers called together the officers as they used to do in peacetime, and the colonel seated on his bay criticised, praising some of them and blaming others. The field kitchens came up and provided a meal, after which the proceedings closed with sports. The staff was invited to dinner at one of the large estates. The colonel expected that after the meal a final criticism of the day's work could be given.

Thomas excused himself, saying that he must leave immediately after the meal, as for a fisherman there was no such thing as a holiday.

He and Bildermann ate with a few young workmen from the town. Thomas mounted his bicycle, but Bildermann asked permission to stay until evening.

As Thomas was passing one of the last groups, he saw the militia captain, and stopped to say goodbye to him. 'Should anyone ask after me, will you please tell them that I have been accustomed to having my meals with my former batman for some years now, and that I would not care to revert to the custom, whether it be in real war or only in make believe, whereby a special meal is served for the officers and the staff. If challenged myself, I should be glad to give this explanation. If not, I should be grateful if you would give it for me.'

'I am sorry that you are going home. It is a great pity that those who ought to be the leaders are not always in that position.'

That autumn the general proposed that Thomas should leave the fishery to Bildermann, move to the castle, and take over the administrative work. The general felt that his age often made it difficult for him to deal personally with everything, and he would be glad to have somebody to take his place when he felt too tired to do anything himself.

Thomas however asked to be allowed to stay on the island. 'I know,' he said, 'that I am capable of doing other work than catching fish and mending nets. But in the last few years I have come to realise that if happiness is ever to be mine, I can only find it in simple work.' The fact that he had written a book and was about to write another seemed to him unimportant, even dangerous; for what he had laid down as his firm conviction might seem highly debatable to others. 'When I have caught a hundredweight of fish, that is a fact which is not debatable, and it is not due to a lucky chance, but to work and industry.

'I am, so it seems to me, born for simple things. In my former life I always made a slight mess of things: in the service, in my married life, with Joachim's education, and so on. But here I generally seem to get things right. Most people will say that I am trying to escape from the responsibilities of life, and that a man of my age should not take refuge in renunciation. However, I don't believe that he who works is an escapist, and I do think that renunciation is permissible to one who has lived in the last decades as I have. For one who has left meaningless words behind him, the plough and the spade are not substitutes for them, but represent reality, a simple, great and unspoilt reality. Men are always displeased with those who do not take part in their games, just as drunkards despise those who remain sober.'

'You ought to be in charge of a training ship, dear Orla, not of a fishing smack.'

'My English friends have written to me about a man who, after having conquered the whole of Arabia and Palestine, laid down his rank as soon as the war was over and worked as a simple soldier in an aeroplane factory. He seems to me to be one of the few wise men the war has left us. Of course, I have not conquered a country, yet I think I have earned the right to occupy this place here and to bring some sort of order into my life. Only when that has been done can good for others come out of our lives. Whenever I went to the theatre in recent years, I noticed that for nearly all the play was over when the last curtain fell. Their everyday face reappeared, and once outside one could not see from their expressions, whether they had come from a dinner party or a football match. But some left with a peaceful expression on their faces, and I don't think they were the worst. It is just like that in war. Many return in "their old freshness", as they call it. But some return with a very strange expression on their faces, as if they had been to a great play; they think of other things than the next performance.'

'You have lost your faith, Orla. I'm sorry. Your life is like a barren field which needs fertilising.'

'That may be so, general. In the last few years we have re-examined so much which we formerly took for granted, that I don't understand why we do not reinvestigate everything. Even the so-called eternal truths might bear scrutiny. A people which has sacrificed two million men on the battlefield has a right to ask God why He allowed this to happen. If they do not get an answer, they need not accept without question the explanation given by the Church. For the Church did not always teach aright those who brought the sacrifice. But if no answer comes with regard to those war victims, it will not come either for the million slain after the war, or for the children who die of starvation at the roadside. Then it would seem that God is unwilling to answer and would remain silent even if it were twenty or two hundred million; a mute God, cold and indifferent like a heartless teacher before children who cry helplessly. Then, general, it may come about, that some of us find it impossible to kneel in front of a stone wall and to hear only an echo instead of an answer to our prayers. Men will ask themselves what sort of love it is that demands sacrifices and remains dumb, that allows oceans of blood to be shed, that hears the groans of victims of all ages, good and bad alike, guilty and innocent; a God who contemplates his work in silence, his head supported in his hands, and still thinks it is good.'

'I have often thought about all this, Orla,' replied the general, 'but you go too far. Children need not be aware of all the motives of their parents.'

'Parents do not slaughter their children, general. And if a parent should happen to kill a child, he does not maintain in court that he did so out of love for that child. I cannot imagine that you, general, would torture your child day by day, and then claim that you had done so from love, or that you would say nothing at all, but make her kneel before a picture on the wall–deaf, dumb and blind–an idol of stone.'

'Orla!'

'It is so, general. We must start from the very beginning. Nothing is gained by negation. Life becomes impossible, if one cannot affirm sometimes. I am like a man who has grown up with bow and arrows and suddenly discovers that my enemies are clothed in armour. I have to invent new weapons, of an entirely different kind. I must go into seclusion and only emerge when I have achieved a new defence. I must start again from the very beginning. The old God I acknowledged is dead, and the new God has not yet mounted his throne. I do not even know what he will be like, but I imagine that one must be a man to be able to face him. However, I must take my time. There must always be time for God in this world. When the old colonel shouts "Hurry up" that may be quite right, as far as he is concerned; for in all probability he is on good terms with his God and naturally concludes that the same is the case with those whom he is commanding. If, however, there is one amongst them who feels differently, then the colonel has no right to tell him to hurry up. In company drill haste may be necessary, but there must be no haste in the search for God.'

'You think too much, Orla.'

'No, general. I only try to make up for the time when I thought too little. We have all thought too little. Since the time of Luther the belief has spread that it is unnecessary to think. We accept what he and his disciples taught. He who refused to do so was a marked man. Have you ever heard of an officer who refused to be married in church? To steal the silver spoons would not have been worse. I do not believe that war is the originator of all things, but that it is the prime mover I will concede readily, or at least that it can be the prime mover.'

'Supposing, Orla, you do not find God. What then?'

'Of that I am not afraid, general. What the savages of Easter Island or New Guinea found, that I can find also. But I will find something different. The God I shall find will not need to be implored or thanked. It will not be necessary to sing an anthem, "All thanks to the Lord" after having slaughtered thousands. For were that so, the others would have to sing "Now let us all curse God". I believe that I shall find an image that is beyond curses and gratitude; perhaps not even an image, perhaps just a law before which we are all equal. The world will have meaning as soon as we abandon the theory of divine love. Even war will have a meaning, although a hard one. Then it will be up to us to love in such a way that we find it impossible to say that war is good. To love as your child loves, who asks me not to forget to sit by this fire so that you, general, should not be lonely.'

'It is a sad world, Orla.'

'Possibly, general, but it is also a brave world. Children must lose their belief in fairy tales, in the ring which one turns to obtain the granting of a wish, in the Sesame which opens all doors, in the magician who can redeem us as soon as he touches us. What will be left is love and the absence of fear. Life is eternal but we are not. The curtain falls, the performance is over. We are not called before the curtain again to give the play a different ending. Other players are waiting ready to take our vacant place. Our beliefs are just as fervent and just as sure as theirs. But for us there is no afterlife which is less painful than this life. We believe that in spite of all vicissitudes LOVE must become more and more profound in this life; for that is all we have with which to oppose the inexorable law. We shall never overcome it or put it to shame, for it does not know shame. We must obey it, but in that very obedience we shall create something which is our very own, and which will illuminate its stony face: our love.'

'You make life hard for yourself, dear Orla. Formerly things were simpler. For King and Country. That was a concept the simplest man could grasp.'

'Certainly, general. But he did not grasp it. He was only obedient. That motto was not his invention. Others found it for him. He only had to obey. It was just the same seven thousand years ago. In those seven thousand years much has been done under the device: "with God". I think it is good for us that we know only the smallest part of it.'

The general's eyes travelled over the portraits of his ancestors on the wall. 'Then all these were wrong, Orla?'

'No, general, none of them were wrong. Their work was good, but He whose instruments they imagined themselves to be was not as good as they thought.'

'And the God you have in mind is good, Orla?'

'Neither good nor bad, general. Those are human but not divine concepts. He just exists and knows as much about us as the sun knows of this grape which it ripens or dries up. He is the ocean but we are the water.'

The autumn gale moaned in the chimney and blew the flames of the fire into the room. The leaves of the oak trees could be heard rustling in the wind.

'Another year, Orla,' said the general. 'It is a long time for an old man to wait. I should like the child to believe in the ocean, not in the water.'

'Nobody will challenge her faith, general. One who loves as much as Marianne does will always have the right faith in my opinion.

'*Drink in the sunshine and sip the light*. She often sang that. As a faith it is beautiful, and we must not interfere with it. It is bad enough, if we lose our way sometimes; old people should know their way even in the dark.'

When Thomas got back, he found Bildermann asleep in front of the fire. His hands were resting on the arms of his chair, his head had dropped on his chest, and even in sleep his face showed the unmistakable traces of the hardships he had suffered. This man had not been led by a God of Love either, or it was an incomprehensible love that had looked after him.

The smoke from Thomas's pipe woke him. His eyes had a faraway look. 'Asleep at his post,' he said, 'court martial.'

'We will sentence you to another hour's sleep, Bildermann. As I was rowing across the lake, I was wondering what made you sacrifice your best years to me and to the island. You have had a nice little legacy and I can give you a bit more. Why do you not start a fishery on your own? Or something else? At sea, of course. I think it would be enough to buy a cutter.'

'Do you think I am superfluous here, captain?'

'Don't talk nonsense, Bildermann.'

'Bildermann made two promises, captain. Once to a wife and once to a little lady. Both times he said: "FOR EVER". He would not like the young lady to raise her eyebrows when she thinks of him.'

'All right, Bildermann, then we will remain on the ocean together.'

CHAPTER TWELVE

WINTER HAD come and gone. A silver mug stood on the cabinet with the masks, and every morning Bildermann took it down and dusted it carefully with a woollen cloth. The inscription on the shining metal stated that Thomas von Orla and Friedrich Wilhelm Bildermann had won the first prize in an ice-sledge race. They had started to build their sleigh on the day following the evening on which Bildermann had fallen asleep by the fire. He had designed it and made most of it himself and had persuaded Thomas to drive to the large lake and compete with the others. It seemed advisable that the captain should mix with other people now and again. Thomas had submitted and had even remained for the distribution of the prizes, but one could see that it meant nothing to him, whether he was presented with a silver mug or a skittle board. At that time he was writing the last chapters of his second book, and as they drove home with the silver mug, he had asked Bildermann whether he liked the title: 'The God of Battles' or whether he preferred: 'Concerning God's Equivocal Attitude to Sea Fights'.

Something seemed wrong with the captain this winter. True, he was busier than ever, and after he had declared war on the foxes, he spent every moonlit night with his rifle in some lurking-place. He had also bought a telescope and often spent most of the night in the leafless top of the oak. But he did not seem really cheerful when he came back from these expeditions. It was as if he had stopped playing and was now searching for the rules that underlie all games. His expression had become more and more serious – like that of a man whose profession forces him to see others die.

'We ought to go to a dance, captain,' Bildermann had said one evening. But Thomas had only looked at him thoughtfully and replied: 'Don't worry, Bildermann, he will ask us to a dance in due course.' And at this his eyes were so strange that Bildermann was ashamed at having made such a silly suggestion.

Winter had come and gone and the island was green once more, as if it had never worn a coat of snow and ice. It surprised them both to see how the land could remain unchanged through years and decades, while the grey strands in their hair became more and more numerous.

On the grave near the forester's house the flowers were already in bloom, and sometimes the forester's melancholy wife stood with her arms on the fence humming her low song without words, and rocking to and fro. She had remained unchanged in all these years, only her face had become paler, as if a ghost was draining the blood from her heart in the long, silent nights. When Bildermann passed – the ribbons of his cap streaming in the wind – she used to stop him and ask him to sing one of his songs for her. She followed each movement of his lips, as if she were deaf and could only see his words instead of hearing them. The spring was hot and sultry; early storms passed flaming over the woods with short, heavy downpours. The heat of the sun hatched out blight, cockchafers destroyed the birch plantations, and old people prophesied the coming of the Antichrist.

On the island they thought that the child would come home after the summer but Thomas was restless and heavy dreams haunted him at night. One evening they found that one of the fish tanks had been forced open and emptied, and although the thief was arrested the next day by Bildermann and a sergeant, Thomas got up a few times every night, went down to the shore and listened attentively over the dark water. More might happen than a theft of fish, and he remembered that he had 'to stand by his employer faithfully at all times'.

Now and again in his dreams he fancied he heard a voice from a distance calling for him or for some human consolation. It was so distant that it must come from the wood or even from beyond the forest. He never understood what it was calling, but it was full of fear and sorrow and that stupor of the senses which one only feels in dreams or in a fever.

Once when he had heard it, he threw on his cloak and untied the boat. He believed that the voice had come from the meadows by the swamp, where high reeds grew round black ditches, and where the reed-warbler called in the evening. Though he was fully awake, a veil seemed to lie before his eyes, and sometimes while rowing he forgot that he was on the lake. In the north-east the sky was turning pink already with an unreal translucence, but on the shore the stiff reeds still stood like a dark wood and the alders in the meadows towered like houses into the white mist that rose from the earth.

The keel of the boat touched boggy ground. Bubbles rose and burst with a dull, sighing sound. Thomas remained sitting and listened closely for any noise that came from the land, but only the water in the ditches was to be heard, as it glided almost noiselessly over roots, and the soft trembling of an aspen which stood invisibly in the mist. The stars faded away, and a soft breeze blew from the swamp over the country. It was filled with the smell of decaying plants, and for a moment Thomas felt as if he were sitting in a boat in the other hemisphere on the delta of one of the mighty rivers which wound lazily into the ocean, as if he were breathing an air saturated with the scent of majestic flowers and with the heavy, fading smell lingering on the tracks of great animals imprinted on the fermenting earth.

The voice that had called in his dream was no longer audible. He got out of the boat and walked into the mist which reached up to his chest. The dewy grasses struck cold to his bare feet, and only when the soil gave way did warmth rise from underneath. He walked on and on without a goal, and during all the time a forgotten, senseless nursery rhyme which rose up from the past moved his lips involuntarily: 'A little man with a hunchback stands in the breeze – and all of a sudden begins to sneeze . . .' beginning and end were lost, but these few words repeated themselves again and again in the rhythm of a montonous lullaby echoed from below the earth, where the bubbles rose under his feet.

This spell lasted until a crane rose with a hoarse cry in front of his feet, and its metallic voice destroyed the mist and the spell. Thomas stood still, staggering with fatigue, and gazed after the body of the bird, whose bluish feathers were shining in the dawn. The mist dispersed, and the trees with their familiar outlines stood on the dewy ground, and at his left the crimson dawn shed its light over the world in grand serenity.

Thomas did not know where he was. He scarcely knew how he had got here, but the dark track in the bright dew guided him back. Before he landed again at the island, the sun had risen over the wood and Bildermann drew up the boat on the sand by the chain. He looked worried, but he did not ask anything, he only tucked Thomas well into his bed and closed the shutters. Yes, he was going to look after the nets alone.

'Perhaps I am ill, Bildermann,' said Thomas, while he was falling asleep. 'There is something wrong out there. . . .'

'People call it mania, captain,' replied Bildermann calmly. 'There are nights when the water calls us, but we must sleep that away.'

'Do you think that the water calls?' asked Thomas. But there was no answer necessary, Bildermann saw that his master had already fallen asleep.

On the shore he examined the boat in which Thomas had rowed away, but he only found the traces of his naked feet on the boards. They were nearly dry, and what was left looked like the trail of some big animal which had walked over the boats at night.

Bildermann bent down and strewed dry sand over the wet marks; he had always been a little superstitious.

Thomas slept well and soundly, following Bildermann's advice. During the summer, the curtain of which the general had spoken dropped twice, and both times it affected the whole district, as if concerned not only with those two whom it covered, but as if a sign were written on the canopy of heaven – high and with flaming letters, so that nobody should overlook it.

At first it dropped from the melancholy woman; it was as if she wanted to remind the people in the district once again of her strange and almost lifeless existence, for the sign of her last hour death wrote in a grand way. In reality her disturbed mind had circled for such a long time round the turret where her child had been burnt to ashes that, without knowing it, her dull thoughts had knitted the threads together again where death had torn and burnt them. Thus the disturbed course of the blood between mother and child was re-established, and her death followed out of his death, just as his life had once been born out of her life.

They had already gone to bed on the island when Thomas thought he heard the castle clock strike. First he imagined that the voice of his dream was calling him again, but when he lifted his head from the pillow, he clearly distinguished the ringing of the fire bell, which was pulled by a rope and now without ceasing rang out some dire need across the water. At the same time he saw the red glow outside the window, jumped out of bed, and called Bildermann.

There was no wind and they had to row. The glow of the fire stood quietly over the wood, only now and again a single flame rose high above the glow, and a sheaf of sparks fell down in a thousand stars which sank slowly to the bottom and went out. The fringed edge of the treetops lay motionless and luminous, and only when they came nearer, the red light fell now and again between the trunks to the forest floor and down to the shore.

'It's the barn,' said Bildermann, 'I think I shall have to dig another grave.'

The roof had collapsed already, only the rafters were still hanging above the walls like a glowing scaffolding. The fire-engine from the castle stood at the gate and played its water on to the roof of the house and the stable. They had put a hose from the fire-engine down to the lake, and the white jets of water hung in the radiant air like illuminated fountains. The forester sat on a plough in front of the open stable door, leaning back his head against the warm wood and staring with fixed eyes into the fire. His hands lay on his knees, and in the flickering, reddish light he looked like a wooden idol which someone had saved from the conflagration and carried into the yard.

The general stood at his side in his long, grey coat, a soldier's cap on his white hair. One of his hands lay on the shoulder of the sitting man, and from time to time he bent down and gently spoke a few words to him. But the man to whom he spoke did not reply.

Bildermann immediately went to the men at the fire-engine. Their faces looked depressed, and before Thomas approached the door of the stable, he had learnt that the forester's wife lay buried under the slowly collapsing beams.

There was no longer any danger. They pulled down the rafters and let the fire burn itself out. Gruber did not want them to use the hose on the barn.

He could tell them nothing as he did not know anything himself. He was asleep when a distant singing awakened him. He always slept lightly. At first he thought she was singing in the attic but then he saw the red glow. He had been able to open the door of the barn, but everything was already ablaze, and her voice was no longer audible. She had been singing the flag song, and he thought he had heard all three verses in his dream. They had sounded loud and gay, not subdued then, as he remembered her singing.

'Eleven years, dear sir,' he said to Thomas without looking at him. 'It takes all that time to turn away from God and lose the desire to live. It was not a hymn she was singing, but He is generous and will have accepted this song. Not many die with a song of praise on their lips.'

Thomas realised that it had been this song he had heard the first night, and he thought it strange that he had not recognised a song with which he had practically grown up. He shivered when he saw the white and yellow smoke rising slowly from the heart of the fire. At her grave, no doubt, they would say that man should submit and not ask for reasons. The old man would be left alone and would perhaps find consolation in the fact that he had given wife and child to his country, all he owned on earth and in the world to come:

they would be commemorated on invisible tablets not deeper than in his heart but lasting longer.

The high vault of the forest below which the sparks hung like stars was now reflecting the slowly sinking fire.

The hoses were rolled up, ladders and hooks strapped on to the fire-engine, and after a while it disappeared in the wood. Only the light of the two lanterns was to be seen above the plantations like two big will-o'-the-wisps.

'You really ought to come along with me,' said the general once more. 'There is room enough for old soldiers in my house. This is not a good place for you.'

But the forester shook his head. He was still sitting, as Thomas had seen him when he arrived – not a heart-broken but an absent-minded man who stared at the smoking grave whispering to himself. 'The saints will have received her,' he said. 'St Florian and his helpers. They do not ask after one's confession, they only ask whether one has suffered. Do you think, dear sir, that she suffered pain?'

'No,' replied Thomas, 'she did not suffer any pain. She went to sleep in the smoke, before the flames touched her. And she was singing, until she went to sleep.'

The forester nodded silently. 'A hard God,' he said. 'He wanted to mutilate one of us, and now he has carried His point. The other fell to dust faster than His hand could reach him, but now He has made up for it. . . . I know what they look like. . . . I have seen a trench through which the flame throwers went . . . they don't look good; but He will change them, when He receives them. He can do so much, practically everything if He wants to.'

The general took off his cap and said a prayer. His white hair stirred lightly in the night wind. Then he went to his horse.

'Please, do go too, dear sir,' said Gruber. 'Bildermann will make a coffin for her, an emergency coffin, and will bring it here, before the day breaks. The others need not see her, but he may. She has always looked out for him and his songs, and he may have seen worse sights in his life than this.'

When he was left alone, he remained sitting for a little while. It was still early and he had plenty of time. He was not cold, for the beams were still glowing. Now and again a soft breeze came from the lake bringing the smell of water and the first green leaves with it. The small flames flickered and the smoke was wafted under the tops of the pine trees. Then all was quiet, and the stars stood in their old places.

It seemed as if he were sitting at a camp fire. The battle was lost, but he had not been hit. Only others were hit. Probably God would be satisfied now – however hungry He might have been. There was not much to be found with him now. Only he himself was left and he did not mind a bit, if He came for him. But the forester knew very well that it was just he whom God did not want. One man had always to be left over to drain the cup, and the dregs were not sweet. There had always been discord among the various confessions, and they had said that his faith was the wrong one, but God seemed to deal with men of all faiths in the same way. It would be quiet in his house now. The floorboard would no longer creak, that grace would no longer be said: 'And what you have burnt on land and drowned in the sea, take it into your hand with glee. Amen.' He had been waiting for eleven years, as if He did not care for the woman with the disturbed mind who had blasphemed Him, as mothers sometimes will blaspheme. But in the end He had stretched out His hand – as an eager God who does not let anything slip from His grasp, not even the distraught.

'May it do you good,' said the man and got up.

He took the fire hook which lay at his side and began to pull the beams and rafters out of the barn. He worked quietly and cautiously and thought of everything. He knew where the machines had stood, and that the right stall had been empty. He found the twisted flywheel of the chaff cutter and the crooked frame of the scales. Otherwise the barn had been empty. She was not there. He stood for some time and felt the heat penetrating through the soles of his shoes. Then he fetched some armfuls of the chopped wood and lit a new fire at the side of the one that was going out. Now he could distinguish whether it was charred wood or something different. As no attempt had been made to put out the fire here, all the boards were burnt and only beams and rafters had kept some of their former shapes. It was not difficult to pull them out over the blackened foundation.

And eventually he found her. She lay at full length on her back, her arms folded under her breast. She seemed to have grown smaller, much smaller. He had to look at her now and again – to prevent the beams from touching her, but he did so with half-closed eyes, moaning now and again.

When he had finished, the Great Bear had passed beyond the zenith. The stall was empty now, except for the body, which lay almost in the middle. He fetched a white tarpaulin with which the sledge had been protected and covered the dead woman with it. They had done that in the war, only their tarpaulins had been grey and brown.

Then he sat down again near the stable door on the plough, whose iron was so cool to his touch, and began to smoke. They had learnt that at the front, too, that one may smoke in the presence of Death. They were so familiar with each other that Death did not mind. He fetched the smokers as well as the others and was not offended by the habits of men.

There was an early dawn; the crested grebes began to call on the lake. Everything was as it always had been. There was no disturbance in the landscape. Only the squirrels in the red-fringed tops of the pines scuttled restlessly up and down and looked down curiously on the empty place with the white tarpaulin.

The forester got up and slowly walked down to the shore. The crimson dawn stood big and clear behind the island, the birch woods had the first flush of green. The boat was already on its way. Bildermann stood in the stern with a long oar and the bright coffin before him on the empty seats. The reflection in the dark water went with him. It was a friendly picture and the old man's eyes dwelt on it. Once it was over, all would be well. The hand of the clock stopped, and the earth was waiting.

They buried her at the side of Gloria's grave. The one-armed vicar had come again and instead of the bullfinches the thrushes were singing in the tops of the pine trees. The vicar spoke and said that mothers were the most faithful people in the world, and that they would be forgiven sins which nobody else would be forgiven. But he did not understand why this had happened. He said with emphasis that he did not understand it. They should bow down – all of them together – but while he said it, his face looked as if he were fastening his helmet under his chin. He said that the old soldiers were still marching and that the dead still fell to the right and to the left. Death had marked them years ago, but only now he had touched their hearts. War beat the drum, and they went up in a fiery chariot like Elijah in his time or like the son of this dead woman. 'Dear Lord,' he concluded, 'are we to fight with you for ever? And don't you realise that you are fighting with yourself?'

It was a peculiar funeral sermon, and the forester did not turn his eyes from the pale face of the vicar that looked into the grave, as if his own mother was lying there.

'They have got power, because the child is away,' said the general gloomily, when all was over. But Thomas shook his head.

'They take what they can get,' he replied.

Gruber was to spend the rest of the day with them on the island, and the vicar said he would like to come too. He had taken to that part of the country, he said, and he would like to be there in spring and see the woods then. So all four rowed to the island.

Bildermann made some coffee, and they drank it at the grey table in front of the house. They all seemed to be battleworn, just as after a fight. Then Gruber went with Bildermann to the smithy. He needed some angle pieces for the open van, and he wished to forge them at once.

'I wonder if those over there will be disturbed, when I use the hammer?' he said to the vicar.

'No, certainly not.'

The vicar said he would like to walk round the island, and Thomas accompanied him. They stopped under the oaks and looked across the water. White clouds sailed over the sky and on the opposite side of the bay the long green branches of the birches were waving. 'I would like to be buried here one day,' said Thomas, 'you could bring the coffin here from over there. You need only read the Ninetieth Psalm, if you must say something.'

'You do not believe?' asked the vicar.

'I bow down, but I do not believe.'

'You ought not to bow down either,' said the vicar. 'You

ought to fight with Him. He can only put your thigh out of joint in a fight.'

'One can fight with God, if one believes in Him; only fools fight against necessity.'

'Nothing is more necessary than God.'

Thomas gently put his hand on the vicar's arm, and they walked on together. 'It took me ten years to get through it,' he said. 'Only a coward turns round when he has seen the face. I am not a coward.'

'Was it the face or the mask?'

'It was the face behind the mask.'

They did not speak of it any more, and before the sun went down Thomas rowed him across the lake.

'If you should call me some time,' said the vicar, when he took leave, 'you must not think that I shall come like a victor who has been in the right. But I don't believe you will call me.'

'Nor do I,' replied Thomas seriously. No, he had no mind to call anyone.

In his memory the forester's wife stood at the gate of his new life, for on that evening when he had first seen her, he had also seen the island for the first time. It was not as if some unknown woman had died in the forest. He meditated whether the call in those nights was heard everywhere, in all houses where sleeping or dreaming people were lying in their beds, or whether only he had heard it. And if it were so, had it come from this woman, and had she called to him for help? But what place could this have in the life he had taken such pains to build for himself?

He finished his book without real pleasure. Somehow he felt it was a mistake to offer his ideas to the world.

And as to his thoughts about God: who was entitled to say: this is my God and you must know what I think of Him? Such was the origin of all religions, and bloodshed had been caused by them all, beause of this origin. Man ought not to preach about God, nor about life, work or love. They should be lived; they radiate light of themselves, if they are within. The word could be a curse; it was the sound which loosened the avalanche; it hindered the march of life. There was no adequate word for bread, battle, generation – they were apart from words. Talking gods were as suspect as talking stones. Divinity was mute like the stars.

He knew so little. He wished to work, perhaps another ten years, until his body gently warned him that this part of his life was already declining. And then he wanted to read. His mind would still be fresh, hungry for all the knowledge that man had acquired, and for his mistakes too. What the intellect of man had built seemed to start up before him like a cathedral, and he felt giddy when he looked up to it. There was the science of the stars and that of the microbes. There were discoveries and conquests, plants and stones, legends and fairy tales, philosophies and religions. There stood telescopes and microscopes, vials and retorts, lovers' oaths and death-masks and behind the illegible signs of the necromancers, those who were insatiable, who wanted to shake the world and operate like gods.

Some day at last, nothing on this earth would be strange to Thomas, who wanted to know without any purpose the miracles of the universe. Everything contained within itself its own purpose, strength, beauty or just law. Sometimes he was simply thirsting for knowledge. He would never misuse it, not he! He would be sitting here like an old magician woven into the mesh of the world, looking and listening until the music of the spheres sounded for him. All around him would be growing up, desiring and hating, loving and forgiving. He knew that all these things were temporal and problematic, beautiful or sad. He would grow old like Peter, the fisherman, and he would remember the Great War when it was no more than a legend, just as Peter remembered the times of the Beresina. The autumn leaves would drop, and the trees would grow green again; tombs would sink down, and children would look for the golden crown. But once perhaps he would hear the music of the spheres, the soft harmony that sounds as the great law turns on its axis. He wanted to see neither God nor the next world, neither Paradise nor Hell. He only wished, at last, to see the whole, the microcosm of the ancients – the mighty, grand and all-powerful – in which men are but as dust on the threshing floor.

Then he would become as quiet as the stone at the bottom of the lake, as the leaf dropped from the oak. And at last his breath would cease and his motion be at an end. They would say that he was dead.

Once more the voice called him in his dream; so it had not been the dark woman. He was restless because he knew nothing about these things. When the young Graf came to see them, around the time of the solstice, Thomas asked him what he thought about the things that come in the twilight. The young Graf smiled in his usual way and said that not much could be done about that by thinking. Did he know that the human heart was hung in the chest at the same angle as the ecliptic of the earth, namely, at an angle of twenty-three-and-a-half degrees?

No, Thomas did not know that, and it frightened him almost, as if he had looked at the great table of the law which reigns over the living and the dead. 'Is there an explanation for it?'

'No, there is no explanation. It is only a breath of the great mysteries between which men go their little way.' But the young Graf wanted to know all he could tell of that call in the night, and he asked rather emphatically, as if such a voice had called him every night of his life. 'You will find a whole bookcase full of such things in my library,' he said at last. 'But it won't help you. Science knows of only one expedient in this sphere – experiment – and experiment has failed. No dead person has spoken so far. And whether those who are dying can call over lands and oceans, I do not know. I know that one can hear a voice calling, but I do not know whether it is another's voice or that of my own excited blood.'

'This year is out of tune,' said Thomas. 'We notice it with the fish. They are different from what they were in former years.'

The Graf nodded. 'Nothing is easier than to become too sure of oneself. Don't worry when the voice calls. It shows that somebody still cares for you. My cousin doesn't hear voices.'

'Who is "somebody"?'

But the Graf only shrugged his shoulders. Later he said: 'Supposing you got a great inheritance one day, which made you quite free and independent, as far as a man can be – would you think of going away from here, Orla?'

Thomas shook his head without hesitating for a moment. 'If I did that,' he replied, 'everything would have been wrong. Perhaps in ten or twenty years when I can hold the oars properly no longer. I'm a man for whom work is a support.'

'And thinking a whirlpool,' completed the Graf. 'The mixture of simplicity and complexity in you is very strange. At first I thought that you had come here to live a dream, but now I understand that you have come here to live and not to dream.'

'I want to know and not to dream,' said Thomas.

'Yes, it is the same with all of us in the beginning, but in the end we realise that we only catch ourselves with the net, not even the golden crown.'

He smiled and got up. 'I must go home,' he said, 'the sun is setting.' But he remained standing and looking at the globe with unheeding eyes. 'Funny,' he added, 'how we talk sometimes – as if we were in a play. . . . I must go home, the sun is setting. . . .'

When he was seated in the boat and had dipped the oars into the water, he turned round once more saying: 'By the way, he appeared to me last night, the meditating one – towards twilight. It was exactly as I read it to you. Only I did not come into the room, but was playing the piano. Chopin, Sonata in B minor, quite a suitable piece. While I was playing the second movement I looked up once, and in that moment he put himself together. I cannot express it differently. He put himself together, as it were, out of his own elements, very transient elements, of course. But otherwise everything was as it should be, even the stroke of the clock – and then he "evaporated like a liquid on the floor".'

He looked at Thomas with his mocking and yet melancholy eyes. 'And I thought I knew that the Lord had looked at me,' he concluded. 'But I didn't know for certain, Orla, do you understand? We people nowadays know so few things for certain.'

Then the first stroke of the oar carried the boat away from the landing-stage.

'Do stay here, Graf,' said Thomas. 'Stay with me over night!' he went to the end of the landing-stage and raised his hand, as if to hold back the departing Graf.

But the Graf only shook his head. With each stroke of the oars, the boat shot out farther into the lake, and the thin, smiling face became more and more indistinct.

'Do you believe, Bildermann, that death can send a warning?' Thomas asked in the evening.

Bildermann looked at him rather worried. 'We had better keep to oar and compass, captain,' he replied.

Thomas slept deep and did not dream, but when the sun had risen, he put his bicycle into the boat and said that he had to go and see the Graf.

It took him two hours, for he got off his bicycle several times to smoke a pipe and to consider whether it was not better to go home again. He was not sure whether he was doing the wisest thing. When he arrived, they had already carried the dead body of the Graf from the home farm into the house and had put the bier down in the passage with the masks. They had laid a cloth over his face and were waiting for the owner of the estate and the police from the district town. The old valet stood with a blanched face at one of the lofty windows through which came the green light from the forest. He knew that the Graf would have expected self-control and silence even from his subordinates. But the bailiff of the home farm sat on one of the low chests with a troubled face and his hands combed through his thick hair incessantly, while he was murmuring that it was not his fault, that by God he was not to blame for the death of the young Graf.

Thomas gently lifted the cloth from the face of the dead man. He was not disfigured and not changed. His eyes were closed and Thomas thought he knew that the same expression of melancholy mockery was under the lids as it was round the thin, colourless lips. The hair at the parting was damp with blood that had not yet clotted. The wound must be there.

He raised his eyes and looked along the grey wall with the masks. The old Gräfin might well be satisfied, her son did not look very different from these. He was in harmony with them. He had tried his best.

He put the cloth again over the face and made a sign to the bailiff and the valet to follow him. When they left the passage, he saw that blossoming twigs of jasmine stood in the blue vase. It was an early summer that year.

Outside he heard how it had all happened. That night the farm workers had been at the village inn, and in the morning they had refused to go into the meadows with the mowing machines, to milk the cows, to feed the horses, and so on. Probably someone from the town had made a speech, for they used jargon which was not in common use on the farm. It was all summed up in the sentence that they were not in a mood today to work for 'reactionary employers'. They did not say so in a serious or stupid way, as at other times, but in an impudent and menacing way, and the under-cowman had been the ringleader.

The bailiff did not know what to do and had gone to the Graf, because his was the nearest house. The Graf had been walking up and down in his garden and had only nodded, as if another messenger had already told him about it. But, he, the bailiff, had been the first. 'So soon?' asked the Graf. Yes, the bailiff would take his oath that the Graf had said that, and then he had looked at him for some time. It had been a peculiar look, but he had often thought that the young Graf sometimes seemed to be hidden behind a cloud.

Then they had walked to the farm together without any hurry, and he had asked the Graf whether he had a weapon on him. But the Graf had answered smiling: 'You don't need a weapon on a trip like this.' Nor had he worn a hat; he had just gone along with him as he had been in the garden.

In the yard the men had been standing in front of the stable door smoking cigarettes. They had not taken off their caps. The Graf had pushed the foremost aside with his elbow, for he had his hands in the pockets of his jacket, and had gone up to one of the ploughmen who looked past him grinning. He, the bailiff, had remained outside the circle.

Everything had happened as quickly as in a dream. The Graf had looked at the ploughman, and in his low, but very distinct voice had only said: 'And you, you rascal, don't you even button your tunic, when you start a revolution?'

The man had quickly seized the top button of his tunic – and in that very moment the under-cowman had dealt the blow. He had been standing behind the Graf, hidden among the others and had had an iron bar in his hand. The Graf was not wearing a cap, and so the blow had struck him with full force. He fell without a sound – head foremost, holding his hand before his face. They had lifted him, but there had been no longer any life in him – he was dead. The homicide had been arrested, and the men had obeyed without a word.

Thomas asked: 'Is there no mistake possible, did the Graf really exclaim: 'So soon?'

'No, no mistake, as I hope to be saved.'

Thomas looked at the old valet and found that his gently supplicating eyes were fixed on him. He nodded almost imperceptibly and then went out to his bicycle. At the gate he exchanged a few words with the Graf's cousin, whom he had met at the wolf hunt, a tall, sober man, and later heard him speaking angrily to the bailiff.

Thomas went down to the river to wait for the inquest. It was better to make his statement here than to wait and be summoned to the town.

The water flowed gently at his feet, and the scent of roses wafted over the river; a little downstream the nightingales were singing. All was as it had always been. But he, the Graf, in whom all this beauty had found a noble reflection as in a precious mirror, had passed away; yet it did not disturb the harmony of all that he had created. Neither the wheels nor the pendulum stopped. The curtain had dropped, but before it dropped a light had flared up through a chink from the abyss, a sudden pale light dying so fast that one could only make out something dark: clouds or gorges, or an empty, icy sea.

'I love it all, even with a heavy heart.'

Thomas saw the Graf standing on the island, the slim figure with bent shoulders looking over the water to where he might have seen the old gods with their amber crowns. He had not taken a gun. He had not been afraid.

When the car from the district town arrived, Thomas made his statement. He confirmed that the bailiff had described the events to him in the same words, and that the Graf had been with him on the island yesterday. No, there was no question of threats.

The district doctor stated that the Graf's skull was so unusually thin that one might have killed him with a ruler. 'Quite an abnormal case,' he said, deeply worried.

'The man with the bar may not have known that,' remarked Thomas.

'Certainly not, certainly not.'

Then Thomas was dismissed. He asked to be informed about the funeral arrangements and then he went. The valet accompanied him to the door. 'He had seen him,' said Thomas in a low voice. 'The evening before yesterday.'

The valet nodded and made the sign of the cross. When the Graf was a child, how often he had sat with him on his knee.

Thomas drove with the general to the funeral. The dead man was lying in state in the castle hall. It was as large as a church. Two officers in the white uniform previously worn by their regiment guarded the coffin. There was an interval before the old Gräfin slowly descended the central staircase to the hall. She came all alone, white-haired, and her stony face looked bloodless. Thomas had been told that she had celebrated her eightieth birthday the previous winter.

She remained standing at the head of the coffin, supporting herself on her stick, and refused the armchair which was pushed towards her. Her bright eyes looked round the room, then she nodded to the clergyman. It was an abrupt, almost haughty movement, and it seemed to Thomas as if it frightened him. He had come from the capital and was the chief dignitary of the district, a stout, comfortable-looking man, and when he began to speak, his voice sounded far too loud in the silent hall.

It was easy to see that he had taken pains, but Thomas gave him black looks. One had to speak in a different way about the dead Graf, even if one had not lost an arm in the war. The Gräfin looked past him through the wide-open door, before which the village children were standing. She supported herself on her stick with both her hands, and not a feature in her face moved. She looked like one of the masks in the grey corridor of the Graf's house not yet singled out by death, but already in the province, submitting to a blind force with a proud indifference, without uttering a word. Only when the clergyman came to the main part of his address saying that here the last of six sons had died for his country and the law, and that his mother at the age of three score and ten, the age of the psalmist, must now stand beside the coffin–like a second Niobe of the Greek myth–only then did the Gräfin knock with her stick on the floor, saying loudly and distinctly without looking at him: 'Do not talk nonsense.'

The clergyman faltered and stopped short, and a movement went through the hall. But then he regained his poise, bowed his head, forgiving even this to her sorrow, and then almost at once brought his address to a close.

There were no more speeches; only the general said

farewell in the name of the army to the soldier, Natango Pernein, in front of the family vault in the park. His voice was clear and sharp as on the parade ground, and his eyes under his white brows stared menacingly at the unmoved faces of the two officers. The Gräfin nodded to him.

When Thomas was waiting for the car at the general's side, the Graf's cousin asked him to go and see the old Gräfin. She wished to have a few words with him.

Above, in the large room with the oval pictures, the Gräfin sat at the window looking out on the park. She pointed to an easy chair opposite her and gazed at Thomas in silence. From near at hand he saw the delicate wrinkles in her rigid face and her big, burning eyes. There were no dreams behind those eyes as there had been behind those of the young Graf, but they were so bright that it seemed that nothing close by was reflected in them–only an empty distance, a white autumn sky perhaps without a single cloud and full of light.

'He despised mankind,' she began at last, 'and it pained him that he must despise them. But he liked to talk of you. Tell me how it was, when he was with you for the last time.'

Thomas did not think of concealing anything from those eyes.

'"I must go home . . . the sun is setting . . .",' she repeated. 'Yes, he despised even death. . . . He was different from the others–quite different. His heart was heavy from birth onwards. He needed more courage to live through each day than most people need for all their lives . . . my Benjamin. . . .'

'He loved much, Frau Gräfin.'

'Yes, I know. He also loved me. He was the only one who loved me, even when he smiled at me. The others were only afraid of me. He might have hated me, for he inherited his heavy heart from me. He might have hated me, as if I had infected him with leprosy. But he loved me. He loved all that was hopeless and he shuddered at our ignoble times; at times which no longer know the sword–only the cudgel. And he was felled by a cudgel. I have only lived so long that he might have somebody with whom he could smile. Now I need not live any longer. Niobe, as that man said. It is a pity that Natango did not hear it. It would have amused him. . . . Do you believe that he saw "him"?'

'Of course,' said Thomas.

'He has never appeared to any woman,' she said. 'It is a pity. . . .'

Then she pressed his hand and begged him to go. 'He was right to speak to you. He was always right. Live in peace and die bravely!'

He left the room quietly. As he shut the door, he saw her sitting upright in her armchair with closed eyes. This death gave Thomas much to think about. He felt as if a wall of his house had crashed down overnight with all the pictures that had been hanging there, and if he did not pay attention it might happen one night that while walking towards where that wall had been he might fall into a bottomless abyss. He took good care of himself, and Bildermann took even more care of his master.

Thomas mourned for the young Graf deeply. It was as if a whole generation had sunk down with him. He felt a sharp pain whenever he realised how irretrievable a living human being is. At the funeral the stout clergyman had said that God would know why such a thing had happened. Certainly He had know it of the Flood, too, and of the Thirty Years' War. 'Do not talk nonsense!' How grand she had been standing there, absolutely detached–like a queen among gossiping market women. Blood was the one thing unquestionable and immortal.

The Graf had been killed just as Thomas might have been killed. He had not carried a weapon and had not hesitated. Death had sent for him, even if only in the shape of the flustered bailiff–and he had obeyed the summons without a cap, without a coat, without a weapon. The open tunic had offended him, the lack of bearing, the untidiness in the decisive moment.

But what about the grey man who appeared before the fire? All was twilight there. Would the Graf have seen him, if he had known nothing about him? If the diary of his ancestor had not existed? There was no answer to this question; nature veiled herself and was silent.

A week later Thomas was summoned by a solicitor in the district town. He learned that the deceased Graf had put down in his will, that he, Thomas von Orla, was to inherit his house and his garden and everything in them. From the interests of a considerable fortune the maintenance of the Graf's property was to be paid for as well as the future wages of all the domestic staff–to whom special legacies were made. After the death of Thomas von Orla the whole was to revert to the owner of the estate. The Gräfin Pernein was entitled to dispose of a number of specified objects and was asked not to contest this will. During her lifetime a number of rooms had to be reserved for her as well as a number of explicit prerogatives. The agreement of the Gräfin was already in the solicitor's possession together with the request that she begged Thomas von Orla to respect and honour this last will in all points.

Thomas asked the date of the will. He was shown the original, and he saw that it had been written on the evening of the apparition.

He agreed to accept the inheritance. He paid a visit to the owner of the estate, found him reserved, but not unkindly, and they talked about matters which resulted from their having become neighbours. Then Thomas sat with the valet on the terrace above the garden. He told him that he would probably live here only a few weeks in winter to read and work. In between he would be a rare guest. Everything was to remain as it always had been, and he expected them to keep the house and the garden as if the Graf might return any day.

Then he asked to be led once more through all the rooms, and he paused for some time at the microscopes, at the physical instruments, in the small chemical laboratory. 'There is an inventory of all the things,' said the valet, 'as well as a catalogue of the library.'

The late Graf had been so methodical in everything; and to be allowed to remain here, was the best the valet could wish for his old age.

Thomas took the catalogue, a thick volume, and put it in his haversack, then he sent for the gardener and maids. He repeated what he had already said to the valet and left it to them to leave his service, should they think it too lonely here. But they all decided to stay on, and the gardener asked Herr von Orla to have a look at the garden now and again. It would be sad if the flowers faded away without giving pleasure to anybody. Besides, he said, he would like to come to the island in autumn and plant new perennials. The Graf had already spoken about it.

In the grey corridor, when Thomas looked once more at the masks, the old valet summoned up his courage. 'Will you please excuse me, captain,' he said, 'that I have not spoken about a certain matter before. I knew it the same evening. I came into the room to draw the blinds when the Graf sat the grand piano. Then he said: "It is time, Friedrich," and made a gesture with his hand. In that moment I knew what he meant. The Lord had looked at him. But he only smiled.'

Thomas stayed for a little while looking at the yellow roses in the blue vase. 'Are we going to smile, too, Friedrich?' he asked.

CHAPTER THIRTEEN

THE CHILD was home again, but she was no longer a child. They both had a shock when she got out of the boat and came up the shore. She had grown and her hair was bound up at the nape of her neck. She did not wear one of her old frocks, for these had become too short. She still walked straight and bowed her head when she greeted them as she used to do, but one could see that she had been 'in the house of the king'.

They received her a little depressed, and Bildermann took off his cap, but she looked from the one to the other, put her left hand slowly on her old necklace of wooden beads and said: 'But don't you love me any more?' And with the familiar movement and the sound of her voice which had become a little deeper, the two years vanished, and life knotted the thread again where the old maid of honour had broken it. The smoke of the potato fire seemed still to be hanging over the island, together with the red gleam of the rowan berries in the grey air: the good, old times without loneliness, violence and death – and Bildermann waved his cap with the well-pressed ribbons now becoming more and more faded and said: 'Little lady, an old spell descends on Friedrich Wilhelm Bildermann.'

They led her into the house, the two who had lived on the ocean, and there were no more ghosts in the room, where Gloria had looked at the quiet globe, where the voice had come through the window, where they had seen the glow of the fire, and where the dead Graf had said that the sun was setting. The model of the island stood on the cabinet with the masks, and the golden star was still glittering on the thin flag mast. The child put her left hand on the circle of the equator and looking at it, and then at the two men, only said: 'Oh, Thomas. . . .' And it did not sound very different from how it had sounded four years before when he had told her a story. Not very different, but the maid of honour would have detected the difference.

They drank their coffee in front of the house, and they both noticed that she took the coffee pot from Bildermann's hands and filled the cups. The air was as grey and calm as it had been when she was here for the last time; the wild pear tree on the shore glowed, and the crested grebes called from the bay. She told them about the two years as gravely as an earnest student. Yes, she could do her shopping and get into a tram on the right side. She could drive a car and could dance all the old and some new dances. She could drop a court curtesy and talk in three languages. She had seen foreign countries and had learned there that victory is not always the crown of war. Besides she had seen some things which were not included in her timetable: poverty of body and soul, guilt and atonement, furrow and plough. She had looked at everything with her calm eyes and kept it in her memory. Not everything that Bergengruen had said was right, but of what he had implied in those hours when she had 'side-tracked' him, there was little to erase.

So the 'Prussian dream'–as the Graf called it–was not something to laugh at. It was surprising, thought Thomas, how the blood of these ancient families still kept on flowing in its old course.

She went with him round the island and admired everything they had accomplished. But under the oaks she suddenly seized his left hand with both hers and said in an almost imploring voice: 'You aren't going to drive me away from here, Thomas, are you?'

He caressed her hands with his free hand. 'Dear child,' he said, 'don't you know how we have been waiting for you?'

She breathed deeply several times, her eyes fixed on his. 'You don't know how I have been longing,' was all she said. 'Nobody knows.'

'But wasn't it good to learn what is going on in the world and get to know things which you couldn't learn at home?'

'Good? Probably useful, but not good. Most of the Platens have been restless and their ways have led from the Beresina to the Oranje River.' But what her ancestors probably did not feel, she felt most passionately, namely, that happiness for her lay only on the shores of this lake.

'And what does it look like, this happiness?'

'Oh, Thomas,' she said, 'I saw at once that you have changed.'

'I have grown old, Marianne.'

'No, not old, that's not true. But you look as if you don't believe in happiness any more.'

He shook his head. 'The reason, Marianne, is that we are not seventeen any more. The happiness in which we believe is serious and silent. Ten years ago it looked different, nay, even two years ago it had a blue ribbon round its wrist. A very thin ribbon, but it was blue.'

'And now?'

'Now it's gone. Now we must do without ribbons. But happiness still exists. You know the men on the ocean don't need much.'

'What do they need, Thomas?'

'Peace, Marianne, and a happy heart.'

She meditated for a while with knitted brows. They were sitting on a bench which Thomas had put up under the oaks. Above them the jays whistled softly among the dry leaves, and now and again a brown, shining acorn dropped down on to the moss.

'You don't pray at night yet?' she asked at last in a low voice.

'No.'

'We pray to God for what you said, Grandfather and I. Who will give you what you need?'

He made a wide gesture with his hand over the lake and the woods. 'They will,' he said. 'They and my books and the stars and your voice when we hear it on the shore.'

She had folded her hands in her lap and looked down upon them. 'Why didn't you move into the house which he gave you?' she asked at last.

'We don't need property,' he replied. 'What we need is work, poverty and a little time. And we still think that we must care a little for you.'

'And Joachim?'

'Oh, Joachim is on his way to the West Indies and thinks that we are two funny men whose mast has broken and who are now creeping along towards their goal behind the victors.'

'Oh, Thomas, why are you so lonely?'

'I will tell you, Marianne, because I belong to another generation, not only the generation before the war, but a much earlier one from the time of the monks. Some of the Orlas were abbots long, long ago, and sometimes the blood preserves such tendencies for a long time.'

'But they didn't receive girls in their cells.'

He smiled. 'They may have received many things that were invisible – which they alone saw.'

'But they prayed, Thomas.'

'I wonder, if you know, little Marianne, what I think when I see Sirius through my telescope?'

She asked him to take her to the two graves and he rowed her over the lake. The barn was already rebuilt, but the forester's door was locked. It seemed to Thomas as if the place still smelt of smoke.

'I went to see her,' she whispered, standing by the graves. 'Just before she came here. I wanted to tell her how lonely you are.'

'I know; she told me.'

'She was very unhappy, Thomas.'

'Yes, she didn't catch up. She was running and running, but she didn't catch up. I was too quiet and too slow for her; I ought not to have married her.'

Marianne did not speak any more and he rowed her to the shore of the park. Only when they reached the wooded point did she speak: 'Do you think that it is true what Aunt Gabriele said, that I must marry, whether I want to or not?'

'Because you are the last?'

'Yes.'

'Even without that you will marry,' he said, smiling. 'And not only so that no stranger should drive us from the island.'

'If I were a Catholic, I would become a nun,' she replied. 'I have heard that in old times the daughters of noble families sometimes became nuns, didn't they?'

'Yes, but not when there were no sons. Also the Orlas were only allowed to become abbots when they had brothers. You mustn't only think of God, but also of your grandfather and your inheritance.'

'I'm not thinking of God,' she said, turning away her face.

Some weeks went by before it seemed to them all that life had gone back to the old way. However, she was no longer the child that rode over the fields for an hour with the general. She had become 'the agricultural student'. She wanted to learn, nothing but learn. Within the next four years, when she would be of age, she wanted to know how 'to manage a farm'. The general had listened to her, at first, a little amused, but then seriously and attentively, and at last he had made out a timetable in which everything that filled the days and the seasons, from the rearing of chickens to book-keeping, found a place.

When after the catch in Advent Thomas came with the year's account to the general, the latter looked it through, as he always had done, but then he said that he must take it to the child. Fishery was down on her timetable too. Thomas had to see how he could get on with the new, young mistress.

Next to the general's study, Marianne had furnished a small room for herself with a large table covered with seed-grain, farming books, maps and agricultural catalogues. Sometimes she wore a white overall here, at which nobody smiled, and at which the peasant women looked full of awe, as if their mistress had become 'a doctor or a chemist'.

Thomas bowed and asked to be allowed to submit the year's account to Madam.

She raised her eyebrows a little, took the sheets out of his hand in silence, pointed to a chair and became engrossed in the columns of figures without saying a word, supporting her head in both her hands.

'In the last week of August there is a remarkable decline in the catch,' she said eventually. 'What is the reason for it?'

'In the last week of August Miss Marianne von Platen wrote to the island that she would come home in four weeks, and both fishermen were unable after that letter to accomplish their work with their usual devotion to duty.'

'Fisherman Thomas von Orla,' said Marianne, smiling, 'you promised to serve your employer faithfully at all times.'

'That's just the reason,' he replied. Then he went round to her and explained the columns and figures. He added that the purchasing power of the people was dwindling from day to day, and that one ought to consider whether it was not advisable to reduce the wages of the fishermen. 'We are not starving and the estate needs every penny.'

She leant her cheek against his arm which was resting on the table and listened with absent-minded eyes. 'Oh, Thomas,' she said, 'when one day all this belongs to me, I shall give you nothing but a thin blue ribbon instead of wages, so that you can see it streaming again. . . .'

'Little Marianne,' he said after a while, drawing himself up slowly, 'you must not dream in a white overall.'

She nodded and bent again over the sheets of paper.

When on the island he clipped them together in order to put them into the file with the others, he saw that at the bottom of the last sheet some figures had been blotted out, and the smooth paper had become crinkly there. He looked at it for a while before he smoothed it with his hand and closed the file slowly. He felt as if some time would still have to pass before he could say of himself that he had found his peace.

They were invited to the castle for Christmas Eve. 'For two years we celebrated Christmas like ghosts,' said the general. 'Now I would like to raise my glass not only to dead or absent ones. The man with the scythe has been busy with us for two years, but it is an old experience that in the long run he does not like to walk in his own footprints. We will pour wine into them, and thus try to reconcile him.'

Thomas would have preferred to remain alone, but the

general had grown old in these two years, and the child had black rings round her eyes, as if even the white overall was sometimes too heavy for her shoulders. So he said that he would be pleased to come.

In the long evenings, they had built a model of the cruiser on which they had fought in the last year of the war. Thomas was often discouraged with the work, especially as all its parts were made of metal, but Bildermann had said that honour was honour, and so they had finished it.

The hulk was made of grey sheet-iron and was nearly a fathom long. The long barrels of the guns projected from the glimmering turrets menacingly; they could be moved up and down and wheeled round, and if you lifted a plate of the deck and lit a special tinder, thick white smoke came out of the funnels. The war flag was hoisted and a tiny blue figure stood on the bridge with a small brass telescope held to its eye. It was a work of art, shining and sparkling, and though it seemed a toy, there was deadly earnestness behind it.

They put the model on a sledge and drew it cautiously over the ice. Then Bildermann carried it wrapped up like a frozen child into the giant's room. There he whispered into Johann's ear that this was an invention of his master, a new construction of a torpedo, and if he pulled the string he would be able to collect the fragments of the castle and his own bones among the stars. 'You always bring some rubbish,' said Johann disapprovingly, but he then lifted one of the floorboards under his bed and presented Bildermann with a flat, four-cornered bottle. 'Savings account,' he said mildly.

Meanwhile Marianne decorated the big tree in the hall and Thomas handed her the candles and the tinsel. The general's sister had arrived and had brought with her a young nobleman with a long name, an orphaned cousin remotely related, who had just come of age and had inherited an immense fortune. He looked through his monocle somewhat surprised at the country and the people but otherwise he was serious and modest and like to avoid the menacing eyes of the general. 'They are rather far to the East here, *chère tante*,' he said to the lady-in-waiting, 'they might well have a fancy to tie me up to the muzzle of one of their guns.' But Fräulein Gabriele blew the smoke of her cigar impatiently over her game of patience which would not work out, and asked him kindly to be as quiet as Daniel in the lions' den. On Christmas morning the general had told her that there were only ice flowers in their part of the country. The young cousin would have liked to decorate the tree with Marianne, but she had replied coolly that the hall door would only be opened when the presents were given.

The big house was as quiet as the grave and Thomas sat by the fire and watched Marianne as she hung the silver stars among the branches.

Outside snow was falling, evening was drawing near, and he thought of his grey roof on the island and of the graves which they had dug in these two years. Sometimes he did not know whether it was really worth while.

Every year the Child in the crib came again but the dead did not come alive, and no tear that had been shed was unshed. Everything might have been arranged a little more comfortably on this earth, and the old Gräfin might have kept one of her six sons without disturbing the heavenly order. And might death not as well have seized this child that was fastening the stars among the branches? Where was any security except in the second that one lived? And while one enjoyed it, might not the bow string twang unnoticed and let the arrow fly which would cut the next second to pieces?

Only he who loved nothing was secure from pain; but he who did not love was dead.

Marianne had finished her work and sat down on the arm of his chair, her hands folded in her lap. It was already so dark that you could imagine that behind the tinsel of the Christmas tree the forest began. In front of one of the labourer's cottages the high-pitched voice of a child rose into the evening air – the song grew fainter and fainter, as if the snow were covering it. The flame in the fireplace burnt bluish along a heavy birch log.

Thomas was leaning his forehead on Marianne's arm. It was time to get up and to announce to the people in the house that all was ready, but this moment would never return. When he got up, he would be old, very old, like the man in the fairy tale who had been under the earth. Then nothing would be left to him but the stars and the stones, the fish and the flowers. There was a narrow frontier, where man had to leave behind play and dreams, so that he could step out to untrodden ground where no companionship was permitted, where the air was clear and cold as over a glacier, and where those things were created which lasted longer than the name of man. Loneliness was more than a poetical word. It was a decision, and it did not come again if once it had been declined.

'It is time,' he said, and got up. Marianne once more stroked his forehead lightly with the palm of her hand and obediently got up too. For the first time it was not the gesture of a child, and he knew that she was grown up now. Neither of them would forget this Christmas Eve.

It took a long time to give out the presents to the children who had come from all over the estate. The general went from table to table looking at all the little hands with his menacing eyes. 'Be obedient . . . . always do your duty . . .

love your family!' he rapped out, as if he were on the parade ground. The farmhands clicked their heels merrily and the maids kissed his hands.

The grey cruiser supported by two wooden struts lay on the blue tablecloth, and Bildermann made the funnels send out smoke. The general sat in front of it, his hands folded over his stick, and asked now and again if he might swivel the gun turrets. The child in her long frock, reaching to her feet, stood at his side and saw how the white clouds were wafted among the branches of the tree. A thread of tinsel slowly floated over the fighting mast. From time to time Gabriele von Platen looked attentively at Thomas's face, and eventually she asked whether the man on the bridge was himself.

'No,' replied Thomas, 'that's the signaller, Bildermann.'

'But there are no ribbons to his cap.'

'No, that is true, time has eaten them away, time is more powerful than streaming ribbons.'

The young cousin said that he had not known that Marianne liked such warlike toys. 'How should you have known it,' she asked, 'as you are here for the first time? Besides it is something much more than a toy to all of us.'

After the Christmas dinner to which all the domestic staff had been invited, Marianne drew Thomas aside and asked him whether they could not take the rich cousin out on the lake and drown him there.

Thomas smiled. 'We old people must not be bloodthirsty,' he replied. 'Those who won't join in the game needn't be drowned, need they? One day there will come a time when you will jump after him to save him – though not exactly this one.'

She looked straight into his eyes. 'Never, Thomas,' she said. He was still smiling.

'Let's go to Aunt Mary,' he begged. 'The tears are very

close under her eyelids tonight, for her "handsome husband" never comes back any more.'

They did not know what it was that was special about this evening, but they felt as if the dark walls had never stood so safe and unshakeable around them. Perhaps it was only because the child in her long frock walked among them, and they saw that a new generation had grown up with a new shield which she raised against the powers of evil. Perhaps it was only because Johann was wearing the bearskin cap which Marianne had given him. Though there was no wind, he had fastened the straps under his chin, and he looked so tall now that *chère tante* said he could collect the shoes in the morning from the guest rooms on the first floor without going upstairs. Perhaps it was only because Bildermann sat near the cruiser singing that song from faraway parts . . . 'Rolling home, my boys, rolling home' . . . and the wise man from the east hummed the second part instead of his melancholy wife, who now no longer wore her black clothes and certainly did not sing any more.

Thomas thought he knew why this hour seemed to be so bright and safe: because they were so many, and when they stretched out their hands, they could form a chain as in a children's game. No one had any foreboding that a voice would call out of the night, nor that the grey man would sit himself down before the fire to meditate. They only visited the lonely ones whether they were awake or asleep. Only the lonely man was given over to them whose outstretched hands found nothing but empty space. But then only he heard those last questions, which were rolled up to him like a black ball. They sang as children sing in the dark, and even though Christ was born this night, he could not have prevented Death from opening the doors, or splitting asunder the hall in order to beckon to one of them. A child was a child, even if he bore a halo on his brow, and it had happened often enough, and not only through the hand of Herod in the land of Bethlehem, that God had pushed the children aside to seize him whom he wished to have.

Thomas looked at them as in a sorrowful dream. Only a few hours ago he had been sitting in his armchair, and he had known that he would get up an old man. Many will feel like this after a serious illness, after a loss or a sudden fall from safety into a bottomless abyss. But it had fallen on him in the twilight as the hoar frost comes at dawn, when the mist rises and the woods are suddenly grey and silvery, and the crimson sun shines on a different world.

He might have kept his young manhood, or whatever it might be called. He need only stretch out his hand. But he had been warned once already. He knew that happiness was not the ultimate aim in life, and that he who seizes the last but one has to renounce the very last. He who stretches out his hand after happiness is like a player in that game of New Year's Eve, when the guests pour drops of molten lead into water and a little later pick out the shapes it has formed from the covered bowl – they may draw out death, or a cradle or money. But nobody could grasp the lot. Only he who did not take part in the game, might win all, and even he was not sure of success. As for himself, Thomas knew that he was grasping the rail of a bridge, but he did not know whether the bridge would hold. He had to collect his last weapons and march forward. He had no longer any illusions. The last face, the face of the ultimate, was all that he would meet now.

'To the Fatherland and those who stand up for it, Orla,' said the general, raising his glass.

'Yes, general.'

He drank the red wine, but he knew that even they were not the last. The last of all no longer had any name.

On Christmas Day towards the evening Thomas was already sitting near the fireplace, where the grey man used to appear. He had just taken his skis and had given Bildermann a few lines for the child. If everything went as he had planned, he intended to stay at the Graf's house until well into February. He would use his time well. In the library on the large table he had put many volumes of a comparative history of religion, a textbook on biology, an introduction into chemistry and a work on the history of evolution.

He did not know whether the choice was right, but it seemed to him as if the roots of all human restlessness might lie here. Besides he was old enough not to expect to get any answers from his reading. He only wanted to put a certain system into his queries and then to approach his goal from different points of the compass. Bildermann would probably have said that he wanted 'to tackle the whole show'. Merely looking through the catalogue of the great library he had realised the depth of his ignorance, and of how many works he knew nothing but the titles.

If he were granted another ten or twenty years, he might make up for some of it. It seemed to him that human thought had travelled too quickly, and the individual could only understand a fragment of the whole. Some time in a far future he would read only one single page out of the great book, the page he had chosen for himself, and nobody would be able to read the whole book. The Faust of the future would despair from the very beginning.

The house was as quiet as the grave and at first he had a fancy that he had no right to sit here. The Graf's presence was still everywhere, an echo of his voice, an afterglow of his eyes. He would always be present in this house, but he had willed that Thomas should live here for a time. He had known that Thomas would continue on his way and consider work the only redemption of mankind, and the Graf had only wished to make this way easier or more complete or perhaps only more gaily coloured. The house was as silent as the island, probably more so, and the late Graf had known that he who wished to gain a happy heart might do so even at the bottom of a well.

Thomas said that he did not need anything more and had dismissed the valet. He was as lonely as the general who raised his glass to 'the veterans of the country'. The quiet people came to see him, too, but no angel led them by the hand. They lived in his memory, and when his memory was extinguished, the quiet people would be extinguished also. Then they would live on in the thoughts of others: in Joachim's or Bildermann's or Marianne's, and when those failed also, they would become quite homeless. They were living as on a raft that was breaking up. At last there would be only one plank left, and then that, too, would sink down into the ocean.

The pendulum of the clock on the mantelpiece went hurrying through the quiet of the house, and every quarter of an hour the little hammer struck a bell. It was a bright silvery sound, which fell into the silence without an echo. Friedrich had put a small fir tree on the table between the windows and had decorated it with tinsel and candles. It stood there like a gift offered to the dead, it was only there in case the Graf or the grey man should come to sit down at the fire. Only a woman could break the spell of this house, Thomas thought. A woman and children who would run over the carpets, and send the bright sound of laughter rippling over the masks in the grey corridor. But the Perneins had had no mind to marry. The roof of the house had become crooked and shaky, and meditation had not given them a happy heart. They had not worked and had not loved. They had not borne fruit, and thus at the end of their lives only the grey man had appeared who sat meditating in front of the fire and evaporated like a liquid from the floor.

Thomas got up and went once more through all the rooms. The apparatus and retorts were shining; the microscopes were covered, but the great rows of books stood there waiting and awake. No, he would not give himself to love either, but to work, and there was also love in work. It was the love for the mystery which barred the clear way, and the greater love for the clear way itself which only the feet of man could tread upon. Even if the deed, the great, unique deed, were denied him, which would wake men and peoples from their lethargy, it would not matter. But he would be able to observe, to look into the confusion of the times and to see the needle which pointed, quivering, to the eternal poles.

Thomas shut himself in his web for more than two months, longer then he had originally intended. It fascinated him, and what he saw for instance under the lenses of the microscope was even more wonderful than he had imagined. In the morning he made all sorts of experiments, and in the afternoons and evenings he read. Before twilight fell, he went on his skis for an hour through the woods and over the vast plains. He wrote no letters and he did not dream, only sometimes on clear nights he looked at the stars through the telescope.

Slowly working from the circumference he began to realise the miracle of creation. That is what he called it, and the name gained greater and greater importance for him. But he did not confound it with the name man had given to the miracle. No demons and no gods penetrated into the bright circle below the lens. He did not interpret the incomprehensible, he did not name it, he only revered it. Slowly he learned what appeared to him to be the greatest achievement:

namely, to look upon the mighty workings of nature, upon the macrocosmos as purposeless. Purposes dimmed the light and tangled up the lines. And the last face still stood there behind everything, but it bore neither human nor divine features; it was beyond space and time, and was beyond any moral glorification. It was different from the *Erdgeist*, and it could not be conjured up. It would probably punish by annihilation.

Slowly he was filled with a deep and quiet happiness. Granted good health, all he needed was time. The span of the circle was infinite, even more infinite than the ecliptic, and effort and hard work were necessary to get from one point to the next. Nor did he possess the gift of intuition that could leap over whole stages. Diligence, patience and reverence were all he had. He knew already that he would never behold the ultimate, but perhaps he could divine it. And while he was filled with awe, he would become like the stones at the bottom of the lake. When he knew the law, he would be satisfied. He would never ask to have his clock wound up once more, never beg for time to penetrate further into a beyond. He knew that the orbits of the stars were not wound up either. He was willing to submit and be obedient. He did not want to rebel, and faith was rebellion. There should be no end, and God was there to see that there was no end. Reason cried out for Him, because it did not want to learn to bow down.

But he wished to learn it, and he knew already several things with which he could prove it.

Marianne came once or twice to see him with Frau von Sperber. He saw that she worried about him, and that at first she looked at the masks and idols with a slight shudder. But then he led her into the laboratory to the microscope and told her a little about his work. No, the grey man who sat down at the fire would not appear to him. The family of the Orlas was not old enough for that, besides they had worked too hard in their lives. As they parted the child half smiled: 'Don't forget that we over there are still alive, Thomas,' she said.

No, he promised not to forget. He would emerge again with the first storms of the equinox, like Faust at Easter, he would remember that he had hands to work with and that men needed bread.

'But I suppose you will not hear the Easter bells,' whispered the child.

'I am sure I shall hear them,' Thomas replied, 'perhaps not like Faust. But then I shall not grasp the dark vial either. There is compensation in every man's life.'

In the first days of March the ice broke and Thomas returned to the island. At first he did not know exactly whether he was on leave or on the ocean again, but already the first evening after they had overhauled the boats and dug up a new piece of land for the garden, when his arms and his back ached before the fire, he knew that he was at home, and that the scales were slowly moving to equilibrium again.

The training ship was on its homeward voyage, and Joachim wrote that he would come at Easter and asked whether he might bring along a friend and for that reason live at the castle. During the day, naturally, he would be on the island.

'The time of the reed huts is past, Bildermann, now comes the time of the palaces.'

'First before the mast, then on the bridge, captain,' replied Bildermann. 'Such is life. Only veterans take the sun, where they can get it.'

Thomas did not like to ask the general a favour, but Marianne said that her grandfather always liked to see young men who were in the forces and especially those who were just under the rank of naval commander.

'Young men are not very lucky with you,' said Thomas smiling.

'My standards are too old probably,' she replied.

She was right. The general was pleased. After the cousin had left, he regarded such visitors without apprehension.

'We must help the young men,' he said to Thomas. 'They only mix with each other. It is good for them to visit old houses. The army list is not a gospel.'

But Thomas knew that 'the young men' sometimes look at each other out of the corner of their eyes and that they do not much like to learn their gospel from generals with white hair – nor from captains with fish-scales in their hair. One must be pleased with such visitors and not expect anything sentimental. The difficulties would begin when they mentioned his second book, which they probably disapproved of – though for different reasons.

It had been published before Christmas, and while this time the seamen called it 'very remarkable', the theologians took exception to almost all of it; it really seemed as if the author had changed from one profession to another, but neither was keen on having him.

This time he did not answer any letters – whether of praise or blame. In the winter months over microscopes and retorts he had learned that it was of no concern whether one knew who had made the blossom of a dahlia. The namelessness of the creator reigned in creation. He who wrote for the present time might sign with his present name. But he who had subordinated himself looked upon himself as a wave on a river. The ancient poets had not signed the parchments with their names either. They knew that their work would outlast them. There was no vanity in the cosmos.

One day after the ice had melted a man arrived in a boat. He said that he came from a newspaper with a worldwide reputation and many of its readers wished to know a little more of a man who had written two rather remarkable books and who, besides, was practising such a peculiar trade.

He was rather a young man with quick movements and inquisitive eyes, and he carried a strange apparatus in his hands which he raised before his face like a small machine gun. But Thomas asked him to put it down. He had earned this island just as much as Robinson Crusoe had earned his, and though he wrote books, nobody had the least right to know what he himself or his house looked like. Otherwise they might just as well be entitled to probe into his handwriting, his horoscope, his dreams, and the colour of his eyes.

The reporter listened attentively (much too attentively – thought Bildermann) but his eyes as quick as a weasel looked round the island incessantly. Wouldn't Thomas allow him to look into the house for a minute? 'No, I will not allow it. For the simple man his house is still a sanctuary and one ought not to lift a curtain in a house where somebody has died.'

'Oh,' said the reporter, 'somebody died here? Naturally, I am sorry, but even the press will respect human feelings; it is better than its reputation.'

'Rejoice in the fine landscape on your way home, and don't look upon this trip as a failure.'

Bildermann slung the small gun over his shoulder when he accompanied the reporter down to the shore. 'If you should think of taking a snap, young man,' he said in a low but clear voice, tapping the shining butt-end of his gun, 'then you go overboard. Do you understand? Hurry up!'

The man laughed a little uneasily, but he did not take his hands from the oars, as far as Bildermann could see.

Some days later the editor sent a copy of the newspaper of 'worldwide repute'. In the illustrations they saw a snapshot with water and clouds and deep in the background a grey shadow which might be an island, a sea mine or a burning captive balloon. 'Visit to Thule' was the title. 'The man who wrote the books . . . a mysterious dead person under a roof of reeds . . . wild despiser of graphology . . . Friday with the sporting gun . . . the saints of the last day. . . .'

'Boy, oh, boy,' said Bildermann, 'if you would only come just once more. . . .'

At the castle they talked a great deal but without coming to any real conclusion about *The Doubtful Attitude of God in Sea Battles*.

Thomas waited for his visitors on the island. The carriage had been sent from the castle to the station, and the midshipman Siegfried von Marschall had seen with some amazement how the giant with the bearskin cap lifted his trunk. 'Good work!' he said. After their voyage abroad they liked to use a clipped style of speaking, which was rather difficult for the layman to understand.

The general and his grandchild stood on the stone steps. 'Young generation,' he said menancingly. 'There is much to put right. I am pleased to see my young friends.'

Before his age and the dignity of his white hair, they stood modestly, while Marianne looked at them attentively. Joachim was a little embarrassed as he remembered their last conversation.

'We are as good as engaged, you know,' he said a little off-handedly upstairs, 'and I'll have to ask you not to get in front of my keel.' And as Joachim's opinion as at school was still an absolute law to his friends, Marschall bowed, a little disappointed, and assured him that thoughts of competition were far from his mind.

'Fair play, Orla,' he said good-naturedly, unlocking his silver-fitted dressing case.

Joachim's sailing boat was lying by the shore and Marianne sailed to the island with them. Before they landed she had heard a lot about the West Indies, and she had also been told that the young men were sometimes of a different opinion from that of their captain. The sun was shining and the thrushes were singing in all the woods; Marianne looked across the lake where the forester's house lay and where the grey boats were moored. One of the high pine trees there had twice let its brown cones fall on the two graves. She wondered whether Thomas would be glad to see them, and in her mind's eye his face appeared as she had seen it in the house of the dead Graf, attentive, yet filled with the soft melancholy of those who try to unveil all mysteries. Yes, they truly must be 'old people'.

You could see that Thomas was happy. They had laid the table for luncheon in front of the house, and young Marschall declared roundly that he thought everything marvellous.

The conversation was monopolised mainly by talk of the West Indies and the somewhat antiquated service regulations on the ship, and that it was high time to have a bit of a purge of the people who were ruling the German nation. Thomas listened attentively and at last he said thoughtfully that one only ought to begin work of that sort when one was absolutely certain of one's own capabilities. Besides, the purging or cleaning out would not be all that had to be done, for an empty house had to be filled again, before you could start living there properly in a new way. We should learn slowly from the people that the hand of man is not the most insignificant tool of creation – even if it had grown a horny skin instead of writing poetry. Nobody should be respected less when he left the life of the so-called educated classes and went to the shores of a lake to dry his nets and dig potatoes. However bad it is for a people to have no poets, it is just as bad if no one wants to dig potatoes.

But the boys said that he needn't worry about that.

They walked round the island and Marianne slipped her hand through Thomas's arm. 'We must be humble now,' he said in a low voice.

She only nodded, but after a while she said: 'Oh Thomas, how terribly old we two are. . . .'

'That's why we must hand over the helm, Marianne. Perhaps new sails are better than old ones.'

They passed by the reed hut and stopped at the blackened camp fire. 'A curious whim,' said Joachim, and told Marschall of that last summer. 'I thought we might run aground somewhere one day, then I would have shown the "Old Man" how these things should be done.'

The others stood still and listened.

Would they like to sail for a few hours, and what was the programme to be afterwards? Thomas said that it would be best if he came to the castle about dusk. There were still a lot of nets to be put in order and the general was sure to enjoy showing them the estate.

'But haven't you got the whole house over there, Father?' asked Joachim. 'Do you still need this?'

'More than ever, Joachim.'

They did not hide their disappointment when Marianne declared that she would rather stay on the island and help with the nets. However she walked down with them to the boats and while Marschall got in she said to Joachim in a low voice: 'The graves are quite near the forester's house.'

'Certainly,' he replied, blushing, 'that's a matter of course.'

It soon became evident that they did not mean to spend the whole day on the island as Joachim had promised. They came every day for some time, shot at a target and turned over the leaves of Thomas's books. He did not show any disappointment. They did not think much of the opinions of 'old servicemen', and the island wasn't an officers' mess where young men had to listen to the ideas of 'old buffers'.

At the end of the first week Marschall unexpectedly turned to Joachim and asked him rather sheepishly how the course he was navigating towards the young lady was succeeding. At any rate she seemed to him to be pretty cool and sometimes even haughty. 'I leave it to you to try your luck, too,' replied Joachim, 'but I doubt whether the princess will think you "any great shakes".'

No, she did not think him so, and when they accompanied her into the fields on horseback and heard her speaking to the bailiff or the farmhands quietly, unassumingly, and always sensibly – they stopped their horses near hers – they felt that their security crumbled away a little, even when they said afterwards that in their opinion these people should be made to feel the curb a little more.

The young horsewoman replied, smiling, that country people generally knew more than seamen about the use of the curb. One of the farmhands – she told them – used to take her on his knees, and he did not need a curb for that, only his big, brown, horny hands, and under his nails there had always been some of the earth of their fields.

Before they left, Marschall had to confess, in spite of his considerable self-confidence, that even in his navigation something was not quite right; however, in the course of the next few years there would be time to clear the turrets for action and meanwhile he had to put up with many things from this overbearing young Orla in order to maintain contact with Marianne.

The last evening, Thomas happened to ask Joachim whether, by any chance, he remembered the verse from the proverbs of Solomon which he had quoted to him on the platform. But Joachim was sorry that he had forgotten it. 'You know, Father,' he said, 'that it's mostly hard work there, and if I should think of reading the Bible, they would look at me in a funny way. Besides – as I seem to notice from your book – you, too, have done with the Bible.'

'I should think it a very sad thing in a man if he had done with the Bible, just as sad as if somebody had done with his mother.

'You mustn't think, dear Joachim,' he added, 'that I have joined a religious sect in the meantime, or that I believe a father ought to give his son a trunk full of good advice on his way. But you see we live here very quietly and have much time for thinking. And when such robust young people come to see us, we are good listeners. We consider what we did wrong in life, and we would like you to make fewer mistakes than we made. You know yourself that you have many talents which I never had – talents which I only possessed in my thoughts but never in my blood, and I dare say I would like to see you manage your good fortune as if you were already fifty years old. That is foolish, of course, and you must overlook it.'

'Dear Father,' said Joachim, 'you are so . . . very decent to me. . . .'

Thomas smiled. 'How should I be otherwise?' he asked. 'But the verse I wished to remind you of was: "He that is slow to anger is better than the mighty." Perhaps you will think about it, too.'

'I remember, father. But being patient at sea is quite a job. Until the Skagerrak they were very patient with us.'

'There is a different patience from that, Joachim, but we will leave it now. There would be little hope if you were not different from us.'

'Fresh winds, Orla,' said the general while they were looking after the carriage. 'They are hard as glass, but that's probably necessary nowadays, so that the flag may flutter again.'

'Now they are going to swim on the ocean, child,' said Aunt Mary thoughtfully, 'and they might have had salt enough . . .'

But Marianne contradicted. Only Thomas and Bildermann were 'on the ocean', the others were 'at sea'.

Soon after the departure of the young seamen the news spread that the fisherman who was about a hundred years old had 'gone home'. None of the simple people who lived round the lakes used any other expression than this. Nobody said that he had died or was drowned, though his boat and his cap had been found one morning drifting on the waves.

They thought that in a gentle and not at all violent manner he had gone home to the creatures whose lives and ways he knew so much about. Yes, many maintained that soon after his death, in calm evenings – the place where he had disappeared was filled with a numberless host of old fish which lay quietly under the surface, their green backs turned downstream and their tail fins scarcely moving. It seemed as if they were looking into the deep where they could see the fisherman sitting upright amidst the creeping plants with his smooth, white hair and the amber rings in his ears, and in his twisted, brown hands one could see now and again the golden crown of which he had sometimes spoken.

They searched for him for a long time, even the authorities took pains, but the water refused to give him back. He was never found.

CHAPTER FOURTEEN

THE CLOCK above the castle yard – centre and measure of all local life – still strikes by day and night throughout the seasons and years. Sometimes the people of the district, turning things over in their minds, think that much has changed in themselves and their surroundings, but the axis of their life has remained the same. However erect he holds himself, the general can be seen to have shrunk somewhat, and the little lady has grown rather taller. The men of the ocean have a few more grey strands in their hair, but the fish go into their nets as they used to do, sometimes more, sometimes less, as wind, weather, or their nature commands. As a day goes by for the ploughman, summer and autumn have passed, and again Thomas has spent over two months in the Graf's house. The blue flame burnt under the retorts, and another bluish light appeared in the vacuum tubes – flickering and mysterious. Crystals sparkled in all colours, peculiar shapes and shadows flashed up under the microscope, and between the leaves of the big books lay small slips of paper covered with almost illegible words and figures. The wise man from the east has taken a farm labourer and a maid into his house, and the tiling of the new roof of the barn is already beginning to turn grey on the weather side. Joachim will be a lieutenant soon and is preparing to sit for his examination. He is diligent, cool and concentrated as always, and the midshipman Siegfried von Marschall has given up writing letters to the Honourable Marianne von Platen since she has informed him that her work does not allow her to carry on a correspondence about the dietetics of the soul.

The eagle still flies three times a day over the wood from the east, swoops down on his prey, and lets fall from the height his sad cry echoing over woods and lakes and disappears again, behind the eastern horizon. On the island, after all these years, they do not know whether it is still the same eagle or a young one; however they are satisfied to call it 'the eagle', for none of its tribe has a special name. Animals are nameless.

Thousands still wander over the roads of the Reich: students and vagabonds, old soldiers and pilgrims with sandals on their feet and a rope round their waist. Bildermann when he is going round the country often meets them, stops them and asks whether the ravens are still circling round the mountains. Then he shakes his head, gives them tobacco and a piece of the bread which he always carries in his pocket, and his eyes follow them for a while as they walk on towards east or west with stooping shoulders and tired feet, the outlaws of the earth who patiently carry the guilt of nations.

Men think much has changed, but only the surface is rippled as on a sheet of water, while in the depths fish and plants and stones lie unchanged, waiting their time.

Because Marianne now has a small, shining car, a present from the old lady-in-waiting, that has not changed anything either in fields and woods. She uses it rarely, but then with much pleasure, and when she drives to the town now and again, she likes best to have Bildermann with her. He knows how to listen and answer well, and knows so much about his master and all the mysteries of a motor into the bargain. The ribbons of his cap stream horizontally above the singing car, and sometimes he recalls with a smile the various ways he has moved forward in his life.

Thomas sees well enough that Marianne is suffering, but he wishes to see it – as the saying is – only out of the corner of his eye. He is not yet safe enough himself. He is like a man who stands on two horses and is galloping round a ring. He must look neither to right nor left. He knows that he grew old that Christmas Eve. This means that he learnt then suddenly to look dccp into his life without trying to deceive himself, but he cannot help a piercing pain sometimes shooting through him – as arbitrary and incalculable as a jagged crack in the ice. He who wants to have the whole is not blind to the part. A dream may appear even on a lonely road. He has to wait till the day when that one who can heal the sorrow will come along. Joachim had not been the right one, still less the cousin or the midshipman Marschall. But nature has a thousand ways and means and will also know how to conquer 'the old standards'.

Marianne is not unhappy. She has her work and her dreams and so cannot fall into the abyss. She also has the old portraits in the hall in front of which she sometimes stands. The lips of the women are silent, but even a silent mouth can be eloquent. You do not lose yourself when you can contemplate the ancestors. And anyway you can still hope, always hope. You can cross an abyss, be it only on a golden thread, if it is God's wish.

Frau von Sperber does not see anything. Her handsome husband is dead, buried in Polish earth, and the world has become empty by his death. How could any man charm now his charm is gone? It isn't a question of men now, but of the salt of the earth.

The only one who seen it is the general. Probably the

young men who were as hard as glass have sharpened his eyes. One might think that he is a severe man, and Bergengruen sometimes thought that he was like a soldier whose roots were still in the Thirty Years' War. But now his heart is filled with compassion, and great as his compassion is his embarrassment. Such a case is not mentioned in any regulation; the regulations for active service have nothing to do with it. Eventually nothing is left but a 'daring reconnoitre'. It is worthwhile for the child's sake to get out of one's trench to see what is happening behind the wood.

'I am an old man, Orla,' he said, sitting at the grey table on the island. 'I must think of the future – even generals are not immortal – how is it with the child?'

Thomas understands immediately. 'Not a word has been spoken, general,' he replied, 'but the child knows that it cannot be.'

'Is not, or cannot be?'

'Is, but cannot be, general.'

The old hands are folded over the stick, and his eyes under the white brows look straight ahead. The eagle is circling above the otter bay, and its reflection can be seen in the water.

'Never, Orla?'

'Never, general. He who sins against nature will not be forgiven.'

'How old, Orla?'

'Fifty, general.'

The fingers on the stick move as if they were counting. Then they are still and folded again.

'What are we to do, Orla?'

'We must come to an understanding, general, and help. In a few years nobody will put a wreath on our forehead any more.'

'Don't go away, Orla!'

'No, general.'

They still remained seated for some time. On the opposite shore Bildermann was casting the bow nets into the water. They saw the bright shining wood, and only after an interval did they hear the sound.

The general got up and shook hands with Thomas. 'I would have died in peace, Orla,' he said, 'with nobody as peacefully as with you. But you are right, you are a gentleman, Orla. . . .'

Then he whistled for Johann, and the giant answered from the oak wood.

This autumn something out of the ordinary happened in the neighbourhood. More than ten years after the grimmest and most ineffective battles of war, a ruined gallery was discovered, buried under the fortress and under the hills with their almost sacred names, and in this gallery the mortal remains of half a company. A year later the lakeside communities were officially informed that there were seven 'missing' soldiers from the same parish among those whose bodies were found in the gallery. The vicar, an old man, whose son was among the dead, did not rest until he had obtained permission by applications, collections and persuasion to convey the seven dead soldiers from the foreign earth to the large military cemetery in their own parish. Here the victims of the first years of the war were buried, and the cemetery was well known throughout the whole province, its three tall crosses being visible at a great distance along the shores of the lakes.

The fight of the parish for their dead (for there was no other name for the tenacious overcoming of regulations and red tape) had created a sensation far and wide and had even moved the hearts of many who lived at some distance from those villages. When it was made known that at the harvest festival the narrow coffins were to be laid to rest below the three crosses, many came crowding on foot and by carriage; some who had given their sons to the country, or some who saw in this act a warning or even an inspiration.

As the cemetery was some distance away, Marianne had asked whether Thomas would go with her in her little car, and he had agreed. He came over early to the castle, and she was already waiting for him on the steps. She saw him in uniform for the first time, and he seemed far removed from her–as if he alone had a right to take part in these proceedings. The sun had just risen above the wood; the dewy fields were sparkling, and numerous flights of ring doves, on their way to the south, rose from the oaks. The old birch trees on the high road still bore their golden leaves and in between shone the red berries of the rowans. From the hills they saw the white sky gradually taking on deeper hues, until at last it stood dark blue above fields, farms and woods.

Thomas remembered the days when he had first come to this neighbourhood, and although it had been spring then, he recognised the features which had captivated him at that time. He told Marianne how he had thought then that he would often stand on these shores with Joachim, that he might learn from these grand and austere lines that in a landscape the will of creation always aims at simplicity. He told her how this plan had failed a little, as often happens, when one intends to fill youth with one's own enthusiasm and likings.

'Often, but not always,' said the child.

'No, and there are no limits, for he who is attentive and patient will always find compensation for disappointment, since life only disappoints us in so far as we try to force our opinion upon it.'

'Do you believe that you will never be deceived any more?' asked the child.

'I hope to have done with the worst deceptions,' he replied. 'As far as things are concerned, I do little more than observe and listen, and I have learnt by now that truth is in the objects and not in our opinions about them. And as for human beings, I have had the good luck that my circle has contracted from one year to the next and now only includes those whose pictures remain as fixed as the stars. While you are young, you think yourself able to change, and raise the standard of a whole profession, even of whole nations, but when your life is on the decline, you are satisfied with less and lend all your strength to making this into something permanent. As to the few who are still about me, I don't need to bother whether I shall be deceived in them.'

Marianne asked him if, when her grandfather died and she married, he would leave the island and move to the Graf's house for good.

'Certainly not. You must remember how I saw you for the first time – delicate and fragile – on the steps of the castle in your black frock and the bead necklace which quivered above your throat. And even if I should live to see you a grandmother with white hair, I would always see you as I saw you at that time. That is true both for Bildermann and myself. We were on the first stage of a new life when we saw you for the first time shining like a little flower in all the darkness and uncertainty of our future. That is unforgettable. There is something written in the Bible about helping and healing, and as long as we can expect to have an opportunity to do either, we cannot go away. This opportunity doesn't end with childhood or youth, it remains until death. So I'm afraid you will have to put up with the fact that the men of the ocean will stay in your domain as long as they can handle an oar or cast a net.'

She looked straight ahead along the white road, and taking her right hand for a moment from the steering wheel, she gently put it on his hand. 'Do you know what I want, Thomas?' she asked. 'I want to be buried on the island . . . . at least, that is what I want.'

The higher the sun rose the busier the lonely road became, and when they arrived in the village it seemed as if the population of the whole countryside had flocked together after so many years, to look once more into the now almost legendary face of war. The people looked intent and serious and waited quietly for an hour, and though there were societies and trade unions with banners and flags in all the streets and the small squares, they tried to get into file without much noise.

Marianne and Thomas parked their car in the stable yard of the large inn in the market square. They asked to have a small table under the trees reserved for lunch and went slowly past the church out of the village on a road bordered by young trees which led up to the hill above the lake. In a corner of the market square Thomas saw the colonel with the aquiline nose, not on horseback this time, but still with his parade-ground voice, though he tried his best to subdue it. Thomas thought he heard the 'Hurry up, hurry up, gentlemen!' with which he seemed to chase the members of his staff into the crowd that filed out of the village. Thomas saluted, and the colonel coldly returned his salute.

'Those are the people who came out of the war "as fresh as paint",' he said to Marianne, smiling, 'and who called your grandfather an old fellow.'

Then they were silent, for at the end of the village the huge crosses became visible, silhouetted against a blue horizon. They were the landmark of a whole district erected on the vast cemetery, and with their narrow arms high up on the shaft they seemed to be breaking up the empty sky – and yet, as it were, supporting it at the same time.

When they reached the top of the hill, the view opened out wide and unhindered over endless fields and strips of blue forest on the land side and over blue sheets of water with empty shores on the other. When the silent vault lay before them with yellow sand thrown up by the grave-digger heaped in great mounds, and at the entrance the seven narrow coffins each covered with a flag and autumn wreaths of garden and wild flowers; when they saw the soldiers who kept guard over the dead – young faces under the stern, grey helmets – and the field altar at the head of the coffins; when they looked into the face of the assembled crowd made up of people of all ages – children as well as white-haired, old people – then Marianne experienced for the first time, very distinctly, the immortality of a great era, the face of death and of its transfiguration which had been incorporated into the conception of the nation, and which included all their lives: the old families as well as the dust of the nameless masses. As in a vision she beheld the three crosses, not empty in the mild autumn sun under a blue sky, but as if the high oaken shafts carried the three bodies of Golgotha: Christ crucified and the two thieves by His side; eternal symbols of a sacrificial death atoning for the guilt of mankind.

She took Thomas's hand and held it all the time, until the coffins with the coloured flags were lowered and covered with the yellow sand.

They knew that in one of the coffins were the mortal remains of the vicar's son. He himself had been dragged away deep into enemy country at the beginning of the war. He had buried his wife and suffered much of the sorrow meted out to men. And when they saw how the soft breeze that came from the lake moved his long, white hair, and when they heard no word of bitterness nor complaint in his sermon, and that with the thanksgiving for the year's harvest he literally included these coffins as the late, glorious harvest of a time of devotion and sacrifice, the harvest of harvests; when he begged them constantly to bear in mind these witnesses, lost sons who had come home late, and to plough their fields still deeper: *then* in an unforgettable way they felt that they were incorporated by his words into the life of this district, and that it was of no importance whether they gave their loyalty different names, for labour, toil and sorrow, all took the same path, no matter what the goal might be called.

By the vicar's wish no speeches were made at the cemetery, so that the discord of the times did not lessen the solemnity of his hour. Only the tolling of the bells sounded from the neighbouring villages, and when the salutes had been fired over the dead, and the crowd had dispersed in silence, and the trades unions with their flags and banners had marched down to the road, then the place became quiet and lonely again, only the gulls circling above it high in the blue air.

Thomas and Marianne stayed for some time up on the hilltop and watched how the gossamer threads of the Indian summer grew longer and thicker on the arms of the crosses, floating like thin, white veils in the air.

Then they followed the others. Marianne had taken Thomas's arm, and when they had reached the entrance of the village she said: 'We young ones will never be anything compared with you, Thomas. We shall always remain debtors and unscathed.'

But he shook his head. 'Nobody knows what life has in store for you,' he replied.

They walked once more across the cemetery, and then sat

down at the small table in the garden of the inn and had their lunch. The colonel and his staff sat under one of the nearby trees – his voice was unrestrained now. A young woman, almost a girl, sat at his side and seemed rather bored by the attentions of the old soldier and the younger gentleman at their table. One could guess with some certainty that she was the colonel's wife.

Thomas then told his experience at the manoeuvres, to which Bildermann had taken him that time, and how the meeting with this old warrior had not been an altogether friendly one. He had not guessed then that the picture of his fire eater would be completed like this.

Marianne looked straight in front of her without speaking, but Thomas noticed that her mind was preoccupied with that little group, and when the old captain of the militia sat down for a while at their table and spoke with great respect of her grandfather, she asked him if it were true – as Herr von Orla had said – that the young lady over there was the colonel's wife.

'Yes, that is true as only the register in a registry office can be. She is quite all right, though still rather like fallow land. On the whole it does not seem to be a happy relationship, and for both their sakes it would probably have been better if it had never happened.' Thomas and Marianne soon said goodbye and steered the car with some difficulty through the vehicles and crowds, but after some time they were on the empty road, which led white and straight to the first woods.

Here in the shade and quiet Marianne slowed down, and still looking straight in front of her she asked: 'Is that the reason, Thomas?'

He had been reading her thoughts all the time, and so he answered without hesitating: 'Yes, that's the reason.'

Not far from the castle he asked her whether she would like to drive with him to the Graf's house. They had plenty of time to have tea on the terrace, and he would like her to take home as many flowers as the car would hold. 'It is sad when they fade there, and I feel that we must remember the Graf too, today, in a kindly way.'

They felt that there was a spell over this piece of land also, though a different one from that on the island. In the light of the setting sun the garden seemed to be a single, many-coloured flame, and the old gardener a magician who walked about unhurt with basket and scissors. The air was so calm that they heard the jays on the distant potato fields and the children's voices on the home farm.

'No human life disappears from its sphere,' said Thomas, 'least of all his. Everything is still aware of his presence, every flower, every shrub, and even the horizon appears to me to be his horizon so much is it formed and filled with his spirit.'

'In what way are we so different from each other, Thomas?'

He led her smilingly to the table which Friedrich had pushed on to the terrace. 'In that you want to see him again in a future life, child, and we do not. You think God has killed him with a club, and we think that such things are far too small for Him to concern Himself with. The late Graf was an unbeliever, and you think that you must believe that he is now in hell. Death did not leave him time to recant, and even if he had had time he would not have recanted. Not he. He went to meet death without a weapon. We think that a hell full of men like him must be a peculiar hell.'

'But those are nothing but symbols, Thomas.'

'Yes, but you recognise the painter when you look at the pictures.'

After tea they went down to the river and sat on a bench by the clear water. The poplars towered stiffly into the blue air and faded leaves which looked like gold in the sunshine glided past them on the river.

'I think it will be fine to be old,' said Thomas. 'On the island or here; but preferably on the island. One must only loosen the ties in time, so that nothing is left for the shears to cut. Then one will be like a leaf falling from a tree. I think that only those are afraid and rebel who have not been able to finish their life's work. But did not the old fisherman prophesy that I shall be able to finish? I see already that I shall not succeed in understanding the whole, but if I recognise that we are not meant to understand it, that creation did not mean us to understand – then there is no pain in it. I must get to the limit, and I shall try to do so.'

'Did you make many mistakes, Thomas?'

'I think I did. Firstly with my profession and then many with Gloria and perhaps also with Joachim. But it was only wrong when one judges by the standards of the absolute, and one ought not to judge like that. Everything was necessary, so that this could be, and all we experience now is necessary so that the future may be shaped. We always walk with somewhat bandaged eyes, but only fools will tear off the bandage.'

Beyond the curve of the river they heard a high-pitched twittering, and the little blue bird shot over the water at their feet so quickly that they could not distinguish the bird from its reflection in the water.

'The bird . . .' she whispered. 'When I was young, Thomas, you made no mistakes then, did you?'

'I hope not,' he replied, looking at her seriously.

'No, Thomas, you shall not regret anything, above all not that time. You mustn't strike anything off, for that is what I am living by, and if you should do so, you would strike it off my life.'

'I will not strike anything off, Marianne,' he said in a low voice.

The sun was setting behind the wood and they got up. A thin haze rose over the meadows, but the evening sun was still reflected red in the garret windows of the house. The boot of the car was filled with flowers, and a bunch of dahlias lay on the seat. Friedrich smoothed the rug over their knees. They both saw how withered his hands were.

'We have given you trouble, Friedrich,' said Thomas, 'but the evening will be quiet.'

The valet smiled. 'I always hear him walking now, Herr von Orla, up and down in the library. And sometimes a string of the piano sounds.'

'You are too much alone, Friedrich.'

He shook his head respectfully. 'We were always alone, Herr von Orla, the late Graf and myself. I always believe that he will send me a message when I sit at the fireplace. But we are too impatient even when we have white hair.' He closed the car door and stood back.

When the road turned beyond the gateway, they saw him once more. He looked small and fragile in front of the big house with the heavy roof, and when he put his hand on the latch to open the door, you could fancy that he was entering a vault and that the stone would fall behind him.

'You must come here with me now and again,' said Thomas, 'houses also will decay when nobody looks at them.'

She nodded, but she said that she would always be afraid. It was a house without God.

'And yet so full of idols,' he said, smiling.

The general was standing at the gate of the park waiting for them. 'It's a long day for an old man,' he said. 'The

Sperber always pictures you crashing into a tree. I told her there are not so many trees as she would imagine for the car to run into.'

They carried the flowers into the hall and Marianne took the car to the garage. 'It looked like a wedding coach, Orla. If only God had distributed the years a little differently. It would have been a trifle for Him.'

'Let us not encroach upon His province,' said Thomas quietly. Later, when all the flowers stood in vases and bowls, and they were sitting in front of the fire, Marianne asked her grandfather whether he knew the colonel who had called him an old fellow.

'Seen him three times,' replied the general. 'His nickname in the West was Ammonia. No eye was without tears wherever he appeared. The young people would have said: "Dashing!" '

'Well, he is married now,' said Marianne, 'to a girl of about twenty. They were sitting at the next table.'

The general glanced at her uneasily.

'It didn't look very nice, Thomas, did it?'

'No,' he said quietly, 'and in ten years it will look still worse.'

'He was three years younger than I,' said Aunt Mary innocently, 'and that was not good either.'

But the general looked at her so angrily that she was frightened and did not say another word. Marianne looked from one to the other. 'We have come to an agreement, we two, haven't we, Thomas?'

He nodded.

'To stand by your employer loyally at all times, was it that, Thomas?'

'Yes, and the employer agreed that he would satisfy my needs of body and soul.'

'And the agreement is unredeemable, Grandfather, do you hear? An agreement for life.'

She got up and walked up and down in front of the row of the ancestral portraits, her hands behind her back, as she used to do when she was a child. Then she came back and set out the Halma-men on the large board.

At the beginning of the following week Thomas got a letter from Joachim. It was longer than he generally wrote, and it seemed as if it weighed heavily in Thomas's hand in a peculiar way. Joachim told him that an awkward thing had happened. 'For quite a long time there had been unrest in the docks. We did not get any leave for some time, and when it was restored we were told to keep together and avoid a clash. A few weeks ago ten of us were invited to the house of one of the instructing officers, and, of course, we had to put on uniform. We did not drink much and went back towards the harbour in an orderly manner though perhaps a little noisily, but otherwise quite all right. The Reds must have known of it, for at the end of the park they suddenly attacked us. We formed up at once back to back and as we had our knives on us, we gave them a rough welcome. In the end we were a little scattered, but they had had enough, and everything would have been fine if one of us had not played the fool. He started holding forth and asked them whether they were not ashamed as Germans to attack Germans, and whether class hatred must persist for ever, and so on.

'One of the Reds took the opportunity to creep up behind him and suddenly raised a club. I had just finished with the last fellow who had attacked me and saw what was going to happen. I called out to the others, but the blow had already fallen. We carried him on board; he is still lying in the naval hospital with a fractured skull. However, the doctors think that he will pull through.'

Thomas dropped the letter and filled his pipe. He knew exactly what would follow and he saw in an almost disinterested way how his hand holding the match was trembling.

'The thing was,' Joachim had continued, 'that the fellow who has been hurt, a certain Count Finkenstein, was always rather at cross purposes with me. Circumstances forced him to enter the Navy rather late in life, so that he was a few years older than most of us; he was gifted and methodical but always kept a little aloof. He read peculiar books, played the violin, and so on. We never liked each other and once when I came off second best, Finkenstein wasn't jubilant, as might have been expected, but took the prize with an absolutely unconcerned face, as if it belonged to him by right and any other result would have been a mistake. Without really intending it we had almost been rivals, and the others formed themselves into two camps behind us.'

'Why does he write all this to me?' Thomas thought with growing disquiet.

'I have visited him, too, of course,' Joachim went on. 'One had got to do that. But when the others were leaving, he held me back and fixed his gaze on me. He was still all wrapped up in white bandages, and his eyes had a queer look. "I would like to know, Orla," he said, "why you didn't prevent it? I looked at you just before the blow was falling, and I saw in your eyes that you knew it. You also saw that the blow was being dealt. I don't regret being knocked down, nor that you didn't help me. I would only like to know the reason. I am interested in it from the psychological point of view. Or from the moral point, if you like." There you have his way of putting things.

'Of course, I talked him out of it. I told him that I had been exhausted, as we all had been, and the attack had happened so suddenly that I reacted to it half a second late.

'"That's fine," said Finkenstein. "I really thought you had looked on and seen it all without preventing it, so that I might be out of your way, at least for the final of this examination. It would have made me very unhappy for your sake."

'And now for the main thing, dear Father. I was of course perplexed at first and really furious. But then I found that I did not want to evade the idea – inwardly – I mean. I tried to remember everything from the start, and I feel quite sure now that I might have prevented the blow. One must be honest like that with oneself. It would not have taken a half second to shout, if it had been another fellow. Do you understand? That is the important thing. Of course, it is nonsense to think that the examination crossed my mind, I give you my word of honour on that. I did not think at all. But I had to overcome the feeling that it was just he. Do you understand me? It is very important for me that you should understand. There was an inhibition not of thought, but of feeling. Only for a few heartbeats, and that was just enough. I am very sorry that it happened, but I suppose nothing can be done now.

'I am writing to you, because I want you to advise me what I ought to do. There is a vague possibility that he may report it, and although I can confidentially repeat what I have written here, it would be very awkward just before the examination. There has been enough stink made about this affair already. I did not go to the hospital again, and I don't mean to.'

Thomas folded the sheets carefully and knocked out his pipe. So that's how it was. It might have been worse, but even this was bad enough. It was not only 'awkward'. However it was very peculiar in what variations fate liked to play. It repeated that other half second of hesitation, even though the motives were different. He had no doubt that Joachim was telling the truth. That he had not only not thought, but had had to overcome a feeling. Only he had forgotten to lay bare the roots of this feeling, and Thomas knew where they sprang from.

He would have preferred it to be Joachim lying wrapped up in white bandages and worrying about the moral point of view. But he worried about his career; he was very much worried obviously – else why this confession? There was no question of morals in Joachim's point of view.

'A child can be as a sword over us,' he thought finally. Then he pushed it aside for a while, took the hose and a basket and went to the potato field.

He answered the letter only that morning. 'I am convinced', he wrote, 'that you told me the truth. I will not probe into whether you have done the right thing as an officer. But I will state that you, as a moral human being, have neglected a duty, according to my old-fashioned standards, please remember. You are young, and our standard should be applied to age, not youth.

'You make a great mistake when you believe that the injured man will report the occurrence. If that is all you are worrying about, you may set your mind at rest. But if you are worried over and above this apprehension (and I sincerely wish you were) I would advise you to go to the hospital immediately you have received this letter and repeat to the patient all you have written to me – without curtailing or extenuating anything. In this way you may make up for part of that second, not for the whole, but for a part of it.

'I don't know whether you will see a warning in this event. I myself see it, but I must confess that it took me forty years to recognise the hand of fate. On the other hand I had nobody to point it out to me. Please, give my kindest regards to the young Graf.'

After a while he added a postscript: 'I am glad you wrote to me about it, Joachim. But I am still more pleased that you have faced up to it yourself. Do not take it too lightly, but do not take it too much to heart. A life can be destroyed starting from the smallest spot of decay. We all emerge damaged from such events, but nothing is lost as long as we emerge with integrity. As long as you tell me such things, I know that we belong to each other.'

On the same day Thomas wrote to the patient and invited him to spend his sick leave on the island if he had time and would like to do so. He was pretty sure that they would get on well together.

Joachim thanked his father, wrote that he had done what he had been told to do, and that in his opinion the whole affair was settled now. Two weeks later Finkenstein arrived.

Bildermann fetched him in the sailing boat, and when they got out, Bildermann nodded merrily to Thomas. His face said that everything was all right about this guest.

After a few days there was nobody who did not think the same. The patient was silent and a little uncertain, as if he had not altogether returned from the dark shores of his fever. But as soon as anyone addressed him, his features opened in an expression of wonderful confidence that was reflected back in the face of the speaker, and it was a matter of course that after three days Aunt Mary told him the sad story of her 'handsome husband'.

Finkenstein had no parents, had been brought up by relatives and had first tried to study law. But immediately, even during the first term, he found that his way of thinking brought him into constant conflict with the precepts he was taught to accept; for he could neither approve of the harshness of former verdicts nor of the vague humanity of modern times. He also confessed that his flesh crept, when he thought of his comrades as future judges. Then he had looked for a profession where human affairs were restrained and restricted to the most simple formulas, and where nothing but cold duty ruled a man's conduct. The profession of an officer, especially a naval officer, seemed to him to be the right one. The latter might even keep the remoteness of primal life through the element to which it was bound.

'Probably some things don't quite tally in your reckoning either,' said Thomas.

Finkenstein conceded this point though with some embarrassment, but said he believed that the fault lay in him more than in the circumstances. He who stood a little aloof ought not to look for all faults in others. He knew that youth nowadays was often like an arrow without a target. The old house had been demolished and the new one had not yet been built. They all behaved like sons of rich parents who had suddenly become bankrupt, and most of them thought that such a thing ought not to happen with decent parents. He himself, however, believed that sons and parents both had to carry their burden, and the sons must carry the heavier load as their shoulders were younger.

'I will not prophesy anything,' replied Thomas, 'but it seems to me that you have still a good deal to learn even for this profession. There is only a limited scope for the individual in all large communities or associations. If one wants to go only one's own way in regard to moral judgments all subordination would appear to be impossible, for one may well adopt foreign customs but never foreign morals. For an officer it it imperative to acknowledge a law above his own judgment – even if it includes things which one does not like to subordinate to a law.'

With a little embarrassment Finkenstein confessed that Herr von Orla's two books had made a deep impression on him and that somehow (and here he searched a long time for the right words) he could not quite fit Joachim into a world where these books had been conceived.

'Do you mean that he appears to you inferior to these books?'

'I would not like to say "inferior", Herr von Orla, but absolutely different; he seems to have no problems, except those of making a good career.'

'You mustn't forget one thing, Finkenstein, that the author produces the book; it is his property alone. The author is father and mother of his book, it is produced solely from his own blood. But whence come our children? Of how many secret sources in their blood composed? Subterranean sources and nobody knows the realm through which they flow, before they emerge into the light of the day? We have wronged every human being of our times, and I have neglected many a duty as far as Joachim is concerned. When I realised it, it was already too late, and I do not even know whether it is not always too late for us. So many things have become problematic to me in these last years.'

'But here, in your realm, Herr von Orla, nothing seems to be problematic. I believe this is the first place on earth I have known, where everything is in the right place, and where even a stranger like myself cannot do anything amiss.'

Thomas shook his head. 'Not everything is in its place, but it is true, we try hard.'

'I think I'll go for a little row on the lake,' said Finkenstein, and Thomas looked after him as he went down to the boat – tall, slim, with quiet movements which reminded him of branches through which the wind blew. He did not hide from himself that his perception of this young man's character gave him a sense of deep consolation, the certainty he felt now that one might quietly pass away – there would always be a few people to put their hands to the plough. One need not tell them about the field in which one had thought to labour, nor of the seed which one had saved. They would plough the furrow to the end and sow the seed exactly where one would have sowed it oneself. There was a guiding thread that ran through the tapestry. Nature took care that nothing was discarded that tried to recognise its inner meaning.

After the harvest had been brought in, Marianne often came to see them. She thought that the visitor fitted well into the life of the island, but she sometimes looked at Thomas out of the corner of her eye, as if she had discovered a new enigma in him. When Finkenstein's leave had come to an end and, the days growing shorter and shorter, the old routine had been taken up, one evening she asked Thomas why he had invited this visitor.

He looked at her in surprise, saw her expressionless face and guessed what she was thinking of. He took Joachim's letter out of his pocket, where he still carried it, and gave it to her. He had never so much as mentioned it until now.

She read it in silence, only the necklace above her throat quivered as it had done when she was a child. Then she laid the letter on the table and looked out across the water. 'Forgive me, Thomas,' she said at last.

Later Thomas remarked that he sometimes wished Joachim had some of this guest's qualities, but those were wishes of bygone times. At the age of fifty, one cannot make up for certain things. This young man had often made him happy, probably in the way an astronomer feels happy when he beholds a new star through his telescope. The infinity of creation becomes clear once more and when we see the bottom of our own glass it is good to know that in countless others the wine is still overflowing. Perhaps not in countless cases, but certainly in two or three.

'Do you see the bottom, Thomas?'

'Yes, child, it would not be good if at the age of fifty one saw nothing but one's own reflection.'

CHAPTER FIFTEEN

AT THE BEGINNING of the winter the general wanted to cut down some pines which were about a hundred and twenty years old. In late autumn he had walked with Thomas through that part of the wood, not far from the shore, and tapping one of the huge trees with his stick had said: 'This one must come down . . . a hundred and twenty years old . . . it has outlived its time.' Thomas said that it seemed a pity, especially as Goethe was still living when these trees were planted. However, it might be right to obey nature's rules, and he was sure that one day somebody would write a psalm on the lives of trees.

'We'll plant a mixed wood here,' said the general. 'First great work for the child . . . it will give her shade when we have been gathered to our fathers, Orla.'

Then they separated. Thomas had gone to his boat, but at the shore he had turned once more and tramped through the hilly district in all directions. In the evening he discussed with Bildermann what he had in his mind, and the next morning he knocked at Marianne's little office.

'I have come to ask you a favour. Really it is your wood – the one that must be felled as well as the other which you are going to plant. I have discussed the matter with Bildermann, and we two would like to fell it. If we keep well and can stick to it, we may have finished by the end of January, then I shall have time enough to move to the house on the river for another two months.'

First Marianne smiled, then suddenly she became serious and gazed out of the window for some time. 'You know, Thomas,' she said at last, 'that you can do anything you want. But why will you do this?'

'We have got too little work to do, Marianne. Of course, Bildermann works all day long, but I am dawdling about, and there is nothing useful left for me to do.'

'And why don't you go to the Graf's house now?'

He shook his head. 'Before I dig myself in,' he said, 'I must be tired. So tired that only my mind is still awake. And I am not yet tired. Summer here is too short. The monks, too, felled and cleaned the ground.'

She still stood at the window looking at him, but his picture became dim with her tears. 'You shall fell it, Thomas,' she said. 'I'll tell Grandfather about it. But I shall come to see you every day and bring you your lunch. And you must take care that no tree crashes down on you!'

'We don't wish to die, Marianne,' he replied. 'We will get over this winter, then we shall be beyond the polar circle.'

So they cut down the wood. Bildermann was an expert in felling trees too. He had brought new axes and a long saw, and when it grew cold early in the first half of November, he also got the laced and lined canvas shoes which people in the villages here still wore. For two days the ice of the lake over which they walked was not very firm, but later it froze hard, and the first snow began to fall.

They got up at dawn and drank their coffee in front of the hearth. Not until they had lit their pipes did they begin to talk. Their bodies were aching, but they laughed at it, and after a week they left the house as merrily as if a Christmas tree were waiting for them under the gloomy pines. They carried their tools on their shoulders, and in their soft shoes they went noiselessly over the ice. A crimson dawn stood above the forest and lit up the lonely track of a hare which ran across the lake to the island. They breathed the cold, pure air deeply, and it was as calm as if they lived at the North Pole.

'A grand idea, captain,' said Bildermann.

They had trodden out two parallel paths, and behind the shore they dived into the woods. They always looked back at the island once more, but it had not disappeared. The house stood motionless, and the reddish smoke rose straight above the low roof. They saw the tracks of game running over their path, and they smelt the fresh wood. Then they were there. The heavy trunks lay as they had crashed down, their branches lopped off. Resin stood in the scars, and the branches were piled up tidily. They looked round full of childish pride. Then Bildermann lit a fire, and Thomas considered which of the giants should be the next to fall. On the trampled snow Thomas saw here and there the impression of a small child's foot, and he looked smilingly down on the track which was trodden every day at noon.

'Happy, Bildermann?'

'Rather, captain. Good idea, that–driving them out of Paradise.'

The fire burnt with a red comforting flame, and the white smoke wafted up to the high treetops. Bildermann stood a saucepan filled with snow in the ashes, and then they started their work. They discussed in which direction the tree was to fall, and then the forest echoed with the strokes of their axes. They kept time, and white chips hung in their hair. The smell of the living wood rose up to them, but they had no time for thinking. The sparkling blades demanded eye and hand, and each blow must fall true in the gaping notch.

'That will do, captain,' said Bildermann.

They supported themselves on the handles of their axes and wiped the sweat from their foreheads. A crimson sun shone through the trees, the snow was sparkling and a woodpecker was tapping in a dry treetop near them. They put the flat pads under their knees and took the two-handled saw. There was a quick echo in the dense forest. From time to time they pushed a wooden wedge into the notch and rested for a while. 'It is nearly done, captain,' said Bildermann. 'It is trembling already!'

The treetop quivered, shaking down the snow into their eyes, and they looked up as they knelt so as not to miss the right moment. 'Look out, captain!' The topmost branches moved to and fro restlessly, and they felt a heavy trembling in the blade of the saw. They jumped up and pulled the saw out of the gap. 'Hoi-oo,' shouted Bildermann. The top of the tree bent over, there was a creaking at the foot of the trunk, then the green tower sagged, at first slowly, then faster and faster, a boisterous wind arose, and in a cloud of powder snow the felled tree thundered down to the ground with a roaring scream that broke the silence far and wide.

Bildermann put tea-leaves in the saucepan. They sat on the felled trunk, smoked a pipe and sipped the hot tea. The world was so simple, whether the sun was shining or snow was falling, and when the east wind whistled, they built a screen of thick branches and held their feet over the fire. 'It's not like Cape Horn,' said Bildermann.

They climbed along the felled trunk and lopped off the branches. It was such easy work that they could smoke while doing it. After that it was the turn of the next tree. They did not look at their watches. They did not feel bored, and when Gruber went by, they felt as if he came from another world.

Thomas was the first to hear the bells of the sleigh, but he did not say anything. She should hear the strokes of the axes or the song of the saw. He knew well how comforting it sounded in a large empty wood when it came from far away over hills and plantations, and when one saw the white smoke hover over the treetops, as it hovers over a kiln.

They had made a seat of pine branches for her and a screen against the wind. She threw an armful of hay to the horse, and took out the double saucepan from the fur rug. Thomas had asked for double saucepans, as the only possible thing. Only townspeople ate off plates in a wood. She walked carefully through the snow and over the trunks holding the saucepan in her outstretched arms. Her happy eyes smiled when she saw how they were enjoying their meal. 'Are you satisfied, men from the ocean?' Yes, they were, not only with the food, but with the quiet hour, the warm fire, the work they had done and the work they were going to do and with the pure face that looked at them. She counted the trunks, but she did not care how many there were, for Thomas was tired, and his eyes met hers quietly and full of faith.

He made it a rule that the food must be very simple. 'You mustn't think that we are playing here,' he said. After the meal they had another cup of tea with a few drops of rum, and a pipe. Then they talked about their work, and about nothing else. Sometimes when there was a big fire Thomas fell asleep in the middle of a sentence. Then Marianne and Bildermann sat quite still and guarded his sleep, and out of a corner of his eye Bildermann saw how the little lady's eyes were riveted on Thomas's relaxed face.

Mostly he was woken up after a few minutes by the low crackle when a glowing branch snapped, or by a movement of the horse which set the bells tinkling. Then his eyes looked as if they had returned from far away; he did not like being caught dozing, 'Court martial, Bildermann,' he would say.

Then Marianne had to leave; he accompanied her to the sleigh, bridled the horse and covered her feet with the fur rug. The bells became less and less audible, and soon after only the stroke of the axes was heard in the wood.

They ceased working an hour before dusk. Bildermann went home first to light a fire and make the coffee, and Thomas tidied up. He collected the branches and piled them up properly, and was absolutely quiet, and often at this time it would start snowing. Sometimes he heard the castle clock. Then he listened until it had finished striking. The snow caught up the sound and muffled it. Later in the twilight under the lofty trees it was quieter still.

Finally he covered the fire with ashes, slung the axe over his shoulder and walked home. His back ached, but when he reached the shore and saw the light shining through his windows, he was happy. The more tired the hand, the clearer life became. He wanted to get over the time when pictures haunted him, and he wished that in the end they would become only pictures hanging on a wall – high and dim as in the hall of the castle, and one could stand beneath them and say: 'So that's what you looked like once upon a time.' There were many obstacles in life which he had not mastered, but this he surely would master.

He changed, had coffee with Bildermann, and then he slept for an hour. It was marvellous to wake up and to see the crimson reflection of the fire under the beams. In the adjoining room someone was softly rattling the rings of the stove, and out of doors there might have been the Taiga or Spitzbergen or Alaska. Nobody would call, only Gruber sometimes, and now and again the child. He heard the steps in the snow, and he knew which it was before the door opened. A book about the totem customs of dying peoples lay on the table, where the sentences were ranged as simply one after another as the treetops of a forest, but from all of them emanated the beautiful twilight of mystery of a country where the sons of kings spoke as simply as the swineherds, and where the young prince was always stronger than the old water sprite. There was an incorruptible rightness about these miracles.

Thomas and Bildermann put out the lamp earlier than usual, and in their first dreams they saw the squirrel escaping from the high, grey trunks at the first stroke of the axe.

On Saturdays the child earnestly counted the money into their horny hands, and when they walked home at noon, they heard the silver tinkling in their pockets.

'I must go to a dance tonight,' said Bildermann, a little embarrassed.

'Never mind, Bildermann. Young people will dance.'

The contours of the hills grew more and more distinct, and at the end of January – as they had planned – the last tree fell. They stood there leaning on their axes, like the last survivors of a battle. They had made no mistake and had not spoilt anything. The trunks would be dragged to the road, and in spring Marianne could plant the new forest. She could give it a name if she liked, and in a hundred years her great-grandchildren could look up to the high treetops and say: 'So this is the captain's wood. It will soon be time for it to fall, too.' All work reached far into the future, and even the men of the ocean could be immortal if they worked with their hands. But Thomas himself would look at the young trees and would call them in his mind: 'The wood of good hope.'

For nearly three months he stayed at the Graf's house. There was still some work from the previous winter to be finished, if 'finish' was the right expression. Then he felt as if he had measured the first meridian around the earth, and the surest knowledge he gained was that there were three hundred and sixty meridians for those who are easily satisfied. For the others however it would be an infinite number.

He was neither disillusioned nor hopeless. He had been able to grasp the idea of infinity and had grown wise enough for it. He saw the thousand buckets ascending and descending, but neither God nor man held the handle. Also idols were drawn out of the depth, rose and sank down, and man was only able to see 'the drops on the bucket'. Something greater, unrecognizable, stood above all – and that was 'the whole'. Who viewed it must become reverent, but there was neither church nor altar for this kind of reverence, no image, no allegory, not even a name. For not even the stars were the ultimate – not even the nebula out of which stars were born, how much less man or his God around whose image bitter quarrels raged, and to whom man gave all the qualities he would have liked to possess: knowledge, power, goodness.

He reflected on how much had been needed before he could arrive at this threshold of silence: father and mother and behind them the grey procession of generations; the house near the fields, the voyages over all the oceans of the world; the learning of many centuries and the fires of a war, which they called 'the Great War'; a pastor with a wooden Christ; a child named Gloria and another named Marianne. Then there was the signpost to the forester's house, where the wise man from the east stood at the gate; the island and the water with the golden crown; the blue shawl with the golden birds and the green forest which they had felled – an endless web intertwined with all ages and zones, and bearing the traces of dead and living hands.

A life full of tears, disordered by fever, tangled by ecstasy and guilt, and in the end humbly smoothed by obedience and quiet submission to the great Law.

And this also he had recognised, that on the revolving canopy of heaven one star set when another rose in the east. At the age of forty or fifty a man should step back into the shade, and should start to give and cease to take. There was only a certain amount of space on this earth and half of it belonged to youth – in happiness, in power and also in pain.

He who asked for more than was granted to his years destroyed not only himself but all that he coveted. 'Charity seeketh not her own' not even in the beginning and how much less when the hair is greying. There was no greater test of manhood than to renounce without bitterness.

Joachim wrote that his examination would be over in June. Then he would like to come once more with two or three friends, before beginning his service in the Navy. Everything was all right, and his prospects were very good indeed.

Thomas wrote to Finkenstein that he expected him, too, on the island. He was a little afraid of so much youth, and he would like to have someone who was as he had been himself – not too perfect and always uneasy lest he might steer his boat on to the next sandbank.

Bergengruen had finished his theological studies and was now to take up his ministry, preaching his first sermon at Whitsun from the pulpit of the church where the general had promised him the living. 'What a long time has passed, child,' said Thomas, 'since I stood on the steps and you came to meet me. I promised you a golden crown, but it still lies at the bottom of the lake, and only now and again I seem to see it shining through the water.'

'But you are wearing it, Thomas,' she replied, 'you alone fail to see it.'

He shook his head and smiled. 'I will be quite satisfied if I wear my helmet honourably and am allowed to take it off a little in the evening. All is well in the world when man wears a helmet and woman wears a crown.'

They stood in 'the wood of good hope' and looked down upon the young trees which were planted on the slopes in long rows. The cuckoo called but Marianne did not count any more. She thought she knew that she would live long. Her children would pick strawberries out of this grass, and here they would wait – gun on knee – for the scurrying game when the house on the island would be standing empty and forlorn. Nobody should live there but herself – when she had grown old. And she wanted to be buried there too.

'The wood will grow, whatever our burden may be,' she said on the way home.

The tree of life was reflected for him in motionless water now, only once before the guests came the reflections quivered, as if the bottom were gently rising, but the circles vanished, and he could see the stones again with young fish playing above them.

They had been sitting under the oaks by the shore discussing how they would entertain the expected guests, who were about to conquer the world. A far-off storm was gathering over the otter bay. Marianne had been hitting out at the gadflies, then she turned and asked whether they should not bathe before the sun was covered by clouds.

There had not been anything unusual in the question, but Thomas had replied that he did not want to, and when she looked at him in surprise, he had added that he thought she was too old for it now.

It was clumsy of him to say that, and he need not have evaded her eyes and looked over the water to where the green dragonflies sat on the sparkling reeds. She had blushed to the roots of her hair and had not said a word, but when they got up eventually and walked down to the boats, the familiar ground seemed to tremble under her feet.

Only in the evening when Marianne stood at the window of her room listening to the Hungarian nightingales did she realise that it had been happiness which had moved the earth under her feet. The ground under the tree of knowledge trembled too when the apple was picked.

In June the young guests came: Joachim, Marschall and two others. They wore their new uniforms, lived in the castle, and assured the general that a new age was beginning. Finkenstein arrived a day later in an old grey hunting suit and slept in Joachim's reed hut. He talked about the examination with good-natured raillery. According to his opinion an examination ought to be held during a battle. They had all been heroes – on paper – even experiencing the requisite fear. He was looking forward to joining the fleet where he would not only have to deal with ships, but also with human beings, and where you could prove whether your good marks had been deserved or not.

In the evenings Marianne came to fetch them, but they always rather delayed their departure from the island and seemed in no hurry to sail off. 'My life is no longer safe over there with all this admiration. Even naval commanders seem to be mortal.'

After his long letter in the autumn Joachim avoided any discussion with his father. But he thanked him for his advice and all his support. He thought that he was over the worst now. He talked to Thomas as to an older comrade and Thomas was satisfied with it. A clean and capable generation was growing up – harder and more alert than his own had been, and now had to look on and watch how they shaped their course. It was a pleasure to see them like arrows on the bow, quivering with impatience, fancying that the far distance which awaited them was hung with laurel wreaths.

The next morning Thomas went quietly to the reed hut, where his guest was not yet awake, sat down on the blackened stones of the fireplace, and looked at the sleeping youth. The face still pale was without tension now, calmly shaped by his character, and Thomas liked to look at it. 'After all, we do want something like ourselves,' he thought, 'first that and only then the next stage. . . .'

He did not worry that Joachim was different. He was only grateful that he could see this, too, and look upon this young man as a much younger brother. Possession or property was not the most intimate relationship in this world.

For the third evening the general had arranged a festivity in honour of the country's young navy. It was midsummer night, and after dinner they wished to light a fire on the shore of the lake.

Pastor Bergengruen was invited too, and in the afternoon he rowed to the island to greet Thomas. His course was not very straight yet.

They were sitting at the old table in front of the house, and once again Thomas seemed to see time rush by without any details and at a breakneck speed. Bergengruen's face was almost unchanged; it would always remain a childlike face behind old spectacles. Even the movements of his hands were the same as those with which he conjured up pictures of the future of mankind, of the kingdom and the peace of God.

'I suppose you have not had any doubts since our last camp fire here?' asked Thomas.

'No, no doubts. A little fear and some annoyance as just now with the young lieutenants who asked after Noah's Ark – but no doubts. I live in God as the stone exists in the fruit. However much I move about I can't fall out of it – any more than the centre of a circle can be flung beyond the circumference – which would be something absurd. I don't know how I have deserved this divine grace – for doubtless it is a grace.'

'You are right,' said Thomas, 'we without grace know that best.'

'Nobody is without grace,' replied Bergengruen in a low voice.

'No, only those who wish to be so.'

'Have you still got the book with the butterflies?'

'Yes, it is there, and it is always there for you, just as the island will not forget the few faithful and good ones.'

'And the child?'

'Oh, the child will marry, and you will christen and confirm her children and marry them, too.'

'She will not marry one of those over there?'

'Probably not.'

'That's all right; for they speak of God, as they would speak of a civilian trespassing on one of their battleships.'

'Seamen usually find God a little late,' said Thomas. 'But you mustn't worry about that. It's rather a difficult matter to explain the connection between God and the military profession.'

Then Bergengruen returned with Finkenstein to the castle.

Thomas sent word that he would only come in the evening. Storms were rising behind the woods, and he laid out all the nets with Bildermann. After his work was done, he swam once more far out into the lake, smoked his pipe on the shore and slowly changed into his uniform. It hung a little loosely on him, and he looked down at his medals thoughtfully. It was long ago he had won these ribbons and crosses. He rowed quite slowly. The world appeared to him to be especially beautiful. He heard the stroke of the clock over the lake. He would be too late if he did not make haste, but he did not want to make haste. The light on the pine trees was beautiful and so was the reflection of the heron in the motionless water. This was a festival of youth, and he was no longer indispensable. He did not care any more for festivals. He had not much time left, and he could be happy without them.

It was fine that Joachim had reached what was to him the first step to glory, and it did not matter that they were no longer one. His son was already the next link in the chain, and only felt a slight, reluctant attachment to the previous ones. He did not look back. Much had been done amiss, in his opinion, and now they wanted to set it right. The world had waited for them. They needed clear, navigable water in front of their keels, and their battles would be fought differently from those of fifteen years ago. It appeared that there must always be battles, that they were unavoidable. Even the young ones could not do anything to alter the pattern of the world. One ought to help them and trust in their stars. One knew so little about the stars which stood above the earth.

Thomas got out slowly and tied up the boat. Behind the curve of the shore, he heard noise and laughter. Probably they were piling up the wood for the fire which was to be lit tonight. Marschall's high-pitched voice was to be heard above all the others. Thomas had forgotten the names of the two friends.

The general sat on the garden terrace in uniform, his hands folded on the handle of his stick. His hair was snow-white, and he looked over the park to the water, as if the quiet people were standing there surprised at the new life.

'It is good to see you, Orla,' he said. 'Sitting here like a back number. I am boring the young people . . . they are bent on a sharp wind. . . .'

'It will be lonely enough on board, General.'

'They don't yet know what loneliness is, Orla. We only learn that when the hair grows grey. I look at them and think how fast the earth is turning – much faster than your coloured globe.'

Thomas nodded and asked after Marianne.

'Absented herself.'

'I shall go and look for her.'

It was already twilight in the large hall. He gazed at the bronze muzzles of the cannon and remembered the spring day when he saw them for the first time. He did not know how many years had passed. Blessings could not be measured by years. But it must be a long time since, a very long time. The young forest was growing, and Bergengruen already laid together the hands of those who knelt before his altar.

The child came down the stairs in a white evening gown, and round her shoulders she wore the blue shawl he had given her last Christmas. 'Good God,' he thought, 'how good it would be to believe in you sometimes and in your almighty protecting hand. . . .'

He took her arm and led her out on to the terrace. 'There is a passage in the *Iliad*,' he said, 'where Helen appears among the old men.'

Behind them Johann struck the gong for the first time.

At dinner Thomas sat opposite the general. The light of the candles in the old candlesticks shone quietly, the windows were wide open, and the nightingale sang on the shore. It was a fine sight to look across the dinner table at the young, brown hands moving on the white cloth, to see the blue uniforms and the bright eyes in which the candlelight was mirrored.

The general rose and drank to the health of his young comrades. What had gone down with flags streaming would rise again with streaming flags. It had been granted to him in his old age to see a new generation before the mast. He did not ask them to respect the old generation too much, but they always ought to have the deepest respect for the 'Reich' and its flag. Then the old soldiers here at the fireside and over there on the island would say goodbye to them with a light heart. And his wish for the younger generation was that they should win in peace and war as happy a heart, nay half as happy a heart, as the man whom he now saw at his table and bore in his heart with pride and honour.

It was a matter of course that Joachim should reply. He was not the oldest, but it was obvious that he had to stand on the bridge. With slight surprise Thomas saw his son rise and begin to speak. 'I would like to be allowed,' he said, 'to thank you on behalf of my comrades and myself for all the kindness we have received in this house. But deeds show a man's true gratitude, so I beg you to wait patiently until the deed is laid ready to our hands. Our youth has not been an easy one. We have to pay interest for debts which we did not incur. But nothing has been in vain, for through our struggles we have gained a different valuation of the world. A harder one (and to some people it seems too hard) but I believe also a more reliable one.

'This house has been like an island sanctuary to us; it gave us gaiety, relaxation and pleasure. But far away roars the ocean which is calling us. We have betrothed ourselves to it and will remain faithful. And even if there is no island sanctuary but only death, we have made up our minds to face death. For honour stands before death.

'I raise my glass to those who in their time guarded this

honour: to the veterans of the war and to all those who belong to them!'

At the end of the meal Thomas stood up. He had not intended to speak, but he felt that he might be silent from now on and that this was the last time he would be called upon. He looked at the general, but in reality he spoke only to himself.

'Many quiet people come to visit this house,' he said, 'the dead and the living, but more dead than living. They do not speak any more; they are only present, and now and again a glass of red wine is raised to them. As I have always been familiar with them, I would like to speak for them.

'All of us in this house rejoice in the new generation which has dedicated itself to the sea and to death, but we would like to see them also dedicated to life and the land. These are as eternal as others, although constantly changing. The final thing a man can do is to change himself.

'There is no need to stand on the shoulders of the living, but it must never be forgotten that you are standing on the shoulders of the dead. The searching and the probing for guilt and mistakes lead nowhere, but the sense of gratitude and responsibility leads along a bright road. A nation must honour its dead, and it has been a dark omen of our times that we did not do so, nay, that we abused our dead.

'You have passed an examination, and it is a credit to yourselves and to us, the veterans. But you have not yet proved yourselves. However, the proof is still to come. You may well be cautious in judgment and sober in appraisal, until the testing time has come. The real test does not always come in the gun turrets, not even for servicemen.

'I have renounced the sea and have become an islander. In this act there was no wish to blame, nor to accuse, nor to protest; all I wanted was to work; for work is the surest blessing of this earth. I even wanted to raise the golden crown from the bottom of the lake. In this I have not succeeded, but there are nights when I see its golden shimmer flash through the water. He who wishes to win it must have a happy heart, be as quiet as the stones at the bottom of the lake, and not want anything for himself.

'Before I have got so far as that I have still a long way to go, and yours will be a long road too. You rather give me the impression that you wish above all to gain glory and honour. That is quite right, and yet I will not raise my glass to your success in gaining it. There is time enough for that and it will come by itself.

'But I wish you to be always the masters of your courage, and if you consider this well, it is rather difficult, but I will raise my glass today to this wish of mine: May it be fulfilled! May you always be the masters of your courage! . . . As far as I know them, I feel that "the quiet people" will also join in this toast.'

Thomas had been standing very upright without moving a finger and had spoken in a low voice. Actually he had not addressed the young men, but had looked over their heads, and only now and again his eyes had turned to the general and Marianne. He was not satisfied with what he had said. After the last word he stood still for a while gazing in front of him with serious eyes. The Hungarian nightingales were singing in the woods, and their song was the only sound that was heard in the great hall. In silence Thomas went round the table, first to the general, then to Marianne, and when he had touched the last glass, the child rose, so giving the signal that the dinner was at an end.

Then they went without delay over the terrace into the park. The cottagers and the threshold servants were there already, standing round the pile of wood. There was summer lightning above the lake, and the reflection from the crimson glow flashed over their faces. There was a smell of rain, but the stars still shone above them.

Bildermann was allowed to light the bonfire, and when the flame shot up glowing to the treetops, Thomas stepped back into the shadow. While the general was making a short speech, he started to walk down to the shore slowly. It was as if the island were calling him, and as if he had to gaze, quite alone, into the lightning that illuminated the horizon. His part was finished; the curtain had dropped over it. Now it was the turn of others. He was standing alone on the vast, dark stage.

As he took the chain off the post, he heard her light, quick steps. She stood right before him, so near that he could see the reflection of the distant lightning in her eyes. She did not say a word. She only raised her bare arms out of the blue shawl, folded her hands about his hair and kissed him on the mouth. He felt her breath gently rising and falling. Her eyes were open and without tears.

He still saw the hem of her white dress, when his boat was already far away on the water. It was shining like the pedestal of a statue, motionless, and he could imagine that the flashing light fell into the pores of the marble.

He walked slowly up to his house. The sky was covered with heavy clouds which moved slowly to the east, but it was not dark. A pale light was dripping down through the gaps between the clouds, but gloom spread over water and land when the flash had died behind the woods. The fish leapt, and the great nightmoth hovered with softly vibrating wings over the honeysuckle.

The house smelt of smoke and dry reed. Thomas did not light the lamp. He changed, put a light coat round his shoulders and walked up to the bench under the oaks. When he struck the match for his pipe, one of the big birds over his head gave a screeching cry, and the heavy beat of wings circled once around the treetops. Then all was quiet as before. Beyond the bay, in the south-east, a red glow hung over the wood. That came from the bonfire around which they were probably still sitting. The fiery flashes from behind the clouds now gleamed in crimson brilliance across the water. A warm breeze blew over the reeds, and when it dropped Thomas heard the low metallic rumble of thunder. Now and then a pale light appeared over the island and the wood, and in between there were wicked, menacing flashes of lightning, which seemed to come from long barrels over a grey wall of steel, then a dazzling flash shot through the sky, and after a long pause the distant thunder rolled for a long time and shook the earth on which Thomas was now sitting in complete darkness.

With wide-open eyes he gazed into the light. He thought he saw foaming water and grey forms rushing forward. He imagined he heard bells, signals, and the rise and fall of human cries. He sat as in a dream, and before his eyes and ears the sum of his past life seemed to rise up, the test of many years, the decision of young, trembling hearts: the battle.

He knew that he had had the same thoughts many years ago, when he had still been young. He had gone through much, and there were other trials besides those under the grey turrets which sent the flashes of light over the woods.

But that had been the beginning and was part of the law just as his sitting here now and feeling the dry thyme under his hand. Everything had its place and order; everything was right as it was and as it would be. It was neither good nor bad. He had a son who would be a credit to him, and it was unimportant that he was not like himself. He had a young sister called Marianne, and it was of no importance that she might have been fifteen or twenty years older. Nature had not willed it, and there may have been reasons enough. It had not willed either that the young Graf should live any longer or the child called Gloria. In due course the seed was strewn and the harvest brought home. As the measure of the seed was the same, the harvest was so too. Man wore his helmet and worked with his hands, and now and again he could take off his helmet and lay his hands in his lap. Not often, but now and then.

And sometimes one could see a calm, crimson shimmer flashing over the water, and one could think that it came from the golden crown at the bottom.

And once too, much later, one might believe that one had a happy heart.

A few raindrops fell and struck the young oak leaves, but Thomas remained seated leaning his head against the hard, cracked bark of the tree, and watched the lightning play higher and higher above the woods.

A third time Yen Hui met Kung-Fu-Tse and said: 'I am progressing.'

'How is that?' asked Kung-Fu-Tse.

'I am free of everything,' answered Yen Hui.

'You are free of everything?' said Kung-Fu-Tse, deeply moved. 'What do you mean by that?'

'I have liberated myself from my body,' answered Yen Hui. 'I have emptied my mind. And as I have freed myself of body and mind, I have become one with the All-Penetrating. That is what I mean when I say that I am free of everything.'

PARABLES AND SAYINGS OF TSCHUANG-TSE

NOTE ON POTATO-FIRE

In Germany it is the custom to burn the haulm, after the potato harvest, and roast potatoes in the embers.

NOTE ON THE QUOTATION FROM THE NINETIETH PSALM

The Lutheran version used by the author translated literally reads: 'We spend our years as idle gossip'; the English Bible has: 'We spend our years as a tale that is told.' In this translation of Wiechert's novel, the Knox version of the Psalms has been used as the meaning is stronger and gives more significance to Orla's conversion.